The Culpepper Misses

Books 1-2

COLLETTE CAMERON

Blue Rose Romance®

Sweet-to-Spicy Timeless Romance®

Attn: Permissions Coordinator
Blue Rose Romance®
P.O. Box 167, Scappoose, OR 97056

www.collettecameron.com

The Culpepper Misses

The Earl and the Spinster
The Marquis and the Vixen
The Lord and the Wallflower
The Buccaneer and the Bluestocking
The Lieutenant and the Lady

Check out Collette's Other Series

Castle Brides
Highland Heather Romancing a Scot
Daughters of Desire (Scandalous Ladies)
The Honorable Rogues®
Seductive Scoundrels
Heart of a Scot

Collections

Lords in Love
Heart of a Scot Books 1-3
The Honorable Rogues® Books 1-3
The Honorable Rogues® Books 4-6
Seductive Scoundrels Series Books 1-3
Seductive Scoundrels Series Books 4-6
The Culpepper Misses Series 1-2

THE EARL AND THE SPINSTER, Book One
An angry earl. A desperate spinster. A reckless wager.

THE MARQUIS AND THE VIXEN, Book Two
A tormented marquis. A vivacious vixen. A deadly foe.

About the Author

The Earl and the Spinster

Even when most prudently considered, and with the noblest of intentions, one who wagers with chance oft finds oneself empty-handed.
~Wisdom and Advice—The Genteel Lady's Guide to Practical Living

1

Esherton Green,
Near Acton, Cheshire, England
Early April 1822

Was I born under an evil star or cursed from my first breath?

Brooke Culpepper suppressed the urge to shake her fist at the heavens and berate The Almighty aloud. The devil boasted better luck than she. My God, now two *more* cows struggled to regain their strength?

She slid Richard Mabry, Esherton Green's steward-turned-overseer, a worried glance from beneath her lashes as she chewed her lower lip and paced before the unsatisfactory fire in the study's hearth. The soothing aroma of wood smoke, combined with linseed oil, old leather, and the faintest trace of Papa's pipe tobacco, bathed the room. The scents reminded her of happier times but did little to calm her frayed nerves.

Sensible gray woolen skirts swishing about her ankles, she whirled to make the return trip across the once-bright green and gold Axminster carpet, now so threadbare, the oak floor peeked through in numerous places. Her scuffed half-boots fared little better, and she hid a wince when the scrap of leather she'd used to cover the hole in her left sole this morning slipped loose again.

From his comfortable spot in a worn and faded wingback chair, Freddy, her aged Welsh corgi, observed her progress with soulful brown eyes, his muzzle propped on stubby paws. Two ancient tabbies lay curled so tightly together on the cracked leather sofa that determining where one ended and the other began was difficult.

What was she to do? Brooke clamped her lip harder and winced.

Should she venture to the barn to see the cows herself?

What good would that do? She knew little of doctoring cattle and so left the animals' care in Mr. Mabry's capable hands. Her strength lay in the financial administration of the dairy farm and her ability to stretch a shilling as thin as gossamer.

She cast a glance at the bay window and, despite the fire, rubbed her arms against the chill creeping along her spine. A frenzied wind whipped the lilac branches and scraped the rain-splattered panes. The tempest threatening since dawn had finally unleashed its full fury, and the fierce winds battering the house gave the day a peculiar, eerie feeling—as if portending something ominous.

At least Mabry and the other hands had managed to get the cattle tucked away before the gale hit. The herd of fifty—no, sixty, counting the newborn calves—chewed their cud and weathered the storm inside the old, but sturdy, barns.

As she peered through the blurry pane, a shingle ripped loose from the farthest outbuilding—a retired stone dovecote. After the wind tossed the slat around for a few moments, the wood twirled to the ground, where it flipped end over end before wedging beneath a gangly shrub. Two more shingles hurled to the earth, this time from one of the barns.

Flimflam and goose-butt feathers.

Brooke tamped down a heavy sigh. Each structure on the estate, including the house, needed some sort of repair or replacement: roofs, shutters, stalls, floors, stairs, doors, siding...dozens of items required fixing, and she could seldom muster the funds to go about it properly.

"Another pair of cows struggling, you say, Mr. Mabry?"

Concern etched on his weathered features, Mabry wiped rain droplets from his face as water pooled at his muddy feet.

"Yes, Miss Brooke. The four calves born this mornin' fare well, but two of the cows, one a first-calf heifer, aren't standin' yet. And there's one weak from birthin' her calf yesterday." His troubled gaze strayed to the window. "Two more ladies are in labor. I best return to the barn. They seemed fine when I left, but I'd as soon be nearby."

Brooke nodded once. "Yes, we mustn't take any chances."

The herd had already been reduced to a minimum by disease and sales to make ends meet. She needed every shilling the cows' milk brought. Losing another, let alone two or three good breeders...

No, I won't think of it.

She stopped pacing and forced a cheerful smile. Nonetheless, from the skeptical look Mabry speedily masked, his thoughts ran parallel to hers—one reason she put her trust in the man. Honest and intelligent, he'd worked alongside her to restore the beleaguered herd and farm after Papa died. Their existence, their livelihood, everyone at Esherton's future depended on the estate flourishing once more.

"It's only been a few hours." *Almost nine, truth to tell.* Brooke scratched her temple. "Perhaps the ladies need a little more time to recover." *If they recovered.* "The calves are strong, aren't they?" *Please, God, they must be.* She held her breath, anticipating Mabry's response.

His countenance lightened and the merry sparkle returned to his eyes. "Aye, the mites are fine. Feedin' like they're hollow to their wee hooves."

Tension lessened its ruthless grip, and hope peeked from beneath her vast mound of worries.

Six calves had been guaranteed in trade to her neighbor and fellow dairy farmer, Silas Huffington, for the grain and medicines he'd provided to see Esherton Green's herd through last winter. Brooke didn't have the means to pay him if the calves didn't survive—though the old reprobate had hinted he'd make her a deal of a much less respectable nature if she ran short of cattle with which to barter. Each pence she'd stashed away—groat by miserable groat, these past four years—lay in the hidden drawer of Papa's desk and must go to purchase a bull.

Wisdom had decreed replacing Old Buford two years ago but, short on funds, she'd waited until it was too late. His heart had stopped while he performed the duties expected of a breeding bull. Not the worst way to cock up one's toes...er, hooves, but she'd counted on him siring at least two-score calves this season and wagered everything on the calving this year and next. The poor brute had expired before he'd completed the job.

Her thoughts careened around inside her skull. Without a bull, she would lose everything.

My home, care of my sister and cousins, my reasons for existing.

She squared her shoulders, resolution strengthening her. She still retained the Culpepper sapphire parure set. If all else failed, she would pawn the jewelry. She'd planned on using the money from the gems' sale to bestow small marriage settlements on the girls. Still, pawning the set was a price worth paying to keep her family at Esherton Green, even if it meant that any chance of her sister and three cousins securing a decent match would evaporate faster than a dab of milk on a hot cookstove. Good standing and breeding meant little if one's fortune proved meaner than a churchyard beggar's.

"How's the big bull calf that came breech on Sunday?" Brooke tossed the question over her shoulder as she poked the fire and encouraged the blaze to burn hotter. After setting the tool aside, she faced the overseer.

"Greediest of the lot." Mabry laughed and slapped his thigh. "Quite the appetite he has, and friendly as our Freddy there. Likes his ears scratched too."

Brooke chuckled and ran her hand across Freddy's spine. The dog wiggled in excitement and stuck his rear legs straight out behind him, gazing at her in adoration. In his youth, he'd been an excellent cattle herder. Now he'd gone fat and arthritic, his sweet face gray to his eyebrows. On occasion, he still dashed after the cattle, the instinctive drive to herd deep in the marrow of his bones.

Another shudder shook her. Why was she so blasted cold today? She relented and placed a good-sized log atop the others. The feeble flames hissed and spat before greedily engulfing the new addition. Lord, she prayed she wasn't ailing. She simply couldn't afford to become ill.

A scratching at the door barely preceded the entrance of Duffen bearing a tea service. "Gotten to where a man cannot find a quiet corner to shut his eyes for a blink or two anymore."

Shuffling into the room, he yawned and revealed how few teeth remained in his mouth. One sock sagged around his ankle, his grizzled hair poked every which way, and his shirttail hung askew. Typical Duffen.

"Devil's day, it is." He scowled in the window's direction, his mouth pressed into a grim line. "Mark my words, trouble's afoot."

Not quite a butler, but certainly more than a simple retainer, the man, now hunched from age, had been a fixture at Esherton Green Brooke's entire life. He loved the place as much as, if not more than, she, and she couldn't afford to hire a servant to replace him. A light purse had forced Brooke to let the household staff go when Papa died. The cook, Mrs. Jennings, Duffen, and Flora, a maid-of-all-work, had stayed on. However, they received no salaries—only room and board.

The income from the dairy scarcely permitted Brooke to retain a few milkmaids and stable hands, yet not once had she heard a whispered complaint from anyone.

Everybody, including Brooke, her sister, Brette, and their cousins—Blythe, and the twins, Blaike and Blaire—did their part to keep the farm operating at a profit. A meager profit, particularly as, for the past five years, Esherton Green's legal heir, Sheridan Gainsborough, had received half the proceeds. In return, he permitted Brooke and the girls to reside there. He'd also been appointed their guardian. But, from his silence and failure to visit the farm, he seemed perfectly content to let her carry on as provider and caretaker.

"Ridiculous law. Only the next male in line can inherit," she muttered.

Especially when he proved a disinterested bore. Papa had thought so too, but the choice hadn't been his to make. If only she could keep the funds she sent to Sheridan each quarter, Brooke could make something of Esherton and secure her sister and cousins' futures too.

If wishes were gold pieces, I'd be rich indeed.

Brooke sneezed then sneezed again. Dash it all. A cold?

The fresh log snapped loudly, and Brooke started. The blaze's heat had failed to warm her opinion of her second cousin. She hadn't met him and lacked a personal notion of his character, but Papa had hinted that Sheridan was a scallywag and possessed unsavory habits.

A greedy sot, too.

The one time her quarterly remittance had been late, because Brooke had taken a tumble and broken her arm, he'd written a disagreeable letter demanding his money.

His money, indeed.

Sheridan had threatened to sell Esherton Green's acreage and turn her and the foursome onto the street if she ever delayed payment again.

A ruckus beyond the entrance announced the girls' arrival. Laughing and chatting, the blond quartet billowed into the room. Their gowns, several seasons out of fashion, in no way detracted from their charm, and pride swelled in Brooke's heart. Lovely, both in countenance and disposition, and the dears worked hard too.

"Duffen says we're to have tea in here today." Attired in a Pomona green gown too short for her tall frame, Blaike plopped on to the sofa. Her twin, Blaire, wearing a similar dress in dark rose and equally inadequate in length, flopped beside her.

Each girl scooped a drowsy cat into her lap. The cats' wiry whiskers twitched, and they blinked their sleepy amber eyes a few times before closing them once more as the low rumble of contented purrs filled the room.

"Yes, I didn't think we needed to light a fire in the drawing room when this one will suffice." As things stood, too little coal and seasoned firewood remained to see them comfortably until summer.

Brette sailed across the study, her slate-blue gingham dress the only one of the quartet's fashionably long enough. Repeated laundering had turned the garment a peculiar greenish color, much like tarnished copper. She looped her arm through Brooke's.

"Look, dearest." Brette pointed to the tray. "I splurged and made a half-batch of shortbread biscuits. It's been so long since we've indulged, and today is your birthday. To celebrate, I insisted on fresh tea leaves as well."

Brooke would have preferred to ignore the day.

Three and twenty.

On the shelf. Past her prime. Long in the tooth. Spinster. *Old maid.*

She'd relinquished her one chance at love. In order to nurse her ailing father and assume the care of her young sister and three orphaned cousins, she'd refused Humphrey Benbridge's proposal. She couldn't have put her happiness before their welfare and deserted them when they needed her most. Who would've cared for them if she hadn't?

No one.

Mr. Benbridge controlled the purse strings, and Humphrey had neither offered nor been in a position to take on their care. Devastated, or so he'd claimed, he'd departed to the continent five years ago.

She'd not seen him since.

Nonetheless, his sister, Josephina, remained a friend and occasionally remarked on Humphrey's travels abroad. Burying the pieces of her broken heart beneath hard work and devotion to her family, Brooke had rolled up her sleeves and plunged into her forced role as breadwinner, determined that sacrificing her love not be in vain.

Yes, it grieved her that she wouldn't experience a man's passion or bear children, but to wallow in doldrums was a waste of energy and emotion. Instead, she focused on building a future for her sister and cousins—so they might have what she never would—and allowed her dreams to fade into obscurity.

"Happy birthday." Brette squeezed her hand.

Brooke offered her sister a rueful half-smile. "Ah, I'd hoped you'd forgotten."

"Don't be silly, Brooke. We couldn't forget your special day." Twenty-year-old Blythe—standing with her hands behind her—grinned and pulled a small, neatly-wrapped gift tied with a cheerful yellow ribbon from behind her. Sweet dear. She'd used the trimming from her gown to adorn the package.

"Hmph. Need seedcake an' champagne to celebrate a birthday properly." The contents of the tray rattled and clanked when Duffen scuffed his way to the table between the sofa and chairs. After depositing the tea service, he lifted a letter from the surface. Tea dripped from one stained corner. "This arrived for you yesterday, Miss Brooke. I forgot where I'd put it until just now."

If I can read it with the ink running to London and back.

He shook the letter, oblivious to the tawny droplets spraying every which way.

Mabry raised a bushy gray eyebrow, and the twins hid giggles by concealing their faces in the cat's striped coats.

Brette set about pouring the tea, although her lips twitched suspiciously.

Freddy sat on his haunches and barked, his button eyes fixed on the paper, evidently mistaking it for a tasty morsel he would've liked to sample. He licked his chops, a testament to his waning eyesight.

"Thank you, Duffen." Brooke took the letter by one soggy corner. Holding it gingerly, she flipped it over. No return address.

"Aren't you going to read it?" Blythe set the gift on the table before settling on the sofa and smoothing her skirt. They didn't get a whole lot of post at Esherton. Truth be known, this was the first letter in months. Blythe's gaze roved to the other girls and the equally eager expressions on their faces. "We're on pins and needles," she quipped, fluttering her hands and winking.

Brooke smiled and cracked the brownish wax seal with her fingernail. Their lives had become rather monotonous, so much so that a simple, *soggy*, correspondence sent the girls into a dither of anticipation.

My Dearest Cousin...

Brooke glanced up. "It's from Sheridan.

As is oft the case when wagering, one party is a fool and the other a thief, although both may bear the title nincompoop.
~*Wisdom and Advice—The Genteel Lady's Guide to Practical Living*

2

What maggot in Heath's brain had possessed him to set out on the final leg of his journey to Esherton Green on horseback when foul weather threatened? The same corkbrained notion that had compelled him, the Earl of Ravensdale, one of the most eligible lords on the Marriage Mart, to miss the peak of London's Season in exchange for a saddle-sore arse.

He pulled his hat more firmly onto his head. The bloody wind tried its best to blast every last drop of rain either into his face or down the back of his neck, and he hunched deeper into his saddle. Fat lot of good that did.

The sooner I've finished this ugly business with the tenant, the sooner I can return to London and civilization.

The road from the village—if one deigned to grace the rutted and miry track with such distinction—lay along an open stretch of land, not a single sheltering tree in sight. He hadn't spotted another living thing this past hour. Any creature claiming half a wit laid snuggled in its nest, den, or house, waiting out the foulness. He'd seen two manors in the distance, but to detour to either meant extending his time in this Godforsaken spot.

People actually *chose* to live here?

Hound's teeth, he loathed the lack of niceties, abhorred the quiet which stretched for miles. The boredom and isolation. Give him London's or Paris's crowded and noisy paved streets any day; even if all manner of putridity lined them most of the time.

Despite his greatcoat, the torrential, wind-driven rain soaked him to the skin. Heath patted his pocket where the vowel proving his claim to the farm lay nestled in a leather casing and, with luck, still dry. He'd barely spared the marker a glance at White's and hadn't taken a peek since.

Reading wasn't his strong suit.

His sodden cravat chaffed unmercifully, and water seeped—drip by infernal drip—from his saturated buckskins into his Hessians. He eyed one boot and wiggled his toes. Bloody likely ruined, and he'd just had them made too. Stupid to have worn them and not an older pair. Wanton waste and carelessness—the calling cards of sluggards and degenerates.

Ebénè snorted and bowed his head against the hostile weather. The stallion, unused to such harsh treatment, had been pushed to the end of his endurance, despite his mild temperament. The horse increasingly expressed his displeasure with snorts, groans, and an occasional jerking of his head against the reins.

"I'm sorry, old chap. I thought we'd beat the storm." Heath leaned forward and patted the horse's neck. Black as hell at midnight when dry, now drenched, Ebénè's silky coat glistened like wet ink.

The horse quivered beneath Heath and trudged onward through the sheets of rain.

Indeed, they might have outpaced the tempest if Heath hadn't lingered at breakfast and enjoyed a third cup of Turkish coffee at Tristan, the Marquis of Leventhorpe's, home.

Leventhorpe actually enjoyed spending time at his country house, Bristledale Court. Heath couldn't understand that, but as good friends do, he overlooked the oddity.

Reluctance to part company with Leventhorpe hadn't been Heath's only excuse for dawdling. Leventhorpe had proved a superb host, and Bristledale boasted the latest comforts. The manor house's refinement tempted far more than venturing to a rustic dairy farm with the unpleasant tidings Heath bore.

He'd won the unwanted lands in a wager against Sheridan Gainsborough. The milksop had continued to raise the stakes when he didn't have the blunt to honor his bet. And it wasn't the first time the scapegrace had been light in the pocket at the tables. To teach the reckless sot a lesson, Heath had refused Gainsborough's I.O.U. and demanded he make good on his bet.

When the sluggard offered a piece of property as payment instead, Heath had had little choice but to accept, though it chaffed his sore arse. A tenant farmer and his family would be deprived of their livelihood as a consequence. No one—including this dairyman, months behind in his rents—should be put out of his means of income because a foxed dandy had acted rashly.

Now he owned another confounded piece of English countryside he didn't need nor want. He didn't even visit his country estate, Walcotshire Park. With a half dozen irritable servants for company, he'd spent his childhood there until fifteen years ago when, at thirteen, he'd been sent to boarding school. Instead, Walcotshire's steward tootled to Town quarterly, more often if the need arose, to meet with Heath.

A ripple of unease clawed his nerves. He shifted in the saddle. Discomfort inevitably accompanied thoughts of *The Prison*, as he'd come to regard the austere house, a scant thirty miles from the path Ebénè now plodded.

For a fleeting moment—no more than a blink, truthfully—he contemplated permitting the farmer to continue running the dairy. However, that obligated Heath to trot down to the place on occasion, and nothing short of a God-ordained mandate would compel him to venture to this remote section of green perdition on a regular basis. Not even the prospect of Leventhorpe's company. The marquis would be off to London for the remainder of the Season soon enough, in any event.

Heath had experienced enough of country life as a boy. The family mausoleum perched atop a knoll overlooking the cemetery held more warmth and fonder memories than *The Prison* did. The same could be said of his parents buried there. A colder, more uncaring pair of humans he had yet to meet. He wouldn't have been surprised to learn ice-water, rather than blood, flowed through their veins.

Besides, he didn't know a finger's worth about cattle or dairy farming other than both smelled horrid. He swiped rain from his forehead and wrinkled his nose. How could his favorite cheese be a result of such stench? The reek had carried to him on the wind for miles. How did the locals tolerate it? An irony-born grin curved his lips. Much the same way he tolerated London's, he'd wager. People disregarded flaws when they cared deeply about something or when convenient to do so.

Gainsborough hadn't blinked or appeared to have a second thought when he put up his land as collateral for his bet. He'd laughed and shrugged his thin shoulders before signing the estate over, vowing the neighbors adjacent to Esherton Green would jump at the opportunity to purchase the farm. Then, snatching a bottle of whisky in one hand and snaring a harlot years past her prime around the waist with the other, he had staggered from the gaming hell.

Heath hoped to God the man had spoken the truth, otherwise, what would he do with the property? A gusty sigh escaped him as he slogged along to make the arrangements to sell his winnings. He should've been at White's, a glass of brandy in one hand and cards in the other. Or at the theater watching that new actress, a luscious little temptation he had half a mind to enter into an arrangement with—after his physician examined her for disease, of course.

Heath sought a new mistress after Daphne had taken it into her beautiful, but wool-gathering, head that she wanted marriage. To him. When he refused, she'd eloped with another admirer. That left a bitter taste on his tongue; she'd been cuckolding him while beneath his protection.

Thank God he always wore protection before intimate encounters and insisted she underwent weekly examinations. Laughable, Daphne daring to broach matrimony when she'd already proven herself incapable of fidelity. Not that married women were better. His mother hadn't troubled herself to provide Father a spare heir before lifting her skirts for the first of her myriad of lovers.

Both his parents had died of the French disease, six months apart.

Heath snorted, and the horse jerked his head. Now there was a legacy to be proud of.

If and when he finally decided to become leg-shackled—at forty or fifty—he'd choose a mousy virgin who wouldn't draw the interest of another man. A chit painfully shy or somehow marred, she'd never dare seek a lover. Or perhaps a woman past her prime, on the shelf, whose gratitude for saving her from a life of spinsterhood would assure faithfulness.

Not too long on the shelf, however. He needed to get an heir or two on her.

Didn't matter a whit that half of *le beau monde* shared their beds with multiple partners. His marriage bed would remain pure—well, his wife would, in any event.

A gust of wind slammed into Heath, sending his hat spiraling into the air. The gale lifted it, spinning the cap higher.

"Bloody hell."

Ebénè raised his head and rolled his big eyes at the cavorting cap then grunted, as if to say, *I've had quite enough of this nonsense. Do find me a warm comfortable stable and a bucket of oats at once.*

Two more miserable miles passed, made worse by the absence of Heath's head covering. Water trickled down his face and nape, and, with each step, his temper increased in direct proportion to his dwindling patience. The return trip to Bristledale Court would be more wretched, given his sopped state, and dusk would be upon him before he reached the house.

He should have accepted Leventhorpe's suggestion of a carriage, but that would have meant Heath's comfort at the expense of two drivers and four horses. He shivered and drew his collar higher. He anticipated a hot bath, a hearty meal, and a stiff drink or two upon his return to Bristledale. Leventhorpe boasted the best cognac in England.

Heath glanced skyward. The roiling, blackish clouds gave no indication they had any intention of calming their fury soon. He wiped off a large droplet balancing on the end of his nose. Strange, he hadn't paid much mind to storms while in Town. Then again, he wasn't prone to gadding about in the midst of frightful gales when in the city either.

Perhaps he could bribe a cup of tea and a few moments before the fire from the tenant.

What was his name?

Something or other Culpoppers or Clodhopper or some such unusual surname. The bloke wouldn't likely offer him refreshment or a coze before the hearth once he learned the reason for Heath's visit. Guilt raised its thorny head, but Heath stifled the pricks of unease. A business matter, nothing more. He'd won the land fairly. The tenant was in arrears in rents. Heath didn't want another parcel of countryside to tend to. He knew naught of dairy farming.

The place must be sold.

Simple as that.

Keep spouting that drivel, and you might actually come to believe it.

Although gambling is an inherent tendency in
human nature, a wise woman refrains from partaking,
no matter how seemingly insignificant the wager.
~Wisdom and Advice—The Genteel Lady's Guide to Practical Living

3

Brooke scrunched her forehead and tried to decipher the words. Not only did Sheridan possess atrocious penmanship, the tea had ruined much of the writing.

...writing to inform you I have...

A large smudge obliterated the next few words. She smoothed the wrinkled paper and squinted.

Esherton Green...new owner.

Brooke couldn't suppress her gasp of dismay as she involuntarily clenched one hand around the letter and pressed the other to her chest.

New owner? Esherton Green was entailed. Sheridan couldn't sell it.

Yes. He could.

Only the house and the surrounding five acres were entailed. Even the outbuildings, though they sat on those lands, hadn't been part of the original entailment. The rest of the estate had been accumulated over the previous four generations and the barns constructed as the need arose. She'd memorized the details, since she and Papa had done their utmost to finagle a way for her to inherit.

He'd conceived the plan to send Sheridan half the proceeds from the dairy and farm, so she and the others could continue to live in the only home any of them remembered and still make a modest income. They'd gambled that Sheridan would be content to pad his pockets with no effort on his part, and wouldn't be interested in moving to their remote estate and assuming the role of gentleman farmer.

And our risk paid off. Until now.

She needed the acreage to farm and graze the cattle. Their milk was sold to make Cheshire's renowned cheese. Without the land, the means to support the girls and staff was lost.

"What does he have to say?" Blaire exchanged a worried glance with her twin.

Blythe pushed a curl behind her ear and slanted her head, her intelligent lavender gaze shifting between the paper and Brooke. "Is something amiss, Brooke?"

"Shh." Brooke waved her hand to silence their questions. The tea had damaged the writing in several places. She deciphered a few disjointed sentences.

Pay rent...reside elsewhere...at your earliest convenience...new owner takes possession...regret the necessity...unfortunate circumstances...commendable job managing my holdings...might be of service

Brooke's head swam dizzily.

"Pay rent? Reside elsewhere?" she murmured beneath her breath.

She raised her gaze, staring at the now-frolicking fire, and swallowed a wave of nausea. Sheridan had magnanimously offered to let them stay on if they paid him rent, the bloody bounder. How could she find funds for rent when he'd sold their source of income? They already supplemented their income every way possible.

Brette took in sewing and embroidery and often stayed up until the wee morning hours stitching with a single candle as light. The twins managed a large vegetable, herb, and flower garden, selling the blooms and any excess produce at the village market each week during the growing season. Blythe put her musical talents to use and gave Vicar Avery's spoiled daughters weekly voice and harpsichord lessons.

The women picked mushrooms and tended the chickens and geese—feeding them, gathering their eggs, and plucking and saving the feathers from the unfortunate birds that stopped laying and found their way into the soup pot.

The faithful staff—more family than servants—contributed beyond Brooke's expectations too. Mabry and the other two stable hands provided fish, game fowl, and the occasional deer to feed them. Duffen spent hours picking berries and fruit from the neglected orchard so Mrs. Jennings could make her famous tarts, pies, and preserves, which also sold at the market. And dear, dim-witted Flora washed the Huffington's and Benbridge's laundry.

Sheridan remained obligated to care for them, save Brooke, who'd come of age since he gained guardianship of the girls. It would serve him right if she showed up on his doorstep, sister, cousins, pets, and servants—even the herd of cows—in tow, and demanded he do right by them.

Brooke didn't know his age or if he was married. Did he have children? Come to think of it, she didn't have an address for him either. She'd directed her correspondences to his man of business in London. Where did Sheridan live? London?

Was he one of those fellows who preferred the hubbub and glamour of city life, rather than the peace and simplicity of country living? Most likely. She'd never lived anywhere but Esherton. However, the tales Papa told of the crowding, stench, and noise of Town made the notion of living there abhorrent.

Heart whooshing in her ears, she dropped her attention to the letter once more.

Expect your response by...as to your intentions.

Her gaze flew to the letter's date. Tea had smudged all but the year. Moisture blurred her vision, and she blinked furiously. The unfairness galled. She'd worked so blasted hard, as had everybody else, and that pompous twit—

"Brooke?" The hint of alarm edging Brette's voice nearly undid her.

Fresh tears welled in Brooke's eyes, and she pivoted toward the windows to hide her distress. After dragging in a steadying breath, she forced her leaden feet to carry her to the unoccupied chair and gratefully sank onto the cushion. However, flattened by years of constant use, it provided little in the way of padding.

She took another ragged breath, holding the air until her lungs burned and willed her pulse to slow to a somewhat normal rhythm. Though her emotions teetered on the cusp of hysteria, she must present a calm facade. The quartet weren't given to histrionics, but something of this magnitude was guaranteed to cause a few waterworks, her own included. Pressing shaking fingers to her forehead, Brooke closed her eyes for a brief moment.

God help me. Us.

"I fear I have disquieting news." She met each of their wary gazes in turn, her heart so full of dismay and disbelief, she could scarcely speak.

God rot you, Sheridan.

"Sheridan..." Her mouth dry from trepidation—*how can I tell them*?—she cleared her throat then licked her lips. "He has sold the lands not attached to the house."

The study echoed with the girls' gasps and a low oath from Mabry.

Outrage contorted his usually jovial face into a fierce scowl. "The devil you say!"

Freddy wedged his sturdy little body between Blaike and Blaire, his soulful eyes wide with worry.

"Told you the day be cursed." Duffen shook his head. Highly superstitious, he fingered the smooth stone tied to his neck by a thin leather strip. A lucky talisman, he claimed. "Started with me putting on my left shoe first and then spilling salt in me porridge this morning."

"Sheridan cannot do that." Blaike looked at Brooke hopefully. "Can he, Brooke?"

"Yes, dear, he can." Brooke scowled at the illegible scribbles. She took her anger out on the letter, crumpling it into a tight wad before tossing it into the fire. "He's offered to let us stay on if we pay him rent."

The last word caught on a sob. She'd failed the girls. And the servants.

She couldn't even sell the furnishings, horseflesh, or carriages. Everything of value had long since been bartered or sold. The parure set would only bring enough to sustain them for a few months—six at the most.

What then? They had no remaining family. No place to go.

She clenched the cushion and curled her toes in her boots against the urge to scream her frustration. She must find a position immediately. A governess. Or perhaps a teacher. Or maybe she and the girls could open a dressmaker's shop. They would need to move. There were no positions for young ladies available nearby and even less need for seamstresses.

London.

A shudder of dread rippled through her. Nothing for it. They would have to move to Town. They'd never traveled anywhere beyond the village.

Did she have the legal right to sell the cattle and keep the proceeds? She twisted a curl beside her ear. She must investigate that posthaste. But who dare she ask? One of her neighbors might have purchased the lands from beneath her, and she couldn't afford to consult a solicitor. Perhaps she should seek Mr. Benbridge's counsel. She couldn't count the times he'd offered his assistance.

Silas Huffington's sagging face sprang to mind. Oh, he'd help her, she had no doubt. *If* she became his mistress. Hell would burn a jot hotter the day that bugger died.

"Did he say who bought the lands, Miss Brooke?" Duffen peered at her, his wizened face crumpled with grief. Moisture glinted in his faded eyes, and she swore his lower lip trembled. "That churl, Huffington?"

Brooke shook her head. "No, Duffen, I'm afraid Sheridan didn't say."

What would become of Duffen? Mrs. Jennings? Poor simple-minded Flora? Queer in the attic some would call the maid, but they loved her and ignored her difficulties.

How could Sheridan sell the lands from beneath them?

The miserable, selfish wretch.

Never had Brooke felt such rage. If only she were a man, this whole bumblebroth would have been avoided.

"Man ought to be horsewhipped, locked up, an' the key thrown away," Duffen muttered while wringing his gnarled hands. "Knew in my aching joints today heralded a disaster besides this hellish weather."

"Perhaps the new owner will allow us to carry on as we have." Everyone's gaze lurched to Blaire. She shrugged and petted Pudding's back. The cat arched in pleasure, purring louder. "We could at least ask, couldn't we?"

A flicker of hope took root.

Could they?

Brooke tapped her fingers on the chair's arm. The howling wind, the fire's crackle, and the cats' throaty purrs, filled the room. Nonetheless, a tense stillness permeated the air.

Why not at least try?

"Why, yes, darling." Brooke smiled and nodded. "What a brilliant miss you are. That might be just the thing."

Blaire beamed, and smiles wreathed the other girls' faces.

Duffen continued to scowl and mumble threats and nonsense about the evil eye beneath his breath.

A speculative gleam in his eyes, Mabry scratched his nearly bald pate. "Aye, if he's a city cove with no interest in country life, we might convince the bloke."

"Yes, we might, at that." Brooke stood and, after shaking her skirts, paced behind the sofa, her head bowed as she worried the flesh of her lower lip.

Could they convince the new owner to let them stay if she shared her plans for the farm? Would he object to a woman managing the place?

Many men took exception to a female in that sort of a position—the fairer sex weren't supposed to concern themselves with men's work.

Hands on her hips, she faced Mabry. "Ask around, will you? But be discreet. See if our neighbors or anyone at the village has knowledge of the sale. If the buyer isn't local, we stand a much better chance of continuing as we have."

What if the buyer was indeed one of the people she owed money to?

Not likely.

She would have heard a whisper.

Wouldn't I?

Something of that nature wouldn't stay secret in their shire for long. In Acton, rumors made the rounds faster than the blustering wind, especially if the vicar's wife heard the *on dit*. The woman's tongue flapped fast enough to send a schooner round the world in a week.

Brooke turned to Duffen. Often loose of lips himself, he *had* to keep her confidence. "We want this kept quiet as possible. I cannot afford to have our debts called in by those afraid they'll not get their monies."

Duffen angled his head, a strange glint in his rheumy brown eyes. He toyed with his amulet again. "Won't say a word, Miss Brooke. Count on me to protect you an' the other misses."

She smiled, moisture stinging her eyes. "I know I can, Duffen."

Wringing his hands together, he nodded and mumbled as he stared into the fire. "Promised the master, I did. Gots to keep my word. Protect the young misses."

"Brooke?" Blythe's worried voice drew everybody's attention. "What if the owner wants to reside at Esherton? What will we do then?"

Only ninnyhammers mistake preparation meeting opportunity as luck.
~Wisdom and Advice—The Genteel Lady's Guide to Practical Living

4

Lifting his head, Heath squinted into the tumult swirling around him. At the end of a long, tree-lined drive, a stately two-story home rose out of the grayish gloom. A welcoming glint in a lower window promised much-needed warmth.

Deuced rotten day.

The indistinct shapes of several outbuildings, including two immense barns and an unusual round structure, lay to one side of the smallish manor. A cow's bawl floated to him, accompanied by a pungent waft of damp manure.

Ebénè must have seen the house and stables too, for the tired horse quickened his pace to a trot, ignoring Heath's hands on the reins.

"Fine, get on with you then."

He gave the horse his head. Splattering muck in his haste, the beast shot down the rough and holey roadway as if a hoard of demons scratched at his hooves.

The thunderous crack of an oak toppling mere seconds after Heath passed beneath its gnarled branches launched his heart into his throat and earned a terrified squeal from Ebénè. The limbs colliding with the earth launched a shower of mud over them. A thick blob smacked Heath at the base of his skull then slid, like a giant, slimy slug, into his collar. The cold clump wedged between his shoulder blades.

Of all the—

Another horrendous, grinding snap rent the air, and he whipped around to peer behind him. The remainder of the tree plummeted, ripping the roots from their protective cover and jarring the ground violently. More miniature dirt cannonballs pelted him and Ebénè.

Could the day possibly get worse?

The horse bucked and kicked his hind legs.

Yes. It could.

Heath lurched forward, just about plummeting headfirst into the muck. Clutching his horse's mane and neck, he held on, dangling from the side of the saddle.

The mud oozed down his spine.

I'm never setting foot outdoors in the rain again.

With considerable effort, he righted himself then turned to look at the mammoth tree blocking the drive. Had the thing landed on him, he'd have been killed.

Another ripple of unease tingled down his spine, and he glanced around warily. Didn't feel right. He couldn't put his finger on what, but disquiet lingered, and he'd always been one to heed his hunches.

He returned his attention to the shattered tree and the ground torn up by the exposed roots. Disease-ravaged. He glanced at the others. Several of them, too. Dangerous that. They ought to come down. He'd best warn the new owners of the hazard.

You are the new owner.

Heath swiped a hand across his face, dislodging several muddy bits. Nothing like arriving saturated and layered in filth to evict a tenant.

He scrutinized the dismembered tree. A man on horseback could traverse the mess, but passage by carriage was impossible. To expedite the sale, it might be worth paying the tenant to remove the downed tree. That meant delaying tours to prospective buyers for at least a day or two. Unless a neighbor familiar with the place was prepared make the purchase at once—a most convenient solution.

Turning his horse to the unremarkable house, he clicked his tongue and kicked his heels.

A few moments later, Heath halted Ebénè before the weathered stone structure. A shutter, the emerald paint chipped and peeling, hung askew on one of the upper windows, and the hedge bordering the circular courtyard hadn't seen a pair of pruning shears in a good while. Jagged cracks marred the front steps and stoop, and a scraggly tendril of silvery smoke spiraled skyward from a chimney missing several bricks. An untidy orchard on the opposite side of the house from the barns also showed signs of neglect.

The manor and grounds had seen better days, a testament either to the tenant's squandering or to having fallen on hard times. No wonder Gainsborough hadn't been reluctant to part with the place. Why, Heath had done the chap a favor by winning. Gainsborough had probably laughed himself sick with relief at having rid himself of the encumbrance.

Ebénè shuddered and shifted beneath Heath.

Poor beast.

Heath scanned the rustic manor then the barns. Should he dismount here or take the miserable horse to the stables? A single ground floor window in the house glowed with light, rather strange given the lateness of the afternoon and the gloom cloaking the day.

The entrance eased open, no more than three inches, and a puckered face surrounded by wild grayish-white hair peeked through the crack. "State your business."

This shabby fellow, the tenant farmer? That explained a lot.

Heath slid from the saddle, his sore bum protesting. The mud in his shirt shifted lower. Shit.

"I'm the Earl of Ravensdale, here to see the master."

A cackle of laughter erupted from the troll-like fellow. The door inched open further, and the man's entire head poked out. He grinned, revealing a missing front tooth.

"Mighty hard to do, stranger, since he's been dead these five years past."

The man snickered again, but then his gaze shifted to Ebénè and widened in admiration. The peculiar chap recognized superior horseflesh.

Ebénè nudged Heath, none too gently.

The remainder of Heath's patience dissolved faster than salt in soup. He jiggled the horse's reins. "My mount needs attention, and I must speak to whoever is in charge. Is that you?"

"Is someone at the door, Duffen? In this weather?"

The door swung open to reveal a striking blonde, wearing a dress as ugly and drab as the dismal day.

Heath's jaw sagged, and he stared mesmerized.

Despite the atrocious grayish gown, the woman's figure stole the air from him. Full breasts strained against the too-small dress, tapering to a waist his hands could span. And from her height, he'd lay odds she possessed long, graceful legs. Legs that could wrap around his waist and...

Though cold to his marrow, his manhood surged with sensual awareness. He shifted his stance, grateful his long overcoat covered him to his ankles. He snapped his mouth shut. Evict this shapely beauty? Surely a monumental mistake had been made. Gainsborough couldn't be so cold-hearted, could he?

Heath snapped his mouth closed and glared at the grinning buffoon peeking around the doorframe. Making a pretense of shaking the mud from his coat, Heath slid a sideways glance to the woman. Probably thought him a half-witted dolt.

She regarded Heath like a curious kitten, interest piqued yet unsure of what to make of him. Her dark blue, almost violet, eyes glowed with humor, and a smile hovered on her plump lips. The wind teased the flaxen curls framing her oval face.

A dog poked its snout from beneath her skirt and issued a muffled warning.

"Hush, Freddy. Go inside. Shoo."

The dog skulked into the house. Just barely. He plopped onto the entrance, his worried brown-eyed gaze fixed on Heath. She neatly stepped over the portly corgi, and the bodice of her gown pulled taught, exposing hardened nipples.

Another surge of desire jolted Heath.

Disturbing. Uncharacteristic, this immediate lust.

Rainwater dribbled from the hair plastered to his forehead and into his eyes. He swiped the strands away to see her better.

"Miss—"

A disturbance sounded behind her. She glanced over her shoulder as four more young women crowded into the entry.

Blister and damn. A bloody throng of goddesses.

Surely God's favor had touched them, for London couldn't claim a single damsel this exquisite, let alone five diamonds of the first water.

Gainsborough had some lengthy explaining to do.

The one attired in gray narrowed her eyes gone midnight blue, all hint of warmth whisked away on the wind buffeting them. She notched her pert chin upward and pointed at him.

"You're him, aren't you? The man who bought Esherton's lands? Are you truly so eager to take possession and ruin us, you ventured out in this weather and risked catching lung fever?"

Bought Esherton's lands? What the hell?

A wise woman refrains from laying odds,
well aware that luck never gives, it only lends,
and will inevitably demand payment, no matter the cost.
~Wisdom and Advice—The Genteel Lady's Guide to Practical Living

5

He's come already.

Brooke's hope, along with her heart, sank to her half-boots at the peeved expression on the man's chiseled face. Much too attractive, even drenched, mud-splattered, and annoyed.

The girls' sharp intakes of breath hadn't gone unnoticed. She hid her own surprise behind a forced half-smile. Her breasts tingled, the nipples pebble hard.

It's the icy wind, nothing more.

She imagined his heavy gaze lingering on her bodice.

Why couldn't he have been ancient and ugly and yellow-toothed and...and balding?

Shock at his arrival had her in a dither. She'd counted on a scrap of luck to allow her time to prepare a convincing argument. To have him here a mere hour after reading Sheridan's letter had her at sixes and sevens. The letter must have been delayed en route, or her cowardly cousin had dawdled in advising her of the change in her circumstances.

She'd lay odds, ten to one, on the latter.

The gentleman still stood in the rain. That would make a positive impression and gain his favor when she broached the possibility of her continuing to operate the dairy and farm.

Come, Brooke. Gather your wits and manners, control yourself, and attempt to undo the damage already done.

"Looks like a half-drowned mongrel, he does." Duffen sniggered, his behavior much ruder than typical.

Brooke quelled his snicker with a sharp look. "See to the horse, please, and tell Mr. Mabry we have a guest. Ask him to join us as soon as he is able."

"Yes, Miss Brooke. I'll get my coat." Duffen bobbed his head and went in search of the garment.

She wanted the overseer present when she explained her proposition to his lordship. After all, although she'd read dozens of books and articles on the subject, Mabry's knowledge of the dairy's day-to-day operation far surpassed hers.

Brooke folded her hands before her. "He'll return momentarily, Mister...?"

The gentleman, with hair as black as the glorious horse standing beside him, crooked a boyish smile and bowed. Yes, too confounded handsome for her comfort. The wind flipped his coat over his bent behind. "Heath, Earl of Ravensdale at your service, Mistress...?"

"Earl?" *He's a confounded earl*?

An earl wouldn't want to run a dairy farm, would he?

She scrutinized him toe to top. Not one dressed like him. His soaked state couldn't disguise the fineness of the garments he wore or the quality of the beautiful stepper he rode. The wind tousled his hair, a trifle longer than fashionable. It gave him a dashing, rakish appearance. She shouldn't have noticed that, nor experienced the odd sparks of pleasure gazing at him caused.

A lock slipped onto his forehead again. The messy style rather suited him. Where was his hat anyway?

She winced as a boney elbow jabbed her side.

"Tell him your name, Brooke."

Ah, Blythe. Always level-headed. And subtle.

"Forgive me, my lord. I am Brooke Culpepper." Brooke gestured to the foursome peering at the earl. "And these are my sister, Miss Brette Culpepper, and our cousins, the Misses Culpeppers, Blythe, Blaire, and Blaike."

His lips bent into an amused smile upon hearing their names, not an uncommon occurrence.

Named Bess, Mama and Aunt Bea had done their daughters an injustice by carrying on the silly B name tradition for Culpepper females. Supposedly, the practice had started so long ago no one could remember the first.

Brooke dipped into a deep curtsy, and the girls followed her lead, each making a pretty show of deference. She wanted to applaud. Not one teetered or stumbled. They'd never had cause to curtsy before, and the dears performed magnificently.

Freddy lowered his shoulders and touched his head to his paws, a trick Brooke had taught him as a puppy.

Lord Ravensdale threw his head back and laughed, a wonderful rumble that echoed deep in his much-too-broad chest. At least, it looked wide beneath his coat. Maybe he wore padding. Silas Huffington did, which, rather than making him look muscular, gave him the appearance of a great, stuffed doll.

A very ugly doll.

"What a splendid trick, Mistress...?" His lordship inquired after her name again.

"It's miss, your lordship." Brette nudged Brooke in the ribs this time. "We're *all* misses, but Brooke's the eldest of the five and—"

Brooke silenced her with a slight shake of her head.

A puzzled expression flitted across the earl's face. He took her measure, examining her just as she'd inspected him, and a predatory glint replaced his bewilderment.

Her gaze held captive by his—titillating and terrifying—the hairs from her forearms to her nape sprang up. Awareness of a man unlike anything she'd ever experienced before, even with Humphrey, gripped her.

A man of the world, and no doubt used to snapping his fingers and getting whatever he desired, including wenches in his bed, Lord Ravensdale now scrutinized her with something other than inquisitiveness. The look couldn't be described as entirely polite either.

He wasn't to be trifled with.

She'd bet the biscuits Brette made today, Brooke had piqued his interest. Why, and whether she should be flattered or alarmed, she hadn't determined. What rot. Of course she was flattered. What woman wouldn't be?

He approached the steps, his attention locked on her. "There's no *Mister* Culpepper?"

Brooke tilted her head, trying to read him. Why didn't she believe the casualness of his tone?

"No, not since Father died five years ago." She pushed a tendril of hair off her cheek, resisting the urge to wrap her arms around her shoulders and step backward. The wind proved wicked for April. Why else did she remain peppered in gooseflesh? "Didn't Cousin Sheridan inform you?"

"Cousin? Gainsborough is your cousin?" Disbelief shattered his lordship's calm mien. His nostrils flared, and his lovely lips pressed into a thin line. His intense gaze flicked to each of the women, one by one. "He is cousin to *all* of you?"

"Yes," Brooke and the others said as one.

The revelation didn't please the earl. He closed his eyes for a long moment, his impossibly thick lashes dark smudges against his swarthy skin. Did he ail? He seemed truly confounded or put upon.

Wearing a floppy hat which almost obliterated his face, Duffen edged by her. He yanked his collar to his ears. "I'll see to your horse, *sir*."

"Duffen, that will do," Brooke warned gently. She wouldn't tolerate impudence, even from a retainer as beloved as him. "Lord Ravensdale is our guest."

Astonishment flitted across Duffen's cragged features before they settled into lines of suspicion once more. Duffen hadn't expected a noble either.

"Beg your pardon, Miss Brooke."

He ducked his head contritely and, after gathering the horse's reins, led the spirited beast toward the stables. Eager to escape the elements, the stallion practically dragged Duffen.

"My lord, please forgive my poor manners. Do come in out of the wretched rain." Brooke stepped over Freddy and turned to Brette. "Will you fetch hot tea and biscuits for his lordship?"

Brooke sent him a sidelong glance. "And a towel so he might dry off?"

"Of course. At once." Brette bobbed a hasty curtsy before hurrying down the shadowy corridor.

Hopefully, she would brew just enough tea for the earl. They were nearly out of tea and sugar, and there would be no replacing the supplies.

Brooke motioned to Blaike. "Please stir the fire in the study and add another log? I don't wish his lordship to become chilled."

Her attention riveted on their visitor, Blaike colored and stuttered, "Ah…yes. Certainly." After another quick peek at him, she pivoted and disappeared into the study a few doorways down.

He'd been here mere minutes and the girls blushed and blathered like nincompoops. Brooke pursed her lips. It wouldn't do, especially not when he might very well be here to put them out of their home. She drew in a tense breath.

Lord Ravensdale stepped across the threshold and hesitated. He wiped his feet on the braided rag rug while his gaze roved the barren entrance. A rivulet of rainwater trailed down his temple. Soaked through. He'd be lucky if he didn't catch his death.

Surely claiming the lands hadn't been so pressing he'd felt the need to endanger his health by venturing into the worst storm in a decade? A greedy sort and anxious to see what he'd purchased, perhaps. Well, he'd have to wait. She wouldn't ask Mr. Mabry or the other hands to show the earl around, not only because the weather was fouler than Mr. Huffington's breath, but Brooke needed the men attending the cows and newborn calves.

Lord Ravensdale exuded power and confidence, and the foyer shrank with his presence. Except for Brette, the Culpepper women were tall, but he towered above Brooke by several inches. He smiled at Brooke, and her stomach gave a queer little somersault at the transformation in his rugged features. Devilishly attractive. A dangerous distraction. He was the enemy. He'd bought Esherton, practically stolen her home, with no regard to how that would affect her family.

Don't be fooled by his wild good looks.

He shoved wet strands off his high forehead again.

Freddy crept closer, his button nose twitching.

Brooke brushed away a few of Freddy's hairs clinging to her skirt, unexpectedly ashamed of her outdated and worn gown. She hid her calloused hands in the folds of her gown. She would wager the Culpepper sapphires that women threw themselves at Lord Ravensdale.

Fashionable ladies dressed in silks and satins, with intricately coiffed hair, and smooth, creamy skin, who smelled perfectly wonderful all the time. Lord Ravensdale's women probably washed with perfumed soap. Expensive, scented bars from France. Pink or yellow, or maybe blue and shaped like flowers.

Brooke couldn't remember the last time she'd worn perfume or used anything other than the harsh gel-like soap that she and Mrs. Jennings made from beef tallow. Their precious candle supply came from the smelly lard too.

Why the notion rankled, Brooke refused to examine. Except, here she stood attired like a country bumpkin covered in dog and cat hair, with her curls tied in a haphazard knot and ink stains on her fingers. She couldn't even provide his lordship a decent repast or light a candle to guide him to the study, let alone produce a dram of whisky or brandy to warm his insides.

Nonetheless, they...*she* must win his favor.

She straightened her spine, determined to act the part of a gracious hostess if it killed her. "Sir, you should take off your coat. It's soaked through."

While his lordship busied himself removing his gloves, she studied him. He had sharp, exotic, almost foreign features. She shouldn't be surprised to learn a Moroccan or an Egyptian ancestor perched in his family tree somewhere. High cheekbones gave way to a molded jaw and a mouth much too perfect to belong to a man. A small scar marred the left side of his square chin. How had he come by it?

She could almost envision him, legs braced and grinning, on the rolling deck of a pirate ship, the furious waves pounding against the vessel as the wind whipped his hair.

Stop it.

Hand on his sword, he would throw his head back and laugh, the corded muscles in his neck bulging; a man in command against nature's wrath.

"The ride here turned most unpleasant."

Lord Ravensdale's melodic baritone sent her cavorting pirate plunging off the side of the fantasy ship and into the churning waves. Brooke clamped her teeth together. What ailed her? She'd never been prone to fanciful imaginations.

After tucking his wet gloves into his pocket, his lordship unbuttoned his tobacco-brown overcoat.

Almost the same color as his eyes.

"A tree fell as I passed by. I'm afraid it left rather a jumble on the drive." He flashed his white teeth again as he advanced farther into the entry.

Retreating, she allowed him room to shrug off the soggy garment. A pleasant, spicy scent wafted past her nose. Naturally, he smelled divine. She peered past him and to the lane. A tree and a tangle of branches lay sprawled on the road to the house. She stifled a groan. How were they to remove that disaster with one horse and a pair of axes?

Releasing a measured breath, she closed the heavy door.

Lord, I don't know how much more I can bear.

"If you'll permit it, my lord, I shall have my cousin take your coat to the kitchen to place beside the stove." She extended her hand. Not that it would dry completely in the few minutes he would be here, but perhaps he would appreciate the gesture.

He passed her the triple-caped greatcoat then removed a wilted handkerchief from his jacket pocket. A slight shudder shook him as he wiped his face. "I'm afraid the elements did rather get the best of me."

As if he'd cued it, a blast of wind crashed into the house, rattling the door and windows. The corridor grew dim as the storm renewed her fury. The pewter sky visible through the windows paralleling the door suggested dusk had already fallen. Brooke furrowed her brow. His lordship didn't dare delay at Esherton. His return journey to—wherever he'd come from—became more perilous by the moment.

And he couldn't stay here.

They hadn't an empty bedchamber to accommodate him other than Papa and Mama's, and a stranger amongst five eligible women might give rise to gossip. Besides, expecting her to house him when he'd arrived to put them from their home was beyond the pale, accommodating hostess or not.

Playacting wasn't her strong suit. Pretending to welcome the earl when she wanted to treat him like a plague-ridden thief strained her good manners and noble intentions. Had she been alive, Mama would've chastised Brooke for her unchristian behavior and thoughts.

"Blaire, please take his lordship's coat to the kitchen and fetch one of Papa's jackets for him."

Papa's coats had been too old to sell, and Brooke refused to make them into rags. It seemed disrespectful, almost disloyal, to treat his possessions with such little regard. She'd allowed Duffen and Mabry their pick. Therefore, the remaining coats were quite shabby. Still, a dry, moth-eaten jacket must be preferable to saturated finery.

"You and the others join us in the study as soon as the tea is ready."

Brooke wanted the quartet present for the discussion. After all, the sale of the lands affected their lives too. Besides, the earl made her edgy. Perhaps because much was at stake, and there'd been no time to prepare an argument to let them continue as they had been.

Her cousin seized the soaked wool, and after a swift backward glance, marched to the rear of the house.

Lord Ravensdale inspected the stark entry once more. Rectangular shadows lined the faded walls where paintings had once hung. He ran his gaze over her, lingering at the noticeable discolored arc at her neckline where a lace collar used to adorn the gown. She hid her reddened hands behind her lest he notice the missing lace cuffs as well. They'd been sold last year for a pittance.

She hadn't been self-conscious of her attire or the blatant sparseness of her home before, but somehow, he made their lack of prosperity glaring. Rather like a purebred Arabian thrust into the midst of donkeys. Pretty donkeys, yes, but compared to a beautiful stepper, wholly lacking.

Freddy crept forward and dared to sniff around his lordship's feet. Then, to Brooke's horror, the dog proceeded to heist his leg on one glossy boot. Yellow pooled around the toe as she and Blythe gaped.

"Freddy, bad boy. Shame on you." Blythe scolded, bending to scoop the cowering dog into her arms. Her cheeks glowed cherry red. "I'll put him in the kitchen, Brooke."

Whispering chastisements, she scurried away, the dog happily wagging his tail as if forgiven.

Mortification burning her face, Brooke raised her gaze to meet Lord Ravensdale's humor-filled eyes.

"Perhaps I might trouble you for *two* towels?" He raised his dripping foot and grinned.

Brooke tried to stifle the giggle that rushed to her throat.

She really did.

A loud peal surged forth anyway. Partially brought on by relief that he wasn't angry, partially because in other circumstances, she might have indulged in a flirtation with him, and partially to release nervous tension.

If she didn't laugh, she would burst into tears.

He smiled while pulling at his cuffs. A bit of dirt fell to the scarred floor. "So what's this nonsense about Gainsborough selling me Esherton? Your cousin lost the place to me in a card game and said you were months behind in rents."

In the event one is unwise enough to venture down wagering's treacherous pathway, decide beforehand the rules by which you'll play, the exact stakes, and at which point you intend to quit.
~*Wisdom and Advice—The Genteel Lady's Guide to Practical Living*

6

Heath clamped his jaw against a curse at the devastation that ravaged Miss Culpepper's. One moment she'd been glowing, mirth shimmering in her gaze and pinkening her face, and the next, her lovely indigo eyes pooled with tears. They seeped over the edges and trailed down her silky cheeks, though she didn't make a sound.

How often had she wept silently so others wouldn't hear? He'd done the same most of his childhood. He brushed his thumb over one damp cheek. What was it about this woman that plucked at his heart after a mere ten minutes acquaintance? He didn't know her at all, yet he felt as if something had connected between them from the onset.

Did she sense it too, or was it only him? Perhaps he'd caught a fever and delusions had set in.

She blinked at him, her eyes round and wounded. And accusing. "We're not behind in the rents. He's been paid on time each month. Except the month I broke my arm."

Shit, another lie. What have I gotten myself into?

Deep pain glimmered in the depths of her eyes, which were too old and wise for someone her age. This woman had clearly borne much in her short life.

And she hadn't known her home had been lost in a wager gone awry.

She'd thought Heath had bought the estate. Though what difference that would have made in her circumstances, he couldn't fathom. Gambled away or purchased, the consequence remained the same for the women. They'd be ousted from their home. At least he held a degree of concern for their wellbeing, unlike their callous cousin.

Surely they must have someone who could be of assistance to them.

What sort of a vile blackguard gave no thought to his kinsmen, especially five females without means? As apparent as the mud on his boots and sticking uncomfortably to his spine, they were poor as church mice. In all likelihood, the holy rodents fared better since they would eagerly accept crumbs. Gut instinct told him the Culpeppers might have little else, but they had their pride and wouldn't accept charity.

Miss Culpepper drew in a shuddering breath and averted her head. She wiped her eyes as her sister entered the corridor bearing a meager tea tray upon which rested a mismatched tea service, a napkin, a single teacup and three small biscuits.

A wave of compassion, liberally weighted with remorse, engulfed him. He'd never experienced poverty such as this, and yet, they offered him what little they had.

Damnation.

He didn't want a blasted dairy farm, even if angels did make it their home.

Composing herself, Miss Culpepper shifted toward a door farther along the hallway and offered her sister a wobbly smile.

Miss Brette—wasn't that her name?—peered between him and her sister, her nose crinkled in puzzlement. Her gaze lingered on her sister's damp cheeks.

Astute woman.

One of the twins trailed Miss Brette.

Heath had no idea what her name was, but she bore a large black jacket and a towel. He strained to distinguish the women's features in the shadowy corridor. Another violent surge of air battered the house, and the women's startled gazes flew to the entrance.

He feared the windows might shatter from the gale's force. A breeze wafted past, sending a chill creeping along his shoulders. The house radiated cold. This drafty old tomb must be impossible to keep heated, but not one of the Culpepper misses wore warm clothing.

"My lord, this way if you please." Miss Culpepper motioned to the doorway the girl dressed in green had disappeared into earlier. "We'll give you a moment of privacy to dry yourself and exchange your coat for Papa's. It's rather worn, I'm afraid, but it should be a mite more comfortable than wearing yours."

The trio filed through the entrance, slender as reeds, each of them. A natural physical tendency or brought on by insufficient food? Mayhap both.

Heath followed, guilt's sharp little teeth nipping at his heels. He glimpsed the tray as Miss Brette arranged it on a table before the fireplace. How they could be charitable, he didn't know, and, had their situations been reversed, honesty compelled him to admit, he mightn't have been as hospitable. Not much better than their snake of a cousin, was he? The notion left a sickening knot in his middle and a rancorous taste on his tongue.

Actually, the foul taste might have been a spot of mud he'd licked from his lip. Pray God the dried crumb was mud and not some other manner of filth.

"Let's give his lordship a moment, shall we?" With a wan smile, Miss Culpepper ushered her wards from the study.

Frenetic whispers sounded the moment they left his sight.

Heath made quick work of exchanging the jackets. The one he donned smelled slightly musty and a hint of tobacco lingered within the coarsely woven threads. Too big around, the garment skimmed his waist. The Culpeppers didn't get their height or svelteness from Mr. Culpepper's branch of the family. Heath tugged at a too-short sleeve, and his third finger sank into a moth hole.

What had brought this family to such destitution?

He'd lacked human companionship and love his entire childhood—and by choice, a great deal of his adulthood also—but never wanted for physical comfort or necessities. Their circumstances appeared the reverse of his. Company and affection they possessed aplenty, but scant little else. Nonetheless, they didn't act deprived or envious, at least not from what he'd observed in his short acquaintance with them.

The truth of that might prove different upon further association. In his experience, the facade women presented at first glance proved difficult to maintain, and before long, they revealed their true character. Rarely had the latter been an improvement upon his initial impression.

Standing before the roaring fire, he relished the heat as he toweled his hair and dried his neck and face again. Heath glanced around the room, taking in the extraordinarily ugly chairs and cracked leather sofa. He'd seen nothing of value or quality in the house. Everything of worth had likely been sold ages ago.

He scraped the cloth inside each ear and came away with a pebble-sized clump of muck from his left ear. Too bad he daren't untuck his shirt and rid himself of the irritating blob resting at the small of his spine like a cold horse turd. He eyed his boots. No, he wouldn't ruin the tattered scrap he held by wiping the filthy footwear. If it weren't wholly unacceptable, he'd have left the Hessians at the door, but padding around in one's stockinged feet wasn't done.

He rolled his eyes toward the ceiling. Much better to soil the floors and carpet instead.

No sooner had he set the cloth aside than a sharp rap sounded beside the open door. Miss Culpepper peeked inside. Her gorgeous violet gazed skimmed him appreciatively. "Better?"

"Much, thank you." Spreading his fingers, he warmed his palms before the blaze. How had he managed to get dirt beneath three nails? He glanced sideways at her. "I don't recall a storm quite this furious."

"Yes, it's the worst I can recollect as well." She glided into the room, perfectly poised. She might have been starched and prim on the exterior, that heinous dress doing nothing for her figure or coloring, but a woman's curiosity and awareness had shone in her eyes when she took his measure a moment ago.

The corgi peeked around the doorframe then made a dash for the sofa. His fat rear wriggling, he clambered onto the couch. Freddy stood gazing up at Heath, panting and wagging his tail, not a jot of remorse on his scruffy face.

So much for banishment to the kitchen.

The four other young women filed in behind Miss Culpepper, their demeanors a combination of anxiety and curiosity.

God above, Heath would relish the expressions on the faces of the *ton's* denizens if these five—properly attired, jeweled and coiffed, of course—ever graced the upper salons and assembly rooms. He had half a mind to take the task on himself, if only to witness *le beau monde's* reaction.

He smiled, intrigued by the notion. Might be damned fun.

There'd be hissing and sneering behind damsels' fans as the milksops, dandies, and peers tripped over one another to be first in line to greet the beauties. One incomparable proved difficult enough competition, but an entire brood of them? What splendid mayhem that would cause. One he could heartily enjoy for weeks...months perhaps.

Heath rubbed his nose to hide a grin.

Yes, the Culpepper misses would provide the best bloody entertainment in a decade.

Course, without dowries or lineage, the girls' respectable prospects ran drier than a fountain in the Sahara.

He firmed his jaw. Not his concern. Making arrangements to sell the farm and return to London posthaste was. And not with five beauties in tow, even if he could persuade them to toddle along.

His gaze riveted on the blondes, Heath perched on the edge of one of the chairs. It tottered, and he gripped the arm as he settled his weight on the uneven legs. What did one call this chair's color anyway? Vomit? He'd seen pond scum the exact shade outside Bristledale Court's boundary. Why in God's name would anyone choose this fabric for furniture?

After sinking gracefully onto the sofa, and nudging aside a sleeping cat in order to make room for two of the young women to sit beside her, Miss Culpepper poured his tea. "Milk or sugar?"

The girl in yellow sat in the other chair while the twin attired in green plopped onto a low stool and, chin resting on her hand, stared at him.

Never had Heath experienced such self-consciousness before. Five pairs of eyes observed his every move. What was their story? His task would've been much easier if they were lazy, contentious spendthrifts sporting warty noses and whiskery chins.

"My lord?" Tongs in hand, Miss Culpepper peered at him, one fair brow arched, almost as if she'd read his thoughts. "Milk or sugar?"

He flashed her his most charming smile—the one that never failed to earn a blush or seductive tilt of lips, depending on the lady's level of sexual experience.

Her eyebrow practically kissing her hair, Miss Culpepper regarded him blandly. The twins salvaged his bruised pride by turning pink and gawking as expected. The older two exchanged guarded glances, and he swore Miss Brette hid a smirk behind her hand.

Heat slithered up his face.

Poorly done, old man.

These weren't primping misses accustomed to dallying or playing the coquette. He doubted they knew how to flirt. Direct and unpretentious, all but the youngest pair had detected his ploy to charm them. Rather mortifying to be set down without a word of reproach by three inexperienced misses.

Miss Culpepper waved the tongs and flashed her sister a sideways glance, clearly indicating she thought him a cod-pated buffoon.

"Just sugar please. Two lumps." He ran his fingers inside his neckcloth. The cloying material itched miserably.

Heath relaxed against the chair, squashing a cat that had crawled in behind him. With a furious hiss, the portly beast wriggled free and tumbled to the floor. Whiskers twitching and citrine eyes glaring, the miffed feline arched her spine, and then, with a dismissive flick of her tail, marched regally to lie before the hearth.

"I'm afraid you've annoyed Pudding." Chuckling, a delicious musical tinkle, Miss Culpepper lifted the lid from the sugar bowl and dropped two lumps into his tea. Four remained on the bottom of the china. "She holds a grudge, so watch your calves. She'll take a swipe at you when you aren't looking."

She passed him the steaming cup then scooted the small chipped plate of biscuits in his direction. Her roughened hands that suggested she performed manual labor. The other cat, its plump cheeks the size of dinner rolls, raised its head and blinked at him sleepily. The animals, at least, didn't go hungry around here. Miss Culpepper's keen gaze remained on him as she settled further into the couch,

The other girls' attention shifted between him and her, as if they anticipated something. They obviously regarded her as their leader. A log shifted, and sparks sprayed the sooty screen.

Heath took a swallow of the tea, savoring its penetrating warmth and pleasant flavor. A most respectable cup of tea, though a dram of brandy tipped into the brew wouldn't have gone amiss.

A branch scraped the window. What he wouldn't give to stay put in this snug study, sipping tea and munching the best, buttery biscuits he'd ever tasted. But Leventhorpe expected him for dinner and had requested his cook prepare chicken fricassee, a particular favorite of Heath's. Still, the return ride, battling the hostile elements after darkness had blanketed the land, didn't appeal in the least.

"My lord, you—"

"Miss Culpepper, could—."

She smiled, and Heath chuckled when they spoke at the same time.

Biscuit in hand, he gestured for her to continue. "Please, go on."

"You said Cousin Sheridan lost Esherton Green's lands to you in a wager?" Smoothing her rough skirt, she crossed and uncrossed her ankles.

Was that a hole in the bottom of her boot? A quick, covert assessment revealed the other women's footwear fared little better.

Heath paused with the teacup to his lips. "Yes."

"Might I ask when?" Her gaze rested on his lips before sliding to the cup. A dash of color appeared on her high cheekbones, made more apparent by the hollows beneath them.

She'd experienced hunger and often.... Still did, given the thinness of her and the others. Compassion swept him. If he were their blasted cousin, they'd never want again. Except, a cousin didn't inspire in him the kind of interest Brooke did.

"You see, I only received his correspondence today and the letter had suffered substantial damage." She shrugged one slender shoulder while running her fingers through the sleeping corgi's stiff fur. "Truthfully, I couldn't decipher half of it, but I had the distinct impression he'd sold the lands, and we'd be permitted to remain in the house if we paid rent. I can prove payment in full through this month."

That's only a few more days.

Her words rang of hope and desperation.

And how would they pay future rent? Open a house of ill-repute?

He skimmed his gaze over the assembled beauties. They'd make a fortune, but a more repugnant notion he'd never entertained. Besides, the house had been wagered as well.

Hadn't it?

Hell, he hadn't read the vowel, but rather made a show of perusing the note. He preferred not to read anything in public, especially not surrounded by *le beau ton.* A hint that he struggled to read the simplest phrase and the elite would titter for months.

But the fact remained that he journeyed here to sell whatever he'd won. Except now, he didn't know precisely what had been wagered. He would have to return on the morrow, after he'd spent the evening studying the slip of paper in—

Blast. The marker lay tucked in his greatcoat.

In the kitchen.

The two women who'd hustled away with his dust coat wouldn't dare go through his pockets. Would they?

Miss Culpepper mistook his silence for encouragement. "You see, Mr. Mabry and I—and the girls as well as the other staff—have run the dairy ourselves for the past five years. Cousin Sheridan received half the proceeds each quarter for allowing us to remain here and operate the farm. We hoped the new owner would permit us the same arrangement."

She raised expectant blue eyes to his. Her hands fisted in her skirt and her toes tapping the floor belied her calm facade.

He swept the other girls another swift glance.

Their thin faces were pale, and worry and fear filled the eyes peering back at him.

A wave of black rage rose from Heath's boots to his chest. When he got his hands on Gainsborough, he'd thrash him soundly. Pretending absorption in chewing the rest of his biscuit, Heath forced his pulse and breathing to slow.

He relaxed into the chair and placed an ankle on one bent knee, smearing his trousers with mud. Hopelessly stained, they'd be sent to the church for the beggars. Drumming his fingers on the chair's threadbare arms, he scrutinized the women again.

Features taut, gazes wary, they held their breath in anticipation of his response.

A litany of vulgar oaths thrummed against his lips. Blast their cousin to hell and back for putting him in this despicable position.

Heath did not want a dairy farm. He did not want to care for or worry about these women more than their own flesh and blood did. He most certainly did not want to *ever* have to venture to this stinking, remote parcel of green hell again. And he didn't have it in him to put these women out of their homes.

"We would work hard, your lordship." The girl in rose—Blaire or Blaike? Maybe he ought to number the lot of them—gifted him a tremulous smile.

Heath rubbed his forehead where the beginnings of a headache pulsed. "I'm sure you would."

God rot you, Gainsborough.

Her twin nodded, a white curl slipping to flop at her nape. "Yes, besides the milk, we also sell vegetables, flowers, and herbs..."

Anything else?

"And eggs, mushrooms, pastries, and jams," Brette finished in a breathless rush.

What no sewing, weaving, or tatting?

She threw her sister a desperate glance. "And I sew and take in embroidery."

Ah, there it is.

"And Blythe..." She pointed to the girl wearing yellow.

Yes, what does Blythe do?

Heath's gaze lingered on the eldest Miss Culpepper.

Or Brooke? *Surely she has a skill to sell too.*

He uncrossed his leg then leaned forward, not liking the direction the conversation had taken, the distress in the girls' voices, or his cynical musings. "You're to be commended and sound most industrious—"

Blythe squared her shoulders, a challenge in her eyes. "I give music lessons, and Flora takes in laundry."

Who the blazes is Flora?

He straightened and cast an uneasy glance at the doorway.

Good God, please tell me not another sister or cousin?

"Brooke maintains the books and manages the production and sale of the milk and cattle." The first twin spoke again.

Devil it, impossible to tell the two apart except for their clothing. Identical, right down to the mole beside their left eyes.

The other twin piped up. "We all—"

Miss Culpepper raised a hand, silencing her. A long scratch ran from her small finger to her wrist. Her ivory face seemed carved of granite, the angles and lines rigid. She slowly stood, her bearing no less regal than a queen's, and the stony look she leveled him would've done Medusa proud.

God, she was impressive.

He pressed his knee with his chilled fingertips. Yes, warm flesh, not solid rock. *Yet*.

"Enough, girls." Resignation weighted her words. They echoed through the study like a death knell.

The four swung startled gazes to her. A rapid succession of emotions flitted across their lovely faces, each one convicting him and adding more weight to the uncomfortable burden he already bore.

Damn. Damn. Damn.

"You're wasting your breath, dears. His lordship made his decision before he arrived." Miss Culpepper angled her long neck, her harsh gaze stabbing straight to his guilty heart.

"Didn't you, Lord Ravensdale?"

A woman of discernment understands that a deck of playing cards is the devil's prayer book, and a gentleman possessing a pack is Satan's pawn.
~*Wisdom and Advice—The Genteel Lady's Guide to Practical Living*

7

Brooke waited for Lord Ravensdale to deny her accusation.

He ran his hand through his shiny hair and stared past her shoulder. A muscle jumped in his jaw.

Tic or ire?

She curled her nails into her palms against the anger and despair sluicing through her veins. If she had to look at his handsome face or listen to his half-hearted platitudes one more minute, she wouldn't be able to keep from whacking him atop the head.

Yes, blaming him seemed unfair, but this situation was too, made more so because she'd kept her end of the bargain these many years and that slug...worm...*maggot* of a cousin had gambled away their lives.

How dare Sheridan?

His lordship turned his attention to her. Did concern tinge in his eyes?

She briefly closed hers to hide the rage that must've been sparking within them, and also to block his lordship's troubled expression.

Don't you dare pretend to care, you opportunistic cawker.

Lord Ravensdale heaved a low sigh.

Her eyelids popped open.

Ought to be on stage so someone can appreciate his theatrics.

He rubbed his nape. "Miss Culpepper, ladies, I—"

Duffen shuffled into the study, scraping a hand atop his wild hair in an unsuccessful attempt to tame the unruly bush. "Miss Brooke, Mabry will come up as soon as he can. A calf's turned wrong. Said he couldn't leave just now."

Brooke simply nodded, not trusting herself to speak. Mabry wasn't needed, in any event.

"I rubbed your horse down, my lord, and saw him settled." Duffen rested his bleary gaze on Lord Ravensdale, his dislike tangible.

His lordship curved his perfect lips into a narrow smile before placing his hands on the chair's arms and shoving to his feet. The signet ring on his small finger caught the fire's glow. "Thank you for your trouble, but I'm set on leaving in a moment. I don't wish to travel after dark. I require a few more minutes of your mistress's time, and then I'll be on my way."

His intense stare heated the top of Brooke's head as surely as if he'd placed his fire-warmed palm there. Refusing to raise her attention from the hole in the carpet, she slid her foot atop it. Had he noticed? She drew in a long, controlled breath. Her composure hung by a fine strand of sheer will, and she'd be cursed if she would let him see her cry again. Or let the girls see, for that matter. She didn't cry in public.

Their faces when Brooke had exposed his lordship's purpose...the despair and hopelessness... God, to have been able to spare them that anguish. They didn't lack intelligence and understood perfectly what their circumstances had been reduced to in the course of these past two hours.

So blasted, bloody unfair. Men didn't have these worries, but women without means had few opportunities.

"Miss Culpepper?" Lord Ravensdale prompted.

Persistent isn't he?

Mud-spattered boots appeared in her line of vision. She followed the lean length of his lordship's leg, past muscular buckskin-covered thighs, narrow hips, and his hunter green and black waistcoat to the pathetic excuse of a neckcloth drooping round his neck. An emerald stick pin glinted from within the folds. She'd missed the jewel earlier.

Firming her lips, she stared pointedly at his faintly-stubbled chin. Must be one of those gentlemen who required a shave twice daily. Humphrey hadn't.

What would it feel like to trace her fingers across his jaw?

Brooke Theodora Penelope Culpepper, have you lost your wits? Cease this instant!

He had the audacity to tilt her chin upward, forcing her to meet his chocolaty gaze.

Why must he be the man to awaken her long dormant feelings? Feelings she thought she'd succeeded in burying. Tears flooded her eyes, and she attempted to avert her face.

He would have none of it, however. "I will call at eleven tomorrow, at which time we can continue this discussion."

"Why?" Brooke jerked her chin from his gentle grasp. She angrily swiped at her eyes and retreated a couple of paces. "Why bother returning? Just send a note round, and tell us when you've sold the lands and what your directives are. I won't have you coming here and upsetting my family or staff anymore."

Duffen angled closer, his eyes gone hard as flint. "Did I miss somethin'? I thought, Miss Brooke, you planned on askin' his lordship if we could carry on like afore."

Brette rose and wrapped an arm around Brooke's waist. She gave it a reassuring squeeze. "Unfortunately, the earl has other plans, Duffen."

"I didn't say that." Lord Ravensdale retreated and planted his hands on his hips. His ebony gaze roved each of them, perused the study, lit on Freddy and Dumpling still sleeping soundly on the couch, before finding its way to Brooke once more. He sent a glance heavenward as if asking for divine guidance. "I'm not sure what I shall do. Give me the evening to ponder and see if I can devise something that will benefit us all."

"I assure you, my lord, I'll not concede our home without a fierce fight and before I use every means at my disposal."

And you can wager with the devil on that.

His lips turned up in a wickedly seductive smile, and he caressed her with another leisurely glance. So sure of himself, the pompous twit. Used to taking what he wanted, consequences be hanged.

A wave of scorching rage swept her. The earl needed to leave. Now. Before Brooke lost what little control she held. She wasn't given to violence, but the urge to punch him in his perfect, straight nose overwhelmed her.

She patted Brette's hand. "Please retrieve his lordship's coat, and take the others with you. I wish to have a moment alone with him."

With a curt nod, Brette whisked from the study as their cousins scrambled to stand. After sending Lord Ravensdale glances ranging from accusatory to wounded, they scurried from the room.

Brooke squeezed her hands together to stop their trembling. She'd only eaten a piece of toast today, and hunger, along with the disastrous afternoon, made her head spin. "Duffen, please see to the earl's mount."

"Did that, an' now I have to go into Satan's playground again?" He stuffed his cap onto his head, and with a mutinous glower, buttoned his coat. "Should've waited by the entrance. I'd have been no wetter or colder."

Muttering, he stomped to the door. "Bet my breeches he'll get lost on the way home, he will. Pretentious cove, strutting about in his fine togs, lording it over the poor gels. Haven't they been through enough?"

Brooke made no effort to chastise him, since her sentiments closely echoed his. She followed him to the doorway. Presenting her back to Lord Ravensdale, she spoke softly for Duffen's ears alone. "Please tell Mabry he needn't bother coming to the house."

Duffen gave a sharp nod. "Why'd he bother to come at all? Upset the young misses, he did. Lord or not, the man hasn't the sense of a worm."

He slashed Lord Ravensdale a scowl that would've laid out a lesser man before disappearing into the dark corridor, still grumbling beneath his breath.

"Yes, why bother coming at all? Couldn't your man of business have seen to the sale? For surely that's what you intend." She crossed her arms and glared at Lord Ravensdale, unable to keep the scorn from her tone. "You don't look the sort to worry yourself about the running of an estate. You probably don't venture to your own holdings unless you make a token visit once every now and again. Probably more concerned with the tie of your cravat or the goings on at White's or Almack's."

I've become a harpy.

His lordship appraised her coolly while exchanging Papa's coat for his own.

No, definitely not padded. Those broad shoulders and chest are natural muscles, more's the pity.

It seemed most unfair that he should be gifted with wealth, looks, and a physique to rival a Greek god's. An attractive package on the exterior perhaps, but the trappings hid a blackguard's treacherous heart.

With a great deal of difficulty, he struggled into his coat, the wetness and tight fit presenting a humorous challenge. Swearing beneath his breath, he wriggled and twisted. Had her life not been shattered, she might've chuckled at his antics.

His elbow caught at an awkward angle near his ear, and he curled his lip in irritation. He glanced her way and opened his mouth.

She arched a brow.

Don't you dare ask for my assistance.

Freddy would fart feathers before she offered to help the earl.

He snapped his mouth shut and a closed expression settled on his features. "You know nothing of me, Miss Culpepper, and your blame is sorely misplaced."

"Indeed. And on whom shall I place the blame then?"

"If you must blame someone, blame your confounded cousin for being a self-centered sot. Blame your father for not providing for you." At last, he rammed his arm into the sleeve. He waved a hand in the air. "Blame The Almighty for making you a woman, and not a man capable of providing for himself and his family."

Too far!

Brooke gasped and narrowed her eyes. She fisted her hands and clamped her teeth together so hard, she feared they would crack.

Forget the blasted cane. She longed to run Lord Ravensdale through with the rusty sword hanging askew above the fireplace, the arrogant bastard. She *had* provided for her family, despite the odds against her, and despite being a woman.

God forgive her, but she hoped the earl did catch a nasty chill or get lost on his journey to wherever he stayed. Or, better yet, fall off his magnificent horse and suffocate on a pile of fresh cow manure. She doubted he'd experienced a moment's discomfort in his entire life, and he had the gall to amble into Esherton today—as if strolling Covent Garden or perusing the oddities at Bullock's Museum—and nonchalantly destroy their lives.

She might be able to forgive him for winning the wager. After all, the rich thought nothing of losing a few hundred pounds, a prized piece of horseflesh, or a millstone of an estate. Josephina assured her gambling was the rage in London's upper salons. But the earl's indifference to their dire circumstances? And then having the ballocks to lay the blame for her predicament on her sex?

How callous and coldhearted could he be?

As coldhearted as Sheridan, and he is your cousin, which makes him the greater fiend by far.

Seething, Brooke pointed to the door. "Take your—"

Brette returned with Lord Ravendale's greatcoat. Mouth pursed, she passed it to him then moved to stand and stare into the waning fire. Her slumped shoulders and bowed head spoke of her distress.

He'd done this to her gentle sister.

Brooke clenched her jaw to quiet her quaking and suppress the vulgar suggestion she longed to make regarding where he could shove his opinions. She continued to shake uncontrollably.

Rage? Cold? Fear? Hunger?

Yes, those had her quivering like the leaves on the tormented trees outside.

Hugging her shoulders, she gazed out the blurry window. The rain had ebbed. Dusk wasn't far off, the mantle of night hovered on the horizon though the afternoon hadn't seen its end. She swept the clock a glance. A jot beyond half-past two. He'd been here a mere half an hour? The disastrous change he unleashed upon their lives ought to have taken much longer. Unfair how one man could snuff what little joy had survived at Esherton in less than a blink of an eye.

After securing his jacket, his lordship donned his damp overcoat. He gave his right chest a light pat, and a slight smile skewed his lips.

Done with the niceties, Brooke faced him fully.

"See yourself to the door, and don't bother us with your presence again. The house and surrounding five acres are entailed. Sheridan had no legal right to use them as collateral. Do what you will with the rest of the property, but understand I intend to seek counsel regarding the ownership of the herd and the use of the outbuildings. They sit on entailed properties, and you won't be permitted use of them. I...*we* haven't labored like slaves for five years to have you destroy everything we've worked for."

Would he call her bluff?

She hadn't any right to make those claims. Only Sheridan did.

Would Lord Ravensdale know that? Would he make an arrangement with her cousin regarding occupation of the house? God, then what?

The two devils would deal well together, she had no doubt.

"Believe me when I say, my lord, I'll cause you no small amount of grief for the havoc you've wrought on my family." How, she had no idea, but when an uneasy look flashed across his features, she relished the small victory her false bravado provided.

Brooke presented her back. If she never laid sight on the man again, it would be too soon.

It infuriated her all the more that she had ever entertained the slightest interest in the fiend.

She closed her eyes and drew forth every ounce of faith she possessed. *We've been through hard times before*. God would see them through this too. *Wouldn't He*? He'd met their needs thus far. *Barely*. He wouldn't fail them now.

He already has.

She opened her eyes, blinking away another round of burning tears, further testament to her overwrought state. Since when did she snivel at the least little thing? Why, until today, she hadn't cried since Papa died.

See what the earl had reduced her to? A weeping ninny.

Freddy snorted and rolled onto his back, still sound asleep. His tail twitched and his paws wiggled. A low whimper escaped him. Likely dreaming of his younger days when he drove the cattle. He'd been quite the herder until old age relegated him to snoozing the day away.

Get up, Freddy, and pee—or worse—on his lordship's boot again.

Brette gathered Pudding from the hearth before settling into one of the wingback chairs. She obviously didn't intend to leave Brooke alone with the earl again. Propriety prohibited it, as did Brette's protective nature.

Thank you, Brette.

The cat curled into Brette's lap, her leery gaze on the earl. She'd not soon forgive him for crushing her into the cushions. Pudding was a pout.

After sending Lord Ravensdale an unreadable look, Brette petted the cat and stared into the fire's remaining embers. No sense adding another log when they'd vacate the room as soon as Lord Ravensdale took his leave.

Brooke whirled around at a light touch on her shoulder.

He stood mere inches away, close enough that she smelled his cologne once more. Such forwardness wouldn't be tolerated. She opened her mouth to say as much, but his chestnut eyes held no hostility, only warm empathy.

She swallowed, wanting to glance away, but her dratted eyes refused to obey. What was wrong with her today? Out of character for her to be mawkish over a man, weep like a child, or wallow in self-pity.

"I will go, for now, because this weather forces me to." Brows pulled into a vee, he looked to the window. "But be assured, I will return with a satisfactory solution, and I intend to communicate with your cousin regarding the matter of the house and grounds."

A bitter laugh escaped Brooke. "Unless your solution involves allowing us to run the dairy farm and remain in our home, I strongly doubt you will have any suggestion I would welcome."

"You will agree to what I propose, Brooke." He ran his forefinger along her jaw and smiled. "You haven't a choice, have you?"

Brooke tried to ignore the flash of sensation his touch caused. Why did this man have this power over her? "We'll see about that, my lord, and I haven't given you leave to use my given name."

He glanced at Brette.

Her eyes shut and head resting against the chair, she appeared to have dozed off. No wonder. She'd been up past midnight finishing a lace collar for Josephina.

Lord Ravensdale edged closer to Brooke and bent his neck, his mouth near her ear. "Oh, I intend to use much more than your name, Brooke."

Always remember, gaming wastes two
of man's most precious things: time and treasure.
~*Wisdom and Advice—The Genteel Lady's Guide to Practical Living*

8

Heath grinned as he marched to the entrance.

Brooke smelled incredible. Not of perfume, but her natural scent. Womanly, warm, and sweet.

He'd wanted to gather her in his arms and bury his face in the hollow of her neck. After less than an hour's acquaintance, he already ached for her. Of course, three months of forced celibacy might have something to do with his randy state.

Cheeks glowing, Brooke had stared at him, dazed. However, a spark had glinted in the center of her eyes, and male instinct assured him the glimmer hadn't been entirely shock or ire. He'd piqued her interest and what's more, she'd responded to him physically.

His remark about using her had ruffled her feathers. True, he had been a mite crude, but she didn't seem the sort who'd appreciate flowery speeches or false flattery. She'd been honest and direct with him and deserved the same in return.

Brette, on the other hand, had scowled at him, not a hint of anything but hostility within her narrowed gaze. Tiny she might be, but Brooke's sister remained a force to be reckoned with and one he didn't want to cross. Much better to have the other four as allies in his newly formed quest to win Brooke over.

A notion had taken hold as they'd sat in the study, one that would provide for her and her family, and allow him to dispose of the albatross he'd won. The whole debacle seemed quite providential when he considered the situation, though he didn't believe in that sort of mythical nonsense. The facts remained: he required a new mistress, and Brooke was desperate for a means to provide for her family.

They complicated things a bit, but could work to his favor too, especially if his contract with Brooke included settling a monthly sum on her that would allow her to continue to care for the other four until the quartet married.

Several delightful ways she might express her gratitude crossed his mind, including a bottle of his finest champagne and a bath teeming with fragrant bubbles.

Why not marry her?

Heath faltered mid-step.

Where had that ludicrous thought come from? The bowels of Hades?

He wasn't ready to marry, didn't want to ever, truth to tell. But if he didn't, his reprobate of a cousin, Weston Kitteridge, would inherit and obliterate what scant remnant of honor and respect the Ravensdale legacy retained. Holding a title wasn't all pomp and privilege. The earldom required him to marry. A martyr for his title.

Eventually.

Heath resumed his progress through the hallway, his pace somewhat slower.

Brooke had intrigued him from the moment she appeared in the doorway. No woman had gotten his attention, snared him, so completely in such a short time. That he couldn't ignore. Not only a delectable morsel, she possessed a keen mind, evident in the years she'd operated the dairy. She had a practical head on her lovely shoulders—shoulders he itched to strip naked and trace with his lips—and she'd already proven she would willingly sacrifice herself for the wellbeing of others.

In all likelihood, she remained as chaste as the day she'd been born, but wisdom dictated an examination by his physician before Heath penned his signature to any agreement between them. He would be generous, of course. Provide her with an annual income and a comfortable cottage once he tired of her.

No doubt she'd prefer the farm, but instinct told him he wouldn't grow weary of her soon. He had no intention of nursing the dairy along in order for her to return to it in a few years, and resume the heavy responsibilities of operating the place. Besides, no woman should have to labor so hard to live in poverty.

He could give her that much at least—a comfortable existence for the rest of her days. Perchance she would even decide to marry after their association ended. Many women made respectable, even exceptional, matches, after being a kept woman.

Daphne's features sprang to mind.

And others didn't bother waiting until they'd been given their congé.

What had started as a miserable outing had proved advantageous after all. Not a direction he'd expected the day to take, but such an opportunity shouldn't be squandered. Some—not him, mind you—might call it a blessing in disguise.

Opening the entry door, he released a soft chuckle.

Taken aback, she'd gaped at him like a cod fish, her blue-violet eyes enormous and her pink lips opening and closing soundlessly. Heath had bent halfway to kiss them when her sister's exaggerated throat clearing had brought him up short. He'd forgotten Brette napped in the chair.

Rather touching, how protective the sisters were of one another. He hadn't experienced that sort of bond with another human. Not that it bothered him. One didn't miss what one had never had. Emotional balderdash and sentimental claptrap he could do without, thank you.

The esteem he held for his friends, Alexander Hawksworth and Leventhorpe, was the closest Heath had ever come to an emotional attachment with anyone, including his mistresses. Must be a family curse handed down from his glacial parents, and theirs before them. The Ravensdales weren't hailed for their warmth and geniality, but that didn't stop them from coupling like rabbits with any partner willing.

He had put a stop to that practice...almost.

Grateful the storm had abated somewhat, he ran down the stoop stairs. An occasional blast of cold air accompanied a thick drizzle. Far better than the monsoon that had blown him here, nonetheless.

Hunched within his baggy coat and oversized cap, Duffen waited at the bottom of the stairs.

Ebénè, however, was nowhere in sight.

Heath scanned the drive before casting a glance at the barns. "Where's my horse?"

"Hadn't the heart to make the poor beasty stand in the rain an' cold. I thought…" Staring at the ground, the servant stuffed his hands into his jacket pockets and shuffled his feet. He darted a quick look at Heath before returning his attention to the dirt. "Thought I might take you to your horse an' give him a few more minutes out of the weather."

He scuffed his boot uncertainly.

"Most considerate of you." Heath shook his head, curling his mouth at the corners. "Ebénè is already miffed at me for the journey here. I'm sure he won't welcome the return trip. Thank you for thinking of his comfort."

Duffen rolled his shoulders before angling toward the outbuildings. "Aint the horse's fault you got a hair up your arse an' set out in weather evil enough to bewitch the devil himself."

Heath scratched his upper lip to cover his smile.

Ought to reprimand him for his impudence.

After turning away, the servant lumbered down the path to the barn. Amusement outweighed propriety and Heath dutifully followed the disgruntled little elf of a man. The pathway forked, and instead of continuing on the trail to the stables, Duffen veered to the other branch.

Heath stopped and looked at the barns. "Isn't my mount stabled in one of those?" He pointed to the buildings. Light shone from the south end of the farthest one. The lowing of cattle echoed hollowly from within the two long structures.

Duffen looked over his shoulder and shook his head. He didn't stop plodding along.

"No, the herd's indoors 'cause of the storm. There's no room. Besides, several cows have newborn calves, and more are in labor or expected to birth their babes any day." He jerked his head toward a beehive-shaped stone building. "Puttin' your stallion in the carriage house seemed wiser. There are stalls in there, an' it's quieter."

That's a carriage house?

Heath would bet Ebénè a carriage hadn't graced the inside of the building for a good number of years. Lady Bustinza's monstrous bosoms drooped less, and the dame was six and eighty if she was a day. He shook his head, and with another brief glance at the stables, raised his collar and continued onward. He wouldn't make it to Leventhorpe's before darkness fell. Traveling at night—the only thing he hated worse than riding in the rain.

Other than a dagger in his boot, he bore no arms. Not that he expected trouble, but a wise man prepared for any eventuality. *Should've taken Leventhorpe's carriage.* He allowed himself a rueful smile. He'd grown soft, too used to the comforts of his privileged life.

Duffen faced forward again but waited for Heath to catch up.

Scrunching his eyes and pulling his earlobe, the servant gave him a sideways glance. Duffen opened his mouth then snapped it closed, glaring past Heath. "Don't s'pose you'd help an old man with somethin'."

Heath grinned. Despite himself, he liked the cantankerous fellow. The poor man shouldn't have been working at all at his age. He could spare a minute or two more. "And what might that be?"

"We store the extra feed and grain in the dovecote 'cause it's harder for the vermin to get to it. The only way inside is through them holes on top and the door." He cackled and shoved his hat upward, exposing his wizened face. "The rats sure do try, though, let me tell you. Caught one gnawin' at the door the other day. Clever little beasts, they are."

"I'm sure." Heath took the servant at his word.

A crow perched on the dovecote's upper edge took to the sky, its croaking call stolen by a gust of wind whipping past. Heath shivered and secured the top button of his coat then dug around in his pocket and found his gloves. Damp leather didn't do much to stave off the chill permeating him, but he tugged them on, nonetheless.

Damn, but he'd never been this miserably cold.

"Dark omen that." Duffen pointed to the bird zig-zagging across the sky. "Bad luck to see a lone crow atop a house."

Heath eyed the dour man and swallowed a chuckle. Like anyone could see the moon tonight with clouds thick as porridge. Not the least superstitious, he didn't believe in fate either. "Well, I don't think a pigeon cote qualifies as a house, so there's nothing to worry about, is there?"

"You city coves don't know much, do you?" Disgust puckered Duffen's face. "It's a house for pigeons an' doves, aint it?"

Not in the last century.

Heath surveyed the ancient structure, and the spots of grass sprouting atop the roof.

Or two.

"Mark my words, my lord. You'll wish you never set foot on Esherton Green's lands afore the moon rises."

Almost sounds like a threat.

Where in God's name had Brooke unearthed the man? Was he the best she could find to employ? She probably couldn't afford to pay him much and no one of substance would work for the pittance she offered.

His patience running thin, Heath strode across the grass. "So what is it you need help with?"

"Can't get the door open. Think it's jammed." Duffen planted his hands on his hips and scowled at the barns. "Mabry an' the other hands don't think I pull my weight round here. I'll be damned—beg your pardon, my lord—before I ask 'em for help."

He begs my pardon now?

"Let's be about it then. I truly need to be on my way." The drizzle had turned into rain once more, though the wind hadn't returned in force.

"This way, your lordship."

Duffen trudged round the backside of the building, Heath in his wake.

Heath obligingly turned down the latch and, levering his legs and shoulders, gave the door a hefty shove. It sprang open with surprising ease. He tumbled to his knees on the circular floor, cracking the left one hard. Pain wrenched the joint.

Damnation.

Eyeing the hundreds of dung-encrusted nesting holes lining the sides, he brushed his palms on his coat. "It didn't seem all that stuck—"

Pain exploded at the base of his head.

A prudent woman holds this truth close to her heart:
gambling is the mother of all lies, and good luck, her fickle daughter.
~*Wisdom and Advice—The Genteel Lady's Guide to Practical Living*

9

After telling Brette she needed a few moments alone and to tell Mrs. Jennings to serve dinner early, Brooke puttered about the study. She banked the fire before closing the drapes and blowing out all but one candle. Brette had taken the cats when she left, and only Freddy remained curled on the couch, dozing. Every now and again, he opened his eyes to make sure she hadn't left him. She'd rescued him as a puppy from an abusive, slick-haired showman at a county fair, and Freddy seldom let Brooke out of his sight.

A flush suffused her for the dozenth time since Lord Ravensdale had left her gaping like a ninnyhammer.

He'd been about to kiss her.

She was positive.

Mesmerized by his beautiful eyes and mouth, she would have let him. *Let him*? Encouraged him.

With her sister sitting right there, watching.

What had come over her?

Brooke had experienced desire before. She'd nearly married Humphrey, though the mild pleasantness he'd stirred in her didn't compare to the wild tempest of sensations his lordship had rioting through her. Thrilling and frightening and certainly not the sensations a practical spinster should've been entertaining.

Must be because he was a practiced man of the world with a swashbuckler's bold good looks and comportment, and Humphrey had been a quiet, mild-mannered man. More of a reserved poet sort than a swaggering, cock-sure, womanizing—*remember that, Brooke...the earl's no doubt a womanizer*—pirate.

Brooke rubbed her fingers against the sofa's roughened backrest as the last embers of the fire faded. Did Lord Ravensdale think her circumstances so desperate, he could take liberties with her? Had she given the rogue cause in the few moments they'd been acquainted to think she'd be receptive to his advances?

Brow knitted, she stilled her fingers, replaying the few minutes he'd been here in her mind. No, she'd behaved with complete propriety, and absolutely nothing about her attire was remotely suggestive or alluring. A nun wore finer, more seductive clothing.

Did the man go about kissing women he'd just met on a regular basis? The notion, much like soured cream, curdled in her belly.

Enough ruminating.

She wanted to inventory the larder before dinner. While they'd waited for the calving to occur, their stores had declined severely. Could she make do for a little longer since she didn't know whether she could sell the calves now?

There's always the bull fund.

Brooke flexed her hands and firmed her lips. No. She wouldn't touch the hoarded reserve. If she did, then she admitted she'd lost Esherton Greens. Her heart wrenched. That she could not do. Not yet. Not until every last avenue had been explored. There must be a way.

Please, God. A miracle would be most welcome.

She pivoted to the door, and her gaze landed on the small package sitting where Blythe had set it earlier.

What a perfectly horrid birthday. Brooke wouldn't celebrate the day ever again. Not that there'd been any real festivities in the house since Mama died. There'd been little time or inclination, and even less money, for such frivolity.

Poverty and grief had denied the girls much.

Brooke lifted the forgotten gift. She turned it over and squeezed gently. Something soft. What had the sweethearts done?

She slid the ribbon from the package. Dangling the yellow strand from a finger, she unfolded the plain cloth—one of the girl's handkerchiefs—and a stocking slid to the floor.

Tears welled again as she bent to retrieve the white length. Where had the dears found the money to buy yarn to knit a pair of stockings? Hers had been repaired so many times, the patched and knobby things scarcely resembled the pair she now held to her face.

A sob escaped her, and she pressed the back of her hand to her mouth to stifle the others scratching up her throat. Tilting on the precipice of hysteria, she drew in a measured breath. Where was the logic Papa boasted of? The common sense Mama instilled in her?

Histrionics solved nothing. Her guide must be calm reason.

And cunning.

She would outmaneuver Ravensdale, the jackanape, one way or another.

Stupid, stupid Sheridan to wager her farm in a miserable card game. For Esherton *was* hers. Perhaps not legally, but in her heart, it had always been hers. She loved the drafty house—crumbling entry and shoddy condition and all—and often daydreamed about restoring the treasure to its former glory. As a child, she'd roamed the meadows and orchard, climbed the gnarled trees, and petted the newborn calves. Every night, the soft moos of the cattle lulled her to sleep, and most mornings a songbird's trill woke her.

Somehow, she must persuade Lord Ravensdale to allow them to stay.

But how?

She fiddled with a loose thread dangling from her cuff.

Stop before you unravel the whole edge.

Could she offer Lord Ravensdale more profit? Use the parure set as collateral? Was there another way to procure funds; anything else they could sell or barter?

She glanced around the office. Not in here, or the rest of the house, for that matter. Oh, to have a treasure buried somewhere on the estate. Alas, her family tree held no buccaneers, addlepated relations ranting of secret stashes of gold, or long-lost kin seeking to bestow a fortune on their surviving family members.

Brooke tapped her chin.

They'd already searched the attic, and hadn't unearthed anything of value. Still, some of her ancestors had traveled broadly, and perhaps an artifact or two that might be pawned or sold remained buried in a corner or trunk. She would send Blythe and Brette above stairs tomorrow to burrow around in the clutter a mite more.

When he'd first inherited, Brooke had asked Sheridan if she might buy the unentailed lands from him, using the parure set as a down payment. The grasping bugger had said no. He'd wanted the regular income and possession of the grounds too.

Would Lord Ravensdale be open to the suggestion?

That only partially solved the problem, though, since Sheridan retained the house and would continue to demand rents. She couldn't afford to make land payments and also send him money monthly. Not on the dismal profit the farm made.

Swiping a hand across her eyes, Brooke sighed, her shoulders slumping.

What a blasted muddle.

She would have to write Sheridan. Discover exactly what he proposed. Bile burned her throat. This helplessness, the lack of control over her fate and the others', nearly had her shrieking in frustration.

Damn the injustice.

She would send a note to Mr. Benbridge, seeking an appointment. He and his wife had been absolute dears after Papa died, despite Brooke breaking their son's heart. They'd assured her they understood her decision to decline Humphrey's proposal. An unpleasant suspicion had always lay tucked in a cranny of Brooke's mind; she hadn't been good enough, of a high enough station for their son. Her refusal had relieved them.

After Humphrey left, Josephina admitted her parents—landed gentry with deep, deep pockets—wanted their children to marry into a higher social class. Mr. Benbridge had refused no less than seven offers for Josephina's hand—none from gentlemen with a title greater than a viscountcy—and now at one and twenty, Josephina feared she'd end up like Brooke.

On the shelf. No offense intended.

However, Brooke hadn't anyone else to ask for advice. Mr. Benbridge would know what direction to point her, and Mrs. Benbridge claimed many connections in London. Her sister, the Viscountess Montclair, was an influential woman, or so Mrs. Benbridge often boasted. Brooke would ask her for a reference and to pen letters on her behalf, should, God forbid, they actually have to leave Esherton.

Brooke dropped the stockings and wrapping onto the desk. Shivering, she sank into Papa's chair. Had she known she would remain in the study longer, she'd not have let the fire die. She placed two pieces of foolscap before her then stared at the paper.

She shoved one aside. Not now. Impossible to write Sheridan today. Too much anger and hurt thrummed through her to pen a civil word to the cull.

She tapped the other piece of foolscap, not certain how to approach Mr. Benbridge about her delicate situation. Best not to say too much. Just send a missive along, ask if she could call in the next day or two, and also, if he might spare her a few moments to ask his advice.

Wiggling her toes against the chill permeating the room, Brooke wrote the brief note. She put the quill away then sprinkled sand on the ink. If the weather cooperated, she would send the letter round with one of the stable hands in the morning.

A short rap on the door preceded Duffen poking his head inside.

Freddy lifted his ears and thumped his tail once.

"Do you have need of me this evenin', Miss Brooke? My bones have ached somethin' fierce all day. This wicked weather is hard on old joints. Thought I'd ask Cook for her sleepin' tonic an' retire early."

Duffen shuffled so slowly, she expected his stiff joints to creak.

"Certainly," Brooke said and smiled. "Please forgive me for the necessity of sending you into the rain twice today."

Grimacing at the new ink stain on her forefinger, she stood. Why couldn't she manage a quill without getting ink on herself? Rubbing her fingers together, she came round the desk and, after gathering her new stockings in her unstained hand, collected the candlestick with her other.

She gave Duffen another warm tilt of her mouth. "Thank you for seeing our guest on his way. Let's hope he doesn't make an appearance again any time soon."

"Don't like the man." He frowned and rubbed his amulet. "Greedy, no good churl."

At his fierce tone, Brooke gave him a sharp look. "I understand you're angry with him. I am too, but we must get him to cooperate with us."

"I aint grovelin' for the likes of that cheatin' bugger," Duffen muttered. "Mebe he'll take you at your word an' not come back."

They exited the study into the unlit hallway, Freddy pattering behind.

"I think he'll return, but I plan on being better prepared the next go round." She raised the candle to look Duffen in the eye. "I promise you, as I told Lord Ravensdale, I shall do everything within my power to keep our home."

"What about...nicking him off?" Duffen averted his eyes and tugged on his earlobe.

Brooke stopped abruptly and stepped on Freddy's paw. "Pardon?"

The dog yelped and scampered away, giving her a wounded stare.

"I'm sorry, Freddy. Come here, let me see. Duffen, hold the candle please." She bent and examined the dog's paw. After assuring herself he hadn't sustained a serious injury, she straightened.

Arms crossed, she regarded Duffen. He did say the most peculiar things at times. What went on in that head of his? "Don't jest about something so appalling. Lord Ravensdale may be our adversary, but I do not wish the man dead."

"He'd let you and the other misses starve." Duffen jutted his chin out, his eyes suspiciously moist.

"That's harsh, Duffen, and I believe you know it. His lordship doesn't realize how dire our circumstances are."

"Beggin' your pardon, but he'd have to be blind not to see our sorry state." He scratched his scrawny chest, frustration glittering in his toast-brown eyes.

Brooke retrieved the candleholder, her heart aching for the old retainer, and they continued along the barren hallway. "He's only acting to better his interests, and it's a wise business move on his part."

"Why are you defending him?" Duffen snorted and gave her a look suggesting she'd gone daft.

Why am I defending him?

She entered the welcoming kitchen, Duffen at her side.

"You don't need to worry yourself, Miss Brooke. I promised your father I'd take care of his girls. I've done what needs be done."

One who desires peace and contentment, neither lays wagers nor lends.
~Wisdom and Advice—The Genteel Lady's Guide to Practical Living

10

Eyes closed, Heath rolled onto his back, and instantly regretted the movement as agony ricocheted inside his skull. He covered his face with an elbow and swallowed. Nausea toyed with his stomach and throat.

Holy Mother of God.

Not dead then. Death wouldn't be painful, would it? Unless this was hell. No, hell was hot. Dank and cold permeated this place. Where was he?

He forced his eyes open a slit.

Ah, the dovecote.

Duffen had clobbered him, the crusty old goat.

At Brooke's direction? What did she say to the servant before he stomped from the study?

Heath squinted at the faint light filtering into the top of the domed ceiling.

Early morning?

He'd been unconscious the entire night. Slowly, afraid any sudden movement might send his head rolling across the grain-smattered floor, he sought the entrance. Closed and likely locked tighter than a convent of giggling virgins.

He sucked in a long breath and wrinkled his nose at the stench. Pigeon *and* cow manure.

Splendid.

He flexed his stiff shoulders and spine. The stone floor didn't make for the most comfortable sleeping accommodations. In the weak light, he scrutinized the culvery. To his surprise, a flask and a lumpy cloth—perhaps a napkin—lay atop a pair of ratty blankets beside a bucket atop bulging grain sacks.

All the comforts of home.

Groaning, he struggled to a sitting position. He removed his gloves and waited for another dizzying wave to subside before exploring the source of pain. Heath brushed a tender fist-sized lump behind his left ear and, wincing, probed the area gently.

No blood.

His skull hadn't been split open, thank God, but he would boast a cracking good headache for a day or two. He coughed, flinching and holding his head as agony crashed through his brain again. Make that a whopping headache for a bloody week.

What had the puny whoremonger bashed him with? A boulder? No, more likely one of the several bricks scattered near the door.

Heath inhaled then released a holler. "Help, I'm locked in the dovecote."

His brain threatened to leave his head through his nose. Shouting like a madman would have to wait a few hours, until he could be certain the act wouldn't slay him.

Would Leventhorpe start searching for him immediately or assume he'd taken refuge at an inn along the way. In that event, his friend might delay until as late as tomorrow to sound the alarm. But sound it, his friend would.

Had he mentioned Esherton Green by name to Leventhorpe?

Heath couldn't remember, blast it.

He could scarcely string two thoughts together. He closed his eyes and sucked in an uneven breath to lessen the throbbing in his head and ease his churning stomach. Neither helped a whit.

He pressed two fingers to his forehead.

Think. What will Leventhorpe do?

Aware of Heath's reputation for fastidiousness, Leventhorpe would dismiss any notion of a woman waylaying him. Besides, when expected somewhere, Heath didn't cry off unless he sent a note round.

Leventhorpe had probably been in the saddle since before dawn. He possessed a dark temper, far worse than Heath's. Miss Culpepper had no idea the nest of hornets she would disturb if the Marquis of Leventhorpe became involved. The chap couldn't abide any form of lawlessness or breach of conduct.

Heath had underestimated Brooke's desperation. What did she think to accomplish by having her servant knock him in the head and confine him, both severe offenses against a peer?

My God, maybe she'd intended to kill him.

Disappointment like none he'd ever known squeezed his lungs. He didn't want to believe that of her.

He slid two fingers inside his right boot. His knife remained sheathed there. His gaze wandered to the supplies. Why bother with food and water if she planned on disposing of him? Perhaps she thought to blackmail him into giving her the lands. He'd have to rethink that mistress notion. Bedding a bloodthirsty wench didn't appeal.

If he hadn't felt so bloody wretched, he would've given vent to the fury heating his blood. No matter. There'd be plenty of time for anger later—after he'd escaped or been freed, for he hadn't a doubt his stay in this oversized birdhouse wouldn't be an extended one. Either she would come to her senses—because he wouldn't bend to coercion—or Leventhorpe would out her scheme.

She'd better hope it wasn't the latter.

Just you wait, Brooke Culpepper.

A crow's harsh call sounded.

Heath lifted his gaze to the ceiling and met the beady, ebony gaze of an inquisitive bird sitting on one of the upper beams. Hopping sideways, the crow eyed him then the supplies. The storm had passed, and jagged rays of sun formed a crisscross pattern within the structure. Nonetheless, the place held as much hominess and warmth as a tomb.

Terribly thirsty, he half-crawled, half-scooted to the flask. His skull objected by cruelly stabbing him with each lurching motion. After unscrewing the top, he took several satisfying gulps of rather tangy water. Better, but food might help settle his stomach more. He pulled the cloth away and revealed two hard rolls, a chunk of Cheshire cheese, and dried apples.

Not the most sumptuous of meals, but prisoners couldn't be persnickety.

Did the Culpeppers break their fast with this simple fare every morning? Probably, and inexpensive porridge too.

Despite the coolness, sweat beaded his brow and trickled into his temple hair. God, he feared he would cast up his accounts. Except he hadn't eaten since yesterday morning, and his stomach lay empty. He sought his handkerchief. Gainsborough's marker crackled inside his greatcoat. After patting his face and returning the hopelessly wrinkled cloth to his pocket, Heath withdrew the paper.

Time to find out exactly what he'd won in that confounded wager.

Sighing, he relaxed against the grain sacks and bent his knees. He unfolded the I.O.U then smoothed the paper atop his thighs. He stared at the writing. One short, sloppy paragraph with Gainsborough's—*damn his eyes*—and a witness's signature affixed to the bottom. His forehead scrunched in concentration, Heath nibbled a roll and squinted at the black scrawls.

Despite the best tutors and regular beatings meant to encourage him to pay attention to his lessons, he could barely read. Heath was known for his sharp wit and droll humor, and few people knew the truth. Those who did, he paid well, *very well*, to keep their silence on the matter.

He traced his forefinger over the top line. The letters on the page didn't always make sense. They appeared turned around, the words and sentences impossible to read. He long ago decided the issue a deficit in him, and the knowledge mortified him to his core. Toddlers scarcely out of diapers could read better than he.

The page blurred. His eyelids felt weighted with stones, too heavy to lift. He blinked drowsily, jerking his neck abruptly when he nearly dozed off. Pain seared him once more.

"Dammit to hell."

His shout startled the crow. The bird screamed in alarm and streaked to the exit atop the dovecote. An ebony feather spun slowly to the floor.

His movements sluggish, Heath crammed the unfolded paper into his pocket. Reading the marker would have to wait. Mouth dry, he licked his lips. He fumbled for the flask, intent on quenching his thirst before resuming his slumber. The cool liquid slid into his mouth, and bitterness assailed his tongue. He went rigid.

Drugged?

He spewed the water onto the floor and hurled the flask against the opposite wall.

Struggling to keep his eyes open, he tugged a horse blanket from the sack beside him. After draping the threadbare length across his chest and shoulders, he slumped against the bags.

Words slurred and chin resting on his chest, he mumbled, "Brooke Culpepper, you'll regret the day you crossed me."

Sleep claimed him a moment later.

Brooke rose before dawn, having lain awake most of the night. While drinking a cup of tea—more hot water than tea—she had poured over the farm's ledgers, searching for the slightest way to afford rent and make land payments at the same time. Even if Lord Ravensdale agreed to sell her the land, which she doubted, it was painfully clear she hadn't enough money to pay both.

Now, midmorning, she sat at Papa's desk, a throw Mama knitted draped over her shoulders. Freddy slept in his favorite corner of the sofa. No fire burned in the hearth or candles in the holders. Heavy shadows hovered in the corners the light from the windows couldn't penetrate.

Similar darkness haunted the recesses of her heart.

She had concocted every conceivable scenario she could imagine, and each resulted in losing Esherton and leaving the only home she'd ever known. Brooke tapped her fingertips together, pondering the pile of notes before her. The funds for a bull lay upon the scarred desktop. Sufficient to see her and the girls to London and settled in inexpensive lodgings, but scant more to live on and no provision for the servants at all.

The parure sat atop the desk too.

She lifted the blue velvet lid, worn thin on the edges from hundreds of fingertips touching the fragile fabric. The sapphire and diamonds winked at her from their secure nests. She lifted the tiara high and rotated the circlet so the stones glittered in the cheery ribbons of sunlight filtering through the window. This set had adorned Culpepper women for five generations, since her blond-haired blue-eyed Spanish grandmother wore it for her wedding. Tragically, she'd died before reaching her new home, but her legacy lived on through the jewels.

Selling the gems…a betrayal of Brooke's and the quartet's heritage. Who could she entrust the set to who knew how to barter and wouldn't cheat her? She must receive top price for the sapphires, and that would only occur in London.

Perhaps the Benbridges would know of someone.

She'd sent Rogers, a stable hand, round to their house with the missive over an hour ago. The girls had headed above stairs straightway upon her suggestion they search the attic one more time after breaking their fast this morning.

A stuffed pheasant missing an eye as well as part of a wing and foot propped the study door open part way. Its remaining eye reproached her for the indignity. Fingering the knobby wool atop her shoulders, Brooke half-listened for a knock at the house's entrance. If Rogers returned with an invitation for her to visit the Benbridges this afternoon, she'd need to change into her best gown and set out at once in the dog cart.

She also wanted to speak to Duffen this morning. His peculiar declaration last night before he trundled to bed still nagged. He assured her he'd only warned Lord Ravensdale to stay away from Esherton Green—not the servant's place at all, as she sternly reminded him—but doubt niggled, nonetheless. One more thing to compound her stress.

Duffen hadn't been happy at her reprimand, and for the first time, turned surly toward her. He'd stomped away, mumbling beneath his breath. Mayhap the time had finally arrived to relieve him of his duties—he had become more confused and difficult of late—but to set him aside would destroy the dear. Especially since he, too, had nowhere else to go.

She returned the tiara to its place on the once-white satin, now yellowed to ivory. Would Lord Ravensdale put in an appearance today as promised, despite Duffen's threat? If his lordship came round, she prayed she'd be at the Benbridges. Otherwise, she'd not be at home to callers.

Fewer than twenty-four hours didn't allow time enough to hatch a fool-proof plan.

Fool proof?

She didn't have a plan except to sell the jewels. Rather difficult to hatch a scheme when something nullified each idea she dreamed up. Elbows on the desk, Brooke closed her eyes, buried her face in her hands, and let the tears flow.

Papa, I vowed I'd take care of the girls, and I've failed you. And them. I don't know what to do. Our situation is impossible.

Raucous pounding at the entrance followed by raised voices in the hallway snared her attention. Brooke swiftly wiped her cheeks. She yanked the ratty throw from her shoulders, and after glancing around for a place to hide it, settled on stuffing the makeshift shawl into the desk's kneehole.

"Excuse me. What do you think you're doing?"

Blythe? She'd answered the door instead of Duffen? Where was he?

Brooke slid open the desk drawer then pushed the hidden latch to the secret compartment. One eye trained on the doorway, she rapidly gathered the money and jewelry case. After cramming them into the small cubicle, she clicked the latch, shoved the drawer closed, and locked it. She returned the key to its hiding place in a slot beneath the chair's seat.

Blythe, a strange inflection somewhere between irritation and awe in her tone, exclaimed, "You cannot push your way inside, you great looby."

Drat, Lord Ravensdale—more persistent and annoying than an itch one couldn't reach.

Still, Brooke's lip curved at Blythe's pluck. "Probably the first time the earl's been called a looby, eh, Freddy?"

Barking, the dog bounded to his feet and then ran up and down the length of the couch, pouncing and yapping.

"Hush, I cannot hear."

Freddy obediently plopped onto his bottom before snuffling his haunch in search of a flea.

Brooke leaped from the chair, smoothing a few wayward tresses into place. She'd been in rather a hurry when she'd piled the mass into a loose knot, mainly because she couldn't stand to see herself in the gown she wore—one of Josephina's cast-offs from several seasons ago. Brooke swept the front of the saffron muslin a critical glance and grimaced. The heinous color washed out her complexion, making her look sallow and sickly. However, her wardrobe consisted of four gowns, and she couldn't be picky. She pinched her cheeks and bit her lips to add a dab of color to her face.

Thankfully, no pet hair clung to this garment, and the cut and fit were acceptable. She stopped short of scrutinizing her reflection in the window to make sure her appearance met the mark. She'd tired of the thin, pale face staring at her from her dressing table mirror.

Why did she care how she looked anyway? She wasn't trying to impress Lord Ravensdale. The opinion of the flea Freddy scratched away at concerned her more than anything the earl might think.

Rubbish.

"I insist upon seeing your master or mistress," a cultured male voice—clearly irritated and condescending—demanded. "And you would do well to show your betters more respect."

Brooke cocked her head. Assuredly not Lord Ravensdale, but two visitors in the same number of days? Unheard of.

"My betters?" A dangerous inflection entered Blythe's voice. "And who might *you* be?"

A theatrical, masculine sigh carried into the study. "Lord Leventhorpe, if you insist on knowing. You really are the most impudent servant."

"And I believe you're the most pompous ars—donkey's rear I've ever had the misfortune of meeting," Blythe retorted.

This man clearly possessed the common sense of a potato, speaking to Blythe that way. She would verbally filet him—in the most ladylike manner possible, of course. Blessed with a quick wit and sharp tongue, Blythe did have a most…eloquent way with words.

Brooke strained to hear their conversation, more amused than she'd been in a long while.

"Again, I must insist on speaking with the proprietor of this… er…house," Lord Leventhorpe said.

"Well, your high-and-mightiness, you can insist all you want, but I already told you before you rudely shoved your way inside, no one is home to visitors today." Exasperation rang in Blythe's voice. "Leave your card, if you must, then take your odious self off."

"I shall do no such thing. I'll remain until I am received." Heavy footsteps tread along the corridor. "Where might I wait? In one of these rooms?"

Doors swished opened then clicked closed in rapid succession.

Snoopy bugger.

"Oh, for the love of God, are you completely dense? Do feathers occupy your skull, or is it altogether empty?" Slightly breathless, as if she'd had to scurry to keep up, Blythe said, "You cannot go poking about in people's homes."

"Then be a helpful chit, and tell me where I might await your mistress or master. A good friend of mine has gone missing, and Ravensdale intended to call here yesterday."

'Tis a simple truth that life depends on probabilities, and those who wager had best be prepared to pay the penalty for taunting fate.
~Wisdom and Advice—The Genteel Lady's Guide to Practical Living

11

Lord Ravensdale. Missing?

Brooke didn't need to see her reflection to know she'd grown pale as milk. She felt the blood rush to her feet, washing her in a wave of dizziness. She'd never fainted before, but feared she might swoon from alarm. Pressing a hand to her forehead, she tore to the study door.

"Duffen, what have you done?"

Rushing through the opening, she barely stopped short of plowing into a giant of a man with fiery auburn hair and a scowl fierce enough to set demons to trembling. She toed aside the pheasant and pulled the door closed behind her.

Freddy didn't need to anoint another lord's boots.

She craned her neck to meet the man's eyes.

And I thought the earl tall.

"I tried to stop him, Brooke." Blythe hurried to Brooke's side, delivering the gentleman a glower as hostile as the one he leveled at the women. "But the pig-headed oaf wouldn't listen."

So I heard.

"I'm aware. I heard him." Brooke met Lord Leventhorpe's cynical gaze, shadowed beneath thunderous brows. "I beg your pardon. I didn't mean you're a pig-headed oaf."

Though your decorum dictates otherwise.

"Yes, he is, and a boorish buffoon too." Blythe gave an insincerely sweet smile, ire radiating from her.

He quirked those hawkish eyebrows, his gaze swinging between Brooke and Blythe before settling, heavy and disapproving, on Brooke.

Judgmental, uppity prig.

"Am I to assume you are mistress here?"

She angled her head in affirmation.

He turned startling blue eyes to Blythe, and stared for a long, rude moment. The corners of his mouth tilted upward fractionally. "And I've blundered and called you a servant. However, you must admit," he flicked a black-gloved hand up and down, "your attire lends one to leap to that conclusion."

As did the cobwebs and dust clinging to her gown from rummaging about in the attic.

Blythe grunted, and thrust her chin out. "Fools jump to conclusions, *my lord*."

Brooke dipped into a reluctant curtsy. False deference peeved her, but Mama had drilled proper decorum into her, and rousing this irritated man further was foolishness.

"I am Brooke Culpepper, and this is my cousin, Miss Blythe Culpepper." Brooke canted her head toward Blythe, who grudgingly bobbed a shallow curtsy. "She and I, as well as our sisters, are the mistresses of Esherton Green."

"Tristan, Marquis of Leventhorpe. My estate is several miles east of here." His attention riveted on Blythe, he bent into the merest semblance of a bow—so short as to be almost insulting.

Seemed Lord Ravensdale chose friends as arrogant and pretentious as he, or did the marquis play a game with her cousin? *Tit for tat*? *Cat and mouse*?

Blythe narrowed her eyes and firmed her lips before averting her gaze. Wise on her part.

They hadn't time for verbal sparring. Duffen must be found at once.

His lordship canted his head in the open door's direction. "Are you aware there's a tree blocking the drive? Rather a mess to traverse."

"Yes, it fell yesterday, and I haven't set the servants to removing it yet." As if she had the manpower for such a task.

"Not bad enough to keep you from intruding." Blythe scratched her cheek, leaving a faint smudge. Attic grime.

His lordship's lips quivered again, and mutinous sparks spewed from Blythe's eyes.

Time to separate them.

"Blythe, we must find Duffen. He was the last to see Lord Ravensdale yesterday. Get the other girls to help you search." Brooke slid a sideways glance to the serious-faced man watching the exchange. "In fact, ask Mabry to have the stable hands look as well. As long as no cows are in labor, that is."

Lord Leventhorpe made a sharp gesture. "I think my friend's disappearance takes precedence over cattle."

The caustic dryness of his words could have set kindling afire.

Brooke folded her arms and returned his harsh perusal. "Not around here, it doesn't, my lord."

Worry crinkled Blythe's usually smooth forehead. She laid a hand on Brooke's forearm. "Do you think something is truly amiss?"

A grunt-like snort exploded from the marquis.

Brooke met his lordship's gaze square on.

Yes, I do, but I'll swallow snails before I admit it without more evidence.

She'd known Duffen three and twenty years and this irksome man three minutes. Her loyalty lay with the servant. For now.

His lordship coolly returned her scrutiny, his features granite hard. He didn't seem the merciful, forgiving sort. No, more like the eye-for-an-eye type of chap.

"Duffen is dotty and prone to muttering beneath his breath, but to suggest he would have anything to do with anyone's disappearance, most especially a lord's, is pure silliness." Blythe brushed at a cobweb on her skirt. "He's always been protective, almost grandfatherly, toward us girls."

"Rather like a decrepit, old rooster trying to rule young chicks and just as comical, I'd wager." His lordship offered this droll opinion, earning him frowns from the women.

"As you've never met him, I'm quite sure I don't know how you arrived at that assumption, my lord." Renewed ire tinted Blythe's cheeks. "Brooke, what are your thoughts?"

"I honestly don't know." If only she could reassure her cousin. She looked to the entrance, still gaping open. A gargantuan russet horse stood docilely out front, awaiting its owner. The sun streamed into the entry, and tiny dust particles danced in the bright warmth. Such a contrast to yesterday. "He did make a peculiar remark last night, and I haven't seen him today. Have you?"

Where were Duffen and Lord Ravensdale?

"No." Eyes wide, Blythe shook her head, setting the curls framing her face to bobbing. "He might be off napping. He's done that oft of late."

Dread knotted Brooke's stomach. She didn't dare contemplate what Duffen might have done. Perhaps the earl's disappearance was a horrid coincidence. *And the cows pooped green gold.*

"I'll notify the girls. Where do you want us to search first?" Blythe pointedly avoided looking at Lord Leventhorpe. Not intimidated easily, her cousin might have met her match in the daunting behemoth. "His usual haunts in the house and on the grounds?"

"Yes," Brooke said. "I'll be along to help as soon as I can."

As soon as she could escape the marquis's suspicious regard.

Blythe spun about then hurried down the corridor, his lordship's fractious gaze never leaving her.

Before turning the corner, she cast a swift glance over her shoulder.

Please let her find Duffen right away so we can sort this out.

God willing, Lord Ravensdale had taken shelter somewhere on the way to the marquis's. Or perhaps he'd been thrown from his horse and lay injured on the route. But wouldn't Lord Leventhorpe have come upon the earl then? Not that she truly wished Ravensdale harm, regardless of the mean-spirited thoughts she'd harbored about him yesterday. But after Duffen's menacing remarks last night...better the earl be lying hurt somewhere than the alarming alternative.

She swallowed a lump of revulsion and fear.

"So you admit Ravensdale called?"

His lordship's terse question wrenched Brooke's attention to the present unpleasantness.

"Certainly. I never implied otherwise. He arrived unannounced, soaked to the skin, I might add. After a small respite before the fire in the study, he went on his way. All in all, he didn't remain above three quarters of an hour." Brooke turned to enter the study. She looked behind her as she pressed the latch. "Would you prefer to wait in here or take part in the search?"

Freddy forced his stout body through the opening. He sniffed the air, and after taking one panicked look at Lord Leventhorpe, ducked his head and retreated into the study. He disappeared around the desk to skulk in the knee well.

His reaction to Lord Leventhorpe caused Brooke no small amount of discomfit. Freddy loved everybody...except the marquis, it seemed. Her unease heightened, she made a mental note of Freddy's reaction. Dogs were good judges of characters. A moist, black nose pressed against the small space beneath the desk's middle panel and sniffed loudly through the crack.

Lord Leventhorpe removed his hat and followed her into the room. “I’d like to ask you a few questions, starting with the peculiar remark this Duffen fellow made.”

Shouts and clamoring roused Heath from a fitful slumber and an equally disturbing dream. A hobgoblin had knocked him on the noggin and locked him in a giant birdhouse, intending to feed him to an elephant-sized gray-plumed bird with violet-blue eyes and a shock of curly white feathers atop its head.

The commotion grew louder and closer.

“Lord Ravensdale?”

“Ravensdale!”

“Yer lordship, can you hear us?”

Heath bolted upright, pain and memories simultaneously assaulting him. He stumbled to his feet, his head throbbing with a crusader’s vengeance.

“In here.” A hoarse croak emerged. He swallowed. “I’m in here. Inside the pigeon cote.”

More commotion echoed outside the building before the door jerked open.

Heath blinked at the outline of several people illumined in the archway. Unsteady on his feet, he waited until they stopped wavering before speaking. “Someone send for the magistrate. I’ve been attacked and abducted.”

A small figure dashed away. Brette. No doubt to warn her sister she’d been found out. He couldn’t wait to hear the elder Miss Culpepper’s fabricated explanation for his treatment.

A fellow Heath didn’t recognize stepped forward. “Your lordship, I’m Richard Mabry, Esherton’s overseer. I’ll send one of my lads to fetch the magistrate straightaway. Are you injured?”

Mouth dry as sand, head stuffed with wool and swollen three times its normal size, and tormented by an invisible hand that jabbed a jagged knife into his skull each time he spoke or moved, Heath barely contained a snarl. “If you consider being wacked on the head with a brick and then drugged senseless injured, then yes.”

Shock registered on Mabry's craggy features before his gaze sank to the toppled bricks left of the entry. "Do you require a physician? Can you walk to the house, or do you need us to carry you?"

Hell of a lot of dignity in that, carted about like an invalid or a babe. Heath lifted an unsteady hand to his stinging face. A cut lay across his cheekbone. He hadn't noticed the scratch the first time he awoke. "No, yes, and no."

Mabry's beetle brows wiggled. "Sir?"

Heath forced his leaden feet to move forward. At least he thought he moved. A slug in molasses moved faster.

"No, I don't need a physician." *Might be a good idea to have one take a gander.* "Yes, I can walk. And no, I do not need to be carried." *You will if you keel over onto your face.*

Mabry gestured to a short, lanky man. "Run to the house, and let Miss Brooke know his lordship has been found."

As if she doesn't know where I've been all along.

The fellow bobbed his head before trotting away.

"I'd feel much better if you'd allow me the honor of assisting you, my lord. Miss Brooke will have my head if further harm comes to you." Mabry tentatively wrapped a burly arm around Heath's waist.

Heath choked on a scoffing laugh. "I doubt that, Mabry."

Nonetheless, Heath leaned into the man, grateful for the support. Lurching outside, he closed his eyes. The sun's glare proved excruciating and increased the ferocious thrumming inside his skull.

"I'll go on ahead and tell Brooke to prepare a chamber for his lordship. He shouldn't travel in his condition."

Heath turned his head in the direction of the voice and cracked one eye open. Blythe, the feisty oldest cousin.

"I would appreciate it." Pretenses be damned. He needed to sit down, before he toppled like a tap house drunkard. Devil it, how far away was the house?

Another sturdy arm wrapped around his other side.

"I see you've managed to make a muddle of things, Raven. Could have sworn you toddled here to sell the place, not take a snooze in a pigeon coop half-filled with shi—er...dung."

Leventhorpe?

Heath squinted at him, the sun's rays slicing straight to his brain. He'd have smiled but wasn't certain the motion wouldn't have split his skull like walnut. "About damned time you showed up."

"And that's the thanks I get for parting with my mattress before the sun awoke. I even missed breaking my fast and my customary cups of coffee." He gave Heath's ribs a gentle press. "You're welcome."

Several torturous minutes later—minutes which left Heath seriously considering asking someone to knock him unconscious again—Leventhorpe and Mabry hauled him up the steps.

Like blond-haloed angels of mercy, the Culpepper misses hovered at the entrance.

Leventhorpe's stride faltered, and he shot Heath a look of such incredulity, he would've laughed if he hadn't been afraid he'd disgrace himself on his friend's overly shiny boots. His reaction upon meeting the women yesterday had been much the same.

"Five bloody unbelievable beauties," Leventhorpe muttered beneath his breath. "My God, five. And not one a hopper-arsed or corny-faced."

Only one snagged Heath's attention. The one that had captivated him from the start, damn his eyes. *Damn her eyes.*

Her face somewhere between ashen and a sickly yellow, and wearing a dress uglier than the one she'd worn yesterday, Brooke met his gaze for an instant before squaring her shoulders and issuing orders. "Mr. Mabry, he needs a physician. Please ride to the village as soon as you've assisted his lordship upstairs."

"I'll notify the magistrate too, Miss Brooke."

Her eyes rounded, the irises growing enormous, and the slim column of her throat worked. "Yes, yes, quite so."

She blinked then blinked again, regaining her composure, but the unsteady hand she raised to tuck a silky curl behind her ear betrayed her true state.

"Blythe, have Flora bring the tea you brewed upstairs, and the hot water and towels too. Oh, and please have Mrs. Jennings heat the leftover stew from last night." She faced the twins. "Everything is prepared in Mama and Papa's room?"

They intended to put him in the master suite?

As one, the lookalikes nodded, but remained silent and exchanged an anxious glance. They turned reproachful gazes on him.

Their silent chastisement grated against his pride. Confound it, he was the victim here.

Not the only one, as you well know.

"Any sign of Duffen?" Brooke laid a hand on Brette's chill-reddened arm.

Why didn't they wear outer garments? He shivered within his greatcoat. Didn't they possess pelisses, or spencers, at least?

"Not yet, Brooke." Brette stepped aside to allow Mabry and Leventhorpe to guide Heath into the entry. "We wanted to get his lordship to the house as quickly as possible. We'll start looking again."

Heath wavered, and Brooke steadied him with a palm to his chest. The contact burned through his garments. She must have felt something too, because she snatched her hand away and rubbed it against her hip. Brow creased, she stared out the doorway.

He detected no mercy in the gaze Brette directed at him. So much for winning the cousins and sister to his cause. The task would be harder without their support. Did he still want Brooke for his mistress? Despite his suffering and the ghastly gown she wore, he couldn't pry his gaze from her pretty face.

Yes, confound it to hell and back again. He did. Why did he want her when any number of females would eagerly warm his bed? He'd address that particular after he determined her guilt. However, everything about her demeanor this moment screamed innocence.

"Where is the chamber you're putting him in?" Leventhorpe's grip tightened. "He's about to collapse."

Acting his overbearing self, as usual. Bossy as an old tabby.

"I am not." Heath took another swaying step.

Brooke whirled to stare at him. Sincere concern shimmered in her dark-lashed eyes, or else she was the best damned actress he'd seen in a long while. Better than that petite morsel he'd contemplated making his paramour. Compared to Brooke, the other woman seemed a tawdry tart.

"Do you need to be carried, my lord?" She wiggled her forefinger, beckoning the stable hands enter who'd followed them to the house.

"No. I am not going to collapse." Wouldn't do to have Brooke think him a weakling. That he cared an iota about her opinion of him gave testament to how hard he'd been whacked. Dashed the sense out of him.

"Stubble it, Ravensdale." Leventhorpe adjusted his support as he assisted Heath up the risers. "A ninety-year old, one-legged crone leans on her cane less than you're hanging on me."

Mabry grunted his agreement. "Not a light cove either."

"True, Mr. Mabry." Leventhorpe hoisted Heath higher. "You might consider a slimming regimen, Raven."

"Shut up, Trist," Heath all but growled, past caring what anyone thought of him. Flecks darted and danced before his eyes. He needed to lie down. At once.

Upstairs, Mabry took his leave, although Heath insisted he didn't need a physician.

"Nevertheless, my lord, I think it wise to have you examined." Brooke fluffed a pillow on the turned-down bed. Uncertainty clouded her indigo eyes. Her gaze flitted to Leventhorpe before she exchanged a telling glance with Blythe. Leventhorpe unnerved her. Good. She wasn't likely to try another stunt with Trist looming over her.

Her cap askew, a timid maid limped into the chamber. Arms twig thin and her gaze riveted on the floor, she bore a wooden tray laden with a teapot, cup, steaming bowl of something scrumptious smelling, two slices of bread, butter, and a spoon and napkin.

His stomach growled when he inhaled the heady aroma.

Brooke cast him a disconcerted glance then gave the servant a kind smile. "Thank you, Flora. Please set it on the table, there."

She pointed to a three-legged table near the toasty fire in the hearth.

Heath held his breath as Flora shuffled to the table, the tray wobbling with each awkward step. She had one leg shorter than the other. He inspected her shoes. A cobbler could build up the left sole, and she would walk much easier. Not a priority when money at Esherton appeared scarcer than frost in Hades.

"Need anythin' else, Miss Brooke?" Head cocked to the side, Flora peeped upward through stubby eyelashes and played with the stringy strand of hair that had escaped her cap.

Brooke offered another encouraging smile. "No. You may go. Make sure you eat luncheon today. You forgot again yesterday."

"I'll do it now." Flora hobbled out the door, leaving it open behind her.

Heath stared at Brooke's lips. What would they taste like? Sweet or fruity?

Why did she have him obsessing over every part of her anatomy? He could find no fault in her appearance, from her oval face, perfectly sculpted rose-pink lips, dove-white hair, surprisingly dark, winged brows, and thick lashes framing astonishing purple-blue eyes to her creamy skin, breasts he guaranteed would overflow his palms, and a backside that begged to be fondled and ridden.

Must be the injury to his head—had him waxing raunchy poppycock.

Leventhorpe propelled him toward the bed, and after urging Heath to sit, tugged off his boots and tossed them on the floor. Arms folded,

Leventhorpe perched a hip on the arm of an overstuffed chair beside the bed.

Clearly exasperated, Blythe faced him, hands on her hips. "My lord, your presence isn't needed. Why don't you wait in the study?"

"Good idea." Brooke nodded her agreement as she dipped a cloth into a basin of water. "I shall come down and answer your questions when Lord Ravensdale's hunger is appeased and he is resting comfortably."

Which hunger?

Heath must've made a noise—*Good God, did I say that aloud?*—for Brooke frowned, and Leventhorpe let loose a hearty guffaw.

"I'm staying." Leventhorpe looked down his superior nose, something he'd perfected over the years to put underlings in their place. One look usually sufficed to send the offender dashing for cover.

Blythe rolled her eyes heavenward, muttering, "Of course you are, obstinate bore."

"I heard that." Leventhorpe removed his gloves then his hat and tossed the lot on the chair's torn cushion.

Blythe offered a syrupy smile. "You were meant to."

He chuckled, and Heath speared him a sharp glance. A roguish grin lingered on Leventhorpe's face. Not a typical reaction from his reticent friend. As Brooke went about removing Heath's greatcoat and jacket, Leventhorpe looked on.

Every innocent brush of her hand or bump of her arm stoked Heath's awareness of her. She bent to her task, and her bodice gapped. He itched to touch the flesh his eyes caressed, but forced his focus away, all too aware they had an audience. Perusing the rather dusty chamber, he caught the sardonic curling of Leventhorpe's mouth.

Brooke tossed the overcoat to the foot of the bed and turned her attention to his jacket. She released the top button. Did her fingers tremble the merest bit?

"I can undress myself," he said, though the way the bedchamber weaved up and down, he wasn't at all certain he could.

Leventhorpe stopped scrutinizing the room—or was it Blythe that he studied?—to quirk a brow at Heath. "Of course you can, but let her fuss over you anyway."

Heath's neckcloth came next. He hated the confounded things. Always felt half-choked, but gentlemen of the *ton* didn't go about with their necks exposed.

"Lie back, my lord." Brooke passed the strip of cloth to her cousin.

At her prompting, Heath reclined against the pillows, and once he'd settled, she drew the bedcoverings to his waist. The pounding in his head lessened to a steady pulsing, and the chamber ceased to dip and sway like a ship on stormy seas.

Her lower lip clamped between her pink lips, she dabbed at the cut on his face.

He inhaled her fresh fragrance. A mole peeked at him from the right side of her neck, and he longed to kiss the small dot then explore the long swan-like column with his lips. The décolletage of her gown hinted at the lush swells of flesh it partially concealed. Would her nipples be pert and rosy or ripe and pink? Unbidden images of him laving her succulent tips with his tongue bombarded him.

His manhood jerked, momentarily stirring the bedcovers.

Busy spreading a pleasant-smelling salve on the scratch, Brooke didn't notice. He hoped. Irritated at his lack of control, and to keep from embarrassing himself, he turned a bland stare on Leventhorpe. The wicked twinkle in his friend's eye said plainly that *he* had noticed. "I don't need you mothering me, Trist. Go below and find someone to pester."

Leventhorpe yawned behind his hand and blinked drowsily. He looked done in. Likely he'd never sought his bed when Heath didn't return last night.

"I've no intention of mothering you, Raven. Removing your boots is the extent of my nurturing skills, I assure you." He inclined his head toward the women. "I'm making sure one of these sirens doesn't slide a knife between your ribs to finish the job."

Harsh gasps escaped the women.

Fury snapped in Blythe's eyes, but censure shimmered in Brooke's.

Bristling with indignation, Blythe whirled to Leventhorpe. Voice quivering, she stabbed a finger at him. "How dare you? We've been nothing but hospitable to Lord Ravensdale, and your ugly insinuations—"

Brooke touched Blythe's arm. "He has the right to worry about his friend."

Blythe pursed her lips and lowered her gaze. "But he doesn't have the right to accuse us of such evilness."

"I agree, but Duffen is in our employ." Brooke's gaze rested on Heath. "If he is responsible—"

Heath gave a derisive snort and paid the price as pain kicked its hind feet against his skull. “He is responsible. He deceived me into helping him then clobbered me with a brick when I turned my back.”

“Then we must make things right.” Her steady gaze met his. Nonetheless, he swore dread lingered in the depths of her unusual eyes. “It’s the honorable thing to do.”

My God, so convincing. She even had him believing her theatrics. He observed her through half-closed eyes. Unless this wasn’t a performance. Perhaps he’d wronged her, and she hadn’t been behind Duffen’s actions. Difficult to believe, but perhaps the gnome truly had acted of his own volition.

Some of the tension eased from Heath.

Duffen, on the other hand, was in it up to his eyeballs. Did he understand the consequences of his misplaced bravado? Imprisonment or worse if Heath brought charges against him. And Leventhorpe would insist upon it.

Brette hustled into the chamber, the corgi on her heels.

Upon spotting Leventhorpe, the stout canine skidded to a halt. His nostrils flared and twitched before he crouched and skulked to hide beneath the draperies. Leventhorpe’s mouth slanted downward, and he scratched his nose. He regarded the snout visible under the frayed window coverings.

Heath pressed his fingertips to the knot behind his head. Dogs usually adored Leventhorpe, but Freddy had clearly taken an aversion to him.

Breathless and pushing a damp lock off her forehead, Brette made straight for her sister. “We found Duffen. He’s in a bad way.”

Brooke paled and clutched the cloth she’d been tending Heath’s scratch with.

“And, Brooke, Rogers has returned from the Benbridges.” Panting, Brette tossed Heath an anxious glance.

Who’s Rogers?

Brooke dropped the wet rag into the basin before reaching for a dry towel.

Heath breathed a mite easier, grateful for the reprieve. Her hovering over him, her breasts and lips mere inches away...pure torment.

“Rogers isn’t alone,” Brette added.

Blythe turned from the teapot, giving Brette a puzzled stare. “He’s not? Did Mr. Benbridge accompany him?"

A nonplussed expression swept Brooke's face.

"Did Mrs. Benbridge and Josephina come to call? It isn't like them not to send a note round first." She shook her head and tossed the towel aside. "I cannot possibly receive them at the moment. We haven't any tea left, and with Lord Ravensdale and Duffen—"

"No, Brooke." Brette drew nearer and clasped her sister's hand. "Humphrey's here. In the drawing room."

Man is a gaming animal by nature, which is why he'll make foolish wagers against impossible odds and still remain convinced he'll come out ahead.
~Wisdom and Advice—The Genteel Lady's Guide to Practical Living

12

Grateful for the interruption in her ministrations to Lord Ravensdale, Brooke would've hugged Brette if her news hadn't been so horrendous.

Touching and smelling him, gazing into his gold-flecked irises scant inches away rattled her senses and strained her composure past endurance. His tense muscles had bunched and twitched while she undressed him, tantalizing her wickedly. The tautness of his jaw and erratic breathing suggested she had affected him as much. Yet he'd uttered not a sound apart from one gravelly groan—quickly silenced—when she'd brushed his torso while unbuttoning his coat.

A shiver of desire had rippled from her breasts to the juncture of her thighs at the guttural noise. What kind of woman lusted after an injured man, and one who sought to deprive her of her home? Perhaps she'd lost her faculties. Perhaps the strain of running the farm and caring for her sister and cousins had addled her at long last.

Add that to the tidings that Humphrey had returned from abroad, and at this moment waited below stairs, and she teetered on the verge of hysterical laughter or frenzied weeping.

Humphrey? For the love of God. Why now?

Could anything else possibly happen to make this day more calamitous?

Brooke took a steadying breath. First things first.

"Where did you find Duffen?"

"In the carriage house. The earl's horse is there too. He's fine, my lord," Brette assured Lord Ravensdale. She spared Lord Leventhorpe a brief glance. "Oh, and I had your mount taken there as well. The barns are full of cattle at present."

Both men murmured thank you, and Lord Ravensdale smoothed the bedding over his lap, as if uncomfortable or in pain.

Guilt prodded her.

"Most wise." Brooke searched her sister's pale face and stricken eyes. She wouldn't be this distraught if matters weren't grave. "What's wrong with Duffen? Does he need a physician as well?"

God's bones, how could she afford a physician's fee for two patients? Her remaining finances dwindled faster than ale in a hot tap room full of thirsty sailors.

On the cusp of tears, Brette nodded. "I think he's had an apoplexy. He cannot move or speak."

Voice breaking, she covered her face and wept.

Dear God.

The day just worsened considerably.

"Losing his home has been too much for him." Her back to the men, Brooke shut her eyes and pressed a palm against her forehead where a vicious beating had begun.

It's been too much for me too.

She sensed the lords' contemplative gazes trained on her and lowered her hand. Had they any notion of the havoc their presence wreaked on this household? Drawing on the last dregs of her composure and fortitude, she schooled her face. She mustn't show signs of feminine weakness, for Lord Ravensdale must be convinced of her ability to operate the farm.

Let it go, Brooke. That dream has died a drawn out, excruciating death.

If only she could turn the clock back to yesterday. Relive the past twenty-four horrific hours. Somehow, some way change the course of destiny.

"See to your man and your guest, Miss Culpepper. I'll stay here until the physician arrives." Lord Leventhorpe spoke to Brooke, yet his attention remained focused on Blythe pouring a cup of tea. He yawned again.

Perhaps a thimbleful of humanity warmed the marquis's blood after all.

"I'll even feed him," Leventhorpe offered with a sly twist of his lips.

"You bloody well will not." Lord Ravensdale levered himself more upright, his shirt rumpling at the neck and exposing a delicious expanse of hairy chest. "I can feed myself."

Brooke swallowed and tore her focus from the black, springy curls. What had she done to deserve such unholy torture? Shouldn't an adversary be reviled? Not in her case. She flitted around him like a moth to a flame. Stupid. Fatal.

"Go, stay with Duffen. Keep him calm and comfortable." Brooke gave Brette a swift hug. "Tell him I'll come as soon as I'm able. Doctor Wilton should be here within the hour."

Wiping her eyes and face, Brette gave a sharp inclination of her head and swept from the room.

Brooke gathered the bowl, napkin, and spoon. How could a man's muscled chest be so devilishly tempting? And why did she notice when disaster raged around them? *Stupid question.* He'd mesmerized her, that's why.

Brooke jerked her gaze to Blythe. "Please go with her. Duffen may need your herbal tea too."

"Of course, although if he's had an apoplexy, I don't want to give him anything until the doctor examines him." Blythe carried the teacup to Lord Ravensdale, seemingly oblivious to his lordship's physical charms. "Sip this slowly. It will ease your stomach. I'm sorry, but I cannot give you anything for your headache until you've seen Doctor Wilton. It's unwise if you have a concussion."

"Thank you." Lord Ravensdale sniffed the light brew. "May I ask what kind it is? It smells minty."

"It is. We grow three kinds of mint at Esherton. It's a favorite of the villagers." She flashed Lord Leventhorpe a mocking glance. "Should I taste it first, my lord? Aren't you worried I might try to poison Lord Ravensdale?"

Those two rubbed each other the wrong way—like flint and steel, sparks and all. Their immediate and intense dislike hadn't lessened a jot.

His lordship moved his hat and gloves to the floor then edged onto the chair's seat. Lines of exhaustion creased the corners of his eyes. He crossed his legs at the knee and, elbows resting on the chair's arms, tented his fingers together. "I regret my earlier accusation. I'm sure the brew is perfectly harmless."

Blythe paused at the threshold, her scrutiny shifting between the men. Her features strained, she searched Brooke's face. "Do you want me to stay with you until you've seen our unexpected guest?"

Bless her. Blythe understood how awkward the encounter with Humphrey would likely be. Brooke shook her head, though facing Humphrey alone after these many years had her palms damp and pulse skittering. "No. Duffen is more important."

"If you're certain." Misgiving resonated in Blythe's voice. Nevertheless, she took her leave after another scathing scowl at Lord Leventhorpe.

Brooke passed Lord Ravensdale the soup, deliberately keeping her attention on his forehead. Her traitorous eyeballs kept trying to sneak a peek lower. "Be careful, my lord. It's hot."

"I'm neither an invalid nor a lackwit, Miss Culpepper." He regarded the cup and bowl he held. "Am I to hold and consume the tea and soup at once?"

Heat singed her face. Ungrateful cur. She bit her tongue. *Be gracious.* No sense riling the ornery bear further.

"No, of course not." She accepted the teacup he extended and, after moving a lamp aside, set it upon the bedside table within his reach.

His rancor took Brooke aback and cooled her ardor as effectively as diving naked into a snow drift. He couldn't be too bad off if he was this disagreeable, could he? She fussed with the items on the nightstand. "I'll return as soon as I know Duffen's condition and see my guest on his way."

She rounded the end of the bed, but paused halfway to the door.

Except for his wan face and a pinched look about his mouth, Lord Ravensdale didn't appear too incapacitated. The pulse in his corded neck beat rhythmically as he regarded her, his countenance indecipherable. A healthy brute like him ought to recover quickly, oughtn't he?

"Please believe me, I honestly had no notion of Duffen's actions." She clasped her hands, when Ravensdale only blinked, his face an impassive mask. Didn't he believe her? More disconcertingly, what did he intend to do when the magistrate arrived? "I am horrified you've been harmed. I pray you recover swiftly."

He slanted his dark head but remained stone-faced and silent.

Hope shrank. Not quite ready to forgive and forget. Not that she blamed him, entirely. She'd be hard-pressed to muster a speck of compassion for a bounder who cracked her on the noggin.

"Who's Humphrey?" Lord Ravensdale's quiet question reverberated as explosive as a cannon in the silent room.

Nearly out the door, she halted and looked over her shoulder. He held her gaze captive as his, accusing and condemning, scraped over her. Leventhorpe appeared to have dozed off, but roused himself to crack an eye open and peer her way.

Busybody.

Her hand on the doorjamb, she whispered, "He's the man I almost married."

Brooke flew down the corridor, Lord Ravensdale's astounded expression etched in her brain. What? Didn't he think her capable of having a beau? Was she too old and unappealing in her cast-off gown that the notion stretched the extremes of his imagination?

The idea hurt more than it ought. Lord Ravensdale's opinion of her shouldn't matter a jot, but confound it all, it did. She sighed. Upstairs lay a man who fascinated her beyond common sense and shouldn't even cause her to bat an eyelash, and below waited a man she should be eager to see, but wasn't.

Humphrey.

Brooke descended the stairway, in no hurry to reach the drawing room. Shouldn't she be more excited at the prospect of seeing him again? She'd loved him beyond reason at one time. Now she felt nothing more than warm sentiment at seeing an old friend. Why had he come, anyway? Could he still harbor a morsel of affection for her?

Her heart fluttered.

Excitement or trepidation? It mattered not. Her circumstances remained much the same, except Papa no longer lived, and paupers claimed deeper pockets than she.

She couldn't wed Humphrey, not unless he could accept the whole bundle that came with her. Why didn't the idea of becoming his wife hold the thrill it once had? Hold up there. Putting the cart before the horse, wasn't she? His visit could be attributed to any number of reasons, and jumping to conclusions generally led to trouble.

What if he had married or was betrothed?

No, his sister would have mentioned it.

Unless either had occurred recently. Possible. Brooke hadn't seen Josephina in weeks. Almost...almost as if she'd been avoiding the Culpeppers.

Nonsense and rot. Goodness. See what fatigue and an overactive imagination wrought.

Unease slowing her steps, Brooke approached the open double

doors. She could do this. Taking a bracing breath, she painted a bright smile on her face and silently entered the same room in which she'd told Humphrey she couldn't marry him.

Unaware of her presence, he stared out the window's narrow leaded glass window. Sunlight played across his features, emphasizing his perfect profile. A crimson riding coat strained across his broad shoulders. Cream pantaloons, tucked into boots, hugged muscular thighs. He held his hat in his right hand and, every once in a while, tapped it against his leg.

"Hello, Humphrey."

He spun to face her.

The same, but different.

He'd filled out, become more striking in a mature man-of-the-world sort of way. His tawny blond hair and hazel eyes hadn't changed. Neither had the charming smile that brightened his suntanned face upon seeing her.

His appreciative gaze stroked her, and then he hurried across the room, his boots rapping a sharp staccato on the bare floor. He lifted her fingers to his warm lips and pressed a light kiss to the knuckles. Scandalous to touch his mouth to an unmarried woman's bare hand, but this man had kissed her lips, so pretending shock would be pointless.

The top of her head and his were almost level. She'd never noticed that before. Probably due to the recent acquaintance of the two towering Titans above stairs.

"Brooke. Even lovelier than I remembered." Humphrey clasped her hand, joy shimmering in his eyes. Her insides gave a strange quiver. "I've missed you, more than words can express. Please accept my belated condolences for the loss of your father."

"Thank you. I miss him still." Moisture glazed her eyes for a moment, not only for Papa's early death, but for what she and Humphrey had lost, and what could never be. She forced a cheerful smile. "So, what brings you to Esherton today? I must say, I was quite surprised to hear you had paid a call."

He offered a sheepish grin, reminding her of the shy, young man who'd courted her.

"I was with Father when your note arrived. I begged him to allow me the honor of responding in person. He and Mother request your company—and the others too, of course—for tea tomorrow at three o'clock." He passed her the invitation, a scented piece of fine stationery.

"We'll send the carriage round for you."

He chuckled, the familiar melodic rumble warming her troubled heart. "When I left, Josephina had interrupted her preparations for London to make a list of sweets she wanted Cook to prepare."

"London?" Bother it all. The London Season. The Benbridges usually departed after the calving ended. Brooke had contacted Mr. Benbridge just in time.

"Yes. My sister is determined to snare herself a husband this Season. My aunt has suggested that a certain marquis would be a brilliant match, poor chap." Humphrey peered behind her. "Where are the others? Josephina said you're all unmarried, as impossible as that is for me to believe. Given your uncommon beauty, I must wonder at the lack of intelligence of the eligible men in the area."

What men? Your arrival home brings the total to precisely one.

Shouldn't she feel a rush of pleasure at his compliment instead of this slight edginess?

He caressed her palm with his thumb. "I'm delighted you didn't find another to take my place in your heart."

There it is.

Her pulse gave a happy little skip, despite her misgivings. His glowing eyes and appreciative smile provided a much needed salve to her chafed womanly confidence. A pair of seductive, black-lashed eyes, a hint of cynicism flashing in their depths, rudely intruded upon the special occasion. She kicked them aside, much the same way she would a mouse attempting to scurry up her skirts. Lord Ravensdale would not rob her of this moment.

"I'm afraid we've had a pair of unfortunate events since I sent my letter round this morning. I'm awaiting the physician's arrival." Brooke gently withdrew her hand from his and then clasped hers together.

Humphrey frowned, genuine concern creasing his forehead. Such a kind man. "What's happened? Is it your sister, or one of your cousins?"

"No, they are fine, but Duffen—you remember him, don't you?"

"Indeed, I do." Humphrey nodded. "Who could forget that crusty devil?"

Brooke gave a half-smile. "Unfortunately, we think he's had an apoplexy. Brette and Blythe are tending him."

"Most unfortunate." He cupped her elbow. No rush of pleasure accompanied his touch.

"You said a pair of events. What else has happened to distress you?"

Humphrey laid a finger on her cheek. "I see the anxiety in your eyes and in the stiff way you hold yourself when you're distraught."

He did know her so very well. Comfortable and safe. He'd always made her feel that way. Not disjointed and tumultuous and confused and...tingly, like the growly beast upstairs did.

"A visitor to Esherton has been injured. He's with his friend above stairs waiting for the doctor to examine him as well."

She couldn't tell Humphrey of Duffen's perfidy. Or that the most alarmingly attractive man she'd ever laid eyes upon now owned the farm, leaving them paupers. Or that two powerful peers occupied her parents' bedroom, and what they might do to her and Duffen turned her spit to dust and stopped the blood in her veins.

"Visitor? A beau?" Humphrey scratched his jaw, appearing a bit uneasy...or jealous?

Ridiculous. He'd been gone five years and hadn't once written to indicate he yet harbored feelings for her. And she wasn't naive enough to think he'd played the part of a monk during that time. Brooke waved her hand and gave a short shake of her head. "No, no, nothing of that nature. He's curious about the dairy operation, that's all."

Ravensdale did have an interest in Esherton's dairy, in a manner of speaking.

Humphrey darted a glance to the window. "You do have some of the finest cattle in the area."

Brooke suppressed a smile. She knew more about distilling whisky than he did about milk cows. He'd never possessed a desire to step into his father's and grandfather's shoes, even if they had become vulgarly wealthy producing the most coveted cheese in all of England.

"What's the nature of his injury?" His regard sank to the expanse of rounded flesh visible above her bodice, and Brooke stifled an urge to tug the neckline higher.

"I'm afraid," Lord Ravensdale said, "I suffered a rather nasty crack to the base of my skull."

Brooke gasped and whirled to face the entrance.

He stood in his stockings, buckskins, and gaping shirt, looking for all the world like the man of the house. Pain darkened his eyes to jet and ringed his mouth in a tense, white line.

The idiot. Brooke feared he'd plop onto his face at any moment. Serve him right, odious man, except he'd probably sustain another injury and blame her. My God, all she needed was for Ravensdale to injure himself further while in her home.

Surely that's what she felt, worry he'd further injure himself, nothing more.

Humphrey's eyes widened as he took in his lordship's dishabille. Gentlemen did not present themselves half-dressed and shoeless. He flashed Brooke a bewildered look. Nonetheless, good breeding and faultless manners prevailing, he bowed.

"Humphrey Benbridge, at your service."

Always the proper, irreproachable, *predictable* gentleman. Where had that unbidden thought sprouted?

Humphrey clasped her hand and raised it to his lips again, almost as if claiming her. Silly man. He needn't worry Lord Ravensdale contended for her affections. A flush heated her cheeks at the absurd notion.

"You must be the visitor Miss Culpepper spoke of. She and I are old, and very dear, friends." Humphrey gave her a jaunty smile and a conspiratorial wink. "And I hope to become much more in the near future."

What? Seriously? He just waltzed in here after five years and wanted to take up where they'd left off? *The gall.*

"Isn't that so, Brooke?" He attempted to draw her to his side, a possessive gleam in his eyes and a challenge firming his jaw. "Our time apart has been quite unbearable."

Yes, and that was why he'd corresponded regularly and hurried home at the first opportunity. Brooke nearly gnashed her teeth at his forwardness and posturing, but instead schooled her features into what she prayed resembled composure. "Mr. Benbridge, may I introduce you to Esherton Green's guest, Heath, Earl of Ravensdale?"

A suitable expression of awe skittered across Humphrey's boyish face. Like his parents, men of rank and prestige easily impressed him. Foolish. A title didn't automatically signify good character. This very moment, Esherton housed two examples attesting to that fact.

Humphrey bent into another fawning bow. "It's an honor, your lordship."

Such shallowness rubbed Brooke the wrong way, and the momentary happiness at seeing her old friend faded.

Lord Ravensdale inclined his head the merest bit, likely afraid further movement would part his head from his shoulders, the fool. Where was that dimwit Lord Leventhorpe? Why had he let the earl out of bed?

Ravensdale sauntered forward, his movements measured.

To the casual observer, he appeared confident and relaxed. Brooke, however, recognized someone struggling to disguise their pain with self-assured cockiness. The set of his jaw, taut shoulders, closed hands, and straight line of his brows all screeched pain. She wasn't catching him if he plunged to the floor. He deserved to be knocked halfway to senseless. Once again, she withdrew her hand from Humphrey's, her gaze trained on his lordship the whole while.

What was he about? Why torture himself by leaving his bed when he obviously suffered?

Lord Ravensdale folded his arms and rested an entirely-too-muscled shoulder against the fireplace. His ebony gaze slashed between her and Humphrey. The predatory glint smoldering in the depths of his eyes hitched her breath and raised the hair at her nape. The urge to flee the room overwhelmed her. Instead, she dug her toes into her boots and defied him with her gaze.

Lord Ravensdale placed a hand at the back of his head.

He's in pain.

His handsome mouth inched upward. "Well, this is rather awkward."

What was?

"How so?" Puzzlement replaced Humphrey's friendly smile. He shot her a questioning glance.

She raised her eyebrows and inched a shoulder upward then angled her head, scrutinizing the earl. She hadn't a clue what he blathered about.

His lordship's magnetic gaze held Brooke's in silent warning. "Brooke's my mistress. Aren't you, love?"

Wagers gone awry at the gaming table
turn friends into foes and lovers into enemies.
~*Wisdom and Advice—The Genteel Lady's Guide to Practical Living*

13

Four days later, wrapped once again in the tattered throw and wearing her gray gown, Brooke leaned against the barn and gazed into the far pasture. Blast, but she wished she could call Ravensdale, the rakehell, out for his scurrilous declaration.

Whirring wings and vibrant plumage announced a cock pheasant's taking wing. A refreshing breeze teased the loose curls framing Brooke's face and set the blushing pink cuckoo flowers bordering a marshy patch to swaying. The morning sun's rays caressed her upturned face.

She would freckle.

She didn't care. Let her fair skin turn bread crust-brown and wrinkled as a crone's.

A few minutes ago, Mabry had let the dappled black-and-white newborns into the paddock for the first time. They explored the thick green grass, never straying too far from their mothers' sides. Occasionally, a frisky calf approached another curious baby, and they'd frolic a few minutes, butting heads and kicking up their heels, before a soft, maternal moo had them skipping to the safety of their anxious parents.

Buford had sired fourteen calves, including a set of twins.

Fourteen, four, or forty, it mattered not.

Not anymore.

There would be no more calves bred at Esherton. At least not beneath her watch.

Most of her hard-earned notes lined Doctor Wilton's pocket, and the rest would soon follow as he returned daily to check his patients' progress. Despair unlike Brooke had ever experienced sank its ruthless talons into her fragile heart and her little remaining hope, tearing them into lifeless shreds.

Two evenings ago, after the magistrate had finally arrived and attempted to question him, Duffen suffered another seizure and lapsed into unconsciousness. Doctor Wilton didn't expect him to survive until nightfall, which meant she'd never know why the servant attacked the earl. Perhaps a misguided notion about protecting the women had coiled, serpent-like, around his fragile mind until the pressure meshed reality with delusion.

She shut her eyes against the disturbing image of him lying, frail and frightened, on his narrow cot. People would do all manner of reprehensible things when driven by desperation. To protect those they loved. She'd already forgiven Duffen for the harm he'd caused, but suspected hard-hearted Lord Ravensdale never would.

No, not hard-hearted. Distant and reserved more aptly described him. An impenetrable shell encompassed the earl. Except his keen eyes. Emotions glittered there, most of which stripped her bare, leaving her vulnerable and uncertain. Yet, she yearned to find a way through his hard exterior, to see if, as she suspected, the man within was warm and caring.

He'd suffered a serious concussion and wasn't permitted anything more strenuous than lifting a fork for a week. His alarmingly brief consultation with the magistrate had Brooke fretting about what they'd discussed. The doctor admitted he'd told Lord Ravensdale that, had his injury been any lower, his lordship would likely have died.

God. Brooke opened her eyes, blinking several times to focus in the glaring sun.

However, Doctor Wilton also reassured her that if the earl obeyed his orders, he would make a full recovery. After his preposterous declaration in the drawing room, he'd fainted dead way, and only Humphrey's quick reflexes had prevented the earl from splitting his head on the cracked tile hearth. He and Leventhorpe—who'd stumbled in half-crazed with worry upon awaking and finding Ravensdale missing—carried Ravensdale upstairs, where he still remained.

Humphrey made his escape shortly thereafter, promising to extend another invitation to tea when things returned to normal at Esherton.

That would be never.

He breathed not a word about Lord Ravensdale's ludicrous declaration, but his gaze, hurt and betrayed, accused her just the same. Had there been a glimmer, an iota of a chance for reconciliation between her and Humphrey, the earl had successfully snuffed that light out and thrust her into bleak darkness once more.

Heaven help her if Humphrey believed the preposterous lie, bandied the falsehood about, told his parents and sister...

He would. Without a doubt.

Social status meant everything to the Benbridges. They'd want no further association with her. Any hope of help or advice from them had gone up in tiny cinders when she burned the unopened tea invitation.

No, when his lordship let loose the colossal lie.

Brooke shuddered and tugged the shawl tighter.

She cared not for her reputation—well, perhaps that wasn't entirely true, but naught could be done for that besmirched travesty at this point—but the quartet's characters could be tarnished by association with her. Rumors that she'd become a kept woman, factual or not, further damaged any hope of them making respectable matches.

Damn the earl. Damn him for winning Esherton and being so eager to sell the farm. Damn him for the wily game he played. And double damn the attraction she felt for him.

Had he given no consideration to the number of lives he ruined with his fabrication? Mistress indeed. As if she'd ever agree to such a sordid arrangement. What in blazes did he hope to gain by sullying her? She sighed and pursed her mouth. Perhaps her ruination had been his sole intent. A perfectly executed revenge for an offense he presumed her responsible for.

Furious beyond civility, she'd left his care to the others, refusing to see him, even when he requested her presence. Then demanded it.

She wasn't a servant he could order about at his whim. Yet, a part of her desperately longed to check on Ravensdale. To brush his hair from his forehead, touch his warm skin, make sure he fared well. Bah, she was hopeless.

When had her emotions become so fickle?

Since she paid his fee, the physician reported the earl's progress to her daily. Seemed his lordship possessed the constitution of a draft horse and the temperament of caged lion, and he'd be up and about—and hopefully, on his bloody way—in no time.

Leventhorpe had forcefully let it be known he had no intention of vacating the premises until his friend could travel. To his credit, the marquis had sent for food and clothing. Likely the sparse meal he dined on the first night, more watery stew, thinly-sliced bread, and a complete absence of spirits of any kind, had alerted him to the desperate condition of Esherton Green's barren larder.

Every able-bodied man had spent the next morning clearing the road to the house. By early afternoon, a path wide enough for a carriage to pass through had been opened and a wagon had arrived, stuffed with food and other supplies, accompanied by not one, but two coaches. A pair of haughty valets, three plump, giggling maids, a monstrous black groomsmen, two footmen—who appeared to be twins and set Blaike and Blaire atwitter—and a French chef, Leroux, had streamed from the conveyances.

For the first time in years, Esherton boasted a full staff and larder. Beside herself with glee, Mrs. Jennings hadn't stopped grinning, despite her missing front teeth.

At least everyone had plenty to fill their stomachs now, except that Brooke possessed no appetite. Worry tended to rob one of the desire to eat, even if the menu boasted the most elaborate meals the household had ever known.

The house overflowed with people, and no room had less than three occupants at any given time. Servants slept in the halls, for pity's sake, hence Brooke's sojourn to the stables for few a moments of much-needed solitude. She'd told no one of her destination, needing a place to grieve in peace.

Fragile as her tattered dignity, her facade of poise and self-control threatened to shatter with her next breath. She rested her head against the barn's splintery wood. In less than a week, her life had crumbled to dust. A fat tear crept down her cheek. Then another. And another.

They poured forth as wrenching sobs worked their way past her constricted throat. Awash in misery, Brooke pressed a length of the shawl to her mouth, shut her eyes, and tucked her chin to her chest, at last giving vent to her desolation.

"Here now, there's no cause for waterworks," Lord Ravensdale's baritone rasped as he enfolded her in his strong arms. He rested his chin upon her crown. "Hush, sweetheart. Things aren't entirely hopeless."

"Yes. They are. Completely and absolutely. You've ruined everything," she whispered against the wall of his chest. She should pull away. Curse him to Hades and hell. Plant him a facer or yank out his splendid hair by the roots.

Instead, she burrowed closer, wrapped her arms around his waist, and wept like an inconsolable infant. Strong and sensible had become wearisome, and she was exhausted from the burden she'd carried for years. So tired of worrying and scraping to make ends meet.

His scent wrapped around her senses, soothing and reassuring as he rubbed her spine and shoulders. Long moments passed, and calm enshrouded her at last. She released a shuddery sigh.

Lord Ravensdale placed a long finger beneath her chin and tilted her face upward. He kissed each tear-stained cheek then her nose, likely red as a pie cherry. Lowering his mouth until it hovered a mere inch above hers, he closed his eyes. He grazed her lips, his warm and firm, at first feather light then more insistent, demanding a response.

Her resistance fled. Moaning, she slanted her head and allowed him the entrance his probing tongue sought. Heaven surged through her, melting her bones, bathing her in a haze of sweet sensation. Humphrey's kisses hadn't been anything more than mildly pleasant, not this mind-wrenching, searing blast of desire.

A cow bawled, and Brooke tore her mouth from Heath's. Head lowered, she stepped from his embrace and dried her damp face on the wrap. She braved flashing him a glance.

Hatless, his black hair gleaming in the sunlight, he wore a sky blue jacket and white pantaloons. Brilliant colors to emphasize his olive skin. He lounged against the barn, ankles crossed and arms folded, looking the perfect picture of health. Perhaps a little wan about his wickedly dark eyes—definitely some foreign blood there somewhere—but otherwise, his handsome self. The scratch on his cheek had faded to a slender brownish ribbon. He observed her every move, those intense eyes of his missing nothing. Like his namesake, the raven.

Why must he be so blasted attractive?

Why did she react the way she did in his presence? To his kisses? She'd never dreamed a kiss could scatter her wits to the stars.

He gave a knowing smile, as if he'd read her thoughts. A man of his caliber and experience probably knew exactly what his kisses did to her.

Adjusting the shawl, Brooke swiveled to gaze at the calves again. Better than making a spectacle of herself. A few strands of hair had worked loose when she'd hugged his chest, and the breeze blew them into her face. She swept the tendrils behind her ear. She should say something, anything, to break the awkward, sensual silence between them.

"What are you doing out of bed? You're not supposed to be up for another three days."

She could have bitten her tongue in half for asking. It was nothing to her if he chose to ignore the physician's orders.

Liar.

"I couldn't stand one minute more confined to that room or Leventhorpe's incessant fussing. My God, who knew the man was such a nervous old biddy?" He chuckled, the low rumble sending delicious tingles along her flesh. "You'd think I'd nearly died."

She glanced over her shoulder then pushed the bothersome strands flitting across her face from her eyes. "You could have. Doctor Wilton said as much."

His lordship grinned, and her stomach lurched peculiarly. Ought to have broken her fast. Needed her wits to banter with the crafty likes of him. Why had he sought her here, anyway? To steal a kiss?

Theirs had been no stolen kiss but given freely.

He tapped his head as his long strides carried him to her side. "No, too stubborn and too hard-headed to cock up my toes. At least that's what my friends tell me."

"Hmph." She wasn't about to dispute his assertion. Add arrogant and indulged to the list too. Oh, and fabricator of enormous taradiddles designed to ruin innocent young women. She compressed her lips, her earlier feelings of magnanimity giving way to irritation.

"So, Brooke, what are we to do?"

"Pardon?" Holding her wayward hair in place, Brooke leveled him an inquisitive look.

Hands clasped behind him, he stared straight ahead. He could do whatever he pleased. She, on the other hand, had as many options as a condemned woman standing on the gallows with a noose tightened round her neck.

He levered away from the barn.

"I'm aware how dire your circumstances are." He flicked her an unreadable expression before boldly tucking a tress behind her ear.

Sensation spiraled outward at his soft touch.

He cupped her head, gently caressing the sensitive area below her ear.

She clenched her jaw against the sigh, or rather the purr, which had the impudence to try to leave her mouth.

He is your foe, Brooke.

She peered at him. "And...?"

"I have a suggestion, a proposition to make that would—"

She released such a loud, unladylike snort, two calves venturing near the fence scampered to their mothers. "Hmph, that mistress nonsense? You don't seriously think I'd consider becoming a kept woman? Especially of a man I met just days ago."

She tilted her head to look directly into his eyes. Damn his beautiful, thick-lashed eyes. They turned her knees to porridge and caused peculiar flickers elsewhere too.

Come now, Brooke. You're made of sterner stuff. Where's your backbone?

"Why would *you* want that, my lord? It makes no sense at all. Is this revenge for what Duffen did to you?" She narrowed her eyes and gestured between them. "Your way of punishing me? I told you, I had nothing to do with his idiotic decision to smack you on your hard head."

Lord Ravensdale bent nearer and trailed his fingers along her jaw. "No, I took a fancy to you immediately."

She gasped. Her legs nearly gave way, and her already frayed nerves burst with longing.

His pupils dilated, nearly covering the iris.

With desire? Had hers done the same? Just in case, she averted her gaze. He already held too much power over her. Had the nature of their acquaintance been different, she might have dared pursue the attraction between them. He stirred her like no other. But the lots had been cast and providence hadn't favored her.

"Immediately?" She rearranged her shawl. "Are you always so impetuous?"

"No, but I made the decision to offer you my protection while sitting in the study the day we met. I decided it was the least I could do to rescue you from your circumstances."

Her attention snapped to him. *He's serious.* Did he think she'd thank him for his chivalry?

"I'm quite fond of you already, though I'm sure you'll find that difficult to believe." He smiled tenderly and brushed his thumb across her lower lip. "You'd be well-cared for, and I'd treat you kindly. I would also provide for your family."

Brooke gawked at him, her befuddlement swiftly turning to blistering outrage.

I'll bet you would, you cawker.

"Just like that?" She snapped her fingers in his face.

Startled, he blinked. Did he think she'd leap at his offer? Throw herself at him and cover his face with grateful kisses? Toss up her skirts and let him have his way with her behind the stables?

"I've taken a fancy to her, so I'll make her my fancy piece?" she mocked in imitation of his deep voice. "How magnanimous of you."

He had the audacity to grin, one hand resting on her shoulder.

Blast his handsomeness.

Ooh, if only she were a man... She'd wipe that smug look off his face.

"Of all the brazen, buffleheaded, conceited things I've ever heard, that tips the scales as the most contemptible. Pray tell me what about me makes you think I'm a loose-moraled strumpet?" Tears stung behind her eyelids. Why did he alone make her cry?

"Quite the opposite, Brooke." His focus sank to her mouth. "It's your innocence and purity I find irresistible."

"If that's meant to be a compliment, I assure you, it fell far short of its mark, my lord." She whirled away from him. Her thoughts rattled around in her head like pebbles in a tin when he touched her. Of all the outlandish—

Her innocence and purity? Not after he finished with her.

What an infuriating, insulting man!

She'd wager he hadn't considered her desires...er, mayhap not her desires, but her wants. Drat, not wants either, her needs. Bother and blast, why did everything she think regarding him sound provocative and lust-filled?

Arms crossed, she spun to face him. She had a proposition for him too. Let's see how willing he was to gamble for what he wanted. She had nothing to lose at this juncture.

She'd risk it all, everything she owned.

Lord Ravensdale regarded her calmly. He possessed the upper hand, and the cur knew it.

She clenched her hands, itching to box his ears. "You won the lands in a wager, so you're obviously a gaming man, my lord. Give me the opportunity to win them back. We have nowhere else to go. This is our home, though I'm sure to you it's rather a hovel. But my sister and cousins, we have each other, and we're content with the little we've been granted."

Not precisely true. The girls wanted more, deserved more, as did the servants, but they'd done the best they were able with the pathetic lot God or providence had handed them. Grumbling and complaining only served to ferment bitterness. Mama had always preached thankfulness and contentment. Easier said than done, however.

"And what do you have to wager?" He arched a dubious brow. "I mean no disrespect, but the house and grounds are bereft of anything valuable."

"I have the Culpepper grand parure set. It's worth a sizable sum." Brooke savored the dash of victory his astounded look provided.

His intense gaze chafed her. "And you would wager the jewels, the only thing you have left?"

"I'd hoped to sell them to provide Brette and our cousins with small marriage settlements, but keeping our home is more important." She notched her chin higher. "Besides, I haven't anything else of worth to wager."

"I disagree."

Brooke frowned. "What? Look around you. You can see we've only cast-offs, worn-out and broken furnishings. I don't know if the cattle are mine to sell, and I own no other jewelry. Trust me when I tell you there are no stores of silver or fine art hidden in the attic."

He slowly swept his heated gaze over her then bent his lips into a lazy smile.

"You mean me?" She released a caustic laugh. "You want me to wager my virtue?"

Beware: wagers are war in the guise of sport,
and there can only be one winner.
~Wisdom and Advice—The Genteel Lady's Guide to Practical Living

14

That's precisely what Heath meant.

Granted, that made him a cur, a blackguard, and a rake of the worst sort. He hadn't come to Esherton Green intending to despoil an innocent, but once the idea formed, he'd pursued it. He'd been an unmitigated ass announcing Brooke was his mistress in front of Benbridge. Jealousy must have loosened his tongue and warped his common sense. He regretted the outburst, even if he couldn't remember a word of it.

He didn't even recall making his way below stairs or anything beyond Brooke leaving the chamber to speak to her former love. Nothing for the next twelve hours either. Leventhorpe took it upon himself to apprise Heath of the sordid details once he'd regained his senses.

Heath would rather have remained oblivious to his stupidity.

It didn't make a whit of sense, his fear of losing her. Still, he offered Brooke the one thing, short of marriage, he had available. From what he'd observed, mistresses generally fared better than wives, anyway. Besides, didn't she realize that tongues already flapped? He and Leventhorpe had been sleeping in her house for days, for God's sake.

Servants talked. Benbridge *had* talked. Tattle had already circulated back by way of Leventhorpe's staff.

Now Heath must see the act done.

Her position was worse than when he'd arrived, and most of the blame lay on his shoulders. If he gave her the money to restore the place, not only was it a horrid business move, people would still assume she'd traded her favors for the funds. The consequences would be the same; she and the girls would be shunned. He'd learned that, if nothing else, in his lifetime. People assumed the worst, almost as if they relished another's misfortune.

Yes, he was selfish. His conscience could raise a breeze and rail at him all it wanted, but he couldn't get Brooke out of his mind, and he intended to have her. And deserting her and her family, leaving them as paupers, her reputation in tatters with no recourse was not an option.

If she wanted a wager, fine by him. Let her believe she held a degree of power. It cost him little enough, and if it helped her salvage a remnant of pride, well, he'd make the concession. He owed her that and much more.

Taking a broken woman to his bed didn't appeal, but introducing this seething temptress to the pleasures of the flesh...that would be worth suffering a scratch or two. Her resourcefulness, her feistiness, even her mutinous violet eyes spewing darts at him this moment fascinated him. He'd enjoy teaching her to channel her spiritedness in the bedchamber. Oh, the wild romps they'd have. His groin contracted in a rush of pleasure.

She'd captured his admiration and his lust.

He had more than enough blunt to set up a house for her and another for her family. He'd allow her servants to tag along if they wanted. However, he had no intention of that brood being underfoot when he introduced Brooke to passion. Therefore, he would mandate separate residences.

Her eyes flashing ire, she pursed her prim little mouth, in all likelihood to keep from telling him to go bugger himself, something he had seriously considered, truth to tell.

Even with his head thrumming severely enough to turn his hair white and grind his teeth to powder, he'd battled arousal for four days straight. She'd consumed his thoughts and dreams. Hour upon hour of lying on the lumpy mattress, constantly thinking of her, imaging all the erotic things he'd like to do to and with her, had him marble hard. If he hadn't shared the chamber with Leventhorpe, Heath would've been tempted to relieve his randy state himself. A perpetual erection ached like the devil.

Why she consumed him, he hadn't the foggiest notion. He'd bedded beautiful women before, many exceedingly intelligent and witty too. But Brooke...something about her, something he couldn't quite name, mesmerized him, bewitched him until he'd become consumed with her.

Her sultry eyes and subtle shudders proved she wasn't immune to him. She'd kissed him freely and, given her heated responses, desire consumed her too. However, she didn't recognize her need for untapped passion, which hinted all the more of her innocence. He'd be glad to teach her to recognize what she felt, and more. Much more.

Warm heaviness weighted his loins. Too bad they didn't have a signed agreement already. Taking her against the barn or over the fence held a provincial sort of appeal. Well, perhaps not with chocolate-eyed calves looking on. He twisted his lip into a droll smile.

Hell, who did he think he fooled? He would take her anywhere, anytime, as many times as he wanted once she'd become his.

Her concern for her reputation was only natural. Women of her character and integrity didn't barter their bodies in exchange for protection on a regular basis. Nevertheless, he recalled a handful who'd been content as pampered Persians with their decision to accept a gentleman's protection.

Besides, Brooke had several people to think of other than herself. Had it been only her welfare at risk, the war Heath intended to wage to win her would've been much more difficult and complex. But instinct told him she'd accept the stakes he demanded for their wager to ensure the others' wellbeing if convinced she would be the victor.

She worried her lower lip and fingered the god-awful cover, which had slipped to her lower spine. Her work-worn hands revealed how hard she'd labored. Never again would she have to do so. He'd see to her comfort for the rest of her days.

He eyed her shabby clothes, the toes of her half-boots worn almost through. First order of business as her protector: hie her to a London modiste and order an entire wardrobe, right down to her unmentionables. Naturally, he'd be present for the fittings.

She heaved a gusty sigh, her full bosom straining against her gown's fabric.

Well, perhaps not the very first order of business. Slaking his desire topped the list.

"Let's be totally candid regarding the stakes, shall we?" She scooted her gaze around the area. Only docile cattle chewing cud peered at her.

Did she worry someone might overhear?

He sent a casual glance to the meadows and the curving path to the house. Alone. No one eavesdropped on their conversation, though a small rotund ball of fur scuttled their way. The corgi had escaped.

"I'll wager my—

Heath raised his hand. "I have one, rather personal question I require an answer to before we proceed."

A confused expression whisked across her face. "And that is...?"

Deucedly awkward this.

He cleared his throat. He had to know if she'd been intimate with Benbridge, damn his jealousy. "I am most selective in the women I take to my bed."

Her fair brows dove together, and a strangled sound, not quite a gasp, escaped her. A rosy glow tinted her cheeks. "I really don't care to hear about the women you've bedded, my lord, since I have no intention of *ever* becoming one of them."

"You've asked for a chance to win your farm. Do you want to hear my terms or not?" Irritation liberally dosed with pain raised its gnarly head. A punishing cadence had begun in one temple a few minutes ago, stealing his patience. Heath rubbed the side of his head in small, circular motions with two fingers.

Brooke glared at him then waved her hand in an arc. "By all means, my lord. Shout it from the rooftops for all I care."

"Are you a virgin?"

The air left her in a long hiss, and her eyes fairly spat indignation. "You mean to tell me you only take innocents as your mistresses? What kind of despot are you?"

"No, if you are, you'll be the first." He nonchalantly straightened a cuff. Damn, but the notion she hadn't slept with Benbridge exhilarated him. Silence reigned, and he lifted his gaze.

Emotions flitted across her features so quickly, he was hard-pressed to identify all of them. Her chest rose as she inhaled a large expanse of air, scorn sparking in her eyes.

"That's it, you cocksure toff. Take your confounded wager and...and stuff it up your stiff arse! I'll find another way to save my home." Brooke hoisted her skirts and spun on her heel toward the house. "Asking about my virginity. My God, who does that?"

She caught site of Freddy scampering their way and frowned.

"I'll take that as a yes." It pleased Heath beyond ridiculous. He would be her first. *And only.*

She whipped around. "You insufferable blackguard. Why, if I were a man—"

"I'm heartily grateful you're not." He winked and gave her an unabashedly wicked grin. "Calm down. I only meant to spare you a degree of embarrassment. I usually have my physician examine my mistresses for disease prior to signing our agreement and regularly thereafter."

She fisted her small hands, an expression of such incredulity on her face, he fought not to laugh aloud. His humor would rile her all the more.

"Please tell me you're not serious? Do you have any idea how utterly degrading and offensive that is?" She patted her thigh, silently calling the wheezing dog to her side.

Heath shrugged. "Nevertheless, I require it, but for you, given your innocence, I'll make an exception."

She rolled her eyes heavenward as she shook her head. "How benevolent of you. What if I'm not? Is our deal off?"

A flicker of jealousy stabbed Heath. Perhaps his earlier joy had been premature.

Freddy plopped to the ground beside her, tongue hanging out and panting as if he'd just competed in the English Triple Crown. How old was the pudgy beast, anyway?

"No, you'll endure an examination before a contract is signed." He didn't doubt she wished him to the devil at the moment. "So, I'll ask you again. Are you a virgin?"

She responded with a terse nod, and another shock of color flooded her cheeks.

He bit the inside of his mouth to keep from smiling.

Brooke folded her arms and cocked her head to the side. "What else?"

"I'll have my solicitor draw up a document which will include provision for you, your family, and the terms of our separation when the time comes. You will relocate to London, and I will sell the lands I won in the wager from your cousin."

Her eyes narrowed to slits, and she pressed her lips together but remained silent. Outrage and frustration oozed from her.

"Our initial contract will be for a year." He'd never kept a mistress longer. Brooke might be the first. "I'll provide a cancellation clause if we don't suit."

"I don't care about your contract poppycock. My word is my oath. But know this, I will not agree to the sale of Esherton Green. Forfeiture of my body and virtue are worth more than the lands."

She had him there.

Brooke planted her hands on her hips, and Freddy licked his chops and wagged his tail.

"Here are my terms, my lord, and they are not negotiable." She shut her eyes for a second before snapping them open. She launched her battle plan. "Should I lose, I will accompany you to London as your mistress, but you will allow everyone else to remain here, including the servants. You will bestow generous marriage settlements on the four girls, and arrange for sponsors for their come outs. You will also permit Esherton to retain the proceeds from the dairy and farm."

Heath folded his arms. Came up with that too damn quickly for his liking. "Is that all?"

"No." She scowled and pushed her wayward hair behind her ear again. "Mabry will carry on as overseer, and you will permit me to hire a respectable woman of quality to act as a companion to my sister and cousins, both here and when they are in London. An annual allowance to further the estate's recovery wouldn't be amiss either."

She paused, appearing deep in thought, her brows drawn together. "Oh, and I shall be permitted at least two extended visits to Esherton Green annually."

Heath should've suspected Brooke wouldn't acquiesce without a skirmish. He didn't half mind her terms, except the stipulation for keeping the blasted farm. But if he didn't have to manage the place, he would concede the point.

"And if you win?" He braced himself for her demands.

My ballocks fried to a crisp.

"If I win the wager, you sign over to me, free and clear, the lands you won from Sheridan."

That's all she wanted? No bulging purse, new wardrobe, household furnishings...or the hundred other things she and the others lacked?

She extended her hand. "Agreed?"

Heath clasped her roughened palm. It fit neatly within his grasp, as if it had been molded to nestle there. "Yes, the instant you win."

She wouldn't be allowed the victory. They had yet to decide on what game to play, but it mattered not. He might not be able to read worth a damn, but he remembered every playing card dealt and didn't lose at the tables.

Across the expanse of deep green, three figures separated from the house and moved toward the barns. Leventhorpe and two of the other Culpepper misses. At this distance, which two Heath couldn't discern. "What's your pleasure?"

"Excuse me?" Her back to the house, Brooke squinted up at him from where she squatted beside the dog, now lying with his feet in the air, eyes closed, enjoying a tummy rub.

"*My pleasure*?" She almost choked on the words. "Awfully confident you'll be the vanquisher, aren't you? Pride goeth before a fall, my lord."

He chuckled. Never short on pithy remarks, was she? "What game of cards do you prefer?"

Her chagrin transformed to cunningness. A shrewd smile bent her mouth. "I never agreed to a card game."

Alarm dug its sharp little talons on his already pulsing scalp. "Not cards?"

Devil it, what had he agreed to?

A horserace? Did she ride? He examined the barn. Did she own a horse? Surely not a drinking game. Visions of Brooke guzzling brandy or whiskey like a saloon tart churned his stomach. Blister it. What did women wager on besides cards? The color of silk best suited for an embroidered flower?

Men gambled on any number of outlandish things. White's betting book overflowed with one ludicrous wager after another, from what soup might be served at Lady Jersey's to how many pups a hound would birth and everything conceivable in between. Once there'd been a stake on the number of gentlemen a certain courtesan could service in one night.

Heath never participated in that sort of rubbish. Irresponsible and a waste of good coinage, especially when London's streets teemed with orphans and beggars. Even a small portion of money gambled away daily would improve the lives of the less fortunate.

He silently saluted Brooke for outwitting him this round. He ought to have realized she wouldn't choose the obvious. Hadn't he learned anything about her? Predictable she was not.

"Very well, what sort of challenge did you have in mind?" Good God, what if she chose a stitching or baking contest or some other such womanly nonsense? "It must be a competition we're equally capable of."

"Sounds as if you're worried, my lord." Her smile widened, and still crouched beside Freddy, she twisted to look at the milling cattle in the paddock.

Mabry exited the barn and made for the far side of the enclosure where a gate hung. The nervous cattle shifted away from him. Freddy wriggled to his feet then ran to the fence. He trotted up and down, snuffling and whining.

"Hold there, Mr. Mabry." Brooke straightened and waved at the servant.

He pivoted toward them and doffed his hat. "Miss Brooke, your lordship, I didn't know ye were out here."

Was that a Scottish brogue? Heath hadn't noticed it before. But then, he'd barely been able to stand.

"We've only been here a few minutes. I wanted to see the calves." She approached the fence. "They are healthy, it appears."

Heath trailed her, his uneasiness increasing. What was she plotting?

"Hearty lot, these calves be." Mabry gestured in the cattle's direction. "Each one sturdy and healthy. Even the twins there."

He pointed to a pair of spotted calves suckling, while their poor mother straddled them.

Freddy yipped, repeatedly looking at Brooke then the cattle, and then placed his front paws on the lowest fence rail. Mabry bent and scratched behind the dog's ears.

Heath winced as the servant stepped in a pile of warm cow dung.

Unperturbed, Mabry scuffed his boot in the dirt several times and laughed. "He wants to herd the beasties. In his blood, it be."

"And so he shall." Brooke turned triumphant eyes to Heath, her exquisite features alight with joy. "I wager Freddy can separate the calves from their mothers and herd them into the barn in under five minutes. Mabry will stand at the door to prevent the calves from reentering the paddock. You may keep the time." Her gaze slid to his torso, and his muscles bunched as if she'd touched him. "You do have a watch, don't you?"

Heath removed the silver time piece and flicked it open.

"Wager?" Mabry scratched his chest and glanced between them, leeriness scrunching his weathered face. "What sort of wager?"

Brooke inclined her fair head at the dog, caressing him with a doting glance. "Freddy is going to save Esherton for us. His lordship and I have agreed on the stakes. If I win, the lands his lordship won from Sheridan belong to us."

"And if you lose, Miss Brooke?" Mabry's penetrating gaze probed Heath's and disapproval laced his voice. Did he suspect the nature of the rest of their bet?

"Not to worry, Mr. Mabry." She smiled and hugged her wrap tighter.

The loose hairs framing her face fluttered in the light breeze. She gave a small shudder. From cold or excitement? “Trust me. I’d never place a bet I wasn’t confident I would win. I’m not a fool.”

The overseer firmed his mouth and gave a sharp nod. “I do trust ye, lass.” His expression sour, he shifted his focus to Heath, “You, sir, I do not.”

Brooke laughed and the sound pelted Heath with another round of...what? What did she make him feel? He’d never experienced the taxing sensation before.

Panting, his fluffy tail wagging furiously, the squat corgi pranced before her, all but begging to take after the cattle.

Heath eyed the old dog then counted the calves. Fourteen. Almost three calves a minute, and Freddy had gasped as if dying from his jaunt from the house. Not bloody likely he could get the calves inside in five minutes.

“Are you sure he’s up to it? He’s not a young pup.” Brooke would never forgive him if the dog dropped dead from exertion.

“I’m sure. And he is too.” Her eyes sparkling with mirth, she broke into an excited grin before stooping again. She gathered the dog into her arms. “So, my friend, are you ready to have some fun, just like you used to?”

Freddy squirmed and licked her face.

Heath had never seen Brooke this happy, and unbidden warmth washed over him at her delight. If only he were the source of her joy, rather than her consternation.

Yes, women coerced into becoming mistresses are generally elated at the prospect and with the men who compel them, idiot. A wife on the other hand...

No. Wife.

She seemed most confident she’d win. What then? He didn’t give a fig if she won the lands. He did care that she might escape his bed, and, even after their short acquaintance, the knowledge that he’d not see her again left him more disquieted than he would have believed possible.

Marry her.

Holy hell, why did the bothersome thought keep bludgeoning him? Marriage didn’t loom on his horizon for many years yet to come. And it wasn’t as if she’d have him now, in any event.

“You’ll not win, your lordship.” She smiled, a sad little twist of her plump lips. “You see, I have too much to lose, while you have nothing.”

Heath rubbed his chin, and ignored the stab of guilt her words caused. "We shall see."

Brooke handed Freddy to Mabry. The little dog, a quivering bundle of concentration, kept his black-eyed gaze riveted on the uneasy bovines.

Freddy in his arms, Mabry moved to the barn's entrance. His stiff-legged gait and cinched mouth revealed he disliked Brooke's decision, but he respected her enough to allow her to carry on.

The cattle shifted and the cows sidled the humans nervous sideways glances. The calves sensed something afoot and huddled near their mothers. Easier or harder for the dog to work them? Heath knew damn little—all right, nothing—about the four-legged pooping machines except how a thick steak covered in onions and mushrooms tasted on his tongue.

Brooke stood on her toes, arms resting on the top rail. Yes, her shoe had a hole in the bottom. She slid Heath a glance then dropped her attention to his pocket watch. "Are you ready?"

Confidence oozed from her. Rather adorable. He, on the other hand, experienced unfamiliar apprehension. Most troubling.

"Once I say start, the clock doesn't stop for any reason. Agreed? There will be no multiple trials." Freddy didn't have more than one go round in his roly-poly little body in any event.

"Of course." She wrinkled her nose and swatted at a fly buzzing about her head. Hundreds of the pesky insects hovered near the animals and manure littered ground. "Why would we need to stop?"

"Just so, but I won't have you crying foul and demanding another go."

Do you hear yourself? You've already cornered her. Show a modicum of empathy, for God's sake.

Brooke's mouth formed a thin-lipped smile, though her gaze rebelled. "I would have the same assurance from you then, my lord."

"You have it."

"Are ye ready?" Mabry called.

She crooked a winged brow at Heath, and he gave a curt nod, his watch at the ready.

"Yes, Mr. Mabry. You may proceed." She scooted closer to the fence, tension radiating from her.

Mabry placed Freddy on the ground by his feet then dropped to one knee beside the trembling animal. Speaking softly, he stroked Freddy, and the dog lay down, his beady gaze fixed on the cows. The next instant, the overseer gave two shrill whistles.

Chunky body scraping the ground, Freddy tore to the cattle, scattering them every which way. With unbelievable finesse, the small dog worked the livestock, separating a calf from the rest. One, two, three—he swiftly isolated the calves and drove the bawling trio to the barn. Whipping about, the corgi headed into the fray of milling hooves once more.

He showed no signs of fatigue, devil a bit.

Sweat beaded Heath's brow.

Brooke chewed her lower lip, her hands clenched atop the rail.

He glanced at his watch when Freddy maneuvered four more calves through the open doors. Heath had assumed the dog would work the animals one at a time. Ignorance on his part. Brooke might very well have him on the gibbet, a rope about his neck.

Then what? He wouldn't let her go.

You'll have to marry her, old chap.

"Will you shut the bloody hell up?" he muttered beneath his breath. Damnable shrew, his conscience.

Brooke gave him a hurried, quizzical look. The clouds overhead reflected in her clear eyes. "I beg your pardon? Did you say something to me?"

"No, just having a bit of difficulty with the sun glaring on my watch."

She fidgeted with the travesty of a shawl across her bosom, her worry evident. "Did you start timing when Mabry whistled?"

Did she fret Heath would cheat? Well, he hadn't shown himself to be an honorable chap, to this point, now had he?

"Not to worry. I started at the whistle."

"What goes on here?" Waving his arm toward the paddock, Leventhorpe planted a booted foot on the bottom rail. The weathered wood shuddered and groaned.

At Leventhorpe's appearance, Brooke's eyes rounded, the irises shrinking to a miniscule ebony dots. She stiffened before her lips split into a welcoming smile for her sister and cousin.

God above, Heath adored her expressive eyes and ready smile.

Facing the now-dusty enclosure, the Misses Brette and Blythe sandwiched Brooke and spoke in quiet tones. Each sent him a glower of such blue-eyed antagonism, he'd no doubt Brooke had shared the terms of their wager. Thank God they weren't men, or he'd be called out at once. Deserved to be run through by all of them.

Heat slithered from his neck to his face.

Accustomed to women's admiration, he'd never experienced such feminine enmity and found the hostility most disturbing. However, he acknowledged he'd brought their censure upon himself. The oddest urge to check his head for horns and his bum for a twitching, pointed tail gripped him.

Contrition lanced sharp and burrowed deep, where, every now and again, it gave him a vicious jab, reminding him what a cur he'd become. He'd proved no better than the men who'd held his title before him. Self-seeking, arrogant bastards, the entire lot.

The stink from a fish lingered long, especially rotten ones. He, too, bore the familial stench prevalent in his lineage. He'd prided himself on being superior to his forefathers, yet today proved he'd become the worst sod of the bunch. Though his ethics, conscience, integrity—whatever the blasted thing was that kept hounding him to do right by Brooke—nagged worse than a fishwife, he couldn't let her go.

"What's the little terror doing to the cattle?" Leventhorpe peered at Heath before scanning the chaos on the other side of the fence.

Heath cleared his throat. "If Freddy manages to get the rest of the calves—" *Damn, only five left.* "—into the barn in the next," he checked his watch, "three minutes, Miss Culpepper takes ownership of the Esherton's lands I won in the wager."

Leventhorpe chuckled and slapped Heath on the shoulder. "You're letting that fat, ancient dog decide something of such importance?"

"So it seems." Heath kept his attention glued to the puffball darting about the pen, yipping and snapping at the bovines' feet.

Leaning over the top rail, Leventhorpe studied the dog's progress. He canted his head toward Freddy. "And if he doesn't get them all inside, what then?"

Heath angled his back to Brooke and murmured, "She becomes my mistress."

Leventhorpe's jaw slackened for an instant. He jerked upright, condemnation blistering in his gaze. "You are an absolute, reprehensible arse, Raven."

"I'm aware."

"I do believe I'm ashamed to call you friend. I should call you out." Shaking his head, Leventhorpe directed his attention to the paddock. "Ho, there, Freddy. Good boy."

Freddy almost had another pair of calves to the barn.

Leventhorpe hollered and clapped his hands. "There's a smart chap."

Scooting around a stubborn cow bent on protecting her calf, the dog stiffened. He skidded to a halt, his nose in the air then spun and faced the fence. One glimpse of Leventhorpe, and Freddy tucked his tail between his legs and bolted for the barn.

A sensible woman realizes that to achieve the greatest advantage in gambling, one doesn't wager at all.
~Wisdom and Advice—The Genteel Lady's Guide to Practical Living

15

"Freddy, no." Brooke's distressed cry was echoed by her sister and cousin.

His craggy face mirroring the devastation that must surely ravage hers, Mabry trotted into the barn after the dog.

I lost. Oh my God, no. I lost.

Pressing close to her sides, Brette and Blythe each wrapped an arm about her shoulders and glared murderously at both men. Brooke was half convinced that, had her sister and cousin possessed a blade, they would have run the lords through. She might very well have cheered them on and helped dig the graves afterward.

Ruined.

Her head swam with dread and disappointment so pungent, she could taste it, bitter and metallic on her tongue.

"Brooke, your lip is bleeding." Brette plucked a handkerchief from her bodice.

Brooke hadn't noticed she'd bitten her lip. She dabbed at the cut as wave upon wave of panic surged ever higher, rising from her stomach, to her chest, and thrumming against her throat.

His mistress. I am...will be...a fallen woman.

She clutched her shawl and swung to glare at Lord Leventhorpe. "You did that on purpose."

His eyes darkened to cobalt. "Miss Culpepper, I had no notion of what went on here when I asked these ladies to point me in the direction my senseless friend had wandered."

The calves Freddy had directed to the barn trotted out and, amid much mooing and lowing, found their anxious mamas. Several set to nursing at once.

"You didn't have to call out to Freddy." Tears clogged her throat, but she refused to cry in front of these scapegraces or her family. "You know he's terrified of you."

"I but encouraged the dog. I assure you, there was no deliberate intent or subterfuge to cause you to lose."

"He did so do it deliberately." Blythe's voice dripped venom. "He and Ravensdale whispered back and forth when we arrived."

The marquis shook his burnished head. "Such a suspicious mind, Miss Blythe. Does it ever become wearisome?"

"Not where you're concerned." Blythe planted her free hand on her hip. "What did you say to him then?"

"I told him he was an absolute a—" Lord Leventhorpe cupped his nape. "Um, that is, a disreputable fellow, and promptly fell to cheering the dog along."

"Hmph. I'll just bet you did." Brette didn't believe his excuses either.

It didn't matter. What was done was done.

Brooke had given her word, and integrity compelled her to keep it. Ironic that. She would lose her virtue because of her honor. The devil must be dancing a jig in hell at her quandary. Had the situation been reversed, and she'd won by means less than laudable, would she have given the earl another chance to best her?

No. Too much depended on winning.

Lord Leventhorpe crossed his arms and addressed Lord Ravensdale. "You should be in bed instead of making silly wagers to ruin young innocents."

Blythe and Brette inhaled sharply.

Did the man have no filter on his mouth? Did every thought gush forth like a muddy river breeching its banks during a flood? However did these two featherheads manage in London amongst the *haut ton*?

Leventhorpe frowned, his keen gaze vacillating between Ravensdale and Brooke. "I, for one, cannot condone this ill-conceived wager."

"Leave off, Trist." Lord Ravensdale raised a hesitant gaze to Brooke. Instead of triumph and gloating, his eyes teemed with compassion and an unfamiliar glint. He snapped the watch closed then returned it to his waistcoat pocket.

Leventhorpe sent a vexed glance skyward. "Why the confounded theatrics? It's a simple enough fix. I'll leave and you can retrieve the mongrel—

“Freddy is not a mongrel, you red-headed baboon,” Blythe snapped.

Blythe acted a constant shrew with Lord Leventhorpe. Why? Dear God, surely not for the same reason Lord Ravensdale flustered Brooke out of her polite decorum.

Brette jutted her chin upward a notch and nodded her head. “To us, he’s family.”

Leventhorpe sighed, a put upon expression on his face. Did he understand what had just transpired? Had Ravensdale explained the whole of it?

“You can start the affair again, and I give my word, I shall stay in the house, out of sight the entire time.” Leventhorpe jerked his thumb in the manor’s direction.

Brooke shook her head as she stepped away from her sister and cousin’s protective embraces. “No, your lordship, we cannot start over. Lord Ravensdale and I agreed to a single challenge, one time only. That, too, was part of our bargain.”

Mabry exited the barn, Freddy in his arms. He approached the fence, his gaze seething. “Cheap shot, that was. I’ve a mind to call ye out, uppity lord or not.”

“You’ll do no such thing.” Brooke took Freddy from him. “I need you to carry on for me until this conundrum is fixed.”

How could she sound composed? Inside, she tilted on the precipice of histrionics. Quaking, Freddy buried his head in her shoulder. Why did Lord Leventhorpe frighten him so? Freddy would’ve won her the wager if Lord Leventhorpe hadn’t intruded. The knowledge she’d set this trap and snared herself...well, it grated her raw.

Ravensdale taking her to his bed didn’t scare her. Or repulse her. Quite the opposite, truthfully. He’d unearthed feelings in her she hadn’t realized existed. She would’ve been lying if she denied that his dark good looks and well-defined muscles enticed her.

Before his outlandish proposal, she’d given up on knowing a man intimately—although if mating proved anything like what she’d witnessed between Buford and the cows, the act seemed rather violent and favored the male of the species. The only benefit to the females, as near as she could discern, was the babes they’d soon bear.

Good God!

What if a child resulted from her union with his lordship? No, she’d insist measures be taken to prevent a pregnancy. Such things existed, didn’t they? She’d ask Doctor Wilton on his next visit and pray he didn’t expire from shock at such a scandalous question from an unmarried woman.

"Miss Culpepper, I would speak with you privately."

Brooke jerked her attention to Lord Ravensdale. Serious and somber, he gazed at her intently. Why the Friday face? He'd trounced her. Shouldn't he be grinning and celebrating? Instead, his eyes, the planes of his face, even his sculpted mouth suggested poignant reserve.

"We've serious matters to discuss." His expression grew grimmer.

Eager to get on with it, the boor. If he thought to bed her at Esherton, butterflies flitted about in his head. She wouldn't bring shame to the family home by lifting her skirts beneath Esherton's roof.

The morning breeze had ceased, and the chorus of innumerable flies within the paddock, in addition to the bees zipping from clover to flower in the fields, carried to her. The faint scent of sandalwood wafted by.

Which of the lords did it belong to?

Leventhorpe.

Raven's…Ravensdale's scent had been burned into her memory, and he didn't smell of sandalwood. Realization blindsided her. Freddie's first owner, the abusive charlatan, had reeked of the scent. No wonder the dog hied for the nearest hiding spot when he whiffed Lord Leventhorpe. If only she'd made the connection sooner. She nearly strangled, stifling her scream of frustration.

Odd that this perfect spring day should portend the onset of her tainted future. Yet, in the innermost recesses of her being, in a miniscule cleft she'd allow no one access to, a bud of relief formed. She'd secured the girls' futures, and the knowledge lifted a tremendous burden from her mind and heart.

A year wasn't so terribly long. And, in fact, she rather suspected she might enjoy her time as his lordship's kept woman. So be it. She'd make the best of this. Mama always said when the bread went stale, add some spices, egg, and cream, and make bread pudding.

"Please take him to the house and give him a treat, poor thing." Brooke passed Freddy to Blythe then kissed his snout. "You did your best, didn't you, my sweet boy?"

He thumped his tail once, his brown eyes apologetic.

Blythe hugged the quivering dog to her chest and murmured into his fur. He crawled up to snuggle against her neck.

Leventhorpe approached and, after a slight hesitation, scratched behind Freddy's ears.

Brooke held her breath as Freddy went rigid, his small eyes leery.

"No need to be afraid. I won't hurt you," his lordship said while petting the dog. At least Freddy hadn't bitten him.

A song thrush swooped to perch atop a post several lengths farther along the fence. The bird cocked its head before flitting to the ground and poking about for insects. Oh, to live the simple life of a bird.

"Brette, go with Blythe, please, and ask Cook to prepare two tea trays. Have one served in the parlor for Lord Leventhorpe and yourselves. Have the other delivered to the study." Brooke tucked her hand in the crook of Brette's elbow and guided her away from the paddock to where Blythe waited.

Brette patted Freddy when Lord Ravensdale moved aside. "Certainly. I believe we've fresh ginger biscuits, Shrewsbury cakes, and tarts baked just this morning."

How long it had been since they'd indulged in such lavishness? The quartet wouldn't go without again. The notion brought Brooke a measure of consolation.

Half-turned in Lord Ravensdale's direction, Brooke said, "I shall meet you in the study in twenty minutes, my lord. I must speak with my overseer. If you will excuse me, please?"

"Brooke. Blythe. Brette!"

Everyone turned to the frantic shouts coming from the house.

Blaire, skirts hoisted to her knees, hurtled through the grass, her white stockings flashing as she dashed to them. Her ragged sobs rent the air. "Duffen's gone. He's dead."

Esherton Green's Cemetery
Two Mornings Later

"Amen." Reverend Avery closed his Bible, the slight thump jarring Brooke to the disagreeable present.

Over already?

She'd been woolgathering, remembering happier times at Esherton with Duffen. Dry grittiness scraped her eyes when she blinked.

Hiring the reverend to preside over the funeral had consumed the last of her money. He'd been most reluctant to perform the ritual. Duffen had once called him an ignorant hypocrite more interested in lining his pockets than saving souls. Brooke rather agreed with Duffen's assessment, but as no other clerics resided within a day's ride, Reverend Avery it must be.

Would Duffen approve? Brooke didn't know, but she couldn't bury him without a ceremony, no matter how brief or coldly delivered by the officiator.

Shouldn't she be crying? Why couldn't she weep? Her heart ached, but no tears would come.

She scanned the huddled foursome's red-rimmed eyelids before shifting her attention to Mrs. Jennings and Flora, also sporting ruddy noses and cheeks. Not a one wore a coat, but instead had a blanket wrapped around their shoulders against the deceptively mild day's chilliness. Mabry's bloodshot gaze gave testament to his sorrow at the loss of his long-time comrade.

Was she alone incapable of grieving? No, she mourned Duffen's loss deeply, but she'd no more tears to shed, and she had the futures of many people to organize in a short amount of time. A niggling headache pinched behind her eyes from the constant strain. His lordship hadn't said when they would depart for London, but she doubted he'd twiddle his thumbs for a couple of weeks.

Perhaps later, when duty and responsibility didn't demand her attention, she could find a private spot to vent her heartache. At present, the manor overflowed with bodies. Why, just this morning, she'd made her way to the kitchen before first light, bent on a cup of the delicious new tea Leroux had brought. In the near dark, she'd stumbled upon a footman sprawled on a pallet and mashed his hand beneath her foot.

The starchy clergyman gestured to the rich mound of soil piled beside the yawning hole in the earth. Steam rose, a silvery-white mist, where the sun warmed the ground. "Miss Culpepper?"

Brooke drew in a fortifying breath. Since Duffen had no relatives, and as the senior woman of the house, the task of sprinkling Duffen's coffin with the same dirt he'd toiled in most of his life fell to her. She'd discarded protocol and allowed the girls to attend the graveside eulogy. Duffen deserved more than a pair of stable hands, Mabry, and herself to bid him farewell.

Lords Ravensdale and Leventhorpe—*would the man never leave*?—paid their respects as well. It rather astounded her and warmed her heart, despite her misgivings about the taciturn pair. Leventhorpe, however, repeatedly checked his watch and glanced to the drive, as if anxious to have the matter done with. Boorish of him, given he attended of his own volition.

Brooke loosened the glove from her hand, one finger at a time, reluctant to bring the simple service to an end and leave the dear little man who'd guarded her and the others fiercely for years. He'd been the grandfather they'd never had. A peculiar little bird of a grandfather, but loving all the same.

Lord Ravensdale waited a discreet distance away, determined to have their postponed conversation today. What did he seek anyway? She harbored no secrets. They had their agreement. Did he fear she'd renege on the bargain? Quite the couple they made, neither trusting the other, but they would share a bed and the most intimate of relationships. She firmed her lips against irony's cutting reproach.

The man had followed her about, much like a nervous puppy, the past pair of days. All solicitousness, almost as if he cared for her, he said little, but watched her every move with his unnerving gaze. His concern and attention warmed her, wooed her, further eroding the crumbling barrier she'd erected to keep him at bay.

Why of all men, flying in the face of everything logical and wise, had her disloyal heart picked him? A shuddery sigh escaped her. She couldn't deny the truth any longer; not even to herself.

She didn't like how vulnerable that made her.

"I'll take your glove, Brooke." Blaire held out her hand.

"Thank you."

Brooke passed the glove and unused handkerchief to her cousin. She crouched and stared at the humble casket. Sighing again, she scooped a handful of damp earth. A day past a week since Lord Ravensdale disrupted their lives.

And Sheridan, don't forget his dastardly part in this misfortune.

She swept the graveyard with her gaze, lingering a moment on the house and barns in the distance. The cattle, like giant dollops of cream, blotted the emerald meadows.

So much had changed in such a short amount of time.

"Kingdoms rise and kingdoms fall in a day," she whispered to herself.

"What was that, Miss Culpepper?" Reverend Avery peered down his nose at her.

"Nothing." After standing upright once more, she opened her fingers and allowed the dirt to drop. The clump hit the coffin, the sound harsh and final. Tears finally welled. Muffled weeping from the others filled the air as the small crowd turned and trekked down the lengthy, wending path to the house.

"Reverend, please join us for our midday meal." Lord Ravensdale extended the invitation. "I would beg a moment of your time afterward to discuss procuring a grave marker for Duffen."

"Yes, yes, of course. Shall I meet you at the house? I'm recovering from a bout of poor health and don't wish to linger outdoors any longer than I must." Prayer book tucked beneath his arm, the long-faced cleric eyed the house in the distance, a hungry glint in his eye. He swallowed, and his over-sized Adam's apple fought to escape the folds of turkey-like flesh drooping his collar.

"Certainly." Brooke brushed her hands together. "We'll be along in a moment or two, after I say my final farewells to Duffen. Have a drop of brandy in your tea. That should help stave off any ill effects of the out of doors."

She had forgotten the sumptuous spread Leroux had promised to have prepared for them after the funeral, at Leventhorpe's request. The marquis's attempts to get into the women's good graces were endearing, if somewhat audacious.

The same couldn't be said of Reverend Avery. She didn't want to suffer the stodgy cleric's depressing presence for a moment longer, but for Duffen, she would. She hadn't the funds for a headstone, and when pride attempted to rear its horned head and object to his lordship's generosity, she slapped the emotion aside like a fly atop a pastry. Duffen's loyalty warranted the honor. Besides, as her protector, Ravensdale was within his rights to make the decision and pay the fee.

Protector.

Despite her acceptance of her new station, and the startling realization she loved him, her stomach quavered. He'd made no demands on her, nor presented a contract either, as yet.

Brooke bent her forefinger and wiped beneath her lower eyelashes, touched by Heath's...Raven's—drat it all—Ravensdale's kindheartedness. How *did* mistresses address their protectors?

My lord? Master?

Not exactly something taught in the schoolroom.

"Here, allow me." His gaze tender, he patted the moisture from the edge of her lashes with the edge of his handkerchief. He did have the most mesmerizing eyes she'd ever seen in a man. After drying her face, he rubbed the dirt from her palm and then each finger in turn.

Such a simple act, but sensual too. Her irregular breathing and cavorting pulse gave testament to her awareness of him as a desirable man. She searched for similar discomfit in him but found unruffled composure.

"How am I to address you?" Heavens, she sounded wanton as a wagtail. Dry mouth, that was why. Brooke swallowed before running the tip of her tongue across her bottom lip. "Do you prefer Ravensdale, my lord... Raven... Heath?" *Good God, babies babble less.* "Please understand, I have no notion of how this mistress business works."

Except for the amorous congress part. One didn't breed cattle and not have a firm grasp of what coupling entailed. Rather undignified to be approached from behind, but under the cover of dark and with one's eyes—*and ears*—firmly squeezed shut, she ought to be able to manage well enough. She pursed her lips when he still didn't answer her.

"What *do* I call you?"

He kissed her forehead, his lips soft, yet firm, at the same time.

"How about husband?"

Understand this: once the die is cast, everything you've gained can be lost.
~Wisdom and Advice—The Genteel Lady's Guide to Practical Living

16

The quandary ricocheting in Heath's mind burst forth like a cannonball scuttling a ship, blasting his defenses wide open and setting him adrift. Yet subjecting Brooke to the degradation he'd proposed gnawed and chafed him until his conscience and soul lay raw and bloody. Seemed he wasn't cut from the same stuff as bounders and scapegraces after all.

He would marry her, though every fiber of his being cringed in trepidation. Cold, unfeeling, heartless—the negative traits of his sire, and the Earls of Ravensdale before his father, haunted Heath, reproachful and condemning. Could he summon the modicum of deep regard or warm sentiment that created satisfied wives and contented children?

Would he endure contention and strife the remainder of his wedded life as his parents had? Their battles had been legendary. Or, God forbid, do to his offspring what they'd done to him?

No, Brooke possessed a loving nature and generous spirit, unlike his mother. The knowledge was a balm to his wounded soul. A soul he'd not recognized needed healing until Brooke forced him to tear open the protective cover, rip off the scars and scabs, and see the festered wound deep within. She would help heal the putrid mess, restore wholeness to him.

Her character and birth alone made Brooke entitled to more than the degrading position he'd offered her. Brooke was nothing like the wife he'd determined would suit him. He feared one day Brooke would break his once impenetrable heart. Exposed and vulnerable, he possessed no protection from the winsome witch. She'd charmed and enchanted, bewitched and beguiled, cast her spell to where he no longer governed his thoughts.

But to lose her…let her go…

No, his noble intentions didn't extend that far. He would give her a choice. The parson's mousetrap, or revert to their original agreement. He must have her one way or another.

What woman wouldn't choose countess before courtesan?

He wouldn't let himself examine his fascination with Brooke past his physical fascination. Too dangerous... terrifying. What did *he* know of love? Nothing. No, better not to scrutinize his feelings too closely.

A week's acquaintance made a feeble foundation for marital bliss, but a few brilliant matches had started with less. Peculiar how seven days ago, marriage constituted nothing more than a business arrangement, a mutually beneficial union of convenience the earldom required of him. Today, he had selected Brooke, for no other reason than he couldn't bear to leave her or face another day without her.

His life prior to this was shrouded in an ash-gray cloud; seeing, hearing, tasting, living life in part, unaware of how much more vibrant and intense each sense—everything, for that matter—might be experienced. Brooke had awoken him to this new brilliance, and he'd lay odds, he'd only had a glimpse of what was possible.

Hell, she'd practically emasculated him. And worse? He didn't mind. Besotted by a violet-eyed, fair-haired Aphrodite with a heart bigger than England's tax coffers.

"What say you, Brooke?" Heath cupped her jaw, and rubbed his thumb across her soft cheek.

"Beg pardon?"

Her pale face, incredulous gaze, and mouth rounded into a perfect O of surprise, suggested she believed him insane, or perhaps he'd sprouted another nose or two upon his face.

Heath glanced around. Alone. The others had trekked halfway to the house already. Good. No one needed to witness Brooke's bafflement or his ineptitude at proposing. Should have done it properly, with flowers or a piece of jewelry. Perhaps a sonnet or a poem.

Women liked that sort of thing.

"Husband? You?" Her strangled squeak echoed with the same finality as the rat he'd seen seized in the jaws of a wharf cat one day at the docks.

"Yes." He grinned when her eyes widened further. "I thought you might prefer becoming my wife rather than my mistress."

High-minded of you, ruddy bounder.

Brooke shook her head. "Wife. Me?"

Had he so dazed her she couldn't string more than two words together? He'd shocked himself, so her stupefied expression didn't surprise him.

She spun away and stomped a few feet before halting to peek over her shoulder as she spoke to herself. "Why would he marry me? I'm a nobody, and he's an earl. We don't know each other, let alone like one another."

He flinched inwardly. Thorny prick, that. Couldn't fault her for her bluntness or the truth as she perceived it. She'd no reason to think he felt anything other than lust. Worse than a stag in the rut, he'd been.

Like, lust, love, luck...all different sides of the same die.

"Perhaps his head injury has addled him?" Hand on her chin, she squinted at Heath for an extended moment. "How does one know, I wonder? Surely there are other signs."

"Am I supposed to respond?"

Emotions vacillated upon her face. She stared, scrunched her eyebrows, and twisted her lips one way then the other. She rubbed the side of her face, blinking several times, and then pressed her mouth into a single, hard line.

He could almost hear the pinging of the thoughts careening about in her head. He cocked his. Not the reaction he'd expected, but Brooke had yet to do anything predictable. Heath strode to her. Best lay it out bare as a baby's arse. He gathered her into his arms, pressing a kiss into the soft hair atop her crown.

She didn't resist, although she trembled like a newborn kitten.

"These past days I've realized there's no woman more worthy of the title of countess than you, Brooke. You are more generous, noble, and self-sacrificing than any female of my acquaintance." He shrugged a shoulder and tweaked her pert nose. "I have to marry, in any event."

"How gallant of you." Mockery dripped thick enough to scoop with a shovel.

"Brooke, are you coming?" The Culpeppers hesitated at the bottom of the sloping hill. They exchanged wary glances before grasping their skirts and clomping up the rutted track. Four damsels to the rescue. A flock of yellowhammers pelted to the sky, yellow smudges against the blue, when the women tramped by.

Deep in conversation, Mabry and the man of God continued on their way. Mrs. Jennings and Flora had made the drive already, anxious to get inside and see to the rest of the meal preparation.

Leventhorpe faced them and planted his fists on his hips. He sent a peeved glance heavenward and lifted his hands. In supplication? Irritation?

Heath chuckled, enjoying his friend's aggravation. The Culpeppers had Leventhorpe at sixes and sevens, and a mouse in a maze fared better than the poor sot.

"I must be mad." Brooke twisted her glove in her hands and darted the oncoming quartet a guarded look. "They'll think me dicked in the nob—my head in the wool pile."

Heath's heart skidded sideways. Would Brooke say yes? He hadn't been altogether sure. Still wasn't.

She wobbled her glove at the others, who'd paused in ascending the hill. "Go on. I'll be inside shortly."

"Are you sure?" Brette's intelligent gaze flicked to Heath then to her sister. "We can stay. It's no bother."

Plucky for someone so tiny.

"Yes, I'm sure. His lordship and I have some, um, business details to discuss."

Business?

Is that how she saw his proposal? Well, why wouldn't she? There hadn't been a hint of anything remotely romantic in the way he asked her. He'd not wooed her, offered any trinkets, or pretty speeches.

Become my wife or mistress? Which will it be?

She presented her sister a tight-lipped smile and gestured at the house. "Go along, and check if everything is in order for our meal. And see that the reverend has a warm toddy."

They turned and obediently trundled in the direction they'd come. Several times one of the blondes either glanced over her shoulder or turned halfway round to observe Brooke. The scowls they hurled at Heath condemned him to a fiery afterlife and eternal damnation. No easy task winning their favor. Or Brooke's, though only her approval mattered.

The women met Leventhorpe on his way up the hill, and he circled one hand above his head. "Oh, for God's sake, are we performing some heathen burial ritual designed to ruin my boots?"

"Yes, your lordship." Her face serious as a parson's, Blythe pointed to the cemetery. "March around each headstone two times, skip through the center of the graveyard, perform a somersault while reciting The

Lord's Prayer, and kick your heels together before taking a hearty swig of pickle juice."

She winked. "That will assure Duffen turns over in his grave."

A chorus of giggles erupted, Blythe's the loudest.

Leventhorpe emitted a rude noise, somewhere between a snort and a growl.

Heath laughed outright.

Brooke couldn't prevent the smile twitching the corner of her mouth. "He's not been around women much, I'd guess. Has he sisters?"

"No, and his mother died when he was a toddler. The marchioness was a dotty dame. Ten years older than her husband, she didn't permit a single female house servant." Heath winked then waggled his brows. "The old marquis had a wandering eye and roving hands."

"Have *you* any sisters? If we marry, you're essentially inheriting four." She set her jaw, and a stubborn glint entered her eyes. "And the dairy farm too. I won't give it up."

Infernal farm and confounded cows. After the week he'd just spent, his favorite cheese could go to the devil with his blessings. He'd never be able to eat the stuff without remembering the dairy's stench.

"No, I haven't any sisters, but I rather like the chaos a gaggle of spirited women stirs up. I've been imaging the response the five of you would garner in London."

"Have you? Why?"

"Let's just say the *ton* has never experienced anything like the Culpeppers."

"Hmm, I suppose not."

They wandered to the cart track used to haul coffins to the graveyard. "I expected you would insist on the farm in your settlement negotiations. I'll make it a wedding gift to you."

Brooke stopped abruptly and stumbled over a root.

Heath grasped her arm to steady her. His fingers completely encircled her upper arm. Too thin. He'd see to it she'd not experience hunger again, darling girl.

"You will? Truly? To do with as I wish?" She clutched his arm, her eyes sparkling with excitement. "Would you allow me to build a simple house on the acreage so there's never an eviction worry again?"

A calf bawled, and a cow answered with a series of lowing grunts. Several more entered the fray, calling and mooing, their cries disturbing the peaceful morning.

Who would want a house nearer that racket?

Heath edged closer until his thigh brushed her skirts. He placed his hands on her shoulders, drawing her further into his embrace.

"Build a mansion, if you like. Anything to make you happy and keep a smile on your face." He touched her lips with his thumb. "Do you know, you rarely smile? Your lot in life hasn't been easy, has it?"

Brooke shook her head, the fair curls framing her face dancing. "I'm not complaining. It's been worth it." She contemplated the retreating women. If she retained regrets, she masked them behind the pride and love shining in her eyes. Her gaze brushed him, hovering an instant on his lips before flitting to a hawk circling overhead. She rolled a slender shoulder. "They needed me."

Simple as that. No excuses, pouting, or compunctions. She'd done what needed doing and did the job a far cry better than most men of his acquaintance would have. Any idiot decreeing women the weaker sex ought to be rapped upon the head with a cane.

"What of that Benbridge fellow? Do you love him?" Heath could have bitten his tongue off for blurting the question. He sounded like a jealous beau. What if she loved the young scamp? Jagged pain stabbed his middle.

Brooke's eyes rounded for a moment before she shook her head. "No, Humphrey is an old friend, but his parents would never permit a match between us. Besides, as I told you, we're a package deal. He had no interest in taking on such a large encumbrance." A forced smile bent her mouth the merest bit. "Truthfully, I cannot say I blame him. They've been a challenge."

"I promise, things will be better from now on. I'll do everything in my power to make your life easier and to make you happy." And by God, he meant it. Could Brooke hear the sincerity in his voice? He'd become a moon-eyed milksop. And liked it. A great deal, truth to tell. He, the reticent earl, known for his restraint and reason, issuing whimsical promises like a love-struck swain.

He almost touched his jaw to make sure it didn't hang slack at the epiphany that jostled his carefully structured life. In one week's time, Brooke had come to mean more to him than anything else: his title, his fortune, his friendships—few though they were—even Ebénè.

Nonsensical fairytales consisted of such fluff.

Stuff and nonsense.

Wonderful stuff and nonsense.

"I..." Her eyes misted, and she blinked as she stared at him, a mixture of awe and wonder on her face. She laughed and threw her arms around his neck in a fierce hug. "Thank you. Thank you. I feel like the weight of the world has been lifted from my shoulders."

He angled away to see her face. "May I take that as a yes?"

Gaze averted and pink tinging her cheeks, she nodded. "Yes, I'll marry you."

"Immediately?"

"Yes, as soon as the banns are read and arrangements can be made." Her flush deepened to rose and her gold-tipped lashes fanned her cheekbones. "But I still don't know how to address you."

"My friends call me Raven, but I like Heath best." He opened his hand, splaying his fingers over her smooth cheek and jaw.

Her focus slipped to his lips, and her voice acquired a husky edge. "When we first met, I would have said Raven suited you better."

"Coming from your lips, the name takes on an entirely different significance." He could almost imagine she'd whispered an endearment. Sap. Captivated, enamored sap. "By all means, call me Raven."

"No." Her eyes had grown sultry. "While it's true they are intelligent birds, they're also associated with dark omens."

"Then call me darling, or my love."

Her mouth formed another startled O, and she tucked her chin to her chest as color flooded her face.

He tipped her chin upward until their gazes met. A quick glance behind him assured Heath the others had almost made the orchard. "A kiss to seal our agreement?"

"All right." She shut her eyes and parted her lips in invitation.

No hesitation.

His soul leaped. How quickly could he secure a special license? Soon his week-long erection would finally be appeased.

The devil it will.

Not with Brooke as his wife. He'd have a perpetual rod jabbing his leg for the next fifty years. Long after his legs became too feeble to support his weight, his eyes too weak to see her delicate features, or his ears too dim to hear her delightful laugh, his penis would jump to attention whenever her scent teased his nostrils.

Her essence...addictive. An aphrodisiac of innocence and

womanliness.

He feathered kisses atop her cheeks and chin, until at last he tasted her honeyed lips.

She sighed and opened her mouth, melting against him like wax above a flame.

Passion laced with a sweetness he couldn't identify engulfed him. A little moan escaped her when he cupped her buttocks and urged her against his hardness. She stood on her tiptoes, nestling her womanhood against the evidence of his arousal.

The jangle of harnesses followed by the creaking of coach springs, clomping of hooves, and snorts of winded horses yanked him from the ambrosia he'd been sampling.

One arm encircling Brooke at her waist—he doubted she could stand on her own, she leaned so heavily on him—he examined the road to the house. Two carriages drew up before the structure, one quite unpretentious and the other a crimson and black monstrosity he didn't recognize.

As Leventhorpe and the Culpepper misses approached the conveyances, the girls' heads dipped together and bobbed a bit. Probably pondering who the passengers were. Leventhorpe increased his pace and, in a few steps, led the small troupe.

"Who in the world?" Brooke shaded her eyes. She gasped and clutched Heath's arm too tightly, her nails biting into the flesh through his coat and shirt. "No, it cannot be."

He covered her hand with his. "What is it? Who is that?"

Pale as the fine blackthorn blossoms amidst the overgrown hedgerow surrounding the graveyard, Brooke turned her alarmed gaze to him. "I cannot be sure because I've never met him, but I think he," she pointed at the man peering from the carriage doorway, "might be our Cousin Sheridan."

Marrying without love is like gaming with an
empty purse; alas you have lost before you begin.
~Wisdom and Advice—The Genteel Lady's Guide to Practical Living

17

"You've met him." Brooke gripped her skirts, raised them ankle high, and matched Heath's stride as they hurried along the path. She sidestepped a muddy patch. Laden with bulging pink blossoms, wild cherry tree branches overhung the roadway, which was littered with the damp remnants of last evening's rain shower. Brooke neatly stepped over a dinner plate-sized puddle. "Is that my cousin?"

Please say no.

"Indeed." Tension firmed the contours of Heath's face into taut lines. "I'm curious why he's here on the heels of losing the wager to me and threatening you with eviction. You say you've never met him?"

He maneuvered around a deep puddle.

"No." What business had Sheridan here?

"Watch your footing. This path is a travesty of ruts and hollows." Heath dipped her a swift glance before regarding the new arrivals. "Gainsborough hasn't visited prior to this?"

Brooke shook her head. "Never. He left the farm's operation and the girls' care to me."

Sheridan yawned then frowned as he examined the house and courtyard. Displeasure contorted his features and curled his upper lip into a sneer. What did he expect? An opulent mansion with manicured grounds on the pittance he allowed them? Upon spotting the girls, he stopped scowling, and a disturbing smile skewed his mouth.

She leaped over a larger puddle. No man should regard his cousins with such speculation, like a commodity to market and sell to the highest bidder. Hound's teeth, she'd been afraid of this. Why did men regard her sister and cousins like delectable fruit, free for the picking and sampling?

"Heath, I don't trust Sheridan. Do you see the way he's leering at the girls?" She hitched her skirts in order to quicken her pace. "He's guardian to them. I cannot help but think his presence here doesn't bode well."

Heath gave a curt nod and quickened his stride. She possessed long legs but had to trot to keep up. They were practically upon the group, although no one appeared to have noticed them.

"That's deucedly unfortunate. How old are they? How old are you?" He regarded Brooke, running his gaze from the worn toes of her half boots, to the dated bonnet atop her head. "Ought to know if I'm leg-shackling myself to a chit long on the shelf."

Brooke's heart skipped an uncomfortable beat. Did he tease, or did he think her too old?

His strong mouth edged upward on one side, and he winked.

Brooke chuckled. "I'm afraid I'm ancient. Three and twenty."

"Tsk, tsk. You'll need a cane and spectacles before the year ends, as will I. I'm eight and twenty. What are the ages of the others?"

Brooke hastily told him.

"Immediately upon reaching London, I'll petition for guardianship." He gave her hand a light squeeze. "My connections reach much farther and higher than Gainsborough's. Your cousin's reputation isn't, shall we say, pristine. Leventhorpe's distantly related to the Lord Chief Justice, and I won't hesitate to request his help. I have little doubt my request will be granted."

"But what happens in the meanwhile?" She sucked in an unsteady breath. "He...he cannot take my sister and cousins, can he?"

Heath slipped an arm around her waist and gave her side a quick caress. "Over my dead body."

Relief flooded her. It had been so long since anyone else had helped bear the burden of the quartet's wellbeing. They reached level ground at the same time the foursome and Lord Leventhorpe gained the horseshoe-shaped courtyard.

Sheridan waited for them, appraising her sister and cousins much the same way a perspective buyer for one of the cows or calves did. She wouldn't have been surprised if he lined the quartet up on the auction block, peered in their mouths, and took a gander at their legs to see if they would bring a high enough price.

Another man, attired entirely in black, climbed from the second carriage.

Four visitors in a week? All male? Had Esherton Green become a favorite destination for men who wished to wreak havoc on the quiet, respectable lives of the Misses Culpepper? They had better not plan on staying in the house. Unless she crammed one on a larder shelf and stuffed the other in the drawing room window seat, no sleeping quarters remained.

The sun glinted on the newcomer's honey-colored head as he too peered around before stretching. Her sister and cousins resumed their covert whispers, taking his measure as assuredly as Sheridan took theirs. The golden man broke into a wide grin and lifted a hand in greeting as Leventhorpe marched to him. They knew each other?

"Blast me, what's Hawksworth doing here?" Heath's question harnessed Brooke's musings.

Winded from her near run—surely that caused her breathless voice and not his lordship's hand curled at her waist—she regarded the Adonis. Josephina had shown her a book portraying Greek gods and goddesses. This man with his curling hair and hewn features very well might have stepped from the pages of the volume. "You're acquainted with him?"

"Yes, he's Alexander Hawksworth. A good friend of Leventhorpe's and mine. He's the rector of a large parish outside London."

A man resembling a mythical god preached about the Christian deity? She'd wager his church's pews didn't sit empty Sunday mornings.

"Perhaps he should marry us." Heath grinned, amusement crinkling the corners of his eyes, but then the humor slipped from his face faster than a hot iron erased wrinkles. "No, never mind. I wouldn't hear the end of it from either of those buffleheads."

At the precise moment Sheridan and Reverend Hawksworth swiveled in her direction, Brooke lost her footing on a slick spot. She clutched Heath's coat and scrambled to regain her balance. One moment she skidded along, legs spread wide, the next, she lay on her back, Heath half atop her. She opened her eyes, and ceased to breath. From knee to shoulder, his sinewy form mashed into her, and she welcomed his weight. The blistering heat in his eyes sent a pang burning from her breast to her nether regions before suffusing her entire body in prickly warmth.

The sensation wasn't unpleasant. Not at all.

"I say, remove yourself from my cousin's person at once." Sheridan charged in their direction, his mouth puckered tighter than an old maid expecting her first kiss. "Get off her, this instant."

Heath whispered in her ear. "Let me handle this, please."

Oh, I don't think so.

She hadn't time to respond before Sheridan descended upon them.

He glared at Heath then turned a vapid gaze on her as she sprawled beneath him. "Which one are you?"

Heath rolled off her, and after standing, extended his hand to Brooke.

"I'll assist her, Ravensdale." Sheridan thrust his square hand at her. "She's my ward, after all."

"Hardly, since I'm of age. Besides, I've never set eyes on you before in my life." Brooke ignored Sheridan's assistance and accepted Heath's. Her cousin would get no quarter from her. If he thought he could troop into Esherton and take over now, he was in for a most unpleasant surprise.

When Heath didn't promptly release her hand, Sheridan's crafty gaze narrowed, but he bent at the waist, nonetheless. "Sheridan Gainsborough, your cousin, come to survey my estate before taking you and your sisters to—"

"Three are my cousins, which you ought to know since my father appointed you their guardian five years ago." God's bones, fury whipped her temper. Who did the lickspittle think he was, showing up unannounced and having the ballocks to dictate to her? "And you only own the house and five acres. Or did you forget you wagered away the rest to Lord Ravensdale here?"

She jabbed her thumb at Heath's chest.

Brooke extracted her hand from his loose hold and glanced behind her at her skirt. Mud-streaked from hem to bum. She skimmed Heath's tight buttocks and long legs. Him too. Nevertheless, she quirked an eyebrow at Sheridan.

Well, she silently challenged him. *Deny it, you cur.*

"Er, yes, quite right." He puffed out his chest and attempted to look down his bulbous nose at her, reminding her of an outraged bantam rooster. All bluster and no might.

Considering she boasted four inches on him, his pretense proved ridiculous.

Heath's lips quivered, and amusement glinted in his eyes. Or mayhap approval lit his gaze.

"Brooke, are you all right?" Brette, wide-eyed with worry, reached her first. The twins and Blythe came next with Leventhorpe and Hawksworth bringing up thc rear.

"I'm perfectly fine." Aside from wanting to lay Sheridan out.

Blaike edged around Sheridan, her eyes averted. Astute girl. She perceived a lecher when she encountered one. She examined Brooke's gown. "I'm afraid the material might be permanently stained. Best we get you into the house and have it laundered at once."

"That rag is hardly worth salvaging." Sheridan scrutinized her sister and cousins. "Every one of you looks like you stepped from the poorhouse. What have you been doing? Gallivanting in the woods? It's a good thing I arrived, cousin. From what I've observed, you have no notion whatsoever of how to run a profitable estate or supervise young ladies of quality."

The hawk screeched. At least Brooke thought the bird had made the harsh cry. It may have been one of the girl's irate shrieks. Or hers.

Jackanape.

Brooke's breath left her on a drawn-out hiss as slurs romped about in her head, begging to be hurled at the oaf. She clenched her teeth and fists to keep from spewing the vulgar filth—a proper lady didn't know such foul oaths—in front of those assembled and to keep from popping Sheridan in his globular nose. Her betrothed didn't need to see or hear her acting the part of a termagant.

"I'd watch my tongue if I were you, Gainsborough. You haven't a pickle's knowledge about the commendable efforts these women," Heath swept his hand in an arc to include all the Culpeppers, "have made to keep this farm operating, no thanks to you."

"And I suppose you do?" Sheridan speared Heath a dark look. "By the by, why are you here?"

"I might ask you the same thing." The devil inhabited the stare Heath stabbed at Sheridan.

Sheridan's bravado wilted. "If you insist on knowing—

"Oh, I do." Silky, but dangerous.

A flush further reddened Sheridan's blotchy cheeks. "I decided to take a break from the London scene and acquaint myself with my cousins."

"Chased out of town by debt collectors or threatened with debtor's prison, I'd bet." Leventhorpe took a position beside Heath. "Have I the right of it?"

A ruddy hue turned Sheridan's ears purple. He shuffled his feet and pulled at his neckcloth. "Um, nothing of the sort."

Ah, the marquis had hit the target, spot on.

The reverend made a leg. "Lovely ladies, please allow me to introduce myself, as neither of my ill-mannered friends has done so. Reverend Alexander Hawksworth, but please call me Hawksworth. I look round for my esteemed uncle when I hear anyone say reverend outside my parish."

Brooke and the foursome curtsied, but Sheridan smirked and made no move of deference.

Heath made the necessary introductions.

"Didn't your uncle skip off with the baker's daughter?" Leventhorpe scratched the back of his neck. "Or was it the tailor's? I cannot quite remember, but the gossip columns buzzed for weeks."

"Neither, you dolt." Hawksworth smiled, a flash of white teeth, and his green eyes crinkled. "Aunt Elspeth was a nun. Terrible scandal. Anglican priest hieing off to Gretna Green with a Catholic nun. But He," he pointed heavenward, "had other plans for her. She had six children at last count. Happy as grigs, they are."

"*Reverend*?" Blaike wiggled her brows at Blaire. "I must say, I didn't see that coming. I thought he commanded the stage or opera. Something much more...colorful, with those looks."

Blaire nudged Brette. "Told you he wasn't Sheridan's valet."

Hawksworth pressed his hands to his chest in mock offense. "Valet, dear me. Really?" He glanced at his somber garb. "It's the togs, isn't it? But the church frowns on me wearing anything flamboyant or ornate. I really rather adore bright colors, particularly blue."

He looked pointedly at her blue gown.

"Enough of this drivel. Might we make our way into the house?" Sheridan swept the structure a disdainful glance while fussing with his waistcoat.

Brooke bristled. He had no right to criticize the staid old manor. Through prosperity and poverty, the building had been a pleasant home and for generations had witnessed the births, lives, and deaths of Culpeppers.

The breeze shifted direction, filling the air with the barn's aroma. Sheridan's bug-eyes bulged and, frantic, he groped around in his jacket. Gasping, he yanked a handkerchief free. He slapped the cloth over his nose. "My God, what is that unholy stench?"

"I said the same thing when I first arrived." Heath gave a hearty laugh. "You'll get used to it."

"Not as long as I draw a breath." Sheridan shook his head. His face pressed into the fabric muffled his words. "Gentlemen, I really must discuss my plans with my cousins."

He notched his nose higher, daring to put on a superior facade. Didn't he realize he ranked the lowest of the men present? Pretentious toady, and with his face mashed into the handkerchief, Brooke found it impossible to take him seriously.

He drew the cloth away and took a tentative sniff, scrunching his nose at once. Considering the size of the appendage, it rather resembled a pleated dinner roll. Not an attractive sight. "I am famished, and I must change from these travel-soiled clothes."

"Not too terribly road-stained as London is less than an hour's coach ride away," Leventhorpe muttered.

Touché.

Sheridan curled his lip but kept silent.

Leventhorpe might not be such a bad sort, after all, once you got past his prickly exterior.

"Indulge me a moment, Gainsborough." Reverend Hawksworth flicked his hand as if Sheridan were a bothersome insect before turning a brilliant smile on Brooke. Each service, his church probably burst with parishioners, and mostly of the female persuasion, or she wasn't a Culpepper.

Sheridan rolled his eyes skyward and huffed his displeasure. Crossing his arms, he tapped one foot impatiently and scowled like a lad denied a bonbon.

Worse than a petulant child.

Reverend Hawksworth lifted her hand, although his mouth remained a respectable distance above it. Good thing, too, since she hadn't donned her glove again. "May I tell you how honored I am to meet the future Countess of Ravensdale?"

How in the world did he know about Heath's proposal?

"Countess?" A chorus of voices echoed, including Sheridan's, which ended on a hoarse squeak. Fury radiated from his rodent gaze.

The quartet swung their confused gazes between Brooke and Heath, before, one by one, they rested their attention on her. Their expressions fairly screamed the questions they didn't voice.

Better his wife than his mistress, righto?

She flashed Heath a sideways glance, distrust and betrayal squeezing her ribs between their vice-like claws. Had he feigned ignorance regarding the timing of Hawkworth's arrival? Possibly. Yet to this point, Heath hadn't been dishonest. That she knew of, in any event.

She scrunched her toes in her boots. Face it. Theirs hadn't been the sunniest of acquaintances from the onset. And she did say yes to his proposal despite that. Had her good sense flown in the face of desperation?

Lovely way to start a marriage.

Forced marriage, Brooke.

No, not forced. Convenient.

Everything about the union smacked of convenience on both their parts. Except, her heart had become engaged somewhere over the course. When, she couldn't quite say. When he'd fallen in the drawing room? Kissed her outside the stables? Followed her around like a trusting puppy after Duffen's death?

Fear kept her from acknowledging in her mind what her heart had insisted for days. Laughable if the situation weren't so pathetic and clichéd. The whole matter screamed of a Drury Lane drama.

The reverend released her hand. "I hope you'll permit me the honor of performing the ceremony."

The claws dug deeper, drawing her soul's blood.

"You knew of Lord Ravensdale's plans to marry me?" How? She'd only learned of them a few minutes ago.

"Indeed." Hawksworth patted his chest. "I have the special license right here."

Brooke whipped round and confronted Heath.

"You pretended to know nothing about his arrival, yet he has a license?" Brooke poked him in the chest. Hard. "You deceiving bounder. What else have you lied about?"

He who mistakenly believes gambling a
harmless amusement has never looked into the ravaged
faces of those made victims by another's wasteful pastime.
~*Wisdom and Advice—The Genteel Lady's Guide to Practical Living*

18

Heath rubbed the back of his head as Brooke and her angel-haired entourage flounced inside the manor. Brilliant. An infuriated, distrustful bride.

Sheridan trailed them like an unwelcome stray, his mangy tail tucked between his legs.

"Am I mistaken, or is all not as it should be between you and your lady, Raven?" A deep furrow creased the bridge of Hawkworth's nose. When the last woman disappeared through the entrance, he turned an expectant gaze on him.

Heath brushed mud from his elbow as he made his way to the house. "How the blazes did you know we'd become betrothed?"

Falling in step beside him, Hawksworth pointed at Leventhorpe. "He sent a message two days ago. Said to get a special license and be here today, ready to perform your nuptials."

Hawksworth cast a practiced gaze to the graveyard. "And a funeral? The same day? Not precisely tasteful. I ran a bit behind schedule in London obtaining the license, hence my tardiness. I did wonder why Leventhorpe, and not you, made the request though, Raven."

"Because he's a bloody, interfering arse." Heath marched to the house, just short of a run. He needed to talk to Brooke, explain the situation to her, convince her he'd known nothing of Hawksworth's arrival until the moment he exited the carriage in all his celestial glory.

What if she changed her mind?

No, with Sheridan's unexpected arrival, she had more reason than ever to marry him.

He hoped.

He'd seen the fear she'd tried to hide. Her cousin frightened her, or perhaps the power he'd been granted over her sister and cousins caused her trepidation. But that didn't mean she wasn't livid with Heath.

"Explain yourself, Trist, and be quick about it." Heath gave Leventhorpe a sideways glare.

Leventhorpe shrugged as the trio climbed the steps, their boots clinking on the stones. "You talk in your sleep, Raven."

Heath snorted. "I do not."

"Trust me, you do, and you snore like a bloody lion in the process of choking on haunch of water buffalo. Your bride has my condolences in that regard. I really ought to warn her, but she might change her mind, and you'd be an even more unbearable sot." Leventhorpe gave a theatric yawn behind his hand. "It's a wonder I'm able to function at all, I've become so deprived of sleep."

Hawksworth chuckled and gestured between Heath and Leventhorpe. "The two of you share a room? That ought to be interesting."

"Yes, and he's been muttering on in his sleep about marrying Miss Culpepper for days now...or, rather, for nights."

"I have not." Had he? Damn.

"Yes, you have. Incessantly. Enough to force me to bury my head beneath my pillow to muffle your nattering and become desperate enough to send for Hawk."

They handed their hats and gloves to the waiting footman. He promptly trotted down the hallway, no doubt to assist in serving the meal.

"I thought I'd give you a nudge, Raven, since your conscience had already made the decision for you. And until last evening, we didn't know if Avery would officiate at the funeral." Leventhorpe inhaled deeply, peering in the dining room's direction. "Hmm, something smells delicious."

"Damned presumptuous of you." Heath scraped his hand through his hair. "Now she's furious with me. Thinks I manipulated her again."

"Again?" Hawksworth peered at him, his gaze teeming with amusement and curiosity.

"Yes, that respectable miss lost a wager to Raven and agreed to become his mistress." Leventhorpe gave Heath a brusque nod. "His terms, by the way."

Shit.

The comment pealed loud and reproachful in the entry.

"You intended to make that young woman your paramour?" Disapproval sharpened Hawksworth voice and features. "Far below par, and you well know it."

"Yes, I bloody well know it, which is why, after the funeral, I asked her to marry me."

Hawksworth grunted and folded his arms, looking very much an avenging angel. "Is there a single romantic bone in your body? Anywhere? I realize you're not a sentimental chap, but proposing on the heels of a funeral service... Damned crass, that."

"Exceedingly gauche." Leventhorpe nodded his agreement, his attention straying down the corridor again. "But when one is desperate..."

"Why marry someone you've only known..." Hawksworth glanced to Leventhorpe for help.

"A week."

"Eight days." Heath promptly regretted the correction when his friends exchanged mocking glances.

"Yes, the extra day makes *all* the difference." Leventhorpe drawled the word, earning him another murderous scowl from Heath.

"I should think a longer acquaintance would be beneficial to both of you." Hawksworth narrowed his eyes, his astute gaze probing. "Intelligent people do not decide to marry after a week unless they fall in love at first sight. Which I find beyond belief in your case. No offense intended."

I'm not supposed to be offended when one of my closest chums insults the hell out of me?

Leventhorpe's shout of laughter muffled Heath's rude noise.

"Raven? Love at first sight? Oh, that's rich." Leventhorpe's shoulders continued to shake. "Lust, yes. But love? Not him. Never him."

He hooted again.

Fine friend, boorish knave.

"Well, I cannot stay here, and I won't leave without her."

Where was Brooke? Heath craned his neck, gawking first along the passageway and then up the stairway. Had she retreated to her chamber to avoid him?

"Neither will I take her with me unless she's my wife. It would spell her ruination."

He peeked in the study. Nope, not there.

"I promised her and her family a better life than they've had, and I mean to keep my word."

Maybe she'd escaped to the barn again.

"And that rat bastard of a cousin will dance naked in court, scrawny ballocks bared for the royals, before a single Culpepper accompanies the sod anywhere."

"Sounds like love to me." Hawksworth lifted a hand and raised his fingers one at a time. "Putting her needs before yours. Unwilling to be apart from her. Wanting to provide and care for her...and her family."

He wiggled his four fingers and waggled his eyebrows like an inebriated court jester.

"Oh, and the desire to protect her." Up sprang his thumb.

"Don't preach to me, Hawk, when you know nothing of love." Was she in the kitchen?

Leventhorpe regarded Heath, a speculative spark in his eye. "Hmm, as impossible as it is for me to believe, Hawk's made some valid points. And you did mumble something that sounded like love in your sleep, though your speech was so garbled—rather like a drunk chewing a mouthful of marbles—I might have been mistaken."

"Don't be an imbecile, Trist." As much as Heath wanted to deny everything Hawk had said, a measure of truth resonated in his friend's words. He'd be hung if he'd admit it to his two smirking cohorts.

Do I love Brooke?

The theory explained much.

Hawksworth shook his head so hard, a shock of hair tumbled onto his brow. "It's either love, or the knock on your head Leventhorpe wrote me about has deprived you of your reason, in which case, I cannot in good conscience perform the ceremony."

"My thoughts exactly." Thumping echoed above, much like a toddler kicking their heels during a fit of temper. Leventhorpe raised his gaze to the vibrating ceiling. "What's going on up there?"

Heath rolled a shoulder and raked his hand through his hair again.

A calculating gleam entered Leventhorpe's gaze. "Did she say yes when you proposed?"

"I did." Brooke stood just inside the drawing room.

A small sigh of relief escaped Heath. He detected no trace of anger. Wasn't she still upset? He ran an appreciative gaze over her. She'd changed into a simple cream gown, with puff sleeves and a wide emerald ribbon below the bust. Pink and green embroidered flowers edged the hemline. An odd combination of vulnerability and determination shadowed her hollow cheeks and wary eyes.

His heart welled with emotion. *Love.* He loved her. Damn, but this pleasure-pain wasn't what he'd expected. It was more, so much more, and it scared the hell out of him.

Had she heard their entire exchange? Her gaze skimmed Leventhorpe and Hawksworth before landing on Heath. Her soul stretched across the room and touched his.

Yes. She had.

A loud crash reverberated overhead, followed by hollering and violent banging. She flinched, her face draining of color.

"What the devil is happening above stairs?" Heath pointed upward.

Anxiousness replaced Brooke's composure. She clasped her hands before her.

"It's Sheridan." After a hurried glance behind her into the drawing room, she glided farther into the entry and lowered her voice. "I'd like us to exchange vows at once."

"You're not still upset that Leventhorpe arranged for Hawksworth to be here? That he has a license?" Heath extended a hand in entreaty. "Please believe me, I didn't know until the moment you did."

Her shoulders slumped, and she sighed. "It's of no consequence. You'd already asked me to marry you, and I agreed. I've explained the situation to my sister and cousins. Although they are not happy with the circumstances, we are in agreement that the urgency of the situation requires an immediate wedding."

The caterwauling and crashing overhead increased in fervor.

Her gaze searched his. "If you are willing, my lord."

"Of course, I am. Nothing would please me more." He spoke the truth. Marrying her had become his greatest desire, more so than bedding her. Heath glanced at his dirty pantaloons. "You don't want me to change first?"

"No." She cast a troubled glance toward the stairs. "Sheridan's determined to keep me from marrying you and forcing us all to return to London with him. He's threatened to raise an objection during the ceremony on the preposterous, and untrue, grounds that I'm betrothed to another. He thinks to delay the wedding long enough to take custody of my sister and cousins, and I haven't a doubt in the world that his intentions aren't honorable."

"Rotten bounder." Murder glittered in Leventhorpe's eyes. "I'd like to see him try."

She thrust her adorable chin upward and squared her thin shoulders. "We've locked him in the twin's bedroom. That's what the commotion above stairs is."

"Well done, Miss Culpepper. A little isolation usually calms the soul." The reverend raised a speculative glance to the ceiling as bits of dust and plaster sifted down. "However, in this case, given the ruckus above, I'm inclined to believe demonic forces might have been released instead."

He stepped forward. "May I ask how old you are? I cannot legally marry you in England unless you are of age."

"I'm three and twenty. I have proof in the study."

"Good by me." He gestured to the drawing room entrance. "Shall we?"

"Um, what of the vicar?" Had everyone but Heath forgotten about the other man of the cloth?

Brooke's lips curved into a closed-mouth smile.

"He's feasting in the dining room. I explained a dear friend of the groom's had arrived and desired to perform the nuptials. I don't know which peeved him more: missing the promised meal or the ceremony fee." She fidgeted with her skirt, her gaze cast to the floor. "I'm afraid I assured him he'd be paid anyway, and I...I don't have the funds."

A ferocious hammering and several unsavory curses sounded from above.

"I'll pay the fee, but I think it's best we get on with the vows, posthaste." Heath took her elbow and guided her into the drawing room. Petal soft skin met his fingertips. Was the rest of her as silky? He would know tonight.

And he'd worship her with his heart and body.

Her family sat primly on the sofa and ugly chairs, Freddy perched on Miss Blythe's lap. Wariness cloaking them, they stood when Brooke and the men filed into the room. The dog eyed Leventhorpe but remained on the sofa where Blythe had placed him. He wagged his tail once.

Progress.

"Hawk, is there an expedited ritual?" Heath gave Brooke's arm a reassuring squeeze.

The sound of wood cracking and more cursing rent the air.

Everyone's attention raised to the ceiling. To the Culpepper misses' credit, all remained composed aside from disconcerted expressions.

"Sheridan's destroying the house," Brooke whispered. "He's a madman."

"Hawk?" Urgency prodding him, Heath bit out the name harsher than he'd intended. "The ceremony?"

"Short and sweet it is." Hawksworth glanced round to everyone assembled. "I'll assume no one here objects to the union?"

Leventhorpe and the Culpepper misses gave negative shakes of their heads.

"Excellent. Ravensdale and Miss Culpepper, join hands."

Heath clasped Brooke's hands.

She raised her gaze to his, her eyes bright and clear, before she flushed and her lashes swept her cheeks. He almost convinced himself something more powerful than desperation and fear warmed her eyes.

Hawksworth faced Heath and Brooke. "Miss Culpepper...what's your full name?"

"Brooke Theodora Penelope Culpepper." Did her voice tremble the merest bit?

Hawksworth cleared his throat. "Why, Ravensdale, I don't know your full name. Three and ten years acquainted and I just now realized that."

"Oh, for the love of God." Leventhorpe stomped to lean against the closed doors. "Do get on with it before that lunatic," he jabbed his forefinger straight up, "interrupts."

"It's Heath Adrian Lionel Sylvester Kitteridge, Earl of Ravensdale." Heath clasped Brooke's cold, damp hands tighter. Yes, she quivered like a newborn lamb.

Hawksworth scratched his chin. "Hmm, five names? Most impressive."

One of the twins tittered, but a stern glance from Brooke hushed her.

"Wise to leave off the preliminary parts, I think." Hawksworth pointed above them. "Wilt thou have this woman to be thy wedded wife, to live together after God's ordinance in the—"

"I will. I take Brooke to be my wedded wife, for richer, for poorer, in sickness and in health, to love and to cherish, till death us do part." Heath bent his head toward Brooke. "Her turn. Hurry."

"Wilt you have this man to be thy wedded husband—"

Footsteps pounded above along the corridor leading to the stairway.

Bloody maggoty hell.

Heath shook his head. "Skip that part."

Hawksworth shot a knowing glance overhead. "Yes, quite. Forget the formal mumbo jumbo too. Brooke, will you take Heath to be your husband?"

She tilted her head and met Heath's gaze head on. "I will."

Thumping on the stairs caused the quartet to gasp and clutch one another's hands, except for Blythe, who bolted to the desk.

Heath slid his signet ring off his little finger. "I'm sorry, it's much too big. I'll purchase you a wedding ring when we reach London. Maybe amethyst to match your eyes."

Leventhorpe snickered but turned the laugh into a hearty cough at Heath's scowl.

Heath slipped the heavy gold onto Brooke's slender finger.

She covered the band with her other hand before shooting the doors a distressed look.

Hawksworth inhaled in a huge lungful of air and raced through the last few lines. "Forasmuch as Heath and Brooke have consented together in holy wedlock, and have witnessed the same before God and this company, and thereto have given and pledged their troth either to other, and have declared the same by the giving and receiving of a ring, and the joining of hands; I pronounce that they be man and wife together. In the Name of the Father, and of the Son, and of the Holy Ghost. Amen."

Hawksworth grinned and wiped his perspiring forehead. "Just barely legal in God's eyes. You may kiss your bride."

"No. Later." Blythe held a quill at the ready. "Hurry, you must sign the license."

Footsteps thundered in the entry.

Hawksworth, Heath, and Brooke dashed to the desk.

Heath snatched the quill as Hawksworth spread the license atop the desk.

He couldn't read the damn thing. No time for pride. "Where do I sign?"

"Just there." Hawk pointed.

Heath scribbled his signature then passed the quill to Brooke.

"And Lady Ravensdale, you sign here." Hawksworth indicated another place on the parchment.

She neatly affixed her signature.

"Let me in. I forbid Brooke to marry that cur." The drawing room door handles rattled violently before the panels shuddered as

Gainsborough smashed something against them.

"I don't believe I care for our cousin, Brooke." Brette frowned at the door.

The others murmured their assent.

"Dammit, I say. Let me in."

"If you insist." Leventhorpe yanked the door open then dodged aside.

Red-faced and sweating, a blob of spittle hanging from the corner of his mouth, Gainsborough plowed into the room. He skidded to a stop and tottered when the carpet wrinkled underfoot.

Growling deep in his throat and hackles raised, Freddy leaped to his feet.

Gainsborough swung his furious gaze from Brooke, to Heath, to Hawksworth then fixed his attention on Brooke. A jeer contorted his features. "I'll never permit the marriage to be consummated. I'll have it annulled."

A small gasp escaped Brooke. She grasped Heath's hand. "I'm of age. He cannot do that, can he?"

"No, he cannot..." Leventhorpe followed Gainsborough into the room's center.

Gainsborough spun to face the other man. "I most certainly—"

"...if he's incapacitated and locked up." Leventhorpe planted Gainsborough a solid facer.

Bone crunched, and Blaire buried her face in her twin's shoulder. Gainsborough teetered, his eyes rolling back into his head, before he crashed to the floor, blood seeping from his nose.

Blythe grinned and clapped. "Well done, my lord."

He swept her a courtly bow.

"I believe this gentleman, and I do use the term with extreme disdain, has a reservation in a dovecote for the next, oh, say three days?" He flexed his fingers then rubbed his knuckles. "Is that sufficient time, Raven?"

"Indeed." He lifted Brooke's hand and kissed the back of her hand. "This time tomorrow, we'll be in London, and I'll be seeking guardianship."

She gifted him with a brilliant smile.

Hawksworth leaned forward and examined Gainsborough's prone figure. "I believe you broke his nose, Leventhorpe."

"Which can only improve the hideous appendage," Brooke said.

"Looked rather like a bull elephant seal I saw in a book once."

After moment of astounded silence, laughter filled the room.

"Ladies, would you care to show me to the dining room?" Hawksworth extended both elbows. "The wonderful smells have tempted me beyond resistance this half hour past."

Blaire and Blaike swooped in like bees to a flower.

Typical reaction to Hawksworth—women making a cake of themselves. Surely The Almighty had a delightful sense of humor, permitting a man with Hawk's extreme good looks to be a man of God. Not that the vocation had been Hawk's first choice, but a parish proved a more desirable workplace if one must earn one's living than the battlefield or the deck of a rolling ship.

"By the by, Raven, I'm grateful you and your lovely bride came to an accord on your own. I asked Hawk to bring a license because I wouldn't have permitted you to besmirch her by making her your mistress. I fully intended to see you marry her, even if it meant I held a gun to you during the ceremony." After winking at Brooke and giving Heath a mocking salute, Leventhorpe offered his bent elbows to Blythe and Brette. Wearing bemused expressions, they, too, departed the room.

A grin etched on his face—Leventhorpe had flummoxed him, by God—Heath directed the footmen to remove Gainsborough to the dovecote and see him secured there.

Brooke stared out the window, her profile illumed by the filtered rays bathing the window. She appeared almost ethereal, her hair a shiny halo in the golden light. Twisting the ring on her finger, she turned soulful violet eyes to him. "Could we wait until we get to London to consummate the marriage?"

Some claim fortune favors the bold. However,
believing such rationality applies to love and happiness
is as ridiculous as wagering against the sun rising each morn.
~Wisdom and Advice—The Genteel Lady's Guide to Practical Living

Brooke ran the brush through her hair, the long strokes soothing her rattled nerves. She'd passed the remainder of the day in a haze except for Heath's response to her question. That she remembered clear as crystal.

"*No. We cannot.*"

His scorching gaze had threatened to singe the ends of her hair and turned her insides quivery and warm. Disturbing, yet tantalizing too. What that man did to her with a simple look...

She trembled head to toe.

"Of course he wouldn't want to wait."

She didn't really want to either, but fear of the unknown made her hesitant.

Brooke glanced at her bed covered in a handmade quilt Mama had sewed many years ago. The small bed had suited her well all these years. With Freddy tucked at her side, dozens of books had been read snuggled beneath the comforting bedclothes. And buckets of tears had dampened the pillows too.

Her gaze swept the tiny chamber meant for use as servants' quarters and scarcely bigger than the kitchen larder. Its ceiling sloped to the eaves on one side. Heath had better watch his head, or he'd be cracking his noggin on a beam. The girls shared the other two larger bedchambers, the twins' now affixed with a temporary door thanks to Sheridan's earlier violence. Brooke didn't mind. She liked her private sanctuary, the one place she could go and be alone. No expectations or demands in this cranny of the house.

Until Heath came to claim his husbandly rights tonight. Thank goodness her chamber was situated on the uppermost floor and the opposite side of the house from the quartet's. Nonetheless, everyone beneath the roof would know what she and Heath were about. Heat consumed her, and she lifted the heavy mass of hair from her neck, allowing the air to cool her nape.

Brooke pondered the bed again. Would his feet stick over the end? "Hardly big enough for me, let alone two people."

An image of them toppling onto the floor amidst the marriage act leaped to mind.

Good God. Every thump and bump would be heard below. She pressed cool hands to her hot cheeks.

Someone, likely Brette or Blythe, had put fresh sheets on the bed and set a vase of flowers on her dressing table. Extra candles had also been placed throughout the room. A wine bottle and two glasses sat upon a tray. Leventhorpe's doing, likely. Brooke jumped to her feet, her nerves threatening to erupt from her skin. She rubbed her hands up and down her bare arms, not to warm her flesh, but to lessen her tension.

Poor Freddy had been banished to the twins' room for the night. He'd slept with her every night of his life. Would Heath forbid it in the future? Maybe he would be one of those husbands who only entered her chamber to conduct his conjugal visits and then returned to his room to sleep. The notion didn't cheer her. Mama and Papa had always shared a bedroom.

Brooke sighed, hugging her arms snugger around her shoulders.

Married to a practical stranger. Yet far preferable to becoming Heath's mistress. She wouldn't lie to herself and pretend she didn't find him deucedly attractive—his raven hair, intelligent eyes, sharp-hewn face, and sinewy muscles... She secretly thrilled that he'd chosen to wed her. And bed her.

Brooke smoothed a wrinkle from the bottom sheet before fluffing the pillows. No palatial chamber here. She straightened the primrose and sage coverlet. Fingering the silky border, she smiled.

How could she love Heath? Ridiculous. Impractical. Unwise.

Affection took time to develop. Didn't one need to know everything about someone to become enamored and fall in love?

No. She'd known Humphrey for years and had intimate knowledge of his likes, dislikes, preferences, and habits. The mild, comfortable affection she'd harbored for him resembled a skiff ride on a calm lake. Only an occasional fish jumping to catch an insect interrupted the serenity.

Heath, on the other hand...what she felt for him: wild, intense, unpredictable sentiments that left her muddled and excited and...yearning. A journey on rolling waves to an undetermined destination, but one she'd gladly travel with him by her side.

A soft *click* as the door closed announced his arrival.

Brooke whirled to face her husband. Her breath left her in a whoosh.

Attired in a black banyan, he held a pink rose. Where had he gotten a rose? The black hairs exposed by the vee of his robe tantalized. Were all women so obsessed with chest hair?

She wiped damp palms on her nightdress. White, unadorned, and nearly sheer from frequent laundering, the garment wasn't in the least alluring, yet his eyes darkened and the lines of his face tautened as he examined her leisurely.

A seductive grin skewed his lips, and he extended the rose, advancing farther into the room. "For you."

"Thank you." Brooke reached for the blossom.

Rather than releasing his hold, he wrapped his other palm around her hand and drew her near. Heath trailed the silky petals over her cheek then lower to her neck and finally brushed the flower across the flesh exposed above her modest neckline.

Brooke parted her lips on a silent gasp, her nipples going rigid. How could such a simple gesture make her want to crawl atop him and kiss him until she couldn't breathe? He couldn't breathe?

"When I touched your arm today, I wondered if the rest of your skin would feel as petal soft." He ran two fingers over her collar bone before dipping one into the valley between her breasts. "It does."

Brooke shivered and closed her eyes lest he see the lust he stirred in her. She'd never considered herself a sensual woman, but Heath wrought cravings and sensations impossible to ignore.

A moment later, his firm lips replaced his exploring fingers. He feathered little kisses and nips behind her ear, the length of her jaw and neck, and then nuzzled the juncture of her throat. A pleasant, aching heaviness weighted her breasts and filled her abdomen and between her legs.

She shifted, restless for something. Drawing away, Brooke smiled at him and laid her palm in the crisp mat on his chest. She rubbed her hand back and forth, enjoying the friction of the curls and the ecstasy on his face. Wanton power sluiced her. She had caused his response.

He groaned and gripped her buttocks, lifting her against his turgid length.

Brooke kissed his chest, pushing aside the silk covering his molded shoulders. She couldn't get close enough to him, couldn't taste enough of his salty-sweet skin. She darted her tongue out, tracing it over one of the chocolate-colored circles on his chest. His nipples were much darker than her pink-tinted ones, though hers were larger by far.

Another gravelly moan escaped him, and Heath tossed aside the rose before scooping her into his arms.

"I feared you'd be reluctant tonight." He traced his tongue across her parted lips. "I see I needn't have been worried." His fingers clenching her ribs and thigh, he sucked her lower lip into his mouth. "Tell me you want me too, Brooke."

He swept his tongue into her mouth, sparring with hers for a moment.

Heady dizziness encompassed her. If his kisses did this to her, what would making love with him do? She would never be the same. Didn't want to be. Heath brought an awareness she hadn't known existed. Hadn't known she'd lacked.

"I want to feel you against me. Your legs entwined with mine." Brooke wrapped her arms around his neck, pressing her breasts against his chest. "I want you inside me—"

He pulled his head back, his expression gone stern. "And just how do you know about that, pray tell me?"

Laying her fingertips across his mouth, she grinned. "I raise cattle. Did you forget?"

"Hmph." His disgruntled expression softened as he carried her to the bed. "Not the same at all."

"At all?" Brooke smiled, twirling her fingers in the long hair at his nape. "How is it different?"

"Animals mate out of instinct, a primitive drive to reproduce and appease lust-born urges. Some humans—most, actually—are little better." Heath's knees bumped the mattress, yet he didn't lower her. His gaze unfathomable, he stared at her, an intensity she'd never seen in his eyes before. "But humans, the few fortunate ones, find love. The act is an expression of their adoration."

His embrace tightened when he said the last words.

Brooke went completely still. Falling in love in a week's time was improbable and irrational. Could Heath—this proud, enigmatic, wonderful man—feel the same for her as she felt for him?

"Brooke... I..."

She laid her hand on his cheek and summoned every ounce of bravado she possessed. “Are you saying you love me?”

What if he says no?

“Yes, although I don’t understand how or why it came to be.” Happiness sparked in his eyes, and he turned his head to place a kiss in her palm. “I only know I couldn’t leave you and return to London alone. Ripping my heart from my chest would be less painful.”

His eyes grew misty and his voice hoarse. “And I was such an unmitigated, unforgiveable arse, suggesting you...” His gaze caressed her face before he bent and kissed her mouth reverently. “Suggesting you become my mistress.”

He rested his forehead against hers. “Dare I hope, in time, you might come to forgive me and perhaps feel tenderness for me?”

Brooke blinked away the tears pooling in her eyes.

“I already have, and I already do.” Unaccustomed bashfulness seized her, and she nestled her face in the crook of his neck. His pulse beat—strong and steady, like him—beneath her cheek.

“Oh, God, I love you.” A shudder rippled through Heath, and he crushed her closer. “I didn’t believe in love, dismissed it as foolish nonsense, didn’t believe it ever possible for the likes of me.”

She nodded against his chest. “I know. I’m as stunned as you.”

He laid her on the bed then fanned her hair over the pillow.

“You have the most beautiful hair I’ve ever seen.” His hands at his waist, he paused in untying the belt. “I know I said we couldn’t wait to consummate the marriage because of the risk your cousin poses, but if you’re afraid, we could delay a day or two.”

Heath loved her. She had wanted him for days. Brooke lifted her arms to him. “I don’t want to wait.”

“Thank God.” A wicked smile curved his mouth as he bent and tugged her night-rail over her head. He inhaled sharply, and his nostrils flared as his ravenous gaze feasted on her breasts in the muted candlelight.

She yanked the covers over her chest, not ready to wantonly display her womanly assets to him. Perhaps in time.

He shrugged from the ebony silk and the garment slid to the floor. As if he sensed her need to become acquainted with his body, he stood like a Greek statue, allowing her to look her fill. She couldn’t detect an ounce of fat on his powerful form. A well-muscled chest and torso, covered in curly raven hair, tapered into a narrow waist and hips. The dense thatch at his groin arrested her attention. From the patch sprang an impressive phallus.

Bloody gorgeous and arousing beyond belief.

His member twitched, bobbing up and down, and grew even larger.

Her mouth went dry. Just how enormous did the thing get, and more on point, could she accommodate something that size?

Heath edged onto the bed and slid beneath the covers. He gathered her into his arms, tucking her to his side and laying one muscled thigh across her legs. His penis, greedy beast, flexed against her hip.

"Aren't you going to snuff the candles first?" Brooke cast an anxious glance at the flickering tapers. They bathed the room in a soft light a more experienced woman might consider romantic.

"No, love. I want to see and worship every inch of you. I want to cherish the expression on your face when I enter you and bring you to completion." He splayed his fingers atop her abdomen. "And I want you to see what you do to me. The power you hold over me."

He reached between them and laid his manhood on her thigh.

"You do this to me." Pressing her hand atop the velvety length, he spread hot, fervent kisses over her breasts. He traced one nipple with his tongue before pulling the tip into his mouth and sucking.

Brooke gasped. Sparks streaked from her breasts to her toes, igniting every pore along the way. "Dear God..."

She arched into his mouth and let her legs fall open to his exploring hand. Heat spiraled higher and hotter, threatening to consume her with each lave of his tongue and flick of his experienced fingers. The warm stiffness of his penis pulsed against her palm. She grasped the flesh and squeezed gently. "It's so soft, yet hard too."

Heath moaned against her neck. "You're killing me."

Brooke stopped fondling him instantly, biting her lip as he slipped his long fingers into her. She instinctively clamped her muscles around him, squeezing tighter as aching pleasure surged to her womb. A throaty cry tore from her.

"No, don't stop." He groaned and ground his pelvis against her hand.

The urge to rotate her hips overtook her with such ferocity, Brooke had no resistance. She bucked and pumped, aware of the hungry, whimpering noises she made, but not caring.

"That's it, sweetheart. You're nice and wet, almost ready for me."

Wet? That was a good thing?

He moved his fingers faster, deeper.

Oh God, yes, wet is good. Very good.

She spread her legs wider.

"Good girl," Heath breathed in her ear.

He positioned himself over her, the tip of his penis bidding entrance. Cupping her face between both palms, he kissed her with such tender reverence, if he hadn't already told her of his love, his kiss would have exposed the secret.

"Look at me, Brooke."

She forced her eyes open, drowning in overwhelming sensation and need.

"Heath? I need..." A throaty groan escaped her. "I want..."

He smiled, the corners of his eyes crinkling. "I know."

Slowly, he entered her, refusing to relinquish her gaze.

Brooke sighed at the rightness of it. *This* was what she wanted. Needed. Yet, it wasn't enough. More. There must be something more. Clutching his back, she wriggled her hips. Almost frantic with yearning, she rubbed her breasts against his chest.

He stopped his gentle invasion into her womanhood and wrapped one strong arm around her shoulders and one beneath her hips. "Now, love. Now."

Brooke surged upward as Heath plunged. A gasp tore from her as stinging pain seared her center. She trained her gaze on him, trusting him as the most marvelous of feelings radiated from where he joined with her.

"It feels wonderful," she whispered, testing the sensations by rocking her hips.

"It gets better, darling." He arched his spine, his corded neck muscles rigid. "Let me take you to heaven, where angels like you belong."

His breathing harsh and heavy, he began a rhythmic thrusting.

Brooke caught his tempo as he ground into her. She wrapped her legs round his waist and let him carry her heavenward. The world ceased to exist around her. Only she and Heath and this moment of incredible bliss mattered. And just when she thought she could bear no more, when her soft whimpers become small cries of desperation, she fractured and screamed his name, convulsing over and over as indescribable ecstasy ravaged her.

A moment later, he roared his fulfillment.

She welcomed each pounding thrust, knowing he enjoyed the same rush of pleasure she just had. Breathing heavily, he flopped onto his back, pulling Brooke atop his sweat-slicked chest. Several moments passed before her ragged breathing and thrumming heartbeat returned to normal. Delicious drowsiness surrounded her. No wonder Buford had rutted until the moment he'd keeled over. Not a bad way to die at all.

"Never, in all my days, have I ever experienced anything that...that incredible." Heath hugged her fiercely, his lips pressed to the top of her head.

Brooke snuggled into his side and yawned. Head on his shoulder, she ran her fingers through his chest hair. "Can we do it again? I should like to try making love the way the cows do, with you from behind."

Heath grinned and tweaked her nose. "In a bit. I need awhile to recover."

The candles had burned to nubs when Brooke finally roused enough to pull the coverlet atop her and Heath. She gazed at his sleeping form. Her husband. She smiled and shook her head then lay down, her head nestled on his shoulder again.

"What are you smiling about?"

She tilted her head to look at him. Exotic eyes regarded her. She really did need to ask him about his heritage. "I thought you were asleep."

"Hardly, with a tantalizing siren beside me. I shall be in a constant state of arousal until the day I die." The bedding shifted above his pelvis.

She peeked beneath the blankets and giggled. "Poor man. That has to be uncomfortable."

He caressed her shoulder and arm. "Why were you smiling when you thought I was asleep?"

"I imagined what I'd tell our children when they asked how we met." She scratched her nose where his hair tickled her. "I'm not sure I want them to know a wager brought us together and we wed after a mere week. Not a very good example, I shouldn't think."

"Ah, but imagine what a romantic tale we've created. It will serve as an inspiration for our children, to believe true love really does exist." Heath chuckled and palmed her breast, gently pinching the peak.

A jolt of pleasure speared her. "It does, doesn't it?"

The wisest of gamblers have this in common:
They quit while they are ahead.
~*Wisdom and Advice—The Genteel Lady's Guide to Practical Living*

Epilogue

London, England
Late May 1822

Brooke drew in a steadying breath and smoothed the satin of her lavender ball gown for the umpteenth time as the carriage lurched to a stop before an ostentatious manor. Nervous didn't begin to describe her state, not only for herself, but her sister and cousins. A horde of insects rioted inside her stomach, making complete nuisances of themselves, horrid little pests.

Beside her, Brette fidgeted with the silk tassels of her reticule, and on the opposite seat, Blythe, Blaire, and Blaike's features suggested they were about to be offered up as human sacrifices. Not too far off the mark, truth to tell.

In their evening finery, hair intricately coiffed, and jeweled to the hilt, thanks to Heath's generosity, the Culpepper misses and her, the new Lady Ravensdale—blast, but it was proving difficult to remember to answer to her new title—were about to attend their first formal ball. Brooke would rather have stood on her head naked in Hyde Park. But as soon as the Season ended, they would return to Culpepper Park, the name they'd dubbed the lands Brooke now owned, to check on the new house's progress.

Sheridan had signed an agreement and greedily accepted a sizable sum to disappear from their lives forever. Hopefully, they were rid of him for good.

Heath squeezed the fingers of her gloved hand and grinned like a Captain Sharp with a winning hand at cards. "Trust me, dear. None of you has anything to fear."

"Easy for you to say. You're accustomed to the predators and vipers in there." She pointed at the house, every window ablaze with light. A good dozen people paused to stare at their coach.

The carriage door swung open, and a black liveried footman placed a low step beside the carriage. His eyes widened to the size of moons when he glanced inside. A delighted smile stretched across his handsome face. He turned and motioned to another footman.

The second footman hurried to their conveyance. Upon spotting the women, he tripped, nearly planting his face on the coach floor.

Heath slid Brooke a smug glance that said, *See, I told you.*

Yes, but gullible footmen were a far cry from the denizens of High Society, who were wont to devour young ladies with the swiftness of piranhas.

As they assembled on the pavement, Brooke took the girls' measure. Heath had suggested the jeweled tones for their gowns. Amethyst for her, light blue sapphire for Brette, jonquil beryl for Blythe, emerald green for Blaike, and pink ruby for Blaire. Superb choices, and with the matching gemstones each wore, truly regal.

A hush settled upon the guests lined up like docile cattle on the pavement and steps to enter the manor. Every eye turned to look at the new arrivals, and the crowd parted to allow them entrance. Heath and Brooke led, Brette and Blythe followed, and the twins brought up the rear.

Brooke's jaw almost bounced off the floor upon entering the glittering mansion. Never had she seen such opulence. Two eight-foot chandeliers blinded her with at least one hundred candles each. She couldn't decide which offended worse: the garish rose marble floor or the abundant gold gilding plastered on practically everything not moving. Even the hostess wore copious layers of gold.

Brooke sent a reassuring smile over her shoulder. The quartet's stunned faces no doubt mirrored her own.

"Steady on, ladies. Chins up and eyes forward. Incomparable, every last one of you." Heath led them to a gaping butler, his jaw sagging so widely, a pigeon might've nested in the cavity.

"Pretty much the reaction I had, too, upon seeing them for the first time, Withers."

Withers drew himself up, his prickly black eyebrows wiggling like caterpillars in the throes of mating...or dying. "Indeed, my lord. A most astounding collection of young ladies, if I may say so."

The majordomo bowed so low, his nose threatened to scrape the floor. Several dandies also made exaggerated bows, while the *haut ton* ladies' fans snapped to attention and waved furiously. Their tongues probably flapped just as fast.

Heath murmured their names into the butler's ear.

"Ah, may I offer my most sincere solicitations, my lord?"

Heath inclined his head. "Thank you."

Withers cast a languid gaze over the crowd then notched his nose skyward. "Lord and Lady Ravensdale, and the Misses Culpepper."

A low buzz built in volume as more people pushed and shoved their way into the entry and peeked from the ballroom, including the flummoxed Benbridges.

Blythe waved her fingers at their neighbors who continued to gawk.

A tall, auburn-haired man elbowed his way through the gawkers. A blond god followed, a merry twinkle in his eyes. Thank goodness. Brooke had never thought the day would come that she'd welcome Lord Leventhorpe's intimidating presence.

"We thought you might need a hand." Leventhorpe grinned and winked.

Reverend Hawksworth chuckled. "I do believe a near insurrection is at hand."

The gentlemen extended their elbows and, with a Culpepper on each arm, led the way into the ballroom. Elbowing and shoving one another in a most ungallant fashion, a score of gentlemen trotted after them. Miffed ladies did too, but for entirely different reasons—to snatch wayward beaus and husbands back to their sides.

Heath placed Brooke's hand on his arm and whispered in her ear. "My love, the Culpepper misses have tumbled the stuffy *ton* tits over arse."

Brooke burst out laughing. "Come, husband. I've a feeling we'll have our hands full with those four. I did warn you before we married and you became their guardian, however."

"I wouldn't have it any other way." He tilted her chin up, and in full view of the scandalized onlookers, kissed Brooke full on the mouth.

The Marquis and the Vixen

A woman of noble character will at all times remember, calm composure flummoxes the schemes of evil-intended people.
~Dignity and Decorum—The Genteel Lady's Guide to Practical Living

1

London, England, Late May, 1822

Flimflam and goose-butt feathers!

One hand hiding her mouth, Blythe Culpepper gaped as she trailed her cousin, Brooke, and Brooke's husband, Heath, the Earl of Ravensdale, into the mansion.

Surely that wasn't authentic gold gilding the ornate cornices? Squinting to see better, she surveyed the grand entrance. *Yes. It is.*

And not just the sculpted cornices either. The plasterwork and practically every other surface, excluding the coffered ceiling's elaborate paintings and the rose-tinted marble floor, boasted the shiny adornment.

Everything pink and gold and glittery. And costly.

"What a despicable waste of money." Flinging Heath a hasty glance, Blythe checked her muttering. It wouldn't do to offend him or their hostess within a minute of arrival.

The peeress, swathed in gold satin and dripping in diamonds—*three diamond bracelets? On each wrist?*—stood beside an enormous urn. Blythe fought the scowl tugging at her mouth and brows. Disgusting, this brazen flaunting of wealth.

Clamping her slack mouth closed, she reluctantly passed a waiting footman her silk wrap. A chill shook her, puckering her flesh from forearms to shoulders. Maddening nerves. She hadn't expected the pomp, or the mob's crush, to affect her.

A simple teardrop-shaped beryl pendant nestled at the juncture of her breasts, and Blythe pressed a hand to the expanse of flesh exposed above her wide, square neckline. Did she dare tug the bodice higher? After dressing, she'd attempted to, but the fabric had remained stubbornly form-fitting, the slopes of her bosoms pushed skyward for the world to ogle at their leisure.

Repressing a scornful grunt, she tipped her mouth a fraction. In twenty years, the smallish, twin pillows had never garnered much ogling. Probably little need to fret in that regard.

Tripping over her gown remained an entirely different matter.

Her secondhand garments had always been too short for her tall frame. Since exiting the carriage, this ball gown—its sheer silk overdress atop the yellow jonquil swirling about her feet—had become snared thrice upon her slippers' decorated tops.

She would have to endure these outings for the remainder of the Season, and she didn't relish sprawling, bum upward, before the *ton's* denizens. Tapping her fan against her thigh, she estimated how many public jaunts the Season might entail and hid an unladylike groan behind an indelicate cough.

God spare her.

The instant the final dance note faded, she planned on trotting back to the country's quiet civility—to the humble, familiar way of life she preferred. Or perhaps she'd contrive a minor scandal. Nothing too ruinous, merely shameful enough to see her banished in moderate disgrace.

Yes, that might do.

This gaudy, glistening parade quite shred her normally robust nerves. A calculated, hasty departure might be just the thing. After all, she hadn't come to London to marry. Acquiring a husband ranked below cleaning the chamber pots and mucking the stalls on her to-do list. Unless, of course, she found a man who adored her the way Heath cherished Brooke.

Fanciful imagining, that. Stuff and nonsense. Fairy-tales. At least for Blythe.

According to Mama, even as a toddler, Blythe had possessed a determined—some might say daunting—personality. Now, as an adult, the unfeminine characteristic chaffed men's arses and patience raw. No one who knew her had ever used acquiescent and her name in the same sentence, and she wouldn't scheme to snare a husband with false biddableness.

Humbly accepting the dowry Heath had bestowed upon her hadn't made the prospect of wedding more tempting, and though grateful for his generosity, she couldn't expect him to provide for her indefinitely. In a month, she'd be of age and free to make her own decisions, which included returning to Culpepper Park and the new house Brooke had commissioned.

Somehow, Blythe would eke out an existence there. A slight shudder rippled the length of her spine. No more giving music lessons though. At least not to spoilt brattlings like the vicar's daughters. For five interminable years, she'd endured that trial.

With a determined tilt of her head, she sucked in a calming breath and returned Heath's encouraging smile.

He and Brooke preceded Blythe and her cousin, Brette, into the immense entry. Blythe's twin sisters, Blaire and Blaike, slowly wandered in wearing identical wide-eyed, stunned expressions.

Taking in the ostentatious manor, and the more flamboyant assemblage, Blythe craned her neck, catching her toe on Brooke's slipper. "Excuse me."

Perchance as boggled by the crass display of wealth, Brooke didn't respond, just slowly swung head this way and that.

Beneath the glaring candlelight of two eight-foot chandeliers, Blythe blinked again, as did her sisters and cousins—five flaxen-haired, gawping country bumpkins brought to Town.

Who could blame them?

They'd been accustomed to starkness, want, and poverty, and the grandiose entry sparkled like the Pharaoh's tomb she'd once seen in a drawing.

The urge to hike her gown to her knees and bolt to the carriage's safe and anonymous confines—like the fairytale character Cendrillon—had Blythe grasping her frothy skirt with both hands, one white-satin-slippered foot half-raised.

Whose beef-witted idea had it been to introduce the Culpeppers to society?

Heath's. Their proxy fairy godmother. He believed it might prove amusing.

To whom?

Her fan clutched in one hand—too bad it wasn't a magical wand with mythical powers—Blythe surreptitiously lifted her gown a fraction and disentangled her slipper's beaded toe from her hem again. At this rate, she'd make a spectacle of herself before she'd stepped onto the dance floor, the singular thing she hadn't dreaded. Musically inclined her whole life, the prospect of dancing didn't worry her. *Much.*

Their ensemble had drawn considerable attention already, some speculation less than affable from the barbed stares and pouting moues slung their way, and tonight's introduction to *la beau monde* was important to Brooke's and the other girls' success.

None of the Culpeppers had relished visiting London, but these past weeks had changed everyone's minds, excluding Blythe's. The streets boasted refuse and manure, and the city stank worse than the dairy barns during summer's peak temperatures. Beggars and orphans abounded, as did women of loose virtue. The stark contrast between the opulent display currently surrounding her and the hollow-eyed, rag-garbed street urchins she'd seen on the drive here grated.

Grossly unfair, the patent disparity.

Perhaps enduring years of hunger and lack had embittered her toward the affluent more than she'd realized.

"Look at the cherubs and nymphs." Her voice low and lilting with amused embarrassment, Brette elbowed Blythe. "They're everywhere and completely naked."

They were indeed.

As the majordomo announced their troupe in an onerous monotone, Blythe answered the smile of a striking man, who dipped his curly, sun-kissed head at her. Broad-shouldered, with a sculpted face, and attired in the height of fashion, he was quite the handsomest man she'd ever seen.

Merriment lit his features, and his smile blossomed into a satisfied grin. His fawn-colored gaze lazily traveled from her insignificant bosoms to her toes then made the reverse journey to once again hover on her breasts before boldly meeting her eyes. His pleated at the corners again, a testament to a man accustomed to smiling habitually.

Her stomach reacted most peculiarly, all floppy and churning.

And her breasts?

Why, under his appreciative regard, the dratted insignificant things swelled and pebbled proudly. Quite forward of them, given their unimpressive size. Warmth skidded up the angles of her cheeks, and she averted her gaze.

Hound's teeth.

First time she'd ever blushed or had her bosoms betray her. Next thing she knew, the perky pair would scramble from her bodice's lace edge and wave a jaunty hello.

Her cousin edged nearer and splayed her fan, concealing their lower faces. She bobbed her fair head to indicate the ballroom entrance where a crowd spilled forth, perusing and prattling about the newcomers. "Look, Blythe. The statues on either side of those double doors are too."

"Are what?" What was Brette yammering about? Oh. Naked. The statues of Greek gods were naked as a needle. "Must be why those silly girls are giggling and pointing."

Raised on a farm, Blaike smirked and Blaire grinned, their pansy-blue eyes twinkling. The male anatomy didn't intrigue them quite as singularly as it obviously did the sheltered society misses. Nonetheless, the statues' manly endowments left nothing to the imagination.

Well, one remained endowed.

The other's male bits had snapped off in a debutante's hand, causing another round of frenetic tittering. From the way their scolding hostess descended upon the women, Blythe would have bet her pendant the god had lost his penis to curious groping before.

"Thought you might need a hand, Ravensdale." A mocking male addressed Heath from over Blythe's right shoulder.

Good God.

Blythe stiffened, refusing to look behind her.

The rumbling baritone could belong to only one man. The insufferable Marquis of Leventhorpe.

Perfectly horrid.

Her first foray into High Society, and he attended the same gathering, his presence as welcome as a crotchety, old tabby cat. He'd rubbed her wrong, and they'd crossed words, ever since meeting at Esherton Green, her childhood home. A more arrogant, difficult ... humorless ... stubborn person than Lord Leventhorpe didn't strut the Earth.

His scent, crisp linen mixed with sandalwood, enveloped her, warning her he'd drawn nearer. Too near. His breath tickled her ear as he mumbled almost inaudibly, "Your mouth was hanging open like a pelican's. Again."

She pressed her lips together and steadfastly disregarded the distracting jolt his closeness and warm breath caused. He'd startled her. Nothing else.

What's a blasted pelican?

Something with a vast mouth, no doubt, but dancing naked atop hot coals was preferable to asking the behemoth to explain.

"What a rag-mannered boor you are to mention it, my lord."

Speaking under her breath and from the side of her mouth, she commanded her lips to curve congenially while examining her family and mentally cursing him to Hades.

For once, no one noticed their verbal sparring.

Looming several inches above her, Lord Leventhorpe's chest—a thick, wide wall of virile maleness—blocked her view. Tempted to shift away, she forced her feet to stay planted. He was the largest man she'd ever met, and as one of Heath's closest friends, she must learn to tolerate Lord Leventhorpe's intimidating presence. Surely sainthood and a seat at the Lord's Table awaited her if she managed the Herculean task.

The auburn-haired devil enjoyed provoking her, and like a nincompoop, she regularly succumbed to his goading. She normally possessed a level head, and that he should be the person to have her at sixes and sevens, exasperated her.

A growl of frustration formed in her throat, and she clenched her teeth and hands.

"Ravensdale, you have your hands full." Leventhorpe skirted her, giving a cynical twist of his shapely lips as he passed. "I would deem it the ultimate privilege to assist you with these exquisite ladies."

She didn't believe his sycophantic posturing for an instant. At Esherton, when he'd accused the Culpeppers of abducting Heath, she'd seen the real Lord Leventhorpe, and this fawning deference concealed a stone-hearted, grim-tempered cawker.

His penetrating gaze—as heated and blue as a cloudless noonday sky in August—probed hers as if he strove to read her mind and emotions. Most disconcerting, and none of his blasted business. Maddening how he scrambled her thoughts and agitated feelings she couldn't decipher.

A spurt of amusement lit his eyes, and she narrowed hers.

Stop staring, you oversized, handsome baboon.

Immediately, Lord Leventhorpe's expression became shuttered and inscrutable. He rubbed the side of his nose and canvassed the entry before offering an enigmatic half-smile. "If you need help escorting the ladies, Hawksworth and I would be honored to assist."

"Reverend Hawksworth is here too?" Blythe peered over her shoulder.

Yes, indeed. Grinning, Reverend Hawksworth wended his way through the throng.

Charming, witty, and the perfect gentleman, he rivaled the fair god who'd smiled at her earlier. She slanted Lord Leventhorpe a contemplative glance. How could such two startlingly dissimilar men—one angelic and one demonic—be Heath's closest friends?

Brette perked up, her cheeks pinkening and eyes sparkling when the cleric joined them. At Esherton Green, Blythe had suspected her cousin's interest in Reverend Hawksworth, and Brette's reaction tonight confirmed it.

Chuckling, he cut his jungle-eyed gaze to the gawkers surging from the ballroom. "I do believe a near insurrection is at hand. Arriving with five incomparables is hardly fair play, Raven. I expect histrionics, swooning, and apoplexy in record numbers this evening. Perchance a bit of fervent, and not altogether hallowed, petitioning of the Almighty as well."

Nodding at something the butler said, Heath grinned. "Ah, I never intended fair play. I would wager from the reaction I'm seeing, the *ton* will never be the same. What say you, Withers?"

"Indeed not, my lord." Something on the room's far side gripped the butler's attention, and his mouth tipped lower as his brows scaled the distance to his receding hairline.

A giggling young lady held the statue's appendage in the air, swinging it back and forth. Their ruddy-faced hostess, Lady Kattenby, tried to extricate herself from the oblivious dame grasping her arm.

Blaire and Blaike giggled until Brooke hushed them with a severe look. "Girls, unseemly behavior isn't humorous, and dangling *that* most certainly is not funny."

Actually, it rather was.

As were the guests' faces, especially the women, most of whom made no effort to avert their rapt gazes from the display.

"I beg your pardon, my lord." Withers gave Heath a brief bow. "I must see to Apollo's ill-used ... er ... limb at once."

Blythe hid a grin behind her fan.

Lord Leventhorpe, Heath, and Reverend Hawksworth burst out laughing.

"A limb's an exaggeration in my estimation." Heath's shoulders shook again.

Brooke tapped his arm with her fan. "Hush, darling. Remember the girls."

Withers marched to the ballroom's entrance and, after retrieving the length of marble, rather than discreetly concealing it in his fist or tucking it into his tailcoat pocket, reverently laid the member atop his flattened palm and strode to an abashed footman.

Gingerly taking the stone between his gloved forefinger and thumb, the mortified servant hustled from the entry, his ears tinged scarlet at the sniggering in his wake.

To stifle the laugh burbling behind her teeth, Blythe bit her lip.

"That's not something you see every day." A grin flashing in his eyes, the reverend extended his elbows to her and Brette.

A most unconventional man of God, to be sure. If Blythe recalled correctly, the vocation hadn't been his choosing. Something to do with the previous vicar, an uncle, eloping with a nun. Quite a scandal ensued.

"Shall we?" Reverend Hawksworth canted his head. "There mightn't be seats left. The benches and chairs tend to fill rather quickly, and there is quite a crush this evening."

Blythe released a relieved huff. Lord Leventhorpe wouldn't be her escort into the ballroom. She'd spent a lifetime wrangling her temper and unruly tongue into submission. Yet, thirty seconds with that abominable wretch shriveled her self-control to a puff of dust, and she became a razor-tongued shrew.

Lord Leventhorpe's impressive brows dove together and twitched before he resumed his normal austere mien and politely bent his arms for Blaire and Blaike.

What went on in that head of his?

Never mind. Blythe truly didn't want to know.

"Ladies, allow me to claim the first two sets, please." Reverend Hawksworth chatted amiably as he guided them to the only remaining seats, a partially occupied bench. He dashed Blythe a contrite smile. "And, Miss Brette, may I request the supper dance, as well?"

Ah, he returned Brette's regard. Her cousin would search far for a man as worthy as the handsome rector.

When Brette didn't immediately respond, Blythe slid her a questioning glance.

"Reverend, to be honest, I'm not sure what's acceptable. Perhaps we should wait until we are seated so that Heath or Brooke may advise me?" Brette procured a hesitant smile. "If they agree, I would enjoy a dance with you."

Strange. Why the reticence? True, Brette fretted about stirring a dust up, but Reverend Hawksworth obviously intrigued her.

Reverend Hawksworth's brows elevated several inches as he peered at the others trailing them through the horde. "I don't recall the last time I saw dancers missing steps to gawk at new arrivals." He gave a bemused shake of his head. "But then, I don't attend many gatherings. I only did tonight because Raven asked Leventhorpe and me to be on hand. Truthfully, I'm surprised Leventhorpe agreed. He loathes large gatherings and comes to Town during the Season for Parliament, not for the socializing."

Perhaps Blythe would be spared Lord Leventhorpe's company more than she had anticipated, if he didn't care for crowds.

Reverend Hawksworth gave Brette a conspiratorial half-wink. "I do believe your brother-in-law finally realized the furor introducing five diamonds of the first water would cause. Never been done before, that I'm aware."

The Adonis from the entry fell into step beside Blythe, and her stomach did that weird, quivery thing again. He was even more appealing than she'd first believed, and his eyes weren't brown at all, rather an unusual topaz with dark green flecks. A deep earthy tone circled his irises, explaining why his eyes appeared brown from a distance.

He flashed a rakish smile, revealing well-tended teeth.

Splendid. She couldn't abide poor hygiene.

"Hawksworth, I beg you. Introduce me to these charming ladies, so I might claim a dance with each." Though the Adonis included Brette in his appeal, his gaze never left Blythe, and the curving of his lips caused another unfamiliar jolt.

The reverend shook his head. "Too late, Burlington. I've already requested sets and the supper dance with Miss Brette." He slightly raised the arm her fingers lay upon. "And Ravensdale ought to make the introductions, not me."

Burlington—was he a mister? A Lord? Something else?—wrinkled his forehead in mock horror. "Troublesome etiquette rules." His brandy-tinted gaze sought Blythe's. "If Ravensdale agrees, would you favor me with the supper dance?"

A trifle forward, but ...

"I would like that." No feigning diffidence. He was an attractive man, and he'd captured her interest in the entry, something unanticipated, truth to tell. "I must confess, I don't claim a substantial appetite."

For years, the Culpeppers had survived on insufficient food, and although they had plenty to eat now, she couldn't manage generous portions. Given her height, she doubted she'd ever possess an enticingly rounded figure like the young ladies occupying the bench farther along. The figures of the older women with them had evolved into rotundness—not something Blythe worried about.

Once the rest of their group made it to the bench—Leventhorpe, a dark, menacing deity dwarfing everyone, his keen, raptor gaze combing the ballroom—Heath made quick work of the introductions.

Blythe's admirer was Mr. Courtland Burlington, the second son of the Earl of Lauderdale. No title, therefore no worries about a lowly gentlewoman aiming her sights too high.

Not that she'd set her cap for Mr. Burlington. Much too soon for that. This was her first assembly, after all. Nonetheless, he presented quite a dashing figure and, given the envious looks regularly flitting in his direction, much sought after by females.

"I'm delighted to make your acquaintance, Miss Culpepper." Mr. Burlington lifted her hand as he bowed, kissing the air above her fingers. A stickler for propriety or affecting courtly conduct? Would he mind awfully that she found decorum about as useful as a well-gnawed chicken bone?

Blythe half-anticipated a frisson or tremor to skitter along her spine as had occurred at Leventhorpe's touch, but Mr. Burlington's fingers pressing hers elicited nothing more thrilling than a mild, pleasant warmth.

Hmm. Disappointing.

Must have been nerves or repugnance that had induced her strong reaction to the cold marquis.

The plainer young lady of the nearby quartet grinned and waved, and Lord Leventhorpe responded with a cordial nod and a warm upturn of his mouth, earning him satisfied smiles from her companions before he angled away.

"My cousin, Francine Simmons, and her friends," he said to no one in particular, though his attention remained upon Blythe as she extricated her hand from Mr. Burlington's.

Miss Simmons leaned close, speaking to the sable-haired beauty beside her. The pretty girl's expression hardened, and she and the older dames—relatives, judging by the strong familial resemblance—pelted the Culpeppers with reproachful, gray-eyed glares.

Why?

As Blythe and the others conversed, the foursome brazenly eavesdropped, frequently dipping their heads together and whispering. A gentleman claimed the lovely girl for the next dance, and Miss Simmons, her shoulders slumped and countenance dejected, plucked the bench's braid edging, wistfully contemplating the dancers.

Prodding Blaike's side, Blaire whispered, "Look there."

"Good heavens." Blaike stared pointedly at two men striding their way.

"Hush," Brooke gently chastised behind her fan. "Whispering is vulgar and unkind. You are neither."

"Ravensdale." Hand extended, a man wearing army crimson, and bearing a fresh pinkish scar along his left cheek, approached their group accompanied by a—for lack of a better description—buccaneer.

Sporting a neat beard, and his ebony, shoulder-length hair tied with a black ribbon, the man appeared to have stepped straight off the deck of a privateer. Blythe expected to see a parade of barefoot, cutlass-bearing pirates behind him.

Heath, Lord Leventhorpe, and Reverend Hawksworth broke into exuberant grins. After much hearty handshaking, shoulder slapping, and laughing, Heath introduced the newcomers. The officer was Lieutenant Julian Drake, and the sharp-eyed, swarthy fellow, Oliver Whitehouse, captain of the *Sea Gypsy*.

Ah, a sea captain. And he appeared part gypsy too.

"Looks more like a pirate to me," Blaike murmured to her entranced twin.

Captain Whitehouse leveled her an indecipherable look. He'd heard her. Nonetheless, bold interest shone in his obsidian eyes.

"How fare you, my friend?" He touched Leventhorpe's arm and jutted his strong chin to indicate the other men. "It's been a good while since we gathered in one place."

Another attractive gentleman approached, his nose flattened peculiarly. He reeked of rosewater, and from his togs and elevated chin, Blythe would eat gravel if he wasn't a peer.

Every man's visage grew guarded, except Mr. Burlington's, and Lord Leventhorpe and Captain Whitehouse exchanged a speaking glance.

The newcomer's oily gaze slid over Blythe then her sisters and cousins, before lighting upon Lord Leventhorpe and turning antagonistic. "Yes. We haven't all been together since Leventhorpe shattered my nose in an unfair fight."

Fate cares not about schemes or plans, and oft' Fortune, not men, deserves credit for good and bad circumstances.
~ *Dignity and Decorum—The Genteel Lady's Guide to Practical Living*

2

Unfair fight, my arse.

"Phillips." Tristan managed not to snarl Seymour Phillips's name, though contempt riddled his tone, earning him a cocked brow from Blythe—*that is, Miss Culpepper*—her sooty-lashed eyes brimming with curiosity and a dab of laughter too.

She mocked him.

"You broke his nose? Like you broke Cousin Sheridan's? Do you make a habit of mashing faces, my lord?" At Phillips's brazen regard, her gaze wavered between him and Tristan, wariness replacing her inquisitiveness and spurt of amusement.

Not short on intelligence, by George. Miss Culpepper recognized a poltroon when she met one. Or possibly, it was Tristan who aroused her suspicion. Given their instant, mutual animosity, the latter seemed more likely, especially since he had broken Sheridan Gainsborough's nose when Gainsborough interfered with Ravensdale's wedding.

"Yes, I did. And no. I don't." Tristan refused to be baited, and her slightly rouged lips thinned a fraction, a mysterious glint shadowing her eyes. At least he assumed her mouth rouged. Too dewy and rosy to be natural, surely, unless she'd dined upon berries recently.

What kind?

A taste of her delicious mouth, made for hungry kisses and sensual smiles, would answer the question. A blast of sensation straight to his groin strangled his carnal musings.

What the hell is wrong with me, lusting after a woman who clearly loathes me?

Fiddling with her fan, she took Phillips's measure, toe to top before scooting Tristan a covert peek. Good manners prohibited her asking the how and why of his corking Phillips. Nonetheless, her expressive eyes fairly shouted for an answer.

How would she respond if he told her?

Well, you see, Miss Culpepper, it started with a pox-ridden whore, and Hawksworth, the reluctant vicar.

"Phillips, when did you return to England?" Ravensdale's question broke the weighty silence and wrenched Tristan abruptly back to the bustling ballroom.

Flouting propriety and drumming his fingertips along the bench, Ravensdale made no effort to introduce Phillips to the ladies. Brilliant strategy upon Raven's part. Without an introduction, Phillips couldn't address the women directly. When he'd married Brooke, Ravensdale had vowed to protect the Culpepper ladies, and his decorum breach proved his seriousness.

Phillips hauled his appreciative gaze from the women, pique sharpening his angular face. "A month ago. And I'm glad I did, else I would have missed this," he gestured to the exquisite blondes, his hint as brazen as a skirtless harlot, "delightful spectacle."

Still not getting an introduction, you bugger.

Phillips offered his usual suave smile.

No Culpepper responded with anything more enthusiastic than a placid gaze. Not even the twins—the youngest, most impressionable of the lot.

Uncanny how two people could look exactly alike. Dressed in identical gowns except for the color, he had no idea who was Blaire and who was Blaike. How old were they again? Scratching his eyebrow, he wracked his brain. Had anyone ever told him? How old was Blythe, for that matter?

She observed Phillips, a marginal pucker between her winged brows.

As if sensing Tristan's scrutiny, Blythe swiftly schooled her features into blandness once more while unfurling her fan. However, she couldn't conceal the spark glinting in her iris eyes. A sapphire-violet fire, waiting to be fanned into flames, smoldered below her composed surface. He'd seen the firestorm more than once—truthfully, he'd caused a conflagration or two—and found her temper invigorating.

How perverse.

A knowing glance passed between Lady Ravensdale and Brette before their nonchalant gazes returned to Phillips as well.

Yes, by God. All five were on to old Phillips and his reptilian wiles.

Good thing too.

He'd fathered more than one by-blow, and suggestions had circulated for years that the serving wenches hadn't willingly engaged in the dalliances. No doubt his female servants lamented his return to London. *Le beau monde* had been blessed with his absence for two—or was it three?—years while the cull toured the continent before journeying to India. At least that was the drivel his sire, the viscount, spread about Town.

Tristan didn't believe a syllable, especially after a highborn young woman became scarce and later hastily married an elderly sot before giving birth to a daughter a mere four months after the nuptials. Tattle had it, Phillips had ravished her.

The woman's father, the Duke of Coventry, had threated to call Phillips out, hence the cur's abrupt departure from England. Awfully convenient, Coventry's dying recently, paving the way for Phillips to scuttle home and muck about in the dank dens he favored. Rumors had circulated that Phillips's father, the doting and blind-to-his-son's-faults Viscount Rotherton, had greased more than one fist to assure his son escaped justice.

Phillips resembled an enormous cockroach—Tristan's nostrils quivered—right down to the sour smell that copious quantities of cologne failed to completely conceal.

"Memories are peculiar things, aren't they, Whitehouse? They're quite dependent upon the perceptions of the person recollecting." Reverend Hawksworth lifted a short, blond hair from his forearm, inclining his head toward Phillips.

Perturbed, Phillips pressed his lips into a pout, his regard of the Culpeppers bordering upon lascivious.

"I seem to recall that after insulting Leventhorpe, Phillips took the first swing." Hand straddling his hip, Hawk regarded Whitehouse.

"Aye, that's my memory as well. What say you, Drake?" Dislike deepened the lines framing the captain's mouth and feathering the corners of his eyes. He flexed his fingers near his waist as if instinctively reaching for a cutlass.

Hands clasped behind his back, Drake nodded, his eyes flinty. "Indeed. That's exactly how I remember it too."

"You were ape-drunk that night, Hawksworth. How could *you* remember anything?" Phillips's mouth slid into a sideways sneer as he bared his craven talons. "Isn't drunkenness one of the sins you preach against?"

Miss Brette's eyes rounded, and her mouth parted as she and the Culpeppers, plus Lady Ravensdale, swung their attention to Hawksworth's flushed face.

Had Phillips forgotten Hawk's pugilist skills? Even a man of God possessed limited patience. From his sharply drawn brows and balled fists, Hawksworth might be near his snapping point.

How would Phillips like his nose shattered again? Or mayhap his jaw this go round? Hawk could easily do either.

"Stubble it, Phillips." Tristan's warning met with an unrepentant, cocky grin.

The one time Hawk had gotten pished, and for a bloody good reason too, and Phillips, the colossal arse, had to humiliate him for it. Typical.

Blythe speared Phillips a scorching glower, muttering something inaudible beneath her breath and behind her fan which sounded suspiciously like cod's head or codpiece.

Knowing her, probably the latter. Tristan rather appreciated the comparison.

"Gentlemen, this discussion is wholly inappropriate, especially with young ladies present." Lady Ravensdale stood and motioned to the younger women, succinctly ending the unpleasantness. "I'll thank you to cease or continue it elsewhere. Besides, I should like to dance with my husband since I haven't had the opportunity. Blythe, would you please act as chaperone until I return?"

"Of course." Blythe offered Mr. Burlington a penitent smile, and annoyance poked Tristan's ribs. Hard. She'd never been half as accommodating or agreeable to him.

What did he care?

A more provoking, outspoken virago he'd never had the ill-fortune to meet. His embittered mother notwithstanding, God rest her tormented soul.

Truthfully, being the primary beneficiary of Blythe's dislike grated.

In response to Burlington's proprietary smile, she curved her lips, her cheeks acquiring the same flushed glow as her mouth.

Perhaps she wasn't that perceptive after all. True, Burlington was a pleasant enough fellow, but as many young blades were wont to do, he generally treated women as passing amusements, something to trifle with and conquer until another caught his fancy. Nevertheless, women had tamed rakehells far worse than him.

Tristan gave a mental shrug. No concern of his.

He'd been asked to help a friend, and that was the only reason he'd accepted the Kattenbys' invitation tonight. Suppressing a yawn, he perused the ballroom, still humming about the Culpeppers.

Bloody insane. That's what Raven is.

One or two beauties might have been manageable, but five? Humor jerked the corners of Tristan's mouth. His friend would rue the day he'd ever entertained this hair-brained notion. Wouldn't surprise him if Raven wound up bald as a billiard by Season's end, and he had nice hair too.

Set the *le beau monde* upon its arse, indeed.

"I shall save the next set for you, Mr. Burlington." The beatific smile Blythe bestowed upon Burlington squeezed Tristan's lungs.

Damnation. And double damn that he'd noticed.

"That won't be necessary, Blythe. You may dance this set." Though Ravensdale's lips slanted, no humor glinted in the astute gaze he raked over Phillips. "Whitehouse and Drake, I would appreciate you escorting a twin onto the dance floor, and I've already given Hawk permission to dance with Miss Brette."

Well done. Tristan indulged in a gloating grin.

Ravensdale had snuffed Phillips's intent to beg an introduction and a dance with one of the sisters or cousins faster than a pinched candlewick. He wouldn't be adding one of their number to his list of conquests.

"I would beg you save me the supper dance then, Miss Culpepper, since I won't have the pleasure of a dancing this set." Tristan couldn't resist goading Phillips, knowing full well Ravensdale would accept Tristan's request as speedily as he'd spurned Phillips's.

Ravensdale's stunned expression was reflected in the other astounded gazes whipping to Tristan.

Hell.

Ignoring the impulse would have been wiser except he'd agreed to dance with each Culpepper. Damn awkward, this doing the pretty balderdash. No more favors for friends. Tristan suspected Ravensdale intended to utilize him, and perhaps poor Hawk, as surrogates to help chaperone and manage the goddesses the entire season.

Not bloody well likely. Tristan truly couldn't abide crowds for extended periods. An hour at most, and he made for the exit.

A disgusting memory assailed him, rendering him mute and immobile for a moment. Swallowing a surge of nausea, he shook his head to dispel the buzzing in his ears and the sudden onslaught of dizziness.

What had they been discussing?

The supper dance.

Had Blythe responded? "Miss Culpepper?"

What else could he say? He hadn't a clue whether she had answered.

Her lively gaze assessing, Blythe slanted her head the merest bit, the amber gems entwined in her curls winking under the chandelier's radiance. "I'm sorry, Lord Leventhorpe, I already promised the supper dance to Mr. Burlington."

"Perhaps a waltz later, then." Tristan flexed his fingers against the desire to wipe the delighted smile from Burlington's face.

Give over, Trist. You'd have the same smirk on your face if she'd said yes to you.

He would've?

The awareness gave him pause.

He would.

Only because it withered his ballocks to have coxcombs like Burlington best him.

"Blythe." Subtle censure tinted Lady Ravensdale's tone. "You've other unclaimed dances."

Tristan almost stuck a finger in his ear and wiggled it to make sure he'd heard correctly. Had she encouraged her cousin to dance with him? Some turnabout there.

"I shall save you the last waltz, Lord Leventhorpe." A corpse displayed more genuine enthusiasm upon being laid in a coffin. Blythe looped her hand through Burlington's elbow and glided away, laughing at something he murmured to her. She'd never appeared more vivacious or beautiful.

Giving Phillips a contemptuous glare—and hopefully a parson's curse damning him to purgatory—Hawksworth offered Miss Brette his arm, and they set out after the others.

A bevy of whispers behind fans and gloved hands trailed the Culpeppers' progress. Gentlemen peered with brazen interest through their quizzing glasses, while ill-disguised envy pinched many ladies' features. A goodly number of friendly smiles greeted them too.

Yes, Raven had stirred a beehive, and when bees are riled, someone is sure to get stung.

Tristan searched for a servant. After that exchange he welcomed a glass of punch. No. He really wanted a finger or two of whisky, but he was a quarter way to bosky already.

"Seems like you and I have been found wanting, Leventhorpe." Phillips glared after the departing couples.

First sting went to Phillips. That bounder could expect many more sharp pricks from Raven and the Culpeppers.

"Don't include me in your company. I spent several days as a guest of the Culpeppers at their country estate." Vast exaggeration there. He'd arrived at Esherton Green looking for Ravensdale and had refused to leave without his friend. And calling their malodorous dairy farm and ramshackle house an estate was equivalent to calling the Prince Regent a Devil's Acre beggar.

"Awful uppity for country wenches." Phillips scratched his prominent chin. "Though I wouldn't mind sampling their charms. I admit a penchant for blondes. That one in yellow is a prime article and seems the most spirited. I've found that trait commonly carries into bedding the gel."

A fury-induced haze momentarily stole Tristan's tongue.

"Makes for a delicious shagging." His voice deepened by lust, Phillips licked his lips. "Especially if they resist."

Would the House of Lords bring charges against Tristan if he disposed of Phillips once and for all? Probably. Even if they celebrated the cur's demise with fireworks and Champagne afterward. Subduing his wrath, he drew his spine upright, fully aware his immense size daunted shorter men.

He scowled down at Phillips. "Unless you want me to break your nose again, I suggest you take your leave. *Now.* And stay away from the Culpeppers—"

"Tristan, dearest." His cousin's singsong voice beset him.

He speared a gaze heavenward, begging God for patience as she, no doubt prompted by her domineering companion, Rosemary Sanford, glided his way. He'd exhausted his reserves of forbearance by not pummeling Phillips and had scant left to cushion his terse response to Francine.

"You were saying, Leventhorpe?" His lips skewed mockingly, Phillips folded his arms.

Francine seized Tristan's forearm. "Tristan, I told Rosemary you would dance with her this evening since you rudely left the last ball without doing as you'd promised."

He hadn't promised.

Francine had pleaded with him to dance with her friend, and he'd said he'd consider it. He'd done so, contemplating the notion for a lengthy two seconds before deciding he'd prefer to go home and cut his already groomed toenails.

Why Francine kowtowed to the likes of Rosemary Sanford, he couldn't imagine. Though irrefutably beautiful, Miss Sanford was an inconsiderate friend, and he'd bet Bristledale Court and his mother's many glittery baubles that she had manipulated Francine to get to him.

That woman hunted for a title this Season, or he was a twiddle poop.

At eight and twenty, his poor, spinster cousin desperately strove for acceptance and regularly made a cake of herself to please her scheming friend.

That nettled more than Miss Sanford's designs on the marquisate.

"Since Leventhorpe is escorting Miss Sanford, may I request the next set, Miss Simmons?" Phillips extended his arm, challenging Tristan to say no.

Phillips clearly baited Tristan, and as tempted as he was to tell Francine not to, she probably hadn't enjoyed more than a dance or two this evening. Most assemblies, she didn't dance except with Tristan. She'd gaze longingly at laughing couples while huddled with the other plain wallflowers.

If she could abide Phillips's sweet and sour odor for the dance's duration, Tristan wouldn't begrudge her a few moments of happiness.

Francine colored, her cheeks two candy-apple red blotches, and grasped Phillips's elbow a mite too exuberantly. "I'd be delighted, Mr. Phillips."

Smiling coquettishly, Miss Sanford blinked her big, brown calf-eyes at him. "You wouldn't snub me in full view of the Kattenbys' guests, would you, my lord?

The wise woman recognizes and
disdains the schemes of pretentious social climbers.
~*Dignity and Decorum—The Genteel Lady's Guide to Practical Living*

3

After wandering down a corridor, Blythe slowly ambled to a stop. This wasn't right. Nothing seemed the least familiar.

Botheration.

She searched the passageway behind her. After leaving the lady's retiring room, she'd apparently taken a wrong corridor. Or two. She had best retrace her steps before she found herself completely turned round.

She possessed a dismal sense of direction. If she ever found herself in the heart of London without an escort, she would wander about in circles for a month. Then again, it might take them that long to find her in this astonishingly vast and complex house.

The next dance belonged to Lord Leventhorpe. She smiled, a trifle impishly. Perhaps her conscience had deliberately misguided her to avoid what was sure to be a trying half an hour. She'd be obligated to bear his touch and converse with him the whole while.

Considering their longest prior communication hadn't been above five minutes, they might scratch one another's eyes out before the music ended. Lifting her skirt to enable her to walk quicker, she grinned. Mayhap she ought to remove her gloves. Her nails were longer. He, on the other hand, was much taller.

Truthfully, her preoccupation leading to her becoming lost could be blamed on pleasurable musings about Mr. Burlington.

Her cotillion with him had been lovely. An excellent dancer, he possessed a ready wit and a readier smile. More importantly, he made her comfortable. They'd conversed and laughed easily, and when their dance ended, Blythe admitted she'd been startled and not a little disappointed. She'd never expected to meet a gentleman of his caliber this early on, and he'd quite assailed her logic and senses.

Usually a pragmatic woman, her woolgathering was as foreign and distasteful as those strange fishy-smelling black beads their hostess had served at a dinner party three nights ago.

Blythe had taken a spin around the ballroom with several distinguished gentlemen. And she'd refused an equal number of disappointed beaux's requests, because she'd already promised the remainder to others. Mr. Burlington's had been the most enjoyable by far.

In his company, she forgot the crowd and hubbub, and she happily anticipated the supper dance and dining with him. Her next partner didn't rouse the same cheery expectation.

Whatever had possessed Lord Leventhorpe to ask for a dance? And a waltz, no less.

More importantly, whyever had she agreed?

He'd stirred her sympathy, she grudgingly admitted. That knowledge practically sent her into an apoplexy. A shiver raised her flesh, and she briskly rubbed her arms above her elbow-length gloves. Gads, just thinking about Lord Leventhorpe agitated her.

Two corridors intersected, and she paused to collect her bearings.

Right or left?

Ah, the marble-topped mahogany table with the heinous vase she'd seen before.

Now I remember.

Whisking along, her slippers silent upon the burgundy Aubusson runner, Blythe passed the table. Another two turns, and she'd be at the landing. She held her breath, straining to hear the music as she marched along.

A quadrille. Not too late after all, devil it.

Lord Leventhorpe would have his troublesome waltz. If she found her way downstairs again.

When she'd refused him the supper dance, she'd glimpsed something startling in the depths of his eyes. So staggering, in truth, that she'd almost gone onto tiptoe and pulled his head down to examine their blue depths closer.

Vulnerability was the last emotion she'd ever expected to see. *Ever*. He hid it well, which piqued her curiosity. What caused a man as outwardly frosty as a winter gale to disguise shyness?

Blythe loved a riddle, and Leventhorpe, it seemed, was more than he presented. "Now to uncover why." His discomfiture shadowed eyes floated before her, and she quirked her lips. "He's an enigma, to be sure."

Head bowed, she toyed with her pendant, deep in reverie as she approached a black-velvet-curtained alcove. At the corner, she bumped into a man. Smelling of rosewater and something else, a peculiar tangy scent—stale sweat, perchance?—he steadied her with surprisingly strong arms, given their wiriness.

Drat.

Mr. Phillips, another inscrutable man. In a crafty, scheming fashion rather than a mysterious, intriguing one. "Do you usually wander corridors talking to yourself?" His languid gaze slithered over her. "An unwise habit for a beauty such as yourself."

"Talking to myself is unwise?" Blythe raised a dubious brow. His lewd implication hadn't escaped her, but she wouldn't give him the satisfaction of acknowledging his crassness.

"No, I meant—" Mr. Phillips smiled and loosened his grip, though he didn't release her. "It's of no import. I believe you may have crushed my quizzing glass."

"I beg your pardon." Barely subduing the urge to recoil and hurry to the retiring room to scrub her arms where his cold, damp fingers touched her, Blythe disengaged herself and stepped backward. She hadn't hit him hard enough to break anything. "I'll replace the piece if it's damaged."

He would have to prove it first. Doubtful he owned a quizzing glass, and if he had one in his possession tonight, he'd tucked it safely away.

The lovely woman she'd seen on the other bench earlier emerged from the alcove, a syrupy smile bending her mouth as the curtain fell into place.

Hmm, interesting. Had he come from there too? Why the need for the lowered curtain?

A *tête-à-tête*?

Swathed in haughtiness, the woman swept to Mr. Phillips's side. "How clumsy of you, though to be expected from a clodpoll newly introduced to Polite Society."

Mayhap she'd like to see what else clodpolls were capable of. How much did she value her hair? Blythe could sheer a sheep in fifteen minutes. She would have those gorgeous coffee-colored locks off in ten seconds.

Much as she would've liked to give the chit a verbal set down, the music below had ceased.

She must hurry, or she would miss the waltz with his lordship. A minute ago, she'd been half-wishing that very thing, and now she was quite desperate to make sure she didn't. Mimicking the woman's lofty mien, Blythe lifted her chin and examined the passage beyond them. "As we've not been introduced, I find it presumptuous to assume you know anything about me."

"Everyone here tonight knows *who* the Culpepper interlopers are." The brunette's retort rang harsh and venom-laced.

They did? How peculiar. Had Society nothing better to occupy their consideration? That was what came of being idle and wealthy. And bitchy.

"Miss Sanford, please allow me the honor of making the introductions." Mr. Phillips offered a ghost of a bow. "Rosemary Sanford, may I present...?" He peered expectantly at Blythe, his lips edging upward into what he, no doubt, considered a charming smile. He resembled an overly sleek, grinning Cheshire cat. "I'm afraid I don't know your given name, Miss Culpepper."

And it's going to stay that way. I'm not completely ignorant of social graces.

"I believe it's proper to wait to be introduced, is it not? And that same decorum prohibits me from speaking further to you." She inclined her head. "If you'll excuse me, I've promised Lord Leventhorpe the next dance."

The rude, inarticulate sound Miss Sanford released could only be described as a hiss of displeasure. Eyes narrowed to wrathful slits, she stared down her nose at Blythe, or tried to. Rather awkward and comical when Blythe stood several inches taller.

"*You're* dancing a waltz with the marquis?" Miss Sanford's mouth curled into a full sneer.

"Yes. He's a *very close* family friend." Not quite the truth, but the jealous chit needn't know that. Besides, Miss Sanford had stood up with his lordship already. Blythe had seen her pressing into him, a seductress's smile slanting her flawless mouth. "I believe I spotted you dancing with him earlier? Why, did he not request a waltz with you also? How utterly disappointed you must be."

Truly wicked of Blythe to taunt, but Miss Sanford rose to the bait readily.

Another disgruntled sound echoed in her throat, and Miss Sanford lifted her fan threateningly.

Did she think to dictate who Lord Leventhorpe danced with? If they were more than mere acquaintances, her vexation might have merit, but on her first night amongst the upper crust, Blythe had no idea if Miss Sanford was a particular favorite of Lord Leventhorpe's. The chit certainly showed possessive tendencies and a dismal temper too.

Lord Leventhorpe hadn't seemed particularly enthralled with her company, but given his skill at concealing his emotions, his lack of exuberance didn't reveal much.

Francine Simmons emerged from the retiring room, a confused sulk marring her forehead. "There you are, Rosemary. I thought you were still inside. You left without telling me? I was waiting in the adjoining chamber as you asked me to. Did I misunderstand?"

"I needed to speak with Mr. Phillips, and I don't have to tell you my every movement, Francine. I declare, you are positively suffocating at times. I don't know how I abide you." With that snide comment, Miss Sanford gripped Mr. Phillips's arm and sallied forth, hauling him toward the stairs.

Toss pots.

He glanced behind him, giving Blythe another disturbing smile. Something queer about that man. Something uncanny—almost eerie or treacherous—in his eyes. She'd hate to bump into him alone in a secluded spot. Why, even now, with other women present, her skin tried to scamper off her bones and cower in the alcove's dark corner.

A sniffle drew her attention to the dejected woman hunched beside her.

"I don't know why I tolerate her." Miss Simmons rubbed her red-rimmed eyes, worsening their appearance. "On a charitable day she's selfish and inconsiderate ... and entirely thoughtless."

"I'm sorry." Oh, to be able to shave that snotty-nosed miss's head bare as a hog's bristly behind. "Is there anything I can do to help?"

"No. I'm just overwrought. I shall be fine in a moment or two." Miss Simmons shook her head and produced a despairing little laugh. "I have fragile nerves, Rosemary says."

Hmm, with that creature for a friend, the Lord himself would require a calming draught. An immense one.

"I'm Blythe Culpepper." Offering a sunny smile, Blythe touched Miss Simmons's elbow. So much for propriety. Blythe fished her handkerchief from her bodice. "Here. Dry your eyes, and I shall walk to the ballroom with you. Who are you here with?"

Miss Simmons wiped her face then blew her nose. "I came with Rosemary, her mother, and grandmother. I live alone, you see. Well, I have a small staff. My parents are dead, and Tristan, that is, Lord Leventhorpe, is my only living relation. We're second cousins." Melancholy tinged her voice. "Rosemary permits me to accompany her to social gatherings as long as I do as she bids."

I'll bet she does.

She patted another tear leaking from the corner of her eye.

"You live alone? Why don't you live with Lord Leventhorpe?" How could he permit this obviously lonely woman to reside by herself?'

"Oh, Tristan has offered, many times, but I want my independence. Mama and Papa left me enough to be comfortable if I economize, and if I lived in the country with him— Oh, dear. I oughtn't to have shared that. Utterly gauche." Her face blooming with color, she hunched a shoulder. "I hold a trifling hope that I might meet a gentleman who would take me to wife. Silly, I know."

Pained rejection reduced her voice to a whisper with her last words, and Blythe's heart wrenched. Mere weeks ago, her circumstances had been desperate and seemingly impossible, until Heath had rescued them. Who would rescue Francine?

Lord Leventhorpe?

Perhaps a word in his ear was in order, though he didn't seem the sort to readily take suggestions. If intervening helped this pitiable woman, the effort was worth annoying his lordship.

"A lovely woman such as yourself, Miss Simmons, should continue to harbor that wonderful dream."

"Thank you. You are most kind." At Blythe's compliment, Miss Simmons's mouth formed a surprised O and color dashed her face again. "Rosemary said beautiful women like you ..." Cheeks deepening to crimson, she cast her gaze to the floor. "Never mind. I'm sure she is mistaken."

Blythe had a pretty fair notion what Miss Sanford had told Miss Simmons.

Miss Simmons's possessed a good complexion, her gray-blue eyes held keen intelligence, and her hair shimmered with the same umber shades as Lord Leventhorpe's. If she wore the right colors and styles—not like the drab oatmeal-colored sack she had on—arranged her striking hair differently, and added the faintest touch of cosmetics, she would be quite attractive. Her self-confidence was an entirely other matter.

Perhaps Blythe and the other Culpeppers might assist in that regard. And keeping Miss Simmons away from that self-serving Sanford banshee seemed the obvious place to start.

The prelude's first few notes drifted up from below, and Blythe quickened her pace. During the dance would be the perfect time to broach the subject of his lordship's cousin.

"Lord Leventhorpe doesn't stay with you when he comes to town?" Probably had a house. Bachelors didn't like the restrictions of living with female relatives. At least her nefarious cousin Sheridan never had. Thank God the Chancery Court had appointed Heath their guardian, ridding the Culpeppers of ever having to deal with Sheridan again.

"No, Tristan has lodgings at White's. He quite loathes London and never stays at his house on Mayfair. I'm not sure he even maintains staff there. He only ventures to Town for important Parliamentary matters." Brushing a tendril away from her eye, Miss Simmons gave a sad smile. "You needn't pity me. I don't mind being alone. I have my charitable meetings and Church. And every now and again, I receive an invitation to call."

When was the last time anyone had listened to the poor dear? Blythe smiled tolerantly as Miss Simmons prattled on, oblivious to the pair of ladies approaching from the other direction. Stepping to the side, Blythe waited for them to pass and answered their friendly smiles with her own.

"And I enjoy reading. Have you been to The Temple of the Muses, Miss Culpepper? Such a wonderful bookshop. Oh, and I quite adore riding. Tristan takes me two or three times a week when he's here. He is a dear underneath his aloof manner. His mother was dotty, you see, and his father ..." Cutting Blythe a hesitant, sidelong glance, she chewed her lower lip indecisively.

"His father?"

Miss Simmons was a store of useful information. It gushed from her like milk from a cow's full teat. There was much more to the reserved marquis then Blythe had imagined. Not that she'd imagined anything about him, of course, other than uncharitable thoughts at Esherton Green when she'd pondered if he'd docked his devil's tail, how often he filed the horns his hair concealed, and how he managed to shove his cloven hooves into boots.

Miss Simmons exhaled a hefty breath and scooted closer. "The former Lord Leventhorpe was a lecherous, depraved scoundrel." Her voice soft and low, she nervously peered around. "Or so I've heard whispered. No one tells a lady anything directly, for fear of our tender sensibilities—most irritating and utterly ridiculous—but for years I've overheard snatches about his deplorable behavior."

Splendid. Miss Simmons had a fiery streak buried in her. Though how could she not when she shared Leventhorpe's blood?

Blythe looped her hand through Miss Simmons's crooked elbow. "I have two sisters, and we have lived with our two cousins since I was eight. The five of us get along famously, but sometimes I crave time alone."

"Miss Culpepper, would you ...?" Miss Simmons screwed up her courage and blurted, "Would you come for tea? Your sisters and cousins, too?"

Evidently accustomed to rejection, her eyes round and anxious, she fiddled with the folds of her fan.

Blythe grinned and nodded. "If you agree to call me Blythe."

"And you must call me Francine." They reached the staircase's bottom. "I was named after Tristan's mother."

Arm in arm, they entered the ballroom, and coppery hair, a head taller than the rest of the guests, snagged her attention. Arms crossed and his countenance one of polite boredom, Lord Leventhorpe leaned a shoulder against an arched windowsill and perused the room. From the black of his cutaway coat and breeches, to the gold and burgundy of his waistcoat, he blended with the decor.

His languid gaze roved the entrance, and he straightened upon spying her.

An amiable smile brightened his face, his attention dipping to Francine before swooping back to Blythe. His lips bent more as he strode in their direction, moving with the lithe, natural grace of an athlete, his long legs rapidly covering the distance.

Had he watched for her?

Upon reaching them, he executed an exaggerated courtier's bow, and Francine giggled.

Even Blythe's lips curved at his silliness. She'd not have believed him capable of the overplayed gallantry.

"Trist, you're uncommonly chipper." Francine touched his arm, peering at him hopefully "Did you enjoy your dance with Rosemary, then?"

Blythe quashed her irritation. It would take time to wean Francine from her dependency upon Miss Sanford's self-serving approval.

"It was unremarkable." Though he answered Francine, his attention remained upon Blythe.

Francine's face fell, her earlier buoyancy evaporating. "Oh. I'd hoped ... Never mind."

He chucked her chin. "But, my dear, I saved the supper dance for you. Now tell me. What have you two ladies been up to?"

"You did? The supper dance, truly?" Francine beamed once more. "Blythe ... I mean Miss Culpepper, has been most kind and graciously consented to come for tea."

Goodness. Miss Simmons's emotions vacillated hot and cold.

Lord Leventhorpe's chestnut brows shot skyward. "Indeed. Might I join you?"

Francine's jaw slackened, and she blinked, rather like a confused owl. "Of course. Why, I believe I shall ask the Culpeppers to call. And Reverend Hawksworth. He's always kind. Oh, and the Wimpletons, of course." She glanced around. "I must find something to write on. Please excuse me." She hustled off, a plump brown wren, decidedly cheerier than she had been upstairs.

"What have you done to my cousin?" Extending his elbow, Lord Leventhorpe stared after her retreating form. "I don't recall when I've seen her that animated." His intrigued gaze dipped to Blythe's, and a sensation much like warm silk caressed her. "Thank you. She needs kind friends."

"She's sweet. I'm going to speak with Brooke about taking her under our wing." Blythe regarded him candidly. "If you're amenable to the suggestion."

"Miss Culpepper, I would be immensely grateful."

To her surprise, they'd reached the dance floor. Why, if they continued to speak of Francine, the waltz might be bearable after all.

"I bumped into Mr. Phillips upstairs. I believe he'd been sequestered in an alcove with Miss Sanford. She left Francine in the ladies retiring room, and spoke rather unkindly to her."

"No surprise there. Miss Sanford's friendship with my cousin is prompted by ulterior motives." An elusive emotion shadowed his lordship's eyes, deepening the blue to cerulean. "Phillips wasn't forward with you, was he? He's ..." He bent his head as they took their place upon the floor. "He's a disreputable sort."

His concern surprised and touched her. Perhaps Brooke was right, and Lord Leventhorpe possessed a heart after all. "I gathered as much. He attempted to extract my given name. I refused."

The waltz began, and Blythe dipped into a curtsy as his lordship bowed, his unusual lion's head stickpin in the folds of his cravat catching her eye. Its ruby eyes and diamond mouth twinkled in the incandescent light. A family heirloom?

Stepping into his embrace wasn't what Blythe had anticipated either. Though not as light on his feet as Mr. Burlington, Lord Leventhorpe proved a superb dancer, especially for such a towering man. She frequently stood taller than men and quite liked having to look upward to meet his eyes.

Mr. Burlington had been on eye level with her.

So?

Like the muscular statues in the entry, his lordship's shoulder was thick and rounded, the sinewy flesh flexing beneath her fingertips. What other parts of his anatomy might be as generous? Heat stole up her cheeks, and her breathing sputtered for a moment.

Oh, for the love of God, Blythe. Stop.

Of a slimmer build, Mr. Burlington had been solid, but didn't boast the marquis's bulging physique.

Nothing wrong with that. He wasn't scrawny or twitchy like Mr. Phillips, repulsive man.

She and Lord Leventhorpe danced well together, their forms nicely proportioned. As they rose and fell to the orchestra's strains, his lordship's subtle scent wafted to her. Swaying in his arms, she took a deep breath. In addition to his usual sandalwood, Blythe detected cloves and fresh linen. And perhaps a hint of brandy?

Mr. Burlington's cologne had been musky.

Both smelled pleasant, yet distinctly different, like the men themselves.

Stop comparing them, for pity's sake.

Lord Leventhorpe fell silent once their dance began, and the delight of being held in his strong embrace was unexpected and disconcerting. A month ago, she'd have believed herself dicked in the nob for entertaining such an absurd notion as enjoying a waltz with him.

Did his thoughts run parallel to hers, confusion meshed with pleasure? She entertained no misconceptions about his prior sentiments toward her.

Blythe slanted her head, and her gaze collided with his half-open sapphire eyes, the tips of his lashes feathered auburn. She stumbled, mashing his toes.

Had he observed her while they circled the floor?

The gentle upward sweep of his mouth sent a frisson to the tips of her toes, and she missed another step. So much for confidence in her dance skills.

He drew her infinitesimally closer, though surely only because of her momentary clumsiness.

She ought to object, but her tongue seemed content to stay silent.

Say something.

"Francine says you take her riding."

His attention dropped to Blythe's mouth before he nodded. "Yes. When I'm able. Because we prefer the park to ourselves, I collect her at seven o'clock."

The music ended, and after a hesitant moment, he released her and gave a short bow.

Well, that hadn't been unpleasant at all.

Blythe curtsied then accepted his arm as she searched amongst the crush for her family. Encountering several hastily averted, speculative gazes, she fought a smile.

Quite a number of busybodies in attendance.

His lordship escorted her to their bench, albeit by a circuitous route. "If you would like to join us, I'm sure Francine would be delighted."

At the nearness of his mouth to her ear, Blythe gave a start. He seemed particularly fond of doing that.

"Alas, I fear I don't ride sidesaddle. I never learned how. There wasn't a need at Esherton Green, nor much opportunity with an old nag fit only for our dogcart." She pulled a face and gestured with her fan. "But I think we must learn now. It's expected, isn't it?"

"Usually, not always. I don't think anyone should be forced to do something they find objectionable." A peculiar inflection entered his voice, and a flash of pain glinted in his eyes for an instant.

With considerable effort, she dragged her gaze from his and located her family.

Mr. Burlington waited with Brooke and Heath. The girls' escorts must have already claimed them for the supper dance. Unaccustomed to dancing all evening, Blythe's feet had grown sore, and she welcomed the opportunity to sit for a while.

As if reluctant to relinquish her, Lord Leventhorpe slowed his pace. "Miss Culpepper, I would be happy to teach you to ride sidesaddle. If you would like to learn."

The man was full of surprises tonight. What next?

A warbling love sonnet for a shy wallflower?

A race through The Green Park in his underthings?

No, he was too taciturn for either, but his unexpected offer touched her.

"You have a sweet-tempered mare and a sidesaddle tucked in your London mews, my lord?" She wasn't going to learn to stay balanced atop that ridiculous contraption while seated astride a giant of a horse. Men should be made to ride on the stupid thing since they insisted ladies do so. No, a sedate pony or donkey would do perfectly until she mastered the skill. "I cannot conceive of you seated upon either. I've seen that immense, russet brute you ride. That beast looks to be descended from a mythological creature."

She grinned at his flummoxed expression. He didn't know she jested. Lord Leventhorpe was too serious by far.

"I raised Bucephalus from a foal." He summoned a grin and scratched his nose. "Buce is named after Alexander the Great's gargantuan steed, said to have had an immense head."

"A most fitting name." They had nearly reached the others. "You've other horseflesh in London too?"

"I have several horses and carriages at a local livery. Raven asked me to let him know if I spotted horseflesh appropriate for women at Tattersalls, and last week, a brilliant mare caught my eye. Perhaps you'd care to accompany me to the auction tomorrow to view the mare?"

And now an offer of an outing? Blythe rather liked this Lord Leventhorpe.

"I'd like to, and the others may want to attend also. That way we can see if the mare suits before Heath purchases her. Is it permissible? I didn't think women were allowed."

"If you are in my and Ravensdale's company, it's acceptable." Lord Leventhorpe lifted a shoulder. "If he doesn't purchase the mare, I shall. She's a rare beauty sporting a champagne coat with a creamy white mane and tail."

"Oh, she sounds gorgeous. Heath has suggested we wait until we return to the country to learn to ride, but, I confess, I crave the outdoors and would adore early morning jaunts. I used to take a lengthy walk with Freddy at dawn each day."

He slanted his brow. "Never had a beast detest me more than that aged, gone-to-fat corgi."

"Brooke thinks your cologne set the dog against you at Esherton. A man wearing a similar fragrance abused him. At the end, Freddy warmed to you." She dropped her hand as they reached the bench. She'd like the feel of his solid forearm flexing beneath her fingertips. "Brooke, Lord Leventhorpe has generously offered to teach us to ride sidesaddle."

An exuberant grin lit Mr. Burlington's face. "One of my greatest pleasures is riding, and I would enjoy sharing the experience with you. That is, if Leventhorpe doesn't object."

The look in his eyes warmed Blythe to her mistreated toes. A handsome man's admiration did bolster one's confidence, yet the intensity in Lord Leventhorpe's gaze while they danced meant more.

Probably because he didn't loathe her any longer. No one relished being disliked.

Mr. Burlington turned his affable gaze to his lordship. "Leventhorpe, would I be imposing? I helped teach my three younger sisters, and would be happy to volunteer my time and services."

"Not at all, Burlington. Unless Ravensdale prefers the ladies wait." Lord Leventhorpe's tone belied his words. Over her head, he regarded Heath, and as certain as Freddy had peed on Heath's boot at Esherton, a silent message passed between them.

She'd done that very thing with her sister and cousins myriad times.

Enough doubt niggled to steal her earlier enthusiasm about the lessons. She cast Lord Leventhorpe a glance, and her heart flipped when she caught him regarding her. What she wouldn't give to read his thoughts.

Was he considering reneging because Mr. Burlington offered to help? That made no sense. She would think he'd welcome another hand. None of the Culpeppers had ever sat a sidesaddle. Though the task might prove considerable, they might as well learn here as at home. And she would be assured of time with Mr. Burlington, affording her the opportunity to become better acquainted. More importantly, riding lessons meant escaping the house and spending time in the outdoors, and after her stay in London, both appealed more than either man.

Liar.

Enough. She refused to examine her musings further.

"I think Lord Leventhorpe may have taken on more than he wagered, and I'm sure he would appreciate any assistance he can gather, Mr. Burlington. I'm quite looking forward to learning, aren't you, Brooke?"

Clasping her hands, and painting a bright smile upon her face, Blythe turned to Lord Leventhorpe. “Is the day after tomorrow too soon to begin lessons?”

Though circumstances appear to confirm schemes laid in advance,
when motives are selfish, expect unforeseen and unpleasant results.
~Dignity and Decorum—The Genteel Lady's Guide to Practical Living

4

"There he is." Tristan pointed to Hawksworth slumped atop a lopsided table in a fusty corner. "Looks practically pickled."

"What's he doing in The Ship & Whistle?" Ravensdale surveyed the unsavory establishment through the grungy window.

"Probably assumed we wouldn't look here. It's a favorite of sailors and servicemen. Cheap prostitutes and cheaper spirits." Tristan dipped his head as they entered the tavern, the stench of unwashed bodies, sweat, vomit, and spilled ale causing a reflexive surge of bile.

"Ho there, Ravensdale. Leventhorpe." Phillips and a handful of his cronies, all foxed to the gills, stumbled into the establishment. "Come to hire a wench for the evening too?"

Never fastidious or selective, Phillips had retained a flaxen-haired running-to-fat tavern harlot. He pinched her full buttocks. "We can share her, can't we, darlin'?"

She leaned into him. "Sure, guv.'"

"No. We cannot." Tristan glowered at Phillips.

Ravensdale shook his head. "I'll pass."

Tristan and Ravensdale each, for entirely different reasons, never entertained light skirts.

"What about Hawksworth? That Friday face looks like he could use a bit of cheering." Phillips's jibe earned him a blank, glassy-eyed stare from Hawk.

"M' lifesh ended now anyway." Hawksworth's slurred speech testified to his drunk-as-a-wheelbarrow condition. "Might ashh well 'urry i' along." Grinning sloppily, he squinted and tried to focus. "Where ish she?"

Ape drunk, Hawksworth wasn't capable of a cockstand.

He wasn't capable of standing at all.

"At least one of you three has a working set of ballocks." Slapping his chest, Phillips chortled and grabbed Hawksworth's arm. "Come on, man. Let's get you upstairs, unless you want to take her here." He slid Tristan a sly look. "Some men enjoy an audience."

Tristan clamped his jaw and balled his hands, sweat beading his upper lip and soaking his armpits. Had Phillips learned of his humiliation? Zounds. How?

Phillips turned to the harlot. "You don't mind, do you, Shelly, sweetheart?"

She grinned, revealing a mouth of yellowed teeth, and drew her grungy, stained blouse low on her sagging breasts. "Naw, makes i' more fun. I charges extra fer peepers, though."

"Up with you, Hawksworth." Phillips tugged Hawk's arm again, attempting to rouse him from his chair and stupor. "Shelly knows her trade and several unique tricks too. You'll not be disappointed."

Bloody eager to watch, pervert.

"Leave him be. Unlike you, he isn't keen on acquiring the pox." Ravensdale glowered at Seymour and his comrades, who'd formed a taunting semicircle around them.

Seven to three. Not the best odds.

Hawksworth slouched with his eyes closed and chin slack against his chest. Make that two. Rather dismal chances, actually. Couldn't be helped.

Shoving Phillips's hand away from Hawk, Tristan sliced Ravensdale a silent message. "We want no part of your doxy."

"Wot's wrong wif ye, luv?" The strumpet sidled up to Tristan, her foul odor revolting. From her stench, she'd already been busy this evening. She rubbed against him, releasing another unpleasant whiff of her unwashed body.

Queasiness twisted his stomach tighter.

"Ya prefer tuppin' gents?"

Doubled up with glee, Phillips choked on his laughter, his drunken entourage also guffawing.

"You haven't always felt that way, Leventhorpe." Phillips grinned nastily and scratched his groin. "I seem to recall something my father let slip. Something your father shared at Brooks's while deep in his cups one day."

Father was usually in his cups.

"Stubble it, Phillips." Ravensdale dragged his hand through his hair, compassion tinting the gaze he sent Tristan.

He and Hawksworth, alone, were privy to the event that haunted Tristan, and they didn't know the whole of it. He had never been able to speak of the horrific humiliation.

"Wasn't there an instance when you had quite a public display of lust, Leventhorpe?" Phillips held up two fingers. "One that involved two prostitutes?"

Tristan's well-placed facer broke Phillips's nose.

Tristan bolted upright, cursing and disoriented. Darkness enveloped him, and for an instant, he didn't know where he was.

God.

He rubbed his face before lying down once more.

A nightmare. Not his usual, though.

Pure fate, Whitehouse and Drake had happened along that evening, in time to prevent Ravensdale and Tristan from getting completely thrashed. They had jumped into the ensuing fray, balancing the odds nicely. The five had been the greatest of chums ever since.

Nothing quite like fighting side-by-side against a common foe to forge unbreakable bonds of friendship. A week later, they'd shared mutual misgivings too, when the same diseased slattern, tortured and beaten to death, washed ashore on the River Thames's beach.

Tristan closed his eyes against his musing and the accompanying disquiet. He kicked off his bedcovers, and after punching his pillow into an acceptable shape, flopped onto his stomach.

Slumber didn't embrace him.

The rhythmic *tick-tocking* of his bedside table clock usually lulled him to sleep. He cracked an eye open and glared at the indiscernible oval face in the pre-dawn half-light.

What time was it?

Too early to rise, by half.

He hadn't heard a peep from Peasley, and the valet took particular pleasure in slinging open the window coverings the moment the first ray of sun brazened the horizon.

In the distance, a dog barked, and a moment later, an answering woof sounded.

Yawning, Tristan stretched his legs, encountering several furry paws despite his mammoth mattress. Clio and Thalia sprawled at the foot of his bed, softly snoring and twitching every now and again.

He ought to make them get off the bed.

Despite regular brushing, the dogs shed terribly, and White's chambermaid fretted when she had to clean the collies' hair from the coverlet and furniture. The extra vails Tristan offered for her inconvenience lessened her vexation a jot. More than once, he'd endured his valet's wrath as Peasley tutted and fussed while ridding Tristan's togs of hair before permitting him to present himself in public.

For the first time, Tristan had stayed until a ball's confounded end—very nearly a miracle thanks to the humiliating experience his despot of a father had foisted upon him at thirteen.

Wide awake and agitated after last night's ball, he hadn't found his bed until after half past two. Yet each time he shut his eyelids, a halo of silvery hair, violet-blue eyes below delicate honey-blond brows, a pert nose, and stubborn chin taunted him. He'd been hard-put not to stare at the firm teacup-sized bosoms teasing her bodice's neckline during their waltz. He'd fallen into an agitated slumber only to have Phillips encroach upon his dreams.

He didn't trust Phillip's, and Burlington's interest in Blythe chaffed worse than a week bare-arsed in a new saddle, though why it should confounded Tristan.

Worry and concern.

That was what this unease centered in his gut was. None of his blasted business, by God. The Culpeppers weren't—Blythe most assuredly wasn't—his concern.

Stop thinking about her, and go to sleep.

His rebellious musings ignored him.

Tristan had told Ravensdale about Blythe's unnerving upstairs encounter with Phillips, and evidently, Raven had conveyed their mutual disquiet to his wife.

For the evening's remainder, Lady Ravensdale had insisted the Culpeppers visit the retiring room *en masse*. Until they became familiar with *haut ton* protocol, and accumulated a set of trustworthy friends, Tristan applauded her decision.

Years of experience guiding the tightknit quartet would serve her, and them, well in London. Tristan admired the Culpeppers' unity. Genuinely kind and friendly, they'd soon have a circle of supporters.

Surely Ravensdale's melon had gone soft for descending upon London with his new family in tow. With that lot churning High Society's staid waters, Tristan might have enjoyed this Season. However, his abhorrence of crowds prevented any such thing. His habit of imbibing a couple of stiff drinks before venturing to a gathering sufficed when he did so once a fortnight at most.

But, *damn my eyes,* Ravensdale had asked for his help, which meant multiple forays weekly.

Mayhap Tristan would purchase a barrel of whisky. He shook his face in his crisp pillowcase's folds. No. He'd not end up a fuddled drunkard like his father.

Then you need to find another way to deal with your dread.

Grunting, Tristan turned onto his back and stared at the inky canopy. He scratched his bare chest before tucking his hands underneath his head.

Promising to teach the Culpeppers to ride.

Had *his* melon gone soft?

Now he'd have to bear Burlington's insufferable presence too. He wanted to hate the man, but couldn't. Not for being a favorite with the ladies and taking advantage of what many offered freely. Tristan, Heath, and Hawksworth were anomalies in that regard, though they weren't monks, just exceedingly selective.

Well ... Heath had been prior to marriage. Now, tits over arse in love, Raven would never betray Lady Ravensdale.

The epitome of discretion when it came to his dalliances, much like Drake and Whitehouse, Burlington didn't possess despicable habits. He came from a long line of respectable peers, and the Earl of Lauderdale was an upright chap, if a bit thin in the pockets. Other than a weak constitution, Burlington's older brother boasted an exemplary character too.

Damme.

Burlington had to have one unsavory practice. He was too bloody perfect by far. Only his lack of title made him less desirable to some women. Others mightn't care.

Did Blythe?

She wasn't the sort, which made Burlington more of a threat.

Clio twitched and whined in her sleep. Probably dreamed of running the fields and herding the cattle at Bristledale. Tristan should have left the dogs there, but truthfully, he missed them and found London lonely.

The blame for that, too, could be plopped at his doorstep.

A stack of unopened invitations lay piled atop the corner secretary where he'd tossed them.

He didn't relish returning to his empty rooms at White's, and since he stayed in most evenings—at least he had until this confounded Season—he found the dogs welcome company. True, he'd rented these quarters for a decade, and they bore his personal touch and preferences, but the pleasant rooms weren't home.

Only at Bristledale Court, away from Town's observant eyes, attending ears, and flapping tongues, did he find a degree of respite.

As for the house bearing witness to his disgrace as a youth, he'd have sold the place and its furnishings for a pittance without an iota of regret within a week of inheriting the marquisate if the damned thing weren't entailed. He couldn't bear to pass the residence and went out of his way to avoid the street altogether.

No matter how many times he told himself what had happened those many years ago wasn't his fault, he couldn't rid himself of the dirty, used feeling. And with Phillips's return, more people might soon know of his degradation.

A thirteen-year-old, even one the size of a grown man, should never be forced to have his first sexual encounter with jaded prostitutes reeking of cheap perfume, and witnessed by debauched lechers. He'd tried to resist, but against the women's well-honed skills, he'd battled in vain. Even as his mind screeched no, and he'd pleaded and screamed for them to stop, his healthy, young body on the cusp of manhood had responded.

Growling deep in his chest, Tristan flopped a bent arm across his face, as if to hide the scene replaying behind his eyes for the thousandth time. The whores' appreciative coos and laughter mixed with the men's vile remarks regarding his immediate and impressive erection echoed in his dreams.

In his waking hours too.

His stomach roiled, and his nostrils twitched. He'd never forget the putrid smells either.

When a sodomite had asked to have him, and his sire drunkenly agreed, Tristan fought loose of the men restraining him. After he broke the bugger's groping hand, he'd fled the house and stayed either at school or as a guest of chums until he acquired his own lodgings at eighteen.

He never saw his father again.

Not even upon his deathbed, when Father repented of his lifetime of depravity and sent word, begging Tristan to visit him in order to make amends before he died. Better that his sire had changed his ways and sought reconciliation and forgiveness when he had time to make restitution. Precisely like the selfish, old marquis to lay the burden of forgiveness on Tristan.

Why should he grant Father forgiveness?

So he could enter eternal slumber with a contented heart and pure conscience? Hawksworth had argued, many times, that forgiving Father would bring healing and peace.

Tristan's loud snort rent the heavy silence, and Thalia raised her head, giving a weak woof.

He would never have peace. Not while he drew breath.

Every day for the past fifteen years, he'd striven for that elusive state. Just when he thought he'd made progress, that he'd finally put the taunting shadows to rest, something stirred them again. Like Phillips last night. And to know Father had spoken of the incident ... How many of the others present had as well?

Tristan gave a savage groan. Devil and damn. The lot, no doubt. His distance from *ton* activities had protected him from the bitter knowledge.

Thomas Gray had it right. "*Where ignorance is bliss, 'tis folly to be wise.*"

Thalia lifted her head when Tristan made another inarticulate sound of revulsion.

By God, when he had children—*if* he had children—he'd be a decent father, far superior to his sire. A deuced better husband too.

Clio crawled up his side then laid her pointed muzzle atop his chest.

The dogs sensed his distress.

Tristan ran a hand down her spine. "I suppose you think I should walk you?" She thumped her tail once. "You do realize I'll have to tie my cravat myself?" Two more thumps and a whine confirmed the dog's need.

Thirty minutes later—Peasley would have apoplexy when he discovered Tristan's rudimentarily tied neckcloth—Tristan slipped his arms into his greatcoat. A serving boy had taken the dogs out while he had eaten a hasty breakfast. For expediency, Tristan had stuffed bacon between the croissants flaky folds before gulping two strong cups of Turkish coffee. After a sleepless night, he'd need the restorative beverage to keep him alert today.

After snapping leads onto the dogs' collars, he collected his cane and made his way outside to his waiting landau.

"Good morning, my lord. Your paper." Jones passed the news sheet to Tristan then stepped to hold the carriage door open. The morning proved brisk, though the first rays of sunshine glinting off the vehicle's azure paint, promised a temperate day later. "The ladies are energetic early, I see."

"Good morning, Jones." Tristan wedged the paper beneath his arm and passed the leads to the driver before stepping into the landau. "They were most insistent we have an early constitutional today."

At his whistle, the dogs bounded into the conveyance. Hopping onto the opposite, blanket-covered seat, they raised their pointed snouts and sniffed. London's air seldom lacked for odors.

"The Green Park as usual, your lordship?" Jones asked as he snapped the reins and, with a slight lurch, the vehicle rolled forward.

"Yes." Crossing his legs, Tristan pulled the folded news sheet free. He skimmed the first pages. Nothing original or fresh. Just the same drudgery rewritten from a different perspective than yesterday's. And the day before's. He'd grown weary of the rhetoric already, and Parliament wouldn't recess soon. *More's the pity.*

Squinting as the conveyance turned in the sun, he scratched his nose. Hiring someone to vote in proxy didn't appeal. Granted, many peers condoned the practice, but until he had reason—other than loathing London—to avoid Parliamentary proceedings, he'd not abdicate his responsibilities.

Clio jumped onto the seat beside Tristan, sending his cane clattering to the floor. Her claws digging into his thigh to stay balanced, she shoved her wet nose underneath the paper, knocking several sheets loose to join his cane. Tail happily wagging, she licked his cheek.

"No. Clio." He pointed to her sister. "You belong there. Off with you."

Head lowered, Clio did as bidden. Lying across the opposite seat, her muzzle resting upon her paws, she watched him soulfully.

"Don't look at me like that. Peasley will have my head if he finds a single strand of dog hair upon my clothing, and I have several calls to make before I can return to my lodgings. Would you have me disparaged?"

She licked her chops, her tail twitching.

As he bent to retrieve his cane and the scattered news sheets, his attention fell upon the natter column. Such claptrap was good for the rubbish bin, a fireplace, or picking up after the dogs' occasional accidents.

He scanned the neat print.

London's first formal glimpse of Ldy R and the four Ms Cs caused a considerable stir last evening. ... Mr. B showed a distinct penchant for the elder Ms C, much to the disappointment of many a fair maid.

He was one gentleman amongst many to pay marked attention to the five diamonds of the first water. Even the reclusive Ld L put in an unexpected, coveted appearance.

No matter how well-intended or magnificent the scheme,
one should occasionally consider the consequences.
~Dignity and Decorum—The Genteel Lady's Guide to Practical Living

5

Tristan snatched the paper from the floor.

One has to wonder if Ld L has finally decided to pursue matrimony with one of the newly arrived blond beauties.

No. He most emphatically had not.

This columnist means to watch Society's reaction and predicts the thwarting of many a well-laid scheme ...

Tristan checked an annoyed grunt and seized his cane. The silver lion's head grip hid a sword handle. He never ventured anywhere on foot without the weapon.

Once he gathered the news sheets into an untidy pile, he laid them beside his leg.

A rather tame assessment and not altogether contrived, discounting the nonsensical twaddle about Tristan pursuing matrimony. Relaxing into the seat, he tapped his fingers on the landau's side as they neared the park.

How long did Raven expect him to help with his newly acquired family?

Tristan could cry off. Except ... he reluctantly admitted to a perverse fascination. He might be almost as eager to see what High Society made of the ladies as Ravensdale.

Le beau monde could be as fickle as a Friday night whore, and her favors bought as easily. All the more reason to be nearby, in case this ill-hatched scheme unraveled.

Tristan would arrange the riding lesson details after calling and collecting whichever of the young ladies wanted to venture to Tattersalls. The landau rolled to a stop and, after alighting and untangling the dogs' leashes, Tristan grabbed his cane. Taking a refreshing breath, he set a brisk pace toward Constitution Hill, waving for Jones to collect him on the other side, as he did each morning.

Whistling softly, Tristan mentally catalogued the day's priorities.

He should call upon Francine and, again, advise her about her choice of companions. Blythe, her sisters, and her cousins were exactly the type of friends Francine needed—kind, decent women—not the string of ambitious chits who continually used Francine for their gain.

Farther along the lane, a short-legged bundle of fur-covered fat pelted between two gnarled trees chasing a cow in desperate need of milking.

A cacophony of shouting, barking, and mooing echoed throughout the park. Ears perked in excited interest, Clio and Thalia tugged at their leashes, tails wagging furiously.

"Freddy. Stop."

"Come back, ya ruddy beasty."

"Stop, Clover. I needs t' milk ye."

Tristan faced the racket's direction.

Blythe, a pink and white confection, her bonnet's ribbons trailing behind her, tore across the green followed by a milkmaid, her skirts yanked to her knees, and a lad clenching a rope in one hand and holding his cap atop his head with the other.

Ah, a bovine escapee from adjacent St. James Park's milk lines, and the Culpeppers' corgi loved to herd cattle. Tristan wagered the little devil hadn't been able to resist the runaway cow.

A teenage groom sprinted past Blythe, slicing a diagonal path, intent on cutting the panicked cow off. Another man, noticing the ruckus, gave chase as well, and beyond him, another chap moved toward the animal, though at a more sedate pace.

Pulling his hat lower, the latter abruptly turned in the opposite direction and proceeded to briskly walk away.

With the sun shining in his eyes, Tristan couldn't make him out. Perhaps he'd decided his help wasn't needed to capture the panicked beast. A wonder she didn't knock her hind hooves from beneath her with her bulging udders wildly careening like kettle-sized, milk-filled clappers.

Tristan whistled an imitation of one he'd heard the overseer at

Esherton Green use with Freddy. He immediately whirled and trotted Tristan's way, his tongue nearly dragging the pavement along with his leash. Failing eyesight and the distance contributed to the dog's inability to recognize Tristan.

Wait until you realize it's me. You'll be off the other direction faster than angels fleeing hell.

The cow continued to dash along, her enormous udders making Tristan wince with each swing.

Thank God he wasn't a milk cow.

Sunshine, golden and bright, filtered through the tree-lined lane, casting interwoven shadows along the path. He bent and, after unclipping Clio's and Thalia's leashes, pointed at the cow. "Fetch."

Panting, her hair flopping onto one shoulder and her bonnet askew, Blythe dashed onto the pavement. Freddy, a doggy grin splitting his gray face, waddled to her. "Naughty boy. Chasing poor Clover."

Tristan approached cautiously. He didn't need the dog tearing off in a panic too. Squatting, he extended a hand. "Hello, Freddy. There's a good chap."

Freddy skulked closer, his haunches practically hugging the ground and sniffed timidly. He licked Tristan's fingertips then peered at Blythe for approval.

Swiping at a tendril tickling her cheek, Blythe crouched, the graceful curve of her mouth sweeping into a pleased grin. "Well done, Freddy." Patting the dog, she seized his lead and turned a brilliant smile upon Tristan. "He doesn't fear you any longer."

"The wayward cow has been caught." Tristan steered his gaze behind her.

Looking over her shoulder, she stood. "I was about to enjoy a cup of fresh milk when a rail-thin urchin startled Clover." Melancholy riddled her voice. "I felt a jot homesick, and the cows reminded me of Esherton Green. I milked cows almost daily at home." She shook her head, causing a few more curls to tumble loose, and gave a little self-deprecating laugh. "I don't suppose that's altogether ladylike."

"I quite enjoy a cup of fresh milk." Not exactly the fact. He did claim a particular fondness for clotted cream and milk in his coffee. Fresh from the cow's teat, and drunk from a communal cup? No. He managed to conceal his miniscule repugnance-born tremor.

The lad led the docile beast, the rope now circling Clover's thick neck, while the milkmaid, obviously his sister given the smattering of freckles also covering her broad face, guided the cow with a hand to her black and white dappled neck.

Thalia and Clio trotted behind, a safe distance from the cow's hind legs, and the groom and other gentleman brought up the rear.

"Miss, I'm afeared I left the cup yonder. To thank ye fer yer help, I'd be pleased to give ye a drink fer no cost ifn ye want to walk back." The girl repeatedly glanced in the vicinity of connecting St. James Park. "It were kind of ye to give the beggar child yer blunt."

Did a father, or perhaps an employer, expect the milkmaid? Would the children be chastised for the loss of a sale? Tristan passed the lad a shilling and the lass two. "You each keep a coin. The other is to pay for the sales you've lost."

The boy's face lit like fireworks above Vauxhall Gardens. He bobbed his moppy head. "Thank ye, m'lord."

"Thank ye, again, fer yer help, m'lord. Miss. Gents." After pocketing her coins and attempting a clumsy curtsy, the milkmaid headed for St. James Park, her brother chatting and gesturing excitedly about what he intended to buy with his money.

"That was kind of you, my lord." With a soft sigh, Blythe turned to her groom as Freddy and the collies sniffed one another in greeting. "Bennett, would you please fetch the carriage?"

Endeavoring to remedy the havoc her adventure had caused to her hair, she shoved a clump below her bonnet. Holding the hat in place, she tucked a few more strands underneath the brim. After tying the ribbons, she brushed ineffectually at her dress. "I fear I must repair my appearance before anyone else comes upon me this disheveled."

Charmingly tousled, she'd never looked lovelier to Tristan.

Stains marred the palms of her gloves, and grass smeared her gown's front near her knees. One long green streak emphasized the delicious mounds of her plump buttocks, testifying to a tumble or two as she chased the cow.

Uneasiness snuffed his appreciation.

God's toenails. Had anyone else seen her?

Tristan stretched to his full height and canvassed the vista. No one in sight. Not even the fellow who'd decided against helping earlier.

Thank the ungodly hour for the park's solitude. Why had Blythe ventured out this early with only a young stable hand for a chaperone? Most imprudent. Doubtless, besotted by her beauty, the whelp hadn't been able to deny her request, despite possibly risking discharge.

She wouldn't want word spread about that she'd been seen with grass-stained skirts. Foul minds might speculate that someone had given her a green gown, and she certainly didn't want the tattlemongers whispering she'd been tumbled in the park.

Likely as not, Raven wasn't aware Blythe had ventured out. A conversation with him seemed judicious. Not altogether safe for her if the man who'd abruptly departed was who Tristan suspected.

"Leventhorpe, is that you?" Wiping perspiration from his brow with his handkerchief, the fellow who'd succeeded in stopping the cow grinned at Tristan.

"Clancy Maddox?" Tristan extended his hand. "By George. It's been a long time. What, ten years or more? Not since university."

"Eleven." He sent Blythe a curious glance. "I was two years ahead of you."

"Allow me to present you." Tristan made the introductions before leashing his dogs.

"Thank you for your assistance, Mr. Maddox." Blythe picked up Freddy. The panting dog sagged against her, tuckered from his jaunt.

Women of refined breeding didn't tote portly corgis about, or run pell-mell through The Green Park. Another thing he needed to address with Lady Ravensdale and Raven. What Blythe might have been free to do in the country would be frowned upon in Town and could lead to wagging tongues. Something they didn't want if they wished successful come-outs.

Sure as fish guts stank, Blythe didn't care.

Kissing the top of Freddy's head, she shifted the dog, and her reticule slid to her wrist. "He thinks he's young, and though he tried to help with the runaway cow, I fear he did more harm than good."

"Where are you staying, Maddox? Are you here for a while?" Tristan jammed his cane between his side and arm then took the dog from her. Freddy eyed him warily, yet after a moment, laid his head upon Tristan's shoulder and released a long, throaty sigh.

So much for not wearing dog hair today.

"I've let rooms on St. James Street." Maddox placed his hat tighter upon his head. "I'm considering staying and opening an office here. A decade in the colonies was long enough for me. The provincials lack England's refinement and culture."

They reached the lane's end as Ravensdale's carriage drew to a stop behind Tristan's landau. A third conveyance leisurely eased past, the team clopping at a sedate pace. The collies loped to Tristan's vehicle, and in a moment, tongues lolling, sat perched atop the seat peering expectantly at him.

Maddox tipped his hat. "It was a pleasure to meet you, Miss Culpepper. I bid you good day."

"Likewise." She fished a card from her reticule. "Please come for tea tomorrow. I wish to thank you properly. This is my cousin-in-law's card. Mine are at the printers."

His brows dipped together as he read the card. "Ravensdale? I wasn't aware he'd wed recently."

"Yes." Cinching her reticule's handle, she turned somewhat away from another slow-passing carriage. "He married my cousin a short time ago."

"Thank you for the invitation to tea." He bowed to Blythe. "I look forward to seeing Ravensdale and meeting his bride."

She nodded a farewell as she made for her carriage.

Awkwardly balancing Freddy and worriedly watching Blythe's retreating form, Tristan shook Maddox's hand. "I lodge at White's. Be sure to look me up."

"I shall." Maddox's gaze gravitated to Blythe. "Will I see you at tea as well, Leventhorpe?"

"I expect so." Tristan canted his head in Blythe's direction. "There are five of them, and Raven's asked me to make myself available to assist with that tribe of beauties."

"Five? *Five*?" Maddox chuckled and shook his head. "Egads, that ought to be something. Glad I'm back in time to see it, I am."

"A common consensus, my friend." Tristan gave a conspiratorial wink.

"Till tomorrow then." With a carefree wave, Maddox, swinging his cane, headed in the direction he'd come.

Careful to keep his staff secured underneath his arm, Tristan adjusted a now-drowsy Freddy.

How much did the little piglet weigh?

A pair of carriages rumbled past, their occupants craning their necks, no doubt curious who else dared the common at this unchristian hour. The park appeared to be a favorite destination for those enjoying an early morning constitutional today.

He deposited the leashes in his landau and gave instructions to Jones before meeting Blythe at her carriage.

Arms akimbo and one toe tapping, she considered Maddox's retreating form. She turned her puckish regard upon Tristan, pinning him with her direct gaze. "You made it sound like Heath's taken on a Herculean task." Pique sharpened her features and voice. "We're not that difficult."

"I didn't imply *you* were. It's the rest of the upper ten-thousand—London actually—that will be difficult to manage. They've never encountered anything like the Culpeppers." He chuckled, and answering humor sparked in her eyes.

"I can well imagine." She scratched behind Freddy's ears, and he opened an eye. "I think you've found a friend."

"He's a good sort." Tristan patted Freddy's haunch and bent his head toward the groom standing ready to hand her into the carriage. "That was well done of you back there."

"Thank you, m'lord." He grinned at Blythe. "I thought Miss Culpepper would outpace me. Never seen a lady run that fast."

"See what I mean?" Tristan whispered in her ear, delighting in the blush infusing her cheeks as she entered the carriage

She extended her arms for Freddy. He groaned and scrambled onto the seat, where he promptly curled into a ball.

Tristan signaled Jones, and with an understanding slant of his head, the driver clicked his tongue and flexed the reins.

"I'll accompany you. I need to speak with Ravensdale." Before she could object with a single syllable, Tristan stepped in right behind her and shut the door with a portentous thunk. He stretched his legs before him. "Pray tell, what were you doing gamboling around London before an acceptable hour with a stable lad as chaperone?"

Scheming seldom results in anything extraordinary
or eternal, for anything worth having is freely given.
~Dignity and Decorum—The Genteel Lady's Guide to Practical Living

6

"My lord, I assure you, you needn't accompany me, and I wasn't 'gamboling' around London. I merely sought to walk Freddy in the park, as it appeared, you also intended with your collies." Blythe ground her teeth in vexation as she settled against the toast-gold, velvet squabs. That she managed to speak and not snipe or shout brought her a modicum of satisfaction. "And Bennet is perfectly acceptable for a chaperone."

Wasn't he? Should she have brought her maid too? She hadn't bothered with that sort of propriety in the country, where the only things that might set upon her were a stray cat or disgruntled crow.

"A peer walking his large dogs, a short sword concealed within his walking stick," Lord Leventhorpe indicated the elaborate staff tucked into the corner by his seat, "is deuced sure safer than a maiden with a fuzzy, waddling walrus and a smitten stable hand, scarcely more than a wet-behind-the-ears lad, for protection."

His cutting wit drew blood, and that he spoke the truth rankled. Nearly blind and missing several teeth, Freddy, the epitome of decrepitude, offered as much protection as the one-eyed stuffed pheasant in Esherton's study.

Picking dog hair from her spencer, she surreptitiously studied Lord Leventhorpe. Alternating sunbeams and shadows filtered through the windows as the carriage rolled past the row of impressive trees. The light played over his rugged features, making it impossible to read his expression.

Austere or staid? Mayhap somber? Taciturn? Grave?

Definitely not giddy. *Never* giddy.

Despite her frustration, a smile tickled her mouth.

Had he deduced she'd left without notifying anyone and decided to take it upon himself to tell them?

Quite possibly.

That fit the self-righteous, overbearing lord she'd met at Esherton. The amiable, enjoyable man of last night had vanished with the moon and stars' disappearance, and the sanctimonious lord, the one who believed it his duty to inform others of their shortcomings, had returned. Weren't demons supposed to prowl about at night and slink into their dank and gloomy hidey-holes at first light, not the reverse?

Did he think her a wholly inconsiderate bacon wit? She'd left a note with Jenkin, their butler, saying she'd gone for a walk, for pity's sake. Suppressing an urge to kick Lord Leventhorpe, she pressed her half-boot's heel against the seat and petted Freddy instead.

Despite her late night, she'd awoken at dawn, a habit she'd not overcome from years of rising early at Esherton. Desperate to escape the house's confines and London's cramped busyness, she'd sought refuge in the singular place remotely resembling Esherton Green. Her sisters—everyone, barring Cook—had been abed when she'd slipped to the mews. Bennet, alone, prowled the stables, and she'd bade him ready a conveyance and accompany her to the park.

He'd eagerly agreed, much preferring that task to mucking the stalls. Biting the inside of her mouth, she pressed her fingers into Freddy's pudgy back. Would her impulsiveness result in Bennet's chastisement?

Bother. Before asking him, she should've considered the possibility.

Cocking a lofty auburn brow at her, Lord Leventhorpe folded his ridiculously muscled arms across his Spanish-brown-encased chest. Slight disapproval gleamed in his blue eyes, more of deep slate at the moment. His mild, clean scent permeated the carriage's confines, which shrank with his hulking presence.

"Miss Culpepper, appearing in public before seven in the morning is not done. Especially with a lad younger than you— Oomph."

A particularly sharp turn sent him sliding his seat's length, and a giggle escaped her as she braced herself and Freddy to prevent the same.

Scooting to his corner, he anchored his shoulders firmly and stabbed a forefinger in the direction of the driver's seat. "Who, from the careening and uneven pace of this vehicle, has likely not driven a carriage. Ever. Not only is it unsafe, your behavior gives rise to gossip."

Bennet's inexperience explained the rocky ride to St. James Park and why she'd anticipated that last jostling corner. She'd blamed poor roads and worn springs. Warning Lord Leventhorpe would have been charitable, but his flailing about trying to retain his seat proved too amusing to forego. On the other hand, Heath would not be pleased that someone inexperienced had handled the matched team and risked damaging an extremely costly conveyance.

"It's well beyond seven, my lord. Much closer to eight, I'd estimate." She didn't own a watch. "I cannot think it too terribly unfashionable, though somewhat unpopular, with sluggish souls reluctant to part with their mattresses before noon."

London's elite were a lazy lot.

Lord Leventhorpe's regard dropped to her grass-stained gown, disapproval fairly oozing from him.

Running in the garment hadn't been the wisest of decisions. She'd done enough laundry to know the delicate fabric was ruined. Regret chastised her at the shameful waste. Next time, she'd wear one of her well-worn gowns and pretend to be a servant. A borrowed maid's cap and cloak could be donned for good measure too. That shouldn't raise eyebrows or give rise to censure.

Grasping the seat as the carriage careened again, she caught a glimpse of her muddy half-boots. Her shoes had been sensible, though, and after a thorough cleaning would be no worse for wear.

"Blythe." His lordship's voice was low and affable, not condescending or judgmental. Something akin to concern tempered his deep baritone.

Chagrin pricked her. Perhaps she'd been off the mark, and he meant to be helpful.

He gestured at her gown. "I won't be specific as to why, but if the wrong person had seen your gown thus ... Well, they may have concluded you immoral or fast, and your reputation would have suffered greatly."

She gaped at him, something she'd done a great deal since arriving in London. "Because of grass stains? What in the world could be construed as immoral or fast about that?"

"Er, yes. Well ... it leads to speculation as to … uh, that is, how they might have been acquired." He peered out the window and clawed at his lumpy neckcloth.

Oh. *Oh*!

Rot and bother. She sought the dirt-streaked floor, certain her cheeks had turned the same shade as her spencer and gown.

He'd used her given name. On purpose? Or had it been a slip of the tongue?

"I need to speak with Ravensdale about arranging riding lessons, in any event, and to inquire if your sisters or cousins wanted to venture to Tattersalls with us today." His mouth curved rakishly, and she caught a glimpse of the charismatic man of last evening.

Hmm. Perhaps he meant to take advantage of their opportune encounter. Last evening he had said he'd call today. "My lord, forgive me if I overstep the bounds. Is it customary to call before breakfast?"

Lord Leventhorpe's wide grin creased the corners of his eyes. "Not at all. Raven's cook makes the most delicious crepes, and I crave them today. They aren't nearly as tasty at White's."

"She does, indeed. I've not eaten and confess I'm hungry myself." Blythe had been so intent upon conversing with Mr. Burlington last night, her food had gone almost untouched.

The carriage pitched, and she and Lord Leventhorpe clutched the sides. Good thing minimal traffic lined the streets. A blind hobgoblin possessed better driving skills than Bennet.

Righting his cane, Lord Leventhorpe settled into his corner once more. "Did you enjoy your first ball? The dancing? Your dinner with Burlington?"

His questions took her aback. Small talk, or was he genuinely interested?

"Yes, more than I expected to, truth to tell." Freddy laid his head in her lap and sighed. Activity outside the window suggested London had awakened fully in the past hour. "What do you know of Mr. Burlington?"

She couldn't ask Heath because he'd tell Brooke, and then there'd be a bevy of questions launched Blythe's way. Why a man she'd newly met fascinated her, she wasn't ready to explain. Perhaps because he was the first to show genuine interest and not suggest an illicit relationship as had been the case when the Culpeppers had been pauper poor.

If Mr. Burlington's temperament mimicked his lordship's, stern and unapproachable, she wouldn't have been intrigued the least. Except she'd caught a glimpse of an entirely different man last evening, one Lord Leventhorpe seemed at pains to conceal.

Why? What tumult went on in that fiery head of his?

Drawing her attention from the street, she tucked another tendril of hair beneath her bonnet.

Lord Leventhorpe regarded her impassively.

Didn't he intend to answer? She'd probably broken a rule asking him about Mr. Burlington. Someone ought to write a book listing the ridiculous social expectations and decrees. They could call it the *Lady's Guide to Proper Comportment*, or some other such drivel.

He sliced a look outside before setting that disturbing azure-eyed gaze onto her. "He's a decent chap. Comes from good stock. No bad habits that I'm aware of." Lifting a shoulder slightly, he adjusted his glove. "Enjoys himself. Not a serious fellow, by any means."

He'd succinctly answered her question but hadn't told her anything, and his last words held a cautionary inflection. Perchance they weren't friends, or he didn't think it his place to discuss Mr. Burlington.

"You've a dab of dirt smearing your cheek, just there." Lord Leventhorpe indicated her cheek with a long finger.

Covered in dog hair, mud, and grass. Perfectly lovely.

Blythe wiped her face. "Did I get it?"

"No. You smeared the blob more." He chuckled and moved his fingers over his cheek, in imitation of where her smudge was. "You look rather like an adorable ragamuffin who's been making mud pies."

Blythe rubbed the spot again then examined her gloves. Earth marred the fingertips. Whether from wiping her face or from her tumbles in the park, she didn't know. Probably ruined her gloves too. "Better?"

"No. Allow me." He swiftly removed his black leather glove. "Lean my way a mite."

Blythe complied, and he bent and brushed his thumb along her cheek a couple of times.

Sensation darted outward, raising the flesh along her shoulders and arms.

The shards of silver in his gaze glittered as he stared into her eyes, and his touch lingered a fraction longer than entirely necessary. "You have the loveliest eyes and the most perfect mouth I've ever seen."

Such was the wonder in his voice, he almost seemed to speak to himself.

Blythe wet her lips, gone abruptly dry as autumn leaves.

His gaze riveted upon her mouth, tension tightened his lips.

He had the most beautifully sculpted mouth she'd ever noticed, and that included the Greek gods from last night's ball. Were Lord Leventhorpe's as warm and firm and tasty as they appeared?

What the blazes did Mr. Burlington's lips look like?

Did he have lips?

He must, of course.

A wheel sank into a hole with bone-jarring force, abruptly interrupting Blythe's mental rambling and pitching her and Lord Leventhorpe headfirst. His hat flew from his head as he tumbled from his seat onto his knees and reflexively wrapped his arms around her to keep her from plunging to the floor.

With a yelp of outraged surprise, Freddy bumped into Blythe's back, somehow managing to scramble onto the seat.

Their faces mere inches apart, Blythe couldn't haul her gaze from the glinting specks in Lord Leventhorpe's eyes. His focus sank to her lips, and his enlarged pupils revealed his arousal.

Would he kiss her?

Did she want him to?

Illogically, yes.

Breath suspended, she remained perfectly motionless. Waiting.

Lowering his head, he tightened his embrace an instant before his lips whispered across hers.

A brilliant light burst behind her eyes, and every bone in her body turned molten. She clutched his lapels, certain if she let go, she'd slither to the floor.

He ran his tongue along the seam of her lips, and, sighing, she readily capitulated and parted her mouth, eager to taste more of him.

They taste even better than they look.

The carriage jerked to an abrupt halt, and his head banged hers as they toppled to the floor, Lord Leventhorpe—Tristan—sprawled atop her and Freddy landing upon him.

The door sprang open almost immediately. "Where have you—"

Blythe craned her neck to peer beyond Tristan's immense shoulder.

"Devil and damn." He swore beneath his breath before lifting his head and twisting to look behind him.

The entire household had awoken, and they'd trooped outdoors upon sighting the carriage.

"Good morning, Heath. Brooke. Girls." Stifling an absurd urge to laugh at their dumbfounded expressions, Blythe wiggled the fingers of her free hand in greeting. The other remained lodged between her and his lordship, trapped against his rigid abdomen. "We had a bumpy ride."

Blaire and Blaike burst into giggles.

Blythe didn't recall ever tittering that much at seventeen. She'd been the serious, sensible one. Except ... she'd giggled at Tristan mere moments ago.

"It must have been an extremely bumpy ride."

One of them snickered, but buried underneath his broad, delicious-smelling, *hard* body, Blythe wasn't sure which one. "Bennet hasn't much practice driving."

"Clearly." A glacier held more warmth than Heath's voice. "Do get off her, Leventhorpe. Your arse splayed upward atop my ward before I've even broken my fast rather annoys me and puts me off my food."

"I rather like it," Tristan whispered, his lips turned up devilishly as he waggled his eyebrows.

I do too.

Blythe gave him a playful shove. "Off before you cause a scandal."

He brushed her breast and hip as he untangled himself—surely unintentionally—yet hot, tiny pulses lingered where he'd touched her. After clambering from the carriage, Tristan righted his clothing, his expression gone unapproachable again.

Hmm, in public he was one man, in private another. Intriguing.

Heath assisted Blythe to the pavement. His brows swooped together upon noticing her soiled attire. The look he shot Tristan demanded an explanation. "We shall discuss this inside."

Replacing his hat, Tristan dipped his chestnut head in acknowledgement.

Heavens. Heath didn't think they ...? Heat suffused her. Utter hogwash.

"Wise, I think." Brooke cut her dark blue gaze to the sidewalk.

Nurses pushing prams and early morning-goers dotted the strip.

Curiosity glimmered in the twin's eyes as they grinned in unison. They'd barrage Blythe with questions the instant they cornered her alone.

"Blythe, you should mend your appearance before anyone sees you." Heath looked to Bennet. "After you've seen to the horses and carriage, I wish to speak with you in my study."

Hat in his hands, Bennet shifted from foot to foot, apprehension furrowing his brow. "Yes, sir."

"Heath, please do not blame Bennet. I asked him to drive me." Blythe gave Bennet an encouraging smile. He mustn't lose his position because of her. "If anyone's at fault, it's me. I should have waited for the driver."

"You shouldn't have gone out alone at all, Blythe. This isn't Cheshire." Brooke stepped closer and lowering her voice, touched Blythe's arm. "You'll have to curb your impetuousness while in London. I know you're not happy here, and I'm sorry. Be that as it may, you cannot take off pell-mell whenever you've the urge. It isn't safe, and there are others to consider."

Blythe tamped her instinctive sharp retort. Brooke was right. Instead, she offered a falsely bright smile. "Of course, Brooke." Shoving her bonnet in place, Blythe searched for Freddy. There he was, already disappearing into the house. She angled toward the steps, eager to get off the street before passersby took notice of anything untoward. "I do hope breakfast is ready. I'm famished."

Thirty minutes later, everyone sat round the dining table. Blythe had changed her gown and repaired her appearance, the whole while inundated by questions from Brooke and the others. Most likely, Tristan had endured the same interrogation from Heath.

Startling how a petal soft wisp of a kiss had her thinking of him as Tristan rather than Lord Leventhorpe. And she hadn't had a single thought of Mr. Burlington in the past hour.

Surely she hadn't already become as fickle and flighty as half of the women she'd met last night.

His plate heaped with crepes, Tristan took a drink of coffee. "Since I promised to call today to discuss riding lessons and our excursion to Tattersalls, I invited myself to join Miss Culpepper in her carriage." A boyish smile curved his mouth as he forked a piece of crepe. "And, I hoped to sample these."

Teacup halfway to his lips, Heath paused. "And you didn't give consideration to the impropriety of sharing a carriage alone with her?"

"We weren't alone. Freddy was there." Tristan popped the bite into his mouth and winked at the twins, who'd erupted into more giggles.

Blythe almost dropped the knife she'd been using to spread strawberry preserves. He'd made a jest. Who was this jovial stranger?

"All right, not my wisest decision. In my defense, I think I spied Phillips at the park, and quite frankly, I had concerns about Blythe returning home alone." Tristan tapped his forefinger atop the lace tablecloth. "I suppose I might have followed in my landau. But I didn't, which I'll admit, may have provided the rumormongers fodder."

He'd done it again, used her first name, and no one as much as blinked. Perhaps because Tristan was such a close friend of Heath's, it was permissible. Or ... after the kiss, did he now think of her in more personal terms, as she did him?

"Heath, no one saw us. No harm's been done." She bit into her toast.

No one barring Mr. Maddox. And the drivers and passengers in the three—four?—carriages at the park. And anyone who'd glimpsed the inside of Heath's carriage as they passed. And those walking the street when they arrived home.

Botheration. A paper-thin line distinguished boldness from folly, and she may have inadvertently crossed it.

Two footmen and Jenkin entered, carrying enormous bouquets of flowers. "Ma'am, the drawing room can hold no more." Jenkin raised a spray of peach roses. "Where would you like these arrangements placed?"

Brooke's mouth curved. "Full? Already? I suppose the green salon then, Jenkin. Heath, have you room in the study? It's barely nine o'clock. I cannot imagine what the house will look like by noon."

"A confounded hothouse." Relaxing in his chair, he gave his head an amused shake. "I don't want to consider how many callers we'll have today." His lips twitching, he perused the dining room. "I may need to purchase a bigger house." Focusing upon each woman in turn, he rubbed his temple. "A *much* bigger house."

Tristan laughed, a melodious deep-throated rumble that teased her ears. The transformation from dour lord to amused rapscallion caused Blythe's heart to stutter oddly. Who was the real man? The affable chap who laughed easily or the caustic fellow? What had caused his prickly façade?

"Didn't you give that consideration before you launched this farce?" Undeterred by Heath's reproving scowl, Tristan indicated the women with a sweep of his hand. "What time will be convenient to take the ladies to Tattersalls?"

"Oh, I adore horses." Excitement lit Brette's eyes, and she leaned forward. "We're allowed to go, aren't we, Heath? I'm quite looking forward to our riding lessons too."

"As am I."

Blythe's fork clattered to her plate as she swung to the dining room's double doors.

Bearing an enormous variety of yellow flowers, Mr. Burlington—looking entirely too virile in a cinnamon-colored coat and beige pantaloons tucked into glossy Hessians, and wearing a confident smile—stood beside a disapproving Jenkin.

Mr. Burlington's God-like good looks drew the women's attention, aside from Brooke. She only ever had eyes for Heath.

They, like her and Tristan, had disliked each other upon first meeting.

Entirely different circumstances though.

"Sir. Madam. Mr. Burlington was most insistent he had urgent news to impart that could not wait until after breakfast, despite my urging that he wait in the drawing room, or better yet, return at a Christian hour."

Offering an apologetic quirk of his mouth—*his lips aren't as full as Tristan's*—Mr. Burlington patted Jenkin's shoulder. "I own, I exaggerated a mite about the importance of my visit. Surely desiring the company of these lovely ladies begs a degree of forgiveness?"

The majordomo's features puckered in further censure.

"Excuse me for calling unfashionably early." Holding the flowers, he approached the table, apparently intending to join them. "I wanted to make sure I was available to assist with the ladies, and Miss Culpepper assured me last night I'd be welcome, despite my forwardness."

His tawny gaze found Blythe and hovered upon her lips before skimming her bosoms.

The pair didn't offer as much as a tiny twitch this morning, and more incredibly, she detected not a jot of remorse for his brazen taradiddle.

He gave a flourishing bow. "These are for you, Miss Culpepper."

"Thank you. Yellow is my favorite color." Her gaze swerved to Tristan.

He regarded Mr. Burlington aloofly, though a hint of mockery tugged one umber brow upward. His gaze gravitated to hers, a question lurking in the ocean depths. Did he suspect Mr. Burlington lied?

"Won't you join us, Mr. Burlington?" Brooke indicated the chair beside Blythe as she bestowed a soothing smile on Jenkin. "Would you please see to a place for our unexpected guest?"

"At once, my lady."

"Oh, Jenkin, put these in water too, will you?" Mr. Burlington thrust the bouquet into Jenkin's arms. A lily brushed Jenkin's aquiline nose, depositing fine orange pollen over the tip, giving him the appearance of a giant duck. "I sincerely appreciate your gracious tolerance of my poor manners."

Jenkin's features softened the minutest amount. "I'll return with them in a few moments, sir."

If putting in an unacceptably early appearance was Mr. Burlington's singular fault, Blythe could forgive the *faux pas*, since she quite loathed tardiness. However, he'd fabricated that tidbit about her, which pricked rather sharply. She couldn't abide liars or contemptable treatment of servants.

After scooting his chair in, Mr. Burlington gazed round the table. "What time are we off to Tattersalls?"

Wickedness and scheming make one unhappy,
and a virtuous woman will avoid both.
~Dignity and Decorum—The Genteel Lady's Guide to Practical Living

7

A week later, as the sun hovered between Hyde Park's horizon and the bright cloudless sky directly overhead, Tristan sat astride Buce, with Ravensdale and Burlington on either side atop their horses. No hint of a breeze teased the trees' lush foliage, and already the temperature promised to be quite warm.

A line of lissome blondes wearing stylish riding habits, each a different rainbow hue, and regally seated aside, negotiated a wide turn about Rotten Row and trotted to Francine.

She laughed, and after reining her horse round, clapped. "Splendid, ladies. You've quite got the knack of it. Well done."

"They're coming along nicely, aren't they? Francine has been a Godsend." Tristan shook his head. "I wouldn't have guessed she'd be such an apt teacher."

"They are enjoying themselves, which is what matters to me." Ravensdale rested an elbow atop his saddle. "They quite abhorred the notion of coming to London, if you recall. Blythe most particularly."

"Truly? I cannot imagine why. London is the epitome of culture, other than Paris, of course. I'd say Miss Culpepper is thriving here." Burlington's appreciative gaze remained fixed upon her.

Shows what you know.

Burlington moved forward a few paces. A newborn, blind kitten sucking a teat was less attached. Wholly besotted, he apparently didn't care who knew. He'd been impossible to deter, and not a day had passed without his company. A bit pompous and prone to embellishing the truth, he was still an amiable sort.

Tristan would have rather he concealed a vile, scandal-worthy secret, since it was difficult not to like the chap, and he'd been a dab hand at assisting with the lessons, even if he was barely short of a popinjay.

The men needn't have tagged along any longer, but none suggested they cease.

Tristan didn't want to stop, nor did he wish to examine the reason why, though a befuddling suspicion jostled about in his mind.

"There are those who prefer the country's calm to London's chaos." *Including me.* "The Culpeppers were accustomed to a much quieter way of life on their dairy farm."

Why Tristan felt the need to explain, to defend Blythe, he didn't examine.

"Dairy farm?" That caught Burlington's attention. He tossed Ravensdale a surprised look. "They possess an estate? Most unusual for women. Do they own equal shares?"

"No." Raven spared Burlington a perfunctory glance. "Their cousin owns the farm. At least part of it. I won the rest from him and deeded it to my wife as a wedding gift."

Disappointment flooded Burlington's features. As a second son, it was no secret he needed to marry a woman with a heavy purse. Ravensdale had generously dowered Blythe, but still, given Burlington's lavish taste, that wouldn't last long—a year or two at best.

Which mattered more to the fop? Blythe or deep coffers?

Adjusting his position in the saddle, Tristan slapped his reins against his palm.

Blythe must be aware of Burlington's infatuation. Did she return his regard? She wasn't a woman to display her emotions, willy-nilly, but kept them secreted. Her eyes hinted at her sentiments, but even an astute person would have to peer closely to see what lurked in their fascinating, periwinkle midst.

Since their kiss in the carriage—rather, since Tristan had stolen a taste of her utterly delicious lips, a kiss he could feel if he closed his eyes and pressed his lips together—she'd acted differently toward him. Her earlier hostility had been replaced by a watchful wariness and tentative cordiality, which seemed to increase as they saw each other daily, often more than once.

She'd granted him a waltz at each ball, something he looked forward to more than these morning rides. The pleasure of holding her tempting, svelte form made attending the nightly circuses almost bearable. He limited himself to a single dance, reluctant to have his thoughts coiled in her silvery tresses, or unable to rid her from his mind or dreams.

At least he no longer feared casting up his kippers or sweating through his shirt at public assemblies. More importantly, for the past three routes, he'd foregone his customary pre-appearance brandies.

What mystic power did she hold over him, that in a matter of weeks, he anticipated the future with renewed enthusiasm? He wanted to spend time with her, conversing, or strolling in serene silence. She wasn't one of those females who needed to fill the tranquility with senseless chatter.

When in her presence, his spirit found a peace wholly foreign to him; a vast contrast to the frequent and disturbing libidinous urges she also roused. Urges which accelerated to an uncomfortable level, sometimes requiring the discreet rearranging or concealment of his nether regions, easier done when not uncomfortably swollen like a Cumberland sausage.

"My lady will soon have to put aside her daily excursions." Ravensdale inched his horse near Tristan, saying in a low tone, "I'm going to be a father, Trist."

Tristan grinned, at once overjoyed for his friend and also experiencing a bewildering, envious pang. "Congratulations." He cut his gaze to Burlington, raptly gawping at Blythe. "I assume you're not making the joyous news public."

"Not yet." Ravensdale gave a short shake of his head then firmed his mouth, a shadow replacing the earlier joy in his eyes. "I heard you had an unfortunate encounter with Phillips yesterday afternoon."

"That's a marked understatement. I threatened to call the bastard out if he mentions the *incident* again." The churl had cornered Tristan as he left his lodgings, almost as if he'd been lying in wait. Retaliation for Tristan mangling his pretty face likely spurred Phillips's obsession. Or else he was an unconscionable bully who delighted in taunting others.

"Why such rubbish should matter to him after all these years, I cannot imagine. I think he finds perverse enjoyment in goading you." Raven waited until two young bucks rode by, animatedly discussing the bevvy of blondes they'd passed. Craning their necks for another glimpse, they collided and almost unseated the other, much to their snorting and prancing horses' displeasure.

Shaking his head, Raven grinned at their retreating forms. He dragged his focus to Tristan. "Because Phillips knows you still suffer the humiliation."

"Well, I refuse to hide my head or be ashamed any longer. I'm not proud of what happened, but I have come to accept I wasn't to blame. Hawksworth will be pleased. He's preached that particular, as well as forgiveness, countless times." Lifting a shoulder, Tristan twisted his mouth into a sardonic smile. "I suppose most adolescents would have been proud. You know that's not my way."

Raven quirked an eyebrow. "True. Monks boast more of their sexual exploits, and England doesn't harbor many monastics."

An exuberant, musical laugh floated across the green.

Blythe.

Wearing a robin's-egg-blue habit, she cantered her mare in a wide circle.

Like a bird to air, she'd taken to riding, and Tristan found himself awaking with renewed expectancy each morning, eagerly anticipating the lessons. No nightmares had plagued him either, despite running into Phillips at several functions and enduring his spiteful taunts. Only Rosemary Sanford annoyed him as much.

She continued to be a pushy, painful carbuncle. Now that Francine enjoyed the Culpeppers' company, Miss Sanford found her less malleable and less available. Unfortunately, that meant Miss Sanford had become tediously forward. Tristan feared she'd set her cap for him, and she had proven as tenacious as a hound tracking a scent. He could scarcely use the privy for fear she'd pop from the shrubberies or be waiting outside when he exited.

A pair of riders joined the women, and in a moment, the group headed to the waiting men.

Squinting, Tristan released a disgusted puff.

Phillips and Miss Sanford. Again.

Raven had finally conceded and introduced his newly acquired family. Perhaps tomorrow's lesson would take place elsewhere since that pair had invited themselves three mornings in a row now, and after yesterday's ordeal, Tristan was done up with Phillips. His continued pursuit of Blythe proved worrisome too, particularly since Tristan had spied him in the park the day the cow wreaked havoc.

Miss Sanford, her seat excellent, galloped her horse ahead, clearly showing off.

Phillips remained with the others, but Lady Ravensdale maneuvered her docile mare, forcing him to the outside, away from her wards.

Undeniably ravishing in a black and plum habit, a breathless Miss Sanford ambled to a stop beside Tristan. "I bid you good day, my lords. Mr. Burlington. Isn't it a glorious morning? Why, I think we may have a delightfully warm summer this year."

In London, that meant stifling and putrid. All the more reason to return to Bristledale Court's fragrant meadows and fresh air.

"Good day, Miss Sanford." Scarcely glancing her way, Burlington bid her a distracted hello as Ravensdale and Tristan exchanged a brief look. Perhaps a proclamation would be forthcoming from him soon.

She wrinkled her nose peevishly at Burlington's lackadaisical greeting.

"Pleasant day to you, Miss Sanford. Excuse me." Touching his hat, Ravensdale kicked his horse's sides and trotted to meet Lady Ravensdale. Likely to watch Phillips too.

"I'd hoped to see you at the Lockwood's soirée last evening." An invitation in her gaze and her lips bent coyly, Miss Sanford took the opportunity to sidle her horse near enough that their legs touched.

Buce dipped his massive head and snorted.

I agree, my friend.

Her cloying perfume assailed Tristan's nose, and he sneezed. "Beg your pardon."

Had she doused herself in the potion hoping to bewitch him? Or render him unconscious so she could have her way with him? Wouldn't do to gag and cough. Turning his head away, he gulped in a fresh breath. What he wouldn't give for a brisk breeze at the moment.

"I confess, I missed your company, my lord." A seductress's smile curved Miss Sanford's mouth, and the tip of her tongue darted out.

"I was otherwise engaged." And would be until naked cherubim, smoking cheroots, danced at Almack's. Her brazenness left him cold, and not a little worried for *his* virtue. He didn't trust her scheming wiles.

"Ho, Leventhorpe. Look who I ran into." Whitehouse and Maddox bore down on them, and Whitehouse half-saluted, half-waved. "Maddox has purchased a building near the docks, and I came upon him on my way here."

"Excellent to see you again, Maddox." Tristan took the opportunity to edge Buce away from Miss Sanford. "I'm glad you've decided to stay in England."

The other riders joined them. Introductions were made and greetings exchanged.

Scowling at Phillips, Burlington made for Blythe like a hawk swooping to claim its prey.

She nodded, a sweet smile stretching her kissable lips. The white feathers affixed to her hat's brim bounced as she responded to Burlington's comment.

Something he'd taken pains to make sure no one else heard.

The desire to push Burlington off his saddle onto his tight arse nipped at Tristan.

Lifting her head, the graceful arch of her swanlike neck stretched high to see above the crowd, she gifted Tristan with a stunning smile before veering her gaze to Francine.

He didn't doubt his huge grin made him look a lack-wit. She couldn't be that enamored with Burlington if she smiled at him that way. Could she?

Burlington noticed the exchange, and a frown briefly tightened his features. He touched Blythe's arm, regaining her attention.

Well, perhaps he'd permit Burlington to stay in his seat. Poor love-sick swain.

You're not far off yourself, old chum.

Twaddle. Tristan wasn't the type to let feckless emotions run rampant.

Cheeks rosy, Francine fiddled with her reins and sent several covert peeks Maddox's way. She'd seemed quite taken with him when they'd met at tea last week.

Tristan heartily approved. Mayhap he could enlist Blythe's help in that regard. What a perfect excuse to call upon her. They could play matchmakers.

Maddox extracted his watch from his waistcoat, and after glimpsing the face, sighed. "I'm afraid I have an important appointment. I'm quite looking forward to dinner tonight, Lady Ravensdale."

"We have special entertainment planned." Lady Ravensdale slanted her head.

"Not special, I'm afraid." Blythe rubbed her mare's sleek neck. "I've been coerced into singing and playing the pianoforte."

"*Adequate* entertainment for a simple evening at home, I'm sure." Miss Sanford's tone and falsely sweet smile indicated anything but.

"You haven't heard Blythe sing, Miss Sanford." Brette lifted her pert nose, a challenge in her tart response. "She's gifted."

"I'm rather anticipating her performance." Burlington turned to Blythe. "Perhaps you'd honor me with a duet?"

Burlington's puppy-like adoration caused Tristan's stomach to toss.

Of course he sang. Probably had a ruddy brilliant voice too. Tristan's could be described as ordinary.

"Miss Simmons, dare I hope you will be in attendance?" Maddox's ears glinted scarlet in the early morning sun.

Blythe's gaze flew to Tristan's and, lips trembling, she wiggled her winged brows. Amusement frolicked in her eyes as she overtly slashed her gaze between Maddox and Francine.

Tristan swallowed a snort of laughter as Francine turned radish red.

"Francine, I assumed you planned to join me this evening." Miss Sanford's mouth formed an unflattering pout. "We're attending the theater tonight. Might you also be, Lord Leventhorpe?"

"No, I've been extended an invitation to dine with the Ravensdales, as has my cousin, and I'm sure I'll enjoy Miss Culpepper's musical performance far more than Othello." He smiled at Blythe. He loathed Shakespeare, an unpopular sentiment among the tragedy-loving upper ten thousand.

"How ... gallant of you." Miss Sanford jutted her chin, scraping her caustic gaze over Blythe and the other ladies. She formed her lips into such a brittle smile, her face threatened to shatter with the slightest bump. "Another time then, my lord." She swung her horse in the opposite direction. "Mr. Phillips, I must return home. Mama and I have a fitting this morning."

"An appointment you've suddenly recalled, I dare say." Phillips smirked at her stormy glare.

"I shall accompany you, if you don't mind. I needed a word with you, Phillips." With a flash of his white teeth, Burlington lifted Blythe's hand. "Until tonight. The hours apart will be unbearable."

To prevent his guffaw, Tristan set his jaw and studied the array of leaves overhead. Why, there must be a dozen different verdant shades.

"I bid you good day." Phillips lifted his hat, and after a final, lecherous ogling of the ladies, and stabbing Tristan a darkling glare, he followed Miss Sanford.

Mrs. Sanford ought to rein her daughter in. Keeping company with gentlemen of Phillips's ilk, even if he was in line for a viscountcy, wasn't to Miss Sanford's benefit.

An almost indecipherable frown furrowed Blythe's forehead when Burlington left. Because she didn't want him to go, or because of whom he'd departed with?

Smoothing her features, she gave Tristan a saucy smile. "You promised me a Gunter's ice when I mastered trotting, and given this warmer weather, I would relish the treat."

"You did promise, Tristan. And she's quite accomplished already." Francine shared a smile with Blythe.

Tristan couldn't have been more pleased at the friendship developing between them.

"Gunter's will have to wait. We have fittings too. Gentlemen, if you'll excuse us." With a regal nod, Lady Ravensdale indicated the women should follow her. Everyone, including Ravensdale and Francine trailed behind her.

"We can discuss a time for your reward tonight, Blythe," Tristan said as she passed him.

"Excellent, my lord. By-the-by, I told Brooke I would sing if you joined me." Laughing naughtily, she tore after her family.

"I'll be damned." Whitehouse chuckled. "You're smitten, Leventhorpe."

"I'm no such thing. I've come to enjoy the company of Raven's new family, and I've found I can tolerate public gatherings far better when they are," *she is,* "nearby."

When he was a child, Mother had forbidden any female house servants due to Father's wandering eye and groping hands. Tristan had believed the lack, in addition to the traumatic loss of his virginity, had predisposed him against females.

The Culpeppers had infiltrated the barrier he'd erected, and while the wall remained, he didn't feel quite the need to protect himself or be constantly on guard. He rose in his saddle to turn and peer behind him. Blythe's splendidly rounded derrière tucked into her sidesaddle bounced softly, earning an appreciative smile from him. The soft mounds would fit nicely in his hands.

Hell. Whitehouse *might* be right.

Was right.

How, in such a confounded short time, had that happened? How had he made room in his bruised heart for her?

Fingering his glass of port, Tristan crossed his legs and relaxed into the gold and navy brocade settee. Blythe sat before the pianoforte, her long, slim fingers dancing atop the keyboard as she sang a lively duet with Burlington. To Tristan's sheer delight, Esherton's bawling calves carried a tune better than the chap.

Burlington hit a particularly discordant note—*make that the sheep and crows too*—and Tristan flinched, though he studiously controlled his features and stared at his glass lest he laugh aloud. No one appreciated being laughed at, but, by God, couldn't Burlington hear himself?

Did Lady Ravensdale fear the cut-crystal mantel lamps might shatter? Or perhaps the diamond-paned leaded glass windows? Daring to shift his attention from his tumbler's scarlet contents for a moment, Tristan inadvertently snagged Ravensdale's eye and the trembling of his friend's lips nearly undid him.

Raven struggled as mightily as Tristan to curb his ill-timed humor. God help them if anyone dared snicker.

Blythe's beau wasn't perfect after all, and Tristan indulged in perverse, child-like satisfaction at the knowledge. Lifting his glass to take a sip, he hid his grin at the swiftly pained and masked expressions, determined and politely set mouths, and the occasional widened or startled eyes Burlington's inept performance produced.

God's toenails. Tone deaf as a flowerpot.

No. The comparison was unfair to the modest vessel.

Francine, more animated and prettier than Tristan had ever seen her, thanks to an extraordinary makeover by the Culpeppers, chatted quietly with an attentive Maddox. A union between the two would be a welcome blessing. Perchance the time had come to have a pointed discussion with Maddox and probe his intentions.

She deserved a decent man, and Tristan hadn't a qualm about Maddox. However, if he didn't have a serious interest in Francine, better to end things at once rather than break her fragile heart. Regardless, it was impossible to deny their absorption in one another. Both seemed oblivious of the camel caterwauling across the room.

Tristan scratched his nose, checking another troublesome sideways tug of his mouth.

Did camels caterwaul?

A silent petition to The Almighty followed lest he lose control of his tenuous grasp.

Despite his unfortunate lack of talent, Burlington sang with gusto. Tristan had to give him credit for exuberance if naught else. Thankfully, Blythe's lovely voice penetrated Burlington's off-key, baritone warbling.

Brette hadn't exaggerated. Blythe was profoundly talented. Rather unfortunate that respectable ladies of station couldn't take to the stage or sing opera. Tristan didn't doubt she'd be tremendously successful—with a bloody mile-long line of suitors waiting to become her protector.

His earlier joviality fleeing, he pinched the bridge of his nose to ease the tension his scowl created. He'd cherished the unexpected truce that had sprung up between them. He deemed few women his friend, yet that description best fit the easy companionship they'd forged.

What you feel for her is markedly more than friendship.

A woman as striking as Blythe wouldn't remain long on the marriage mart, and the way Burlington diligently pursued her, Tristan had expected an offer by now. Why he hadn't made one perplexed more than a little.

Why Tristan minded confounded a great deal.

You know why.

He ought to forbid himself to ponder it. After all, *he* wasn't shopping for a marchioness. Yet. Still, he couldn't toss aside his disquiet like last month's gazette, which aggravated all the more.

Do shut up.

Blythe ended the piece with a flurry of notes, and everyone broke into applause and polite words of appreciation. Oblivious that the praise wasn't for him, Burlington beamed and nodded as if he'd made a stellar debut presentation and didn't budge from her side.

Blasted cheery ... tenacious ... grinning barnacle.

"Leventhorpe, I distinctly heard Miss Culpepper say she agreed to perform if you joined her." Whitehouse leaned a shoulder against the fireplace's Italian Bardiglio marble mantel, his mouth pulled into a slight smirk. "I don't believe I've had the pleasure of hearing you sing."

Pausing in her perusal of the sheet music, Blythe lifted her head, a silent plea in her gaze. "Yes, your lordship. I'd quite appreciate it."

Freddy's howling would've been preferred if it spared her Burlington's grating bellow in her ear as she'd endured the past three songs.

"I'm afraid I don't sing." Tristan took a hefty swallow of wine. Not precisely true. He rather enjoyed singing and played the piano and violin too. Just not in front of an audience. True, the dinner had been intimate, and only a dozen people occupied the cozy, tastefully decorated drawing room, but he couldn't bear spectators.

Not since ...

"I understand." She bit her lower lip's outer corner, her shoulder slumping the tiniest bit. She flipped a couple more pages, hesitating briefly every now and again, before riffling through a few more. Probably trying to anticipate precisely how awful Burlington's contribution would be. "I'll find something suitable in a moment."

Suitable for a croaking bullfrog?

Blythe had graciously borne the evening's entertainment burden and had to have tired. Earlier, the women had harmonized to *The Joys of the Country*, and Drake, an accomplished pianist in his own right, had expertly played a Pleyel sonatina. Nevertheless, she'd played diligently for nearly an hour now.

"Heath tells me you have talent yourself, my lord." Lady Ravensdale looked up from the ... whatever it was she stitched—probably something for the babe given the tiny shape—and smiled at Tristan.

Bending his lips guiltily, Raven scratched his jaw. "I might have mentioned it in passing."

Miss Blaike—or was it Miss Blaire?—clapped her hands. "Do humor us, my lord."

The pained look her twin slid Burlington said what no one dared.

For the sake of everyone's hearing and sanity, Tristan's resolve wavered.

"Please, Tristan," Francine implored sweetly. Desperately.

Ah, so she had been aware of the yowling.

"Oh, very well, if you agree to a game of loo afterward, Miss Culpepper." That relieved Blythe of further entertainment duties. Someone else would have to step in, or those present would have to find another activity to pass the time.

Please God, anything but charades.

"Bravo, Leventhorpe." Drake raised his glass in a mock salutation.

Tristan finished his wine and after setting the glass upon the marble-topped end table, blew out an extended, silent breath. *Get on with it, old man.* He swung his foot to the floor. "I'm not accomplished by any means. Feel free to chat throughout, or cover your ears with your hands or pillows. I shan't be offended."

Could he ask them to look in the other direction too? Or remove themselves to another room?

"You're humility is admirable, my lord." A trifle reticent this evening, likely due to Hawksworth's surprising absence, Miss Brette rubbed Freddy's belly. "I'm sure your performance will be most pleasurable."

He gave her a gallant bow. "I shall endeavor not to disappoint."

Or break out into a cold sweat.

A grateful smile wreathed Blythe's face, and his stomach, or heart, or something in his torso, flopped uncomfortably.

He was almost certain the cause wasn't indigestion, nerves, or a fatal illness, though he didn't rule out poisoning. Phillips had been at the adjacent table at Brooks's when Tristan met Drake and Whitehouse there this afternoon. Fortunately, for once the cull had kept his mouth shut.

Through hooded eyes, Tristan indulged in a lingering appraisal.

God, Blythe was beautiful.

More than beautiful—exquisite—with her eyes glinting brightly in the candlelight, a slight flush of pleasure pinkening her cheeks, and her mouth berry red from nibbling her lips. A mouth formed for bewitching smiles and honeyed kisses.

Blythe had blossomed in recent weeks, and glowed from plenty to eat, enough rest, and happiness. Her gown, a soft white with fine embroidered vines and purple flowers, the same vibrant shade as her eyes, hugged her ribs and emphasized the tempting flesh peeking above the neckline. Her skin couldn't possibly be as silky and soft as it appeared.

He'd never explore those rounded bits of loveliness.

Listen to him. Even his thoughts waxed poetic, and he didn't like poetry. Ridiculous, confusing, emotional drivel and rhyming poppycock written by infatuated, corkbrained ninnies.

"The vanquisher claims the plunder," Drake murmured, giving Tristan a devilish wink as he strode past *accidentally* kicking Drake's foot and earning him a wicked chuckle.

He was one to talk. That conversation wasn't fit for mixed company.

At the pianoforte, Tristan stood to the side, making it clear Burlington should move. "If you wouldn't mind? I need to stand there to read the music. My seat on the settee is available ..."

Burlington reluctantly conceded, but not before seizing Blythe's *ungloved* hand and ardently pressing his lips to the knuckles.

Bold, indeed, and outside the bounds. Tristan rather envied his audacity.

"Thank you for the duet." Her gaze narrowed almost imperceptibly as she extricated her hand and then smiled round the room before meeting Tristan's eyes. "Do you know *The Last Rose of Summer*?"

"I've heard it often enough, and I can read music." On the pretext of studying the music, he bent nearer. In truth, he wanted to sniff her perfume. She wore something different tonight, a light, musky scent with a hint of mint and vanilla? The glimpse of the lush valley between her breasts came as an unexpected treat. "You're wearing different perfume?"

She started, a half-smile bending her mouth. "Why, yes. It was an early birthday present from my sisters and cousins. They had a custom scent created for me. I'd been using a scent Heath gave Brooke since I had no perfume of my own."

"Might I sit rather than stand?" Giving in to impulse, he flipped his tails out of the way and eased onto the dainty bench's edge. Much less intimidating than standing and being the object of everyone's focused attention. Besides, Blythe sat closer to the others, and created a sort of human barrier.

Hiding behind a woman. How ungallant. He sneered inwardly. *Poltroon. Coward. Nidgit.*

"Of course." She scooted over, yet his rear hung halfway off the rectangular stool.

Claiming all but an inch, scarcely enough to be considered a respectable distance between them, he cleared his throat, now dry as parchment. This mightn't't' have been a clever notion after all. A glass of anything cool would have been advisable given the more delectable view of her breasts as she bent forward to arrange the pages. His fingers twitched, yearning to explore the gentle slopes. The thin material of her gown did little to hide her long, slender legs, and the knowledge her bum rested so close to his caused an embarrassing rise in his trousers.

Think of something else.

"Your birthday is coming soon?"

"In ten days' time." Satisfied the pages were placed to read easily, she set her slender fingers to the keys. Veering him a sidelong look, she began the introduction. "The Wimpletons' have graciously agreed to host my birthday ball since Heath's house doesn't have a ballroom. You were sent an invitation."

Probably in the stack with his other unopened correspondences. He must hire a secretary. Or lease a house in Town and retain a butler. Dammit. He'd never entertained that idea before. What had beset him?

A whiff of perfume teased his nostrils and assaulted his senses.

Blythe had.

Dangerous entertaining such whimsical notions. No good could come of it. It was almost better when they'd been at constant odds. "And I most assuredly will be attending. Someone has to protect you ladies from the ne'er-do-wells."

"I'm sure Heath's counting on it. He's looking a trifle haggard these days." She chuckled, that throaty purr unique to her. "Miss Sanford too."

Tristan turned to her so swiftly, he almost lost his seat and grabbed the pianoforte's mahogany edge to keep his balance. He could use a nip of something. Anything. Tepid tea would do. He swallowed then gave a small cough. "Why do you say that?"

"I overheard her speaking, or venting, rather, to her mother at the modiste the other day. Quite by accident, I assure you." Coyness filled Blythe's indirect gaze, and a peculiar inflection shaded her tone. "I got the distinct impression she intends to be the next Marchioness of Leventhorpe. By Season's end."

With that unnerving disclosure, Blythe lifted her voice in song.

Tristan fell off the bench.

Of this one can be certain: there is always someone
with a mind more devious and a scheme more sly than yours.
~*Dignity and Decorum—The Genteel Lady's Guide to Practical Living*

8

A week later, sitting in Tristan's barouche, Blythe took in the bustle outside Gunter's Tea Shop. Given the number of carriages parked below the maples, many others had craved a cool ice on the warm day.

"What flavor do you recommend, my lord?" Patrons in the curricles beside Tristan's enjoyed an assortment of extravagant confections including a frozen berry-tinted treat and one that surely must be chocolate ice cream.

Though they'd operated a dairy farm, she hadn't tasted ice cream. None of the Culpeppers had ever indulged in anything extravagant or decadent. How did one choose from such an array of heavenly treats?

Tristan glanced up from his position beside his burgundy barouche's wheel. A few auburn curls dared to caress his beaver hat's rear brim. Attired in a cornflower blue jacket—an exact match to his eyes—black pantaloons emphasizing his long, muscular legs, tucked into slightly dusty Wellingtons, and a black and royal blue striped waistcoat encircling his torso, he cut a dashing figure.

Much too dashing for her to remain immune.

"I'm quite partial to the bergamot myself. It's a citrus similar to an orange. The barberry is also tasty." Tristan removed his gloves, and after acknowledging the greeting of a gentleman leaning against Berkeley Square's railing with a slight tilt of his head, laid the buff-toned leather on his equipage's edge. "I suggest you do the same, even if it's not the thing. When the ices melt, they can become quite messy. Your gloves are sure to become sticky and soiled."

"I'd like a barberry, please." Blythe drew off one glove. Wearing new cream kid-leather half boots, a soft green, almost white chintz overlaid with ivory lace and embellished with scalloped edges, and a brushed velvet eggshell-toned spencer, she resembled a giant gardenia. "Do you know what flavor you'd like, Blaike and Blaire?"

"Vanilla," they said in unison before bursting into giggles.

Of course they'd want the same flavor.

"Two vanillas, one barberry, and one bergamot." Tristan passed the young waiter a few coins.

"Yes, my lord." After another lingering look at the striking twins, the servant trotted across the square, dodging conveyances on his circumventive route.

Blythe might have accompanied Tristan to Gunter's alone without fear for her reputation—propriety allowed the excursion—but Brooke had deemed it wise to have the twins join them.

He hadn't objected to the extra company when he'd come to collect her and make good on Blythe's promised reward.

She had chaffed a mite at the forced chaperonage. After all, she'd been anticipating a precious hour or two alone with Tristan, and with the twins in tow, she'd be acting the part of governess. Though sweet, and not difficult of temperament, they possessed typical seventeen-year-old flightiness.

Mayhap not typical.

Blythe had never been featherbrained.

"Blythe, our friend Lady Claire is waving for us to join her and her grandmother. Might we?" Blaire indicated a cheerful redhead seated in a barouche farther along the square.

An elderly matron wearing a ghastly contraption teeming with ribbons and feathers atop her gray-peppered head smiled indulgently as Lady Claire, bouncing in her seat, waved and gesticulated enthusiastically at the twins.

"We can see you and his lordship. No one can suggest anything untoward." Blaike gathered her reticule and parasol, her gaze straying hopefully to her bubbly friend.

"I have no objection, but—" Blythe shook her finger as the twins leaped to their feet before she finished. "Mind your deportment."

Cause no scandal had been drilled into her these past weeks until she mumbled the phrase in her dreams.

Tristan assisted them to the pavement and chuckled as the grinning girls linked arms and hurried to their waiting friend.

"How do you tell them apart? They even have the same mole beside their left eyes." A slight crease lined Tristan's high forehead as he stared after them. "I have to memorize what they're wearing each time I see them, and that's after someone else addresses each, and I've deduced who is who."

Blythe laughed and shook her head. "If you spent more time with them, you'd notice they have distinct features and characteristics. Blaire also has a mole below her right nostril. Blaike is more gregarious."

"Ah, good to know." He rested his elbows atop the barouche's side. "You seem to be enjoying London now."

A more youthful, relaxed man had replaced the stern one she'd met at Esherton. Removing her other glove, she slanted her head in contemplation. "I suppose so. More than I'd expected, honestly, and I've met a few charming people. I do loathe the constraints imposed on women here. I crave the outdoors, and I cannot even go for a walk by myself. The riding lessons have made my stay bearable."

As had his company. Once he'd stopped being a cross-as-a-bear boor. He and Heath were two of a few men who enjoyed and participated in intelligent conversations with her.

Tristan's expression grew pensive, and he cut her an indirect gaze.

Ah, the intriguing bashfulness again. What a paradox.

Almost as puzzling as why she went all soft and warm inside whenever he gazed at her like that.

"I have ..." He scratched his ear and cast his focus to the pavement.

A breeze caressed the maple leaves overhead, sending them cavorting and dancing to a soundless melody, their gentle rustling nature's harmony.

"This is the first Season I recall that I haven't been ready to depart for Bristledale Court upon a week of arriving in London."

Squinting, Blythe wiggled her toes in vexation. Guineas to goiters that was not what he'd been going to say at all.

Almost as if nervous, he drummed his square fingertips along the barouche's gleaming edge, his focus flitting here and there ... everywhere except on her.

"Oh? And why is that?" She'd pry the truth from his lips by one means or another. Blinking coyly and forming a moue in the same fashion she'd seen other wide-eyed misses gaze at their beaux, she almost choked on an inward snort.

Tristan stared at her as if she'd sprouted a disagreeable growth on her chin.

Her attempt at flirtation had fallen flatter than an oatcake. Seems neither she nor Tristan was adept at the art.

Now what?

Laying her gloves beside her atop the cherry-toned leather seat, she swept him a casual glance. And almost swallowed her tongue at the heat simmering in his azure eyes. Blue eyes ought to be cold, icy, yet molten lava tinged his irises.

Good heavens. Did he imply ...?

Surely he hadn't meant *she* was the reason. Had he?

Pleasant tremors tickled her spine and arms. What a stupendous, utterly wonderful notion. One that might alter her perception of London and her future dramatically.

His lips tilted almost shyly, and he clasped the carriage door in a white-knuckled grip. "I—"

"Here you are, sir. Miss." The servant passed Blythe a dainty cup brimming with pinkish deliciousness. He handed Tristan his then looked about in bewildered disappointment for a moment. "Where are the other misses?"

Another conquest for her sisters.

"They've joined Lady Claire." Blythe indicated the black and gold carriage. She wanted to dump her barberry ice atop his neatly parted hair for interrupting Tristan. Now she mightn't ever know what he'd intended to say.

"Yes, I see them." Tendrils of sweet vanilla dribbled down the glass's sides as the waiter scurried to the twins.

Blaike and Blaire had taken to London much better than she. Their enjoyment was genuine, hers a practiced pretense, made more bearable by Tristan's regular company. The girls seldom spoke of returning to Esherton ...well, the newly constructed house there. It wasn't quite finished. Brooke wanted to make the final decisions regarding the interior.

Did Blythe alone long to escape the city?

"Might I ask why you all have names that begin with a B?" Tristan winked and gave her a crooked grin. "It's rather unusual and a bit confusing."

Relaxing against the squab, Blythe raised a brow good-naturedly. "My mother and aunt wanted to continue a long family tradition. Every woman has been bestowed with a name beginning with the letter B. As you've no doubt discerned, Mother and Aunt Bess had to resort to some, ah, creativity. Poor Brette and Blaike have feminized male names. I don't think I'll bother with the custom when I marry. I already stutter and stumble saying our names half the time"

"Oh, I don't know. I'm partial to Brenna, Brownen, Brianna, and Byrony." He took a bite, and Blythe couldn't haul her gaze from his pursed lips.

How delicious a kiss would be from his slightly reddened mouth at this moment.

Tristan took another bite, closing his eyes and making a contented sound.

God help her.

She scarcely checked the urge to lean forward and brush his lips with hers. Instead, she swallowed and attempted to gather her scattered thoughts. Spooning a taste of her ice, she savored the sweet coldness tingling on her tongue and cooling her overheated senses.

Grinning, he lifted his spoon. "You could expand the tradition to your sons. I rather like Bradford and Beauregard."

"Those are nice, I agree, and thus far, we've been spared a surname beginning with B. But gads. Can you imagine the confusion then?" Chuckling, she shook her head while enjoying another taste of her ice. "This is splendid, Tristan. Thank you."

"Blythe, I ..." A shadow darkened his face, and he shrugged. "I made you a promise, and I always keep my word."

Polite coolness had replaced the earlier velvety warmth of his tone, and she glanced at him sharply. In the past few seconds, something had changed drastically. His countenance grew aloof once more with the exception of a few stray sparks lingering in his gaze that he hadn't yet extinguished.

What the devil?

Taking another mouthful, she scoured her mind for a reason for his abrupt transformation. How had talking about names beginning with B caused him to retreat behind his staunch comportment again?

Might as well see what he'd been about to say, even if it made her a forward hussy. She preferred candid speech to polite ambiguity or subtle intimations. "You were about to say something, my lord?"

His expression bland, he finally met her gaze straight on. Every hint of anything other than formal civility had vanished. "It was of no importance."

Dash it to Hades.

"If you're through, I have another appointment."

The nugget of hope that had had the audacity to raise its pathetic head shriveled in her chest and retreated to a safe cranny to bashfully hide once more.

Stupid heart.

Stupid him.

"That's the longest set, and possibly the most energetic cotillion, I've ever danced." Laughing and breathless, Blythe sank into a curtsy on the Wimpletons' ballroom floor. Her birthday ball was well-attended, a crush, truth to tell, and she'd been dancing nonstop for the better part of an hour.

Mr. Burlington, a fine sheen of sweat on his upper lip, bent above her hand. "Quite the most enjoyable one I've ever been privileged to share with someone as beautiful as yourself. Would you do me the honor of another set?"

A third? That wasn't done unless ... Did he intend to propose?

She pressed a hand firmly to her middle to ease her sudden collywobbles.

Anticipation or dread?

A month ago, she'd have predicted anticipation. Now ... Trepidation better described the peculiar sensation assaulting her middle.

Yes, wouldn't readily pass her lips. As clichéd as the phrase was, she needed more time. To get to know him better. Get to know Tristan better, especially after their outing to Gunter's Tea House. To decide whether she could abide Town life for more than this Season.

"I'm afraid the rest of my dances are already promised." She shouldn't have been relieved, and guilt kicked its petulant heels hard against her ribs. Wouldn't a woman desperately in love hurl convention aside to be with their sweetheart?

She would. But Blythe didn't love him.

"Ah, I should have anticipated that." Winking devilishly, he straightened and fished his kerchief from a pocket. "Next time I shall claim them all."

Acceptable if they were betrothed.

He dabbed his forehead, and after finishing, tucked the cloth away.

Placing her hand into his crooked elbow, he guided her toward the terrace. "Would you walk with me outdoors for a spell? It's rather overwarm inside."

"A splendid idea." Unless he had another purpose for the suggestion.

Nonsense.

Even if he intended to propose, he wouldn't publicly. He'd been the embodiment of politesse these weeks past. She'd no reason to expect he would be otherwise tonight.

Besides, she feared her underarms were damp, such was the crowd, and her ball gown was an original. Hopefully, her perspiration wouldn't stain the fabric.

The Wimpletons, in collaboration with her dear cousins and sisters, had hosted an elaborate birthday ball in her honor. The house overran with yellow, peach, and white flower garlands and bouquets, as well as people wishing her well. She'd never had a grand birthday celebration, certainly nothing of this magnitude, and found herself overwhelmed and uncharacteristically emotional at the generosity and kindness.

A month ago, London and Society had rather appalled her, and now, the Season held more appeal than she'd ever foreseen. That didn't mean permanent residence in the malodorous city enticed. Visiting with the knowledge she'd be leaving and not returning was one thing. Staying on, enduring the continual scrutiny and rigid structures set by Society ... She shuddered slightly. And to think, some people thrived in this environ.

As Heath had predicted, the Culpeppers had niggled their way into *le beau monde's* good graces, after first rendering the *ton* off balance. Now they'd become wildly popular—as if she cared a beggar's purse about that sort of approval—and choosing what assemblies to attend had become a daily ordeal. A quiet evening at home had become a coveted thing of the past.

Such an abundance of flowers and sweetmeats arrived each morning, they'd started sending the previous day's tributes to local hospitals and orphanages.

The situation proved more amusing than flattering. Several gentlemen had called upon her, yet only two had captured her interest. Between Mr. Burlington's marked attention and having developed an unusual, yet comfortable, friendship with Tristan, deciding which gentlemen's company she preferred flummoxed her more than a little.

No. That was a fribble's nonsense.

Mr. Burlington affections were as transparent as new glass. He constantly complimented her, and in recent days had hinted strongly of a future together, yet Lord Leventhorpe—the deucedly complicated enigma—continued to rouse her curiosity, and she feared, had engaged her heart.

One man was pleasant and predictable, like summer weather. The other, a discordant winter tempest. Given the choice between an easy-going, cheerful, good-natured god and a reticent, sometimes surly, impossible-to-figure-out man, the choice was obvious to a blind crone.

Only it wasn't. And that vexed her all the more.

Logic and reason clearly weighed in Mr. Burlington's favor, so other than patent foolhardiness, why did she prefer Tristan?

Yes, he had a splendid physique, and reliving their world-tilting kiss had kept her awake many nights, but muscles and a well-formed mouth weren't criteria for selecting a husband.

They could be. If he was the man.

Mr. Burlington hadn't approached Heath to ask for her hand—not that he had a say now that she'd reached her first and twentieth birthday—but, as surely as burning wood snapped and popped, a proposal would be forthcoming. She was as positive as Friday following Thursday it would be soon, too. Very soon. Perhaps tonight even.

She could be happy with Mr. Burlington, perhaps not blissful, but more than comfortable. Couldn't she? Everyone expected her to accept his proposal. Catching her lower lip between her teeth, she peeked at him through her lashes. He doted on her, rather in a smothering fashion at times, and seemed anxious to please. And he was gallant and strikingly handsome.

Why then, did something unidentifiable niggle at the recesses of her mind, enough to keep her from admitting to herself that her response to him was anything more than physical attraction? Maybe her lack of experience with men was to blame, although in recent weeks, she'd been exposed to all manner of males. Charming, witty, shy, awkward, arrogant, even a few who'd tried to steal a kiss and whose toes she'd tromped in response, or whose acquaintance she'd preferred to have been spared.

Mr. Phillips's taunting smile encroached upon her contemplations.

The last two balls, he'd attempted to maneuver her into isolated niches. No surprise that he'd identified each nook and cranny, every hidey-hole and dark corner in the grand homes they'd been invited into. Pests and vermin always found the best places to lurk.

Mr. Burlington patted her gloved hand as they approached the terrace. "I'll find you a seat, and then I'll fetch us something to drink. We can take our walk after we've had our beverages."

Ever the considerate gentleman.

A bead of sweat trickled between her breasts, and she unfurled her fan. Enthusiastically waving her fan, she welcomed the cooling breeze, insufficient as it was. "That sounds lovely. I'm fair parched."

"As am I." He smiled down at her, a sensual glint in his russet gaze.

After exiting the French windows, they paused for a moment beyond the threshold, and she inhaled the mild, blossom-scented air. Framed by flowering shrubs, roses, and an assortment of other blooms, the terrace would be stunning in the daylight. Lanterns, scattered here and there, lit the lawn and illuminated a quaint, fairy-like footpath. She yearned to explore the wending, moonlit trail through the manicured shrubberies.

They rounded the house's side, and Blythe smiled in delight. A carved stone bench beckoned. It sat nestled between another pair of French windows and a pillar topped with a Grecian pot overflowing with flowers and greens. A faint light gleaming behind the partially drawn drapes revealed an unoccupied paneled library. No one milled this darker side, suiting Blythe fine. She relished a few moments of solitude, one of the things she'd craved most since leaving Esherton. "Perfect. I shall wait here."

Mr. Burlington lifted her hand, and after bestowing a fervent kiss upon the back, gently embraced her. His eyes darkened to jet-black shards, and his breath quickened.

He was going to kiss her.

She ought to object, yet her curiosity demanded satisfaction. Would his kiss be as devastating as Tristan's?

"Blythe." Mr. Burlington's mouth grazed hers, tentatively then more forcefully. He made a satisfied sound in his throat and sidled nearer, trailing his lips to her ear. "So beautiful."

Pleasant, though not world-tilting.

Blythe should've been disappointed, and yet she couldn't summon the false emotion.

"Please stop." She lightly shoved his shoulders. "Someone might come upon us."

A kiss in the garden wasn't likely to get her bundled off to the country, was it?

Breathing harshly, he released her. "I'm sorry. I've no excuse except that I was overcome by your beauty and the romantic setting. I've wanted to kiss you since the first moment I saw you." He flashed a boyish smile. "Please forgive my forwardness. I've been desperate to ask you—"

A laughing couple ran off the corner steps, likely seeking privacy as well. From what she'd glimpsed, the elegant garden provided several ideal locations for clandestine trysts.

"I should have stopped you sooner, but I confess to being curious." No sense pretending maidenly shyness. She'd wanted to know, and now she did.

His tawny brows peaked, and his lips curved into a gratified smile. "You were? And ...?"

Jiggling her closed fan at him, she laughed and sank onto the bench. "A lady never kisses and tells." Particularly if the kiss had merely been adequate.

Unlike Tristan's pulse-skipping, thought-scrambling assault on her senses.

"Please fetch our beverages, and then we can take a pleasant stroll." Perusing the tidy yard and neat flower beds, she pointed her fan at the flagstone walkway. "I'd like to explore that charming path. Do you know where it leads? "

"No, I've not had the occasion to wander it." His gaze skimmed the garden, the corners of his mouth tilting downward. "Are you certain you wish to remain here alone?"

Blythe relaxed against the seat's granite back. "I'm not alone. More than a score of people are a few feet away. I need simply call for assistance should I require it."

She could wrestle a calf or a sheep to the ground, so escaping a beau's unwanted attentions, should the need arrive, didn't concern her overly much.

"True. I'll return shortly." Mr. Burlington nodded slowly, before his face brightened, and he strode away, a perfect combination of male grace and refined breeding.

You could do far, far worse, Blythe.

She closed her eyes, and breathed in the perfumed air. Somewhere in the garden, honeysuckle bloomed.

The air escaped her in a frustrated puff.

Marrying into the upper crust hadn't been part of her plans when

Heath towed them to London. She'd assumed she'd marry a simple man with simple ways and simple wants. Mr. Burlington, though not titled, came from a distinguished family and was accustomed to a privileged life. More on point, he adored living in London, relished the hubbub, the assemblies, the noise.

How would he support a family? Her dowry would only go so far, and she'd eat her slippers before she'd accept another groat from Heath. Perhaps Mr. Burlington possessed his own wealth or had an income or allowance from another source.

She couldn't ask him though, now could she?

No, but she could ask Heath.

Blythe didn't mind hard work, and economizing was second nature. They could live modestly ... Well, she could. Could Courtland?—Mr. Burlington? She wasn't ready to call him by his given name yet which revealed much.

What about love?

Her eyes shut, she waved her hand before her nose, chasing away a persistent insect.

Perhaps her pleasant feelings toward Mr. Burlington would grow into something more. It was feasible. Why, a few short weeks ago, she couldn't abide Tristan.

He hadn't indicated interest beyond friendship, and he still kept a part of himself reserved ... almost as if he concealed a great secret or objectionable characteristic.

For a few moments that day at Gunter's she'd ventured to think he held her in esteem, until he'd donned his impenetrable mask again. She'd love to get beyond his exterior and have a glimpse of the real man. For the umpteenth time, Blythe tried to analyze her fascination.

"What is it about you, Tristan?"

"I cannot imagine why you whisper of one man when you've scandalously kissed another." Miss Sanford's haughty sneer nearly sent Blythe toppling off the bench in much the same way Tristan had tumbled onto his bum the other night.

Blythe bolted upright, her eyes popping open. "I cannot imagine why *you* think it your concern."

The chit had seen the kiss and wouldn't keep her painted lips sealed. Blythe peered beyond Miss Sanford's rigid posture. Had anyone else seen?

A dark figure, arms crossed, rested his shoulder against the house's corner.

Phillips.

Double Hades and purgatory.

Those two spent far too much time skulking about together for a couple not engaged romantically. Most peculiar given Miss Sanford's determination to leg-shackle poor Tristan.

Miss Sanford tromped to the bench's end, all pretense of civility gone. She placed her fists against her ivory and turquoise silk-clad hips and glowered. "Did Mr. Burlington propose?"

Of all the unadulterated gall.

Blythe made a pretense of smoothing her already wrinkle-free satin skirt embroidered with gold spangles before half-spreading her French painted brisé fan. The impulse to verbally flay Rosemary Sanford overwhelmed her, and she had to lock her teeth and take a pair of deep, calming breaths. Apparently, Mr. Phillips and Miss Sanford had been close enough to see the kiss, but not hear her conversation with Courtland.

"Well. Did he?" Miss Sanford stamped her foot.

Petulant child.

Blythe could have sworn no one had been nearby when she'd arrived on this side of the terrace. What had Phillips and Miss Sanford been doing? Lurking in the greenery? Something was off with those two.

Blythe offered a noncommittal smile and ran her fingertips along the fan's lace edge. "I can't imagine why you think it your affair."

Her face contorted with loathing, Miss Sanford bent near Blythe. "It is my business if you intend to continue to throw yourself at Lord Leventhorpe. He's mine, you ... you country ... *neep*."

"Neep? Calling me a turnip's the best you can do?" Blythe stood five feet, ten inches tall. Did the diminutive nit think she intimidated her? She shoved Miss Sanford aside as she rose

Phillips stiffened and slowly eased upright, yet made no move to intervene.

Weasel.

Blythe elevated her chin, drawing her spine to its full extension. God, how she wanted to slap the termagant's hoity-toity face. "I have a word of advice for you, and if you've an ounce of common sense in your spiteful, conceited, prettily-styled head, you'll listen."

"I'm sure you've no advice I'd ever consider taking." Miss Sanford swallowed audibly and flung Phillips a hasty glance. "Why don't you and your hick sisters take yourselves back to the country where hobgoblin scarecrows like you belong?"

"Two of those *scarecrows* are my cousins, including *Lady* Ravensdale." Blythe unfolded her fan fully and made a pretense of drawing a finger down the delicate ribs to the handle. "We used to kill our own chickens. Do you know how?" She spared Miss Sanford a fleeting glance. Blythe hadn't killed a fowl, but she'd seen it done many times. Farm girls didn't have time for squeamish stomachs.

Miss Sanford clasped her throat, her eyes round as twin British crowns. "I'm sure I don't—"

"Like this." With a twist and a jerk, Blythe snapped her fan's handle, the crack echoing eerily loudly in the terrace's isolated corner.

Miss Sanford's jaw dropped as she took a stumbling step backward with a strangled shriek. "Mr. Phillips!"

Phillips remained alert, yet disregarded her plea.

What did she think? He'd suddenly become gallant? What exactly was their relationship?

"You'd better disabuse yourself of notions where Lord Leventhorpe is concerned. A few days ago, he told me succinctly that, 'cows will produce whisky before I'd ever marry Rosemary Sanford.'" Blythe's jubilant smile held no warmth. "His words, not mine, dear."

"That's a foul lie!" Miss Sanford released an infuriated gasp and swung her arm.

Blythe seized her palm in mid-air.

"I *shall* hit you back, and I promise you, your nose won't be the same." Blythe jerked her head toward Phillips. "Do you wish to look like him? Or worse?"

"You ... you trollop. Why am I not surprised you'd resort to such violent measures?" Miss Sanford yanked her hand free. "I'm going to tell Mama."

Tattling toddler.

"Please do. And be sure to explain why you are prowling around unchaperoned with Mr. Phillips and how you tried to strike me first." Blythe tossed her broken fan onto the bench. "Consider carefully who my cousin-in-law is and who's in Lord Ravensdale's inner circle before you make an enemy of him. You mightn't find a single peer or respectable man willing to court you."

"Ooh. Ooh!" Miss Sanford fisted her hands and growled—*really growled*: a frustrated, infuriated suppressed roar—before turning on her heel and stomping across the terrace. She pushed Phillips hard in passing, and he laughed.

"Miss Sanford, I told you not to cross that vixen." Lust laced his sinister chuckle.

Where was Mr. Burlington? Shouldn't he have returned with her ratafia by now?

Well, Blythe wasn't dimwitted enough to loiter here with Mr. Phillips nearby. She might have the scandal she had wished for weeks ago, and now she wasn't quite ready to quit London.

She gathered her ruined fan—more wanton waste. When would she learn to control her temper?

"Miss Sanford is accustomed to having her way." Phillips meandered toward her, his bearing alert and predatory.

Botheration. Blythe had rid herself of one menace, merely to be confronted by another.

She rounded the bench, intent on gaining the stairs leading to the yard. Unfortunately, that meant moving farther away from those assembled along the veranda and circumnavigating the shrubberies, which completely concealed her from view until she made the patio's other side.

"No need to scurry away. I simply want to ask you a question." He angled across the stones to the other set of stairs.

Blast.

He would cut her off, and finding herself cornered by that cawker spelled ruination. Heath had candidly warned them of Phillips's propensity to deflower innocents.

Waiting until he reached the top riser, she whirled and bolted toward the French doors.

"Dammit." Phillips sprinted after her. "Wait."

Blythe's hem tripped her, but she managed to regain her balance. The ruffled border ripped when she tore it loose. The gown could be repaired. Her reputation couldn't. She must make the library.

The slight hesitation gave Phillips the fraction he needed to reach her. He snaked an arm around her waist, and before she could twist free, crushed her to his chest. Chuckling lecherously, he panted against her neck.

"Let go, you oaf." Blythe reared away as she brought her knee up, jabbing his groin and shoving his chest with all her strength. The instant his grip loosened, she sprang free.

Cursing, he grabbed his crotch and doubled over. He tottered away a couple of steps, hunched like a hundred-year-old crone. "You'll pay for that, bitch."

She seized her skirts, and after hauling them to her knees, kicked him in the arse, sending him into the bushes below. "Touch me again, and I'll see you castrated faster than snipping a baby bull."

Shaking, more from fury than fear, she sprinted to the French doors.

Empty, thank God.

Panting, she eased the door open and slipping inside, took care to slide the lock home, even though Phillips wouldn't follow her any time soon. She needed a few moments to compose herself, and then she'd go in search of Heath and tell him what Phillips had attempted.

Dash it all. She couldn't.

As certain as sheep grow wool, he'd challenge Phillips. She pressed a hand to her forehead. The annoying ache that she'd attributed to nerves and excitement thrummed full on now.

Truthfully, she wanted to find Tristan and fall into his arms and ask him to break Phillips's nose again. Break a lot more than his nose. She summoned a wry grin. She'd become bloodthirsty of late.

She drew one side of the drapes closed and had grasped the second panel to do the same, when upset voices penetrated the door.

Blythe froze mid-movement.

"She tried to hit me, Mama. If I hadn't dodged her, she'd have broken my nose as she threatened to do."

Lying virago.

"Shh, Rosemary, hush. Here, step inside, and I'll tell you what must be done. That Culpepper chit will not hinder our well-laid plans. You *will* be Lady Leventhorpe."

The devil she will.

The door handle dipped.

Blythe dove behind the drawn drape. Drat, her toes stuck out, and she could be seen from outside. Under cover of the velvet and obscured by an oriental screen, she dashed to the corner beside the window. Cowardice didn't compel her concealment. Quite frankly, she wanted to know what those conniving women planned.

Tristan must be warned of their scheming.

Ears straining, she held her breath as the door swished open followed by the soft clacking of two pairs of heels.

"Rosemary, we must up our strategy immediately." The door clicked shut. "The Season is almost at an end. We'll arrange for you to be found in a compromising situation with Lord Leventhorpe. Tonight."

One who acts with integrity and love will always be
victorious over another's calculating and conniving schemes.
~Dignity and Decorum—The Genteel Lady's Guide to Practical Living

9

Where was Blythe?

Ridiculous, this need to know her whereabouts. Or how much pleasure he drew from simply watching her ... listening to her.

Sipping champagne, Tristan stretched his neck and perused the colorful crowd swirling about the floor. The mirrored walls made the teeming room appear more crowded. Resting a shoulder against a Grecian column, he examined the ballroom and what he could see of the veranda, card room, and entrance from his strategic position.

Nothing.

She hadn't returned after exiting with Burlington, though he'd re-entered several minutes ago and chatted with that American heiress, Margaret Hemple.

Why had he left Blythe outside?

Perhaps he hadn't, and she'd come inside by way of another door. The house did boast three other entrances from the garden.

Should he go in search of her?

He flexed his jaw.

She might not appreciate his interference or the knowledge that he supervised her whereabouts.

Mrs. Hemple laughed and stepped closer to Burlington, placing her hand on his arm and fluttering her eyelashes.

He murmured something while delivering one of his charming smiles, and her upturned face pinkened. Bending nearer, he covered her hand in a proprietary manner as he whispered in her ear.

Brows faintly scrunched, she flung a fleeting glance at the doors and slowly nodded.

After another brilliant smile, and pressing an indecently long kiss to her hand, he finally made his way outdoors once more.

Frowning a touch, Tristan took another sip of the sparkling wine and combed the room. *Again*. Fourth time in as many minutes. *Hopeless sot*.

He'd seen Burlington and Mrs. Hemple driving together in Hyde Park two days ago, and three days prior to that, he'd come upon them at Gunter's. Thank God it hadn't been the same day he'd treated the Culpeppers to ices.

Did Blythe know her beau's devotion had strayed or at the least was divided?

Should Tristan tell her? More on point, would she care? Would Burlington's perfidy devastate her?

He derived no satisfaction from having at last discovered Burlington's flaw.

Blythe seemed quite entranced with him, and if the cur meant to toss her over for a wealthy widow, better it happened now. Damnation. Too blasted bad he couldn't blacken Burlington's eye if he did. Pursuing her and engaging her affections if he didn't mean to act honorably was outside the bounds.

To be fair, Mrs. Hemple had only arrived in London a fortnight ago, and Tristan's subtle questioning of Ravensdale and the Culpepper misses revealed that Burlington still sent Blythe bouquets daily and called as frequently. In recent days, he'd accompanied the Culpeppers to several gatherings as well. He couldn't have progressed to anything more than a flirtation with Mrs. Hemple, could he?

Did he mean to court two women simultaneously?

Blythe needed to know about Burlington's duplicity, yet Tristan didn't want to be the one to crush her heart. He cherished their amiable truce, and hurting her would be twisting a jagged, rusty knife in his chest too.

If Burlington wasn't trustworthy during courtship, would he stray after marriage?

Undoubtedly. Men of that ilk inevitably did.

Tristan stifled a yawn, rubbing the bridge of his nose with two fingers.

He hadn't been sleeping well again lately, except nightmares weren't the cause. Each time he dozed off, a vivacious, silver-haired, lilac-eyed, laughing nymph cavorted across his drowsy mind, jarring him awake. He couldn't quiet his mind or musings *or primal urges* when it came to

Blythe.

Now he had a fresh concern regarding her.

She was going to get hurt. It couldn't be helped. Either she was told now or, far worse, she'd learn of Burlington's treachery later.

It wasn't his business, Tristan reminded himself for the umpteenth time. Fat good that did. His conscience and desire guffawed in unison.

If it hadn't been for his promise to Raven, and how seriously Tristan took his position in the House of Lords, he would've been tempted to make for Bristledale Court straightaway. He had no right entertaining fanciful musings about his closest friend's ward when Tristan wasn't looking to wed yet. That was why, other than a single snatched kiss, Tristan had steadfastly kept his acquaintance with Blythe a casual friendship, nothing more.

Except, the bond was much more. At least to him. Fate recklessly trod a path of destruction over his well-laid plans and laid siege to his heart.

He canvassed the room again.

No sign of her, or Phillips and Miss Sanford, blister it. They'd disappeared outside also, after exchanging a brief word with Burlington when he'd returned without Blythe.

Pathetic, Tristan knowing those trivialities. Everything regarding Blythe interested—*fascinated*—him. Attending these deuced functions didn't intimidate nearly as much with her present. Even if he wouldn't claim more than one dance, and his gut churned constantly with disquiet wondering if Burlington would propose, and she'd accept.

Particularly since Burlington's eye had strayed in recent days.

Perhaps his excursions with Mrs. Hemple meant nothing, and he intended to offer for Blythe, which made him an unconscionable knave for encouraging Mrs. Hemple's hopes.

A betrothal would put an end to Tristan's friendship with Blythe. No man approved of his wife keeping company with bachelors. He'd miss their witty conversations and her delightful, throaty laugh. No other woman compared to her.

If Burlington made her happy and content, Tristan wished them well. Who was he to reveal Burlington's perfidy? Perhaps Blythe didn't want to know. She wouldn't be the first woman to turn a blind eye to her husband's indiscretions.

Tristan couldn't offer her anything until he'd abolished his demons, and a sweetmeat tossed amongst starving urchins would last longer than

Blythe on the marriage mart. She sensibly preferred Burlington's amiable personality, and Tristan knew full well others regarded him as unapproachable fellow.

He *had* been reserved prior to meeting Blythe. He hadn't smiled or laughed as much before becoming acquainted with the charming, strong-willed, vexing, sharp-tongued, wholly enchanting vixen.

Whitehouse had the right of it.

Tristan was smitten, and there wasn't a hell-fired thing he could do about it.

Still, caring for Blythe's wellbeing at assemblies was the least he could do for her and Ravensdale. Raven could scarcely watch all the moon-eyed swains and cocksure-blades swarming the other Culpeppers. One less woman to fret about would ease his mind and Tristan's.

He snorted softly.

God, listening to his vacillating, mental claptrap made him want to slap himself. With a cudgel.

Phillips's persistent interest in Blythe proved disconcerting.

Hence at social functions, Tristan spent half his time following the unsavory cull, and the other half evading Miss Sanford's dogged pursuit. Why didn't the two leave off when the objects of their attentions didn't return their regard? Hadn't she or Phillips a morsel of pride? Or could they be so self-absorbed that they disregarded the other party's feelings? Not a healthy mindset and one that would certainly result in disappointment.

If it hadn't meant he would've had to enter into the parson's mousetrap, he would've claimed a secret betrothal to rid himself of Miss Sanford.

"Looking your usual pensive self tonight, I see Leventhorpe. Must be really enjoying *this* ball. I think it one of the better assemblies this Season, personally." Hawksworth's lopsided grin belied his sarcastic comment. Squinting, he scrutinized the ballroom's far side. "What the deuce have you been glaring at by the French windows the past fifteen minutes or more?"

"I see you finally escaped your parish." Tristan spared him a sideways glance. "How'd you manage that?"

Hawksworth chuckled, pulling his earlobe. "My official duties brought me to this side of Town, and Drake cordially invited me to accompany him." He cocked his head, quirking a brow. "And don't think you can avoid answering the question by distracting me. You've downed two flutes of champagne, danced not at all, and the darkling scowls you've directed at Burlington and the benign beveled panes there," he jerked his head indicating the room's other end, "have more than one tongue wagging."

Tristan wasn't about to tell Hawksworth. "I'm contemplating whether I can make my escape."

Outside, to find Blythe.

Hawksworth shrugged and looked over his shoulder. "With this throng, I don't think our hosts would notice. There's hardly room to mill about. Smashing success." His keen gaze bored into Tristan. "How are you managing? You look all-in."

"Fine, as long as I keep my senses dulled." He paused in raising his empty glass when Phillips stomped past, a leaf poking from the hair above his ear, a smudge, suspiciously resembling dirt, along his knee, and ire smoldering in his eyes.

Blythe. If Phillips touched her...

Phillips made straight for Miss Sanford as she whispered to her mother and grandmother, all three staring pointedly in Tristan's direction.

That trio of Medusas couldn't be conspiring anything good.

Thrusting his glass at Hawksworth, Tristan swiveled toward the French windows. "See if you can discover what Phillips has been up to. He looks like he's been frolicking in the shrubberies. Be discreet."

Jaw set and gut knotted, Tristan strode to the exit, dodging dancers and earning more than one vexed pout and scowl of displeasure.

Phillips's rumpled appearance, and his reputation for forcing women, as well as Blythe's continued absence, wreaked havoc upon Tristan's usually stoic conduct.

A glowing Francine and beaming Maddox intercepted him at the threshold.

Bloody he—

Tristan barely prevented the oath tapping irately at his teeth.

"Just the person we've been searching for." Francine fairly bubbled, her eyes sparkling and her cheeks rosy. "I ..." She gave Maddox an adoring gaze and nestled nearer him. "We wanted you to be the first to know."

"Am I to assume felicitations are in order?" Nothing of interest on the terrace beyond them caught Tristan's attention; therefore, he momentarily put aside his worry and offered a congratulatory smile.

Maddox's mouth lifted at one side as he slipped Francine's hand into his elbow's crook. "I hope you aren't offended I didn't approach you first, Leventhorpe. We were strolling the gardens, and I couldn't wait another moment to ask Miss Simmons, Francine, to become my wife."

"Not offended at all. I'm delighted." Tristan shook Maddox's hand and then pressed a quick kiss to Francine's forehead while surreptitiously scouring what he could see of the veranda and lawn. "My sincerest happy wishes to you both."

Dammit, where is Blythe?

"We want to marry straightaway, as soon as the banns have been read." Francine laid her hand on Tristan's forearm. "Tristan, would you give me away?"

A surge of emotion rendered him speechless. He swallowed and cleared his throat. "I would consider it a tremendous honor."

"Splendid. Come, darling, let's share our joyous news." Maddox led her away, and a crowd of well-wishers promptly gathered about them, though Miss Sanford wasn't amongst them.

Francine and Maddox made a brilliant couple and they were smitten with one another. Tristan found their devotion charming and truly touching. Perhaps his pessimistic nature had softened.

A trifle more light-hearted than he had been mere minutes before, he turned onto the veranda. A quick sweep of its length confirmed Blythe's absence. Hands braced at his hips and jaw tense, he turned one way then the other.

Which should he search first?

The garden, the pathway, or the veranda's other side? What about the lane to the mews beyond the fence?

He scratched his nape. Come to think of it, he hadn't seen a single Culpepper, or Raven, for that matter, for a good while. Not that he'd have noticed, intent as he'd been on seeking Blythe.

Besotted. Thoroughly and entirely. And doomed to disappointment.

"There you are, my lord. I worried you meant to stand me up for my dance." Lady Ravensdale glided his way, a vision in cream and lavender, a mischievous smile brightening her lovely face. "Although, I suspect you'd prefer my cousin to partner you."

She knows?

Tristan managed to keep his jaw from unhinging and crashing into his chest.

Winking, she swept nearer. "Your secret is safe with me, Lord Leventhorpe."

"I wouldn't be so inconsiderate as to miss our dance, my lady." Actually, he'd completely forgotten the commitment. He wasn't about to address her second statement. If the day ever came that he admitted to what she insinuated, it wouldn't be in public.

"I'd offer to let Blythe dance in my stead, but I don't believe I've seen her since her set with Mr. Burlington. She's quite in demand tonight. It is her birthday celebration, after all."

Had the inflection in her voice altered the merest bit when she said Burlington's name?

Placing her hand upon his extended arm, Lady Ravensdale accompanied him inside. The blast of heat and body odors of a hundred people crowded into the insufficient space assailed him.

"Perhaps she's in the retiring room having a lie down." Lady Ravensdale smiled at a group of matrons chatting in hushed tones to one side of the windows. "She was feeling peaked earlier."

"She's unwell?" Had something happened with Phillips or Burlington to cause her malaise? Tristan could barely restrain himself from bolting upstairs and asking.

"No, nothing of that nature. She claimed a slight headache from the excitement. I advised her to take a powder and lie down with a cold cloth upon her forehead." Giving him a sympathetic smile, she curtsied prettily as the strains of a waltz filled the air. "I've sent her sisters to check on her and expect her to join us shortly."

"I'm relieved to hear it. I grew concerned when she didn't return after venturing outdoors with Burlington." Why didn't he blather a little more—go ahead and confess his infatuation?

"My lord, it's not my place to tell you, and I abhor gossip ..." Lady Ravensdale bit her bottom lip, and cast a guarded look about as he guided her past other swaying couples. "I overheard Mrs. Hemple a short while ago, quite inadvertently, I assure you." Her lavender-blue eyes so like Blythe's, Lady Ravensdale raised her pained gaze to his.

"What has you distressed, my lady?"

"Mr. Burlington has asked to pay his address to Mrs. Hemple, which must mean he has decided she would make a suitable bride. I'm afraid Blythe will be made a laughingstock."

Tristan missed a step, but quickly recovered and swung his head to the gaping French windows. Then why the hell had Burlington gone outdoors? To deliver the unpleasant news to Blythe? "Please forgive me, Lady Ravensdale. Are you certain? Burlington seems most devoted to Miss Culpepper."

She nodded, the curls framing her face pirouetting at her exuberance. "Oh, yes. I was in the retiring room suffering from a bout of nausea. They weren't aware I was behind the screen, and I was too discomfited and disturbed by Mrs. Hemple's announcement to make my presence known afterward." A blush tinted her face. "Mrs. Hemple confided her 'joyous news' to Lady Wimpleton. I think they are distant cousins, but I may have that wrong. I have no reason to believe she lied. I do want Heath to speak with Mr. Burlington before I tell Blythe in case I heard incorrectly."

Tristan would bet Buce she hadn't.

God rot Burlington, the unscrupulous knave. Tristan maneuvered Lady Ravensdale round Mrs. Sanford and her portly partner.

Miss Sanford's mother summoned a brittle smile and tilted her head before dragging her partner, huffing and puffing and sweating like a lathered horse, off the dance floor.

Had she overheard?

She'd practically followed Lady Ravensdale and Tristan as they'd danced at the expense of Mrs. Sanford's rotund partner who appeared about to expire from exertion. A naked doxy delivering a sermon from Hawksworth's pulpit claimed more subtlety than the eavesdropping Mrs. Sanford.

Damn. Tristan needed to find Blythe and tell her before that she-cat or her gloating daughter did. "Raven told me your wonderful news, my lady. Congratulations."

"We are very happy." A glorious smiled wreathed Lady Ravensdale's delicate features.

Their dance ended, and they went through the perfunctory bow and curtsy. Her eyes clouded when she gazed past him.

"Botheration. Heath has heard as well, I'll wager." Lady Ravensdale waved shortly at Miss Brette standing beside Ravensdale, a troubled expression tugging his black brows together. "My lord, I know it's not my place, nor yours, and I don't wish to impose or make you uncomfortable. But if you care for Blythe as much as I suspect you do, perhaps you can help ease her mortification and salvage her pride a degree?"

Given the wry twist of her lips, Tristan's astonishment must have reflected upon his face. “How so? We’ve established a truce of sorts, but Miss Culpepper is not exactly fond of me.”

His heart twinged as he spoke, and she laid her hand on his forearm. “You’re wrong in that regard, my lord. Very wrong.”

A man consumed with love or lust schemes more than countless criminals, and a diligent woman guards herself against his ploys.
~Dignity and Decorum—The Genteel Lady's Guide to Practical Living

10

Blythe waited several interminable seconds after the library door clacked shut before daring to move. Tristan must be warned of Miss Sanford's intent to entrap him. Blythe ought to have exploded from behind the curtains and stopped the ill-hatched plotting, and had she not been utterly flabbergasted, she'd have corralled her wits sooner and done so.

Now she understood her instinctive dislike of Miss Sanford from almost the first moment she'd met her. The pert hussy possessed a warped soul.

She'd not sink her sorceress's talons into Tristan if Blythe could help it.

Edging along the drapery, she finally reached the door. She fumbled with the blasted lock until it slid loose then whipped the door open. After a quick glance about the room and veranda, she slipped outside. No sooner had she shut the door then Mr. Burlington strode across the veranda, his eyes crinkled at the corners in excitement.

"Please forgive my tardiness." He drew his golden brows together a degree and sliced a swift glance behind her into the library. "I was detained. I hope you didn't become impatient, darling."

Darling?

Surely that meant he intended to propose.

Not now.

She didn't have the time to gently turn him down, for refuse his offer she must. He didn't stir anywhere near the kind of intense emotions or turmoil Tristan did, and those few minutes in the library overhearing Miss Sanford's wicked intentions had compelled Blythe to face what she'd denied for weeks now.

Stupidly, and against her better judgment, she'd gone and fallen in love with crotchety, obstinate, impossible Tristan. Her perverse heart had chosen the one man she could never have.

Love had an irregular sense of humor.

Casting about for a reason to stall the inescapable, she waved at Mr. Burlington's empty hands. "Where are our drinks?"

His cheerful expression faltered momentarily, and he gave a contrite laugh. "Eager to return to you, I forgot them."

What had he been doing then? He'd been gone upward of fifteen minutes.

He took her hands and gave her a sensual smile, calculated to soothe her ruffled feathers, she'd wager.

"You know I adore you, don't you, Blythe?" Advancing a pace, he cupped her upper arms, and brushed his thumbs back and forth, his eyes darkening to mahogany. "You captured my heart from the first moment I saw you. I knew you were refreshingly different from the coy misses. You're singularly unique. Special."

A bit overdone, there.

"Mr. Burlington ... Courtland ..."

"I want to marry you, dearest heart, I do—"

"I know you do, and I am honored—"

"But," he dipped his golden head as if intending to kiss her again, "I'm sure you also understand why I cannot ask you to be my wife."

Blythe leaned away and squinted at him. "You cannot?"

He continued to give her that roguish smile, the one that had set her heart aflutter and her bosoms puckering the first night she'd met him.

Nothing fluttered or puckered or gave the tiniest twitch.

"Cannot?" she croaked again. A dim-witted parrot sounded more intelligent. Blythe almost stuck a finger in her ear or shook her head to make sure she'd heard him correctly.

He had said, *cannot*, hadn't he?

And he expected her to understand why?

He seemed nonplussed for a flash.

Kicking her tangled emotions to next year, she narrowed her eyes further and examined every plane and angle of his handsome face, scrutinizing his countenance objectively for the first time.

How had she missed the slightly petulant turn to his mouth or the shrewd glint in his arresting eyes these past weeks? Those characteristics had been there, surely? Naiveté couldn't be blamed entirely. Truth to tell, she'd not wanted to see past his attractiveness and his apparent devotion. He *had* been courting her. She was neither slow-witted or given to fanciful imaginations.

Icy tendrils slithered round her shoulders and arms as she eased from his embrace. Shivering, she hugged herself. No honorable man called a woman darling when announcing he couldn't offer her marriage. What was his game?

"Please humor me and explain why we cannot marry." This should prove highly enlightening.

Courtland recovered his composure, or rather summoned his most engaging air, and closed the distance between them. Touching her cheek with his forefinger, he trailed it to her ear. "Surely you understand these things. My brother is not well. I'll likely inherit the title, and though I'm sure your dowry is quite adequate for a commoner ..."

Blythe slapped his hand away. What she yearned to do was plant him a facer. Right in his too-perfectly-straight, noble cork.

"Are you saying I'm not rich enough for you to marry, Courtland, or is it my lack of position that's objectionable? Or perchance both? I'm not wealthy *or* highborn?"

He blinked stupidly, as if surprised by her reaction. "Sweeting, don't take on so. No need to kick up a dust. I didn't expect to love the woman I take to wife."

How forward thinking of you. Dolt.

Tapping her chin, he delivered another of his disarming smiles.

Instead of his touch sending giddy ripples along her nerves, she fought the urge to cast up her accounts upon his gleaming shoes. She wrapped her arms tighter about her shoulders and drew her chin away.

He cradled her cheek in his palm. "You hold my affection, darling. I do love you, more than I believed I'd ever love a woman, and I am determined for us to be together. And I know you love me too. I've seen it in your eyes and the way you smile at me. You haven't been the least coy or reserved. Why, it's apparent, even to others. Several have congratulated me on my good fortune."

Had she been that humiliatingly obvious?

Stupid, stupid, *stupid* green girl.

"Although we cannot wed, Blythe, I have contrived a way for us to be together."

Did he not see the visual daggers she was hurling at him or the tense line of her mouth as she battled to subdue the curses she'd overheard in Esherton's barns?

His arrogant confidence raised her ire another notch. Fine then. Sent it hurtling heavenward, screeching in livid umbrage. "Do tell, Courtland. You've clearly thought this through. I'm most anxious to hear what you have *contrived*."

He nodded a mite too eagerly, and she curled her toes and fingers tightly to maintain her composure. How would he like a nose like Phillips's? With precisely the right angle and enough force, she was certain she could manage something similar ...

"Such arrangements are not uncommon, and with a rich wife, I can indulge your every want." He brushed her cheekbone with his thumb.

"How ... generous of you."

"I know you were dreadfully impoverished in your prior life, and must covet the fineries you've been denied." He cast a hasty glance around and dared sidle a pair of paces closer. Indecently close, truth to tell. "I'll treat you far better than my wife, I assure you. I merely want her money, nothing else. She's simply an inconvenience I must endure." He skewed his mouth to the side. "Well, I'd have to beget an heir. Perhaps a spare as well to assure the title continues."

Why stop at two? Try for a half dozen.

Blythe went rigid and dropped her clenched hands to her sides as her stomach pitched to her shoes. Pasting a falsely sweet smile upon her face, and carefully modulating her tone, she unfurled her fingers. Better to scratch his deceiving, conniving, treacherous ... blackguard eyes out. Good God. What had she ever seen in this conceited, self-centered lout?

"Are you suggesting..." She sucked in a slow, steadying breath.

Lord, help me not to attack him.

Cocking her head, she forced the foul words past her tongue. "Are you offering me carte-blanche? You're suggesting I become your mistress?"

She pressed a hand to her roiling middle. Pity women couldn't fight in affairs of honor. She'd call the ruddy cur out, except she neither knew how to brandish a sword nor fire a pistol. Heath did, and would challenge Burlington in a blink if she told him about the affront. With a babe on the way, that bloody well wasn't going to happen.

"Yes." Courtland grinned excitedly, moving forward and compelling her to retreat until she bumped into the pillar beside the doorway. "It's the flawless solution—"

Flawless? *No.*

"—don't you agree?"

Agree? *When cows poop gold.*

"Phillips suggested the brilliant remedy. We can be together, sweeting, and I can do my duty to my title and family." He reached for her again, but she evaded him, fervently looking about for something to clobber him with in lieu of a club.

How could a man be so dense? Thick as oak and ignorant as a rock. Did he think she'd grasp the chance? That the honor of becoming his paramour held such appeal she'd toss her reputation and her family's into the gossips' cesspool?

Courtland winked conspiratorially and waggled his eyebrows. "I've already selected an heiress."

Poor woman, whoever she was.

"Oh. Is she someone I know?" The pillar shuddered, and the pot atop it rattled when Blythe—intent upon dodging Courtland's grasping hands—bumped into it.

Uneasiness creased the edge of his mouth, and he slowly shook his head. "I don't believe so. She's an American widow, and tonight, she agreed to allow me to court her."

Hence his tardy return. Did he expect Blythe to wish him joy?

He tipped his mouth into a boyish, almost bashful smile. "That's what delayed me. I'm sorry I wasn't forthright from the beginning. I worried you might take offense and react peevishly, but you're such a sensible woman—"

"How considerate of you." Tarring and feathering was too good for the likes of him. Nipping his ballocks off might be appropriate.

She dropped her broken fan, and he promptly bent to retrieve it.

Ever the gentleman.

She seized the potted plant, staggering from its surprising weight. She lowered her voice seductively. "Courtland?"

"Yes, darling?" He glanced up, his brandy-colored eyes widening in shocked comprehension.

"I wouldn't be your *whore* if the king decreed it." She released the plant atop his head, smiling in satisfaction when he toppled like a foxed-to-the-gills tippler.

Happy birthday to me.

Two laughing couples swept up the steps, stumbling to a stop and bumping pell-mell into one another upon spying him. A startled yelp escaped a woman as she clutched her companion's arm.

With the exaggeration of someone who'd practiced the art repeatedly, the other lady pressed her hand to her bosom, shut her eyes, and swayed dramatically. "Is he ... dead?"

One could hope, but if so, the gibbet awaited Blythe. She'd likely only concussed Mr. Burlington though. A few more curious passersby peeked above the bushes before breaking into frenetic whispering.

One fellow raised his quizzing glass and peered through the lens, as if he needed help distinguishing a man's prone form splayed upon the pavers, dirt sprinkled upon his face, and a red geranium upright upon his forehead. "I say, what happened to Burlington?"

"I declined his proposal." He had made a proposition, all right. Just not an honorable one. "As you can see, he didn't take the refusal well. Keeled over straightaway."

With her assistance.

He moaned and moved his head slightly, earning him sympathetic murmurs from the quartet.

Blythe neatly stepped around him. She couldn't dredge up an ounce of remorse. "You might want to summon a physician."

Or don't. Let the bugger rot.

She'd ruined her chances of making a suitable match. Whether Burlington was a cur or not, plopping pottery atop aristocratic heads, especially gorgeous, eligible ones, didn't fly well with the upper ten thousand.

Just as well.

She'd allowed the pomp and flattering male attention to woo her, fool her into thinking Society wasn't horrid after all. People did, indeed, see what they wanted to see. Well, no more. Succumbing once to foolhardiness might be excused. Doing so again made her fair game and she deserved everything slung her way.

She inhaled deeply. Enough self-castigations for now.

No one knew better than she how gullible and susceptible she'd been. There would be plenty of time to dwell upon her foolishness and chide herself to purgatory and back. Right now, she must alert Tristan. It might be too late already.

Fearing what she'd eaten today was about to make a reappearance, Blythe lifted her skirts and bolted into the library. Stumbling over the threshold, she yelped in alarm when a hand clamped onto her arm.

Phillips.

And he wasn't alone. Miss Sanford also occupied the room. Vengeance glittered in their hardened gazes.

Why in blazes did Blythe keep encountering these miscreants? Did Fate simply have a rancorous streak?

"Unhand me!" She wrenched free of his grasp and spun to flee whence she'd come, except Phillips sprinted to the door ahead of her.

He smiled—equally gloating, arrogant, and merciless—and shoved it shut with an ominous thud. The lock slid home disconcertingly loudly, but the rasp of him dragging the curtains closed caused the hairs along her nape to lift.

Hopefully, Phillips slamming the door alerted the foursome outside. Would they notify anyone? They might think Blythe was simply having a fit of temper. Or were they too focused on Mr. Burlington to have noticed?

"Precisely the person we sought." Miss Sanford's expression settled into crafty lines, and half-seated upon the divan's gold and taupe damask rolled arm with her arms crossed, she slanted Mr. Phillips a sly glance. "So, Mr. Burlington threw you over, did he? Cannot say I blame him. Personally, I found it astonishing he'd deemed to wallow in muck."

"Tsk, tsk." Mr. Phillips stood with his arms akimbo, eyeing Blythe toe to top. "Serves you right, putting on airs. He's picked another mark, has he? Someone with a much flusher purse. His family might possess an old title, but they're pauper-poor, and he has to marry for money. Some of us have been blessedly spared that obligation."

Had Mr. Phillips and Miss Sanford been listening at the door? How else would they have known what had transpired between her and Mr. Burlington?

"I'll allow, I did rather admire his other clever notion." Leering at Blythe's bosoms, Phillips ran his tongue over his protruding bottom lip. "Wait. I suggested the idea."

Every part of Blythe tried to shrivel to escape his lewd appraisal. If only she had her shawl to shield her cringing flesh. She thrust her chin upward and marched to the interior door. They could bugger themselves before she rose to their bait. Miss Sanford's presence in the library gave Blythe hope she hadn't yet succeeded in cornering Tristan.

With an unladylike snarl, Miss Sanford leaped to her feet. Blocking Blythe's path, she jabbed a forefinger at her. "You're not going anywhere. I'm tired of you interfering. It's taken me the better part of two Seasons for Lord Leventhorpe to pay me any note."

Blythe released a snort worthy of a bull's admiration. "Vain imaginations from a chit too dull-witted to see the truth."

"You're not going to destroy what I've striven for. I won't be forced to marry that ancient, smelly, doddering fool my uncle has selected for me because he insists I gain a title." Flapping her hand, Miss Sanford sneered, her face contorted like a child in the midst of a tantrum. "Especially since Mr. Burlington has tossed you aside."

Her exultant smirk proved she relished Blythe's situation.

Find Tristan.

As Blythe sidestepped to go past, Phillips seized her from behind, trapping her with an arm below her breasts and his other pressed across her chest in a crushing embrace. "You're staying here with me, in order for Miss Sanford to snare herself a lord."

Not if Blythe wanted to keep her virtue, she wasn't.

From the satisfaction shining in their evil gazes, it didn't take a scholar to discern that was precisely what Phillips and Miss Sanford intended.

My total ruination.

He licked her ear, pressing his forearm into her breasts until she feared they'd breach her bodice.

Revulsion sluiced through her and sent her scalp puckering.

Stomping upon his foot with her heel—blast, what she wouldn't have given for her sturdy half-boots—she gulped in a huge breath, prepared to let loose with a banshee's screech meant to peel the paper from the walls, warp the coffee-and-emerald-toned marble encasing the fireplace, and bend the brass tools propped to one side.

Phillips anticipated her scream and slapped his sweaty, dirt-streaked palm over her mouth.

Writhing against him, she gagged and choked.

Chuckling, the sound gravelly and deranged, he dragged her, struggling and attempting to bite his hand, away from doorway. His sour odor sent another surge of burning bile to her throat. Blythe's lighter weight and his iron grip prevented her from wriggling free.

The key clasped in her gloved fingertips, Miss Sanford glided from the library with a triumphant smile and mocking wave.

Now how would Blythe warn Tristan?

An instant later, the lock turned.

The witch had locked Blythe in the library with Phillips. How could anyone be that calculatingly evil?

Miss Sanford had arranged for Phillips to despoil her because she mistakenly believed Blythe competed for Tristan's affections?

Nipping her neck hard, Phillips seized her embroidered muslin gown at the nape. His breath coming in ragged gasps, he ripped the fabric down her back, accidentally giving her the small amount of slack she needed to slip free.

His debauched laugh as she sprinted away toppled her stomach. Her neck throbbed where he'd bitten it though she didn't think he'd broken the skin. She didn't dare touch it to find out. She needed both hands to preserve her modesty.

"I hoped you'd be a fighter. They're the best to bed. Not the chits who whimper and beg for mercy. They concede too easily." The crazed glint in his eyes intensified. "I'll wager you'll fight until the end."

He's utterly mad.

She darted behind the settee, trying to keep her breasts somewhat covered while searching for a weapon with one eye and keeping her other trained on Phillips.

Grinning evilly, he stalked forward. "No one knows you're in here except Rosemary, and I'm certain, for once, her lips are tightly sealed. Both doors are locked. You cannot escape me, Blythe."

God, please.

Blythe crept along the settee. She had one chance, and it meant baring her bosoms to Phillips's lascivious scrutiny. Scooting another few inches, she bit her bottom lip and deliberately let her bodice dip lower, revealing her insignificant *décolletage.*

He paused midstride, his gaze flicking to hers before gravitating to her breasts again. He licked his lips, his face gone taut with lust. "If I didn't know better, I'd think you were teasing me with your tits."

Disgusting, crude pig.

"You won't get away with this. Heath will kill you." Her gown slid to her elbow, the golden embroidery threads shimmering where the lamps atop the fireplace mantel cast their glow. She left the torn material where it gathered at her crook, the entire side of her breast visible.

His gaze remained riveted to her exposed flesh. Just the distraction she needed.

A few more inches.

Phillips was almost upon her.

She released her dress, and the lace-encrusted cloth bunched at her waist.

Jaw sagging, he gaped.

She seized the poker.

Understanding dawned, and head down, like an infuriated, thwarted bull, he lurched forward, blaring profanities.

Shrieking, she thrust the poker with all her might as he collided with her, slamming her head into the marble at the same instant the French window shattered and a madman's bellow filled the room.

Dropping the poker, she slumped to the floor, Phillips's weight crushing her, as something warm and sticky gushed down her face. She struggled, trying to call for help.

"Tris ... tan."

"Blythe, sweetheart." A moment before she slipped into the frothy black fog wreathing her head and senses, torment-filled ocean-blue eyes hovered above her.

God can't stand schemers; therefore,
the poor and rich alike fall into the pit they dig for others.
~Dignity and Decorum—The Genteel Lady's Guide to Practical Living

11

"Blythe, darling? Can you hear me?" Disregarding the crowd merging into the study from both entrances, Tristan roughly shoved Phillips off Blythe.

Phillips moaned, but didn't move.

Tristan didn't spare him a second glance as he stripped off his coat then gently laid the cutaway upon her chest and torso, providing her a modicum of modesty.

Pulverizing an unconscious man was outside the bounds, but, God help him, he ached to render Phillips a beating he wouldn't recover from. Tristan gritted his teeth against his rage. "Hell."

Blood oozed from a gash on the side of her head.

When he'd heard her scream and broke the door ... He would kill Phillips if she hadn't already.

Pressing his handkerchief to the wound, he attempted to staunch the blood's flow and shield her from the curious onlookers. "Sweeting, wake up."

"Tristan? Miss Sanford ... don't trust ..." Moaning, she opened her eyes briefly, her gaze black and panicked, before they fluttered closed again, and she fell insensate once more.

The library continued to fill with snoops and gossips, and perhaps, a few truly concerned people. Their voices rose and fell in undulating waves of speculation, distress, and censure.

Without fail, the busybodies would take it upon themselves to jump to conclusions and render a judgment then eagerly pass the falsehoods along before knowing what had actually happened.

The intruders' comments melded together in a grating mélange.

"What happened?"

"Is she dishabille under his lordship's coat?

"Why is Phillips lying there?"

"Is he bleeding?"

A woman gasped. "He looks ... *dead.*"

"Stuff and nonsense. His chest is rising and falling," a man calmly advised.

"Oh dear, you don't suppose he ...?"

"Compromised her?"

"She does rather look set upon."

"What's Lord Leventhorpe about?"

"Whatever was Miss Culpepper doing alone with Phillips? Surely she knew better."

"Perhaps it was an arranged *tête-à-tête* that went too far."

Nothing of the sort. A coddled, scheming wench and a black-hearted whoremonger merely conspired to ruin an innocent.

The prattle droned on as guests tossed conjecture about like confetti at a wedding until Tristan bit the inside of his cheek to keep from shouting for the lot to bugger off.

Drake crouched beside Tristan and swore softly. He touched Tristan's shoulder, speaking low. "Whitehouse went to fetch her family and the Wimpletons. Hawksworth and I shall deal with Phillips."

"No. Leave him." Tristan met Drake's acutely troubled gaze, but refused to grant Phillips a glance. If the bloody arse weren't already dead, Tristan wasn't sure he wouldn't strangle him on the spot. He meant to reserve that pleasure for the field of honor.

A fireplace poker, the tip bloodied a good four inches, lay beside Blythe. Her blow hadn't been a missish swat. She'd meant to impale Phillips, and had done a hell-fired job.

"Is he still alive?" Tristan ground the question out between clenched teeth. Maybe Phillips's earlier groan had been his last.

Drake gave a terse nod. "Regretfully."

"Will you act as my second?" Tristan took Blythe's cold hand in his. He was a useless nurse. His luncheon tried again to reappear, and he swallowed the burning scraping his throat. "Can't see Hawksworth in the role. Man of God and all, and I won't put Raven in that position."

"Aye. You mean to call Phillips out then." It wasn't a question.

"Better me than Ravensdale. He has a passel of women he's responsible for and a child on the way."

"Really? I'd not heard. Still, Miss Culpepper's not your responsibility." Drake shifted, glaring over his shoulder and gesturing away inquisitive guests venturing too near. He turned to Tristan. "Some will question your purpose."

Tristan sat on his heels, chin tucked to his chest and palms pressed to his thighs. He spoke discreetly. "She'll have to be married at once. You know that. The scandal will be monumental. Who better than me to wed her? I've spent a great deal of time with the family since their arrival in Town. If Raven can be convinced to claim Blythe has agreed to wed me, that gives me the right to demand satisfaction. Announcing our betrothal will validate her refusing Burlington, and we can spread it about that's why he set his sights on another."

Burlington wouldn't refute the falsehood. It might ruin his chances with his fresh conquest.

"Dear God, what has happened?" Lady Ravensdale and the Culpepper misses descended on Blythe like avenging angels, crowding around her and forcing Tristan to move aside. Face wan, Lady Ravensdale motioned to Ravensdale, thunderous rage sparking in his eyes and hardening the angles of his face. "Heath, please have Lord Wimpleton send for a physician at once. And someone, hand me that knitted throw on the armchair there."

Hawksworth swiftly complied, and in moment the blanket protected Blythe from prying eyes.

Damn, Tristan would have liked to call for the magistrate too. A waste of time, though. A peer would never see the inside of Newgate much less have his aristocratic neck draped with a noose. Phillips stood a better chance of mysteriously disappearing, something Tristan wasn't averse to. All the more reason to meet Phillips upon the dueling field. Theirs would not be a match to first blood match. Someone should have dispatched Phillips long ago.

Tristan would meet with his solicitor in the morning and change his will. Better to err on wisdom's side and be prepared.

Would Phillips choose pistols or swords?

Pistols.

He was too cowardly to risk a test of blades.

Clasping his nape with one hand, and resting the other upon his hip, Tristan stood above the women surrounding Blythe, their pretty faces ravaged by angst and apprehension. He wasn't family, and he had no right to remain, excepting his impulsive intent to claim Blythe as his newly betrothed. But his feet, as if weighted with loadstones, refused to move.

Blythe remained motionless, her face ashen and her glorious hair, red-tinged on one side, spilling about her head.

If Whitehouse hadn't overheard the commotion between Blythe and Burlington and promptly sought Tristan ...

He'd almost been too late.

Scorching fury nearly choked him, the blazing heat setting his blood afire. He made an inarticulate sound, half growl and half oath, causing Miss Blaike—or was she Miss Blaire?—to flick him a confused look. He hadn't experienced hatred this intense since ... No. Not even when he'd been victimized and publicly shamed.

His need to protect Blythe, now more than ever, diminished everything else.

"We need handkerchiefs." Brette thrust her dainty chin upward and extended her hand. "Now, if you please."

Several ladies and gentlemen obliged, including Hawksworth.

"Let's allow Miss Culpepper and her family some privacy, shall we?" Lady Wimpleton took charge and ushered the curious gawkers from the library. "We've supper to eat, and the musicians continue to play. Go along now. I shall keep you apprised of the situation, but Cook will have my skin if her preparations have been in vain. A footman will watch for the physician and deliver him here straightaway." Her gaze scooted to Phillips, and scorn twitched her lips. "I shall send a servant with linens, though I'm sure the carpet is beyond redemption."

With a sharp-eyed, telling glance at her husband, she followed their guests from the room.

Lord Leventhorpe looked askance at Phillips, making no effort to assist him. "Ravensdale, have you any idea what has transpired?"

Ravensdale nodded curtly as he veered his attention to the women. "I've a suspicion, but would prefer not to discuss it now."

"Just so. My thoughts as well. My support is yours, of course, in whatever manner you should need it." Wimpleton's attention fell upon the pillar lying beside a bookshelf. "I see you made good use of that wretched thing at last."

Tristan didn't dare look at where Hawksworth and Drake had dragged Phillips. If Blythe's blow hadn't knocked the bastard off his feet, Tristan would have leveled him.

He closed his eyes and clamped his teeth until they ached.

Rustling behind him drew his attention. Prodding with one foot, Whitehouse nudged Phillips in the side, none too gently. "Wake up, you piece of ..." He slung a shielded glance at the women hunkered around

Blythe. “Odious lump of horse excrement.”

Blaike raked Phillips with an infuriated glare. “That’s much too polite a description for the likes of him. A barnful of ripe, maggoty cow manure is less offensive.”

“Is there water to be had? Or spirits? I imagine a splash or two ought to revive this rabble.” Whitehouse examined the room before poking Phillips harder. “What about smelling salts or a vinaigrette?”

The Culpeppers shook their blonde heads, and Brette said, “We don’t faint, and I don’t recall a single instance where we’ve needed salts.

How badly had Blythe speared Phillips? Brilliant on her part. She had to have been terrified. Another rush of wrath heated his blood. The dastard would use his injury as an excuse to avoid the duel, and Tristan had no intention of allowing Phillips to escape the repercussions of his actions this time.

Phillips cracked an eye open and weakly shoved at the tormenting shoe. “Leave off trying to crack my ribs, you bloo—”

“Stubble it.” Whitehouse jabbed Phillips’s side once more. “There are ladies present.”

“Not all present are worthy of the title, I can assure you.” Groaning, Phillips crawled to his knees, one had clasping his crimson-stained lower abdomen. Curling his lower lip, he glowered and jerked his chin in Blythe’s direction. “That one’s a teasing wh—”

Whitehouse planted his foot on Phillips’s chest, sending him flying onto his back.

“Damn you, Whitehouse.” Phillips struggled into a sitting position, white-lipped and shaking.

Tristan was upon him in three strides. He hauled Phillips to his feet, and tugged him within an inch of his nose, snarling into the sod’s frightened face. “That’s my betrothed you’re maligning.”

Phillips blanched and sputtered, his frantic gaze circling the room. “I ... I ... didn’t know.”

“What’s he talking about, Heath?” Confusion riddled Lady Ravensdale’s harried whisper.

A cunning edge replaced Phillips’s unease. “It seems no one did. How very peculiar.”

“You accosted and compromised the woman I’ve pledged to marry.” Tristan had to swiftly establish his right to demand satisfaction, even if he lied like Zeus in the process. He’d worry about Blythe’s reaction later.

If she found marriage to him abhorrent, he would at least have protected her from dishonor by giving her his name and a marchioness title. He'd allow her to live where she chose and provide for her the rest of her days. Hell, he'd grant her a divorce, though they were harder to come by than King Solomon's treasures.

"Blythe's to marry Lord Leventhorpe?" one of the twins said. Impossible to tell which with his back to the women. "When did that occur? Why didn't anyone tell us?"

"I thought Mr. Burlington held her affections." The other twin?

Bad enough they looked exactly alike, but identical voices too?

"A ruse, perhaps?" Brette hit the mark closer than Tristan liked.

Did she suspect he spoke out of turn?

"Or perhaps, there's no betrothal at all. I hadn't heard a word of it. Why would an affianced woman agree to meet me privately?" Phillips stood a mite straighter, confident in his smug arrogance.

Perchance Blythe had merely nicked him, more's the pity.

Tristan shook him, and Phillips winced, pressing his other hand to his groin.

"Surely she understood what such a clandestine arrangement with me entailed, and she chose ruin regardless."

The men's outraged exclamations mixed with the women's shocked gasps.

"Considering I have you in my grasp, you're an utter beef-wit to continue to besmirch her honor." Giving Phillips a mocking slap, Tristan permitted himself a gratified smirk and stepped away. "I demand satisfaction. Name your second."

"Leventhorpe, no. That's my place." Ravensdale's vehement protest was muffled by a ruckus in the corridor and Lady Ravensdale's quickly stifled cry of protest.

The door exploded open, banging into the shelving beside it and sending several volumes tumbling to the floor. Everyone's attention hurtled to entrance.

Miss Sanford plowed into the library, followed closely by her thin, stern-faced elderly uncle, the Earl of Marfontaine. She rapidly scanned the room, her focus alighting upon Blythe. "I told you, Uncle Rupert, she was in here with Mr. Phillips." Miss Sanford pointed a shaking finger at Blythe. "After rejecting his proposal, she clobbered poor Mr. Burlington and, wanting to be alone with Mr. Phillips, demanded I leave."

What was she about? Dragging her uncle in to witness Blythe's disgrace? Was this another attempt to discredit Blythe? Pathetic and contemptible.

"As I explained earlier, and as Miss Sanford has this instant confirmed, Miss Culpepper was more than willing to accept my advances." Keeping his distance from Tristan, and clutching his stomach, Phillips, pale and sweating, edged toward the door. "I tried to warn Burlington of her duplicity, but the man wouldn't listen."

"Stay right where you are, Phillips." Ravensdale shut the door in the face of goggle-eyed, eavesdroppers, preventing Phillips's escape.

No doubt several guests also stood beyond the drawn drapes listening at the shattered French window. The pillar's convenient location had enabled Tristan to hastily break in. Otherwise ...

Sure enough, glass crunched and someone hurriedly shushed another lurker. Whitehouse tramped to the drapes and, notorious for his devilish glowers, stuck his dark head between the folds. The noise of scurrying footsteps and muted voices filtered through the heavy fabric.

"And stay away." Whitehouse took a position at the mangled window, acting as a deterrent if others dared to venture near enough to listen.

It didn't matter. The gossipmongers wouldn't stop talking about tonight for a decade.

A partially disrobed woman, bleeding from her temple, found alone in a library with a man skewered in the gut, and both lying upon the floor unconscious provided tattle simply too delicious not to bandy about. And Phillips's reputation as despoiler of innocents was the Devonshire cream atop the gossip's cocoa.

Triston shut his mind against the names people would be calling Blythe else he would finish Phillips now.

"I'll be going then." Phillips unsteadily sidled closer to the door.

"You've been challenged to an affair of honor. And if my ward had been 'more than' willing, as you vulgarly claim, pray tell me why she's unconscious and you've been stuck with a poker? I don't believe you for an instant." Ravensdale crossed his arms and slid Tristan a sideways glance. "You will name your second before leaving, or I shall demand satisfaction as well."

"I tell you, no duel is necessary." Phillips waved a hand in an exaggerated gesture. "I pardon Leventhorpe for striking me. I understand he's in a dudgeon. There's no need for such extremes over a woman.

She's not even highborn."

Every Culpepper's gaze pelted him with blue-violet darts.

Maybe Tristan would save them a great deal of trouble and run Phillips through with the poker now. He searched the room. Where had the tool gotten to?

Hawksworth, ankles crossed and one hip resting against the black walnut, leather-topped desk, rested one hand upon the brass length, a knowing gleam in his eye.

Knows me too hell-fired well.

"Did you hear me? I pardon you for striking me." Perspiration beaded Phillips's forehead and upper lip.

Caused by pain from his injury? More likely a coward's fear of looking down a pistol barrel.

"How magnanimous of you. I assuredly don't pardon you, especially since I can think of nothing more worthy of defending than the virtue of the woman who shall soon be my wife."

By God. I mean it too. I shall willingly forfeit my life for Blythe's honor.

Tristan must marry her before the duel, to assure she was provided for if Phillips proved lucky.

A rivulet of sweat trickled from Phillips's temple to his jaw. Fear, most assuredly. "Well, as for Miss Culpepper's injury, we became too rough in our play. I shall make my apologies when she is recovered."

"That's outside enough! I shan't permit another lascivious word spoken in the presence of my sister and cousins." Lady Ravensdale angled her chin proudly and decapitated Phillips with her affronted gaze. "Gentlemen do not discuss such uncouth matters in the presence of innocent young ladies."

"But Miss Sanford just proved I spoke the truth." Phillips sounded quite desperate. Men that preyed upon women and those weaker than themselves frequently revealed themselves limp-spined cravens when faced with equals or someone stronger.

Phillips cowered before Tristan's more formidable figure.

"Balderdash and poppycock. My lying niece didn't validate your sorry tale, and she is not without fault in this." Marfontaine gave her a severe look. "Rosemary, I heard you conspiring with your mother."

He seized her elbow when she shook her head and opened her mouth to protest.

"Be quiet, chit. It took me threatening to cut your Mother off to finally pry the truth from her. As it is, she'll not get a groat for the next month." He sketched a brief bow to the Culpepper misses, his wiry fingers clamped Miss Sanford's arm. "Permit me to introduce myself. The Earl of Marfontaine. I humbly apologize for my niece's involvement in this bumblebroth. Rest assured, she will be dealt with severely."

"Uncle ..." She twisted her arm, trying to break free. "You don't understand."

"Enough." He gave her a slight shake. "I've already spoken to Lord Bexley. You will be married by special license the day after tomorrow."

"No. No! I'm sorry." Weeping noisily, she clawed at his hand. "Please, Uncle Rupert. Mr. Phillips forced me to help him. He threatened me, said he'd beat and despoil me or worse as he had dozens of other women if I didn't. If I helped him, and kept quiet about my involvement, he promised he'd make sure Lord Leventhorpe was made to marry me. He gave me his word."

The word of a scheming cur—worthless.

Miss Sanford had outed Phillips, made him an enemy, and Tristan almost felt a jot of sympathy for her. Good thing he intended to meet Phillips in two days' time, or he feared what might happen to her. Phillips possessed a violent, vengeful streak.

"Tell them, Mr. Phillips," she wailed. "You bragged about your conquests. Said you had at least a dozen by-blows."

More offended gasps and ire-laden noises escaped those present.

The wintry stare Phillips skewered Miss Sanford with caused Tristan's heart to trip. There was the ruthless villain Phillips took such pains to conceal. Evil shadowed his eyes before he veiled his hatred.

"That's utterly despicable." Lady Ravensdale presented her back, giving him the cut as Blythe stirred and put a hand to the side of her head.

Swinging to Tristan, Miss Sanford extended her free hand, fat tears leaving dual paths down her pale cheeks. "Please. I love you. I'll do anything. Don't let him make me marry that odious old man. He farts and belches constantly." She hiccupped and swiped at her wet face. "And he smells of cabbage and tobacco."

"You'll marry him, or I'll ship you off to a convent in France or Spain." Marfontaine's mouth bent a fraction, and he chuckled, the rasping drier than straw in August. "You like your luxuries far too much for that stark way of life, my dear."

"Miss Sanford, as I've tried to explain to you numerous times, I have never entertained any notion of courting or marrying you." Tristan cut Blythe a rapid glance.

She appeared to be rousing. Eyes open, she blinked in confusion.

"It's because of her, isn't it?" Thrusting her arm at Blythe, Miss Sanford laughed, a high-pitched cackle tinged with desperation or madness. "She's completely compromised. No one will have her now."

"I shall." Tristan's attention remained on Blythe.

Her unfocused eyes widened slightly, and her lips parted.

Marfontaine propelled Miss Sanford to the door. "Gel, if you don't leave off, I'll commit you to Bedlam instead of foisting you on poor Bexley. Might be better for him in any event. He'll likely cock up his toes within a year to escape your shrewish tongue."

Phillips waited until Marfontaine opened the door. "By-the-by, Miss Sanford ..."

She flung him a belligerent scowl, snapping, "What?"

A purely evil smile arced his mouth. "Leventhorpe claims he and Miss Culpepper are trothed."

Phillips's gleeful announcement had the desired effect.

Miss Sanford collapsed into Marfontaine's arms, sobbing.

"But why would Lord Leventhorpe say he and Blythe are to be married if they aren't?" Brette addressed the question to no one in particular.

"We are."

The faint response had every eye in the room ricocheting to Blythe propped against Lady Ravensdale.

It can be plainly confessed of the old and
young, he wise and the ignorant,and the rich and the
poor, that despite their best schemes, circumstances far
more often govern mankind, than man controls circumstances.
~Dignity and Decorum—The Genteel Lady's Guide to Practical Living

12

"Lord Leventhorpe waits in the drawing room." Brooke tentatively touched Blythe's arm as she gazed out her upper story bedroom window. "You must see him. There's much to discuss and put to right about last night."

"Yes. I know." Blythe let the lace panel fall into place as she swiveled and smiled at Brooke. "Don't look pensive. Everything will work out." *How, I have no idea.* "The situation isn't a complete catastrophe." *Pretty dashed close, however.*

Groggy and muddled, Blythe had believed the scene in the Wimpletons' library part of a wretched dream when she'd agreed to the betrothal. His desperation, or perhaps the emotion in the depths of his vivid blue gaze had been pleading. Nevertheless, it had silently called to her across the distance, drawing the response from her before she'd considered the consequences.

Once she'd regained her wits, there'd been plenty of time to consider the magnitude, and her foolish impulse, though propelled by compassion and a befuddled state of mind, had further complicated the impossible situation.

Uttering those two little, yet significant words, "We are," had been immensely satisfying. Miss Sanford's reaction to Blythe's verbal blow, even more so. Shame pricked her conscience. Deliberate unkindness wasn't a trait she normally exhibited.

What had possessed Tristan to declare they were betrothed?

Compassion? Pity?

She dared not hope he felt something more.

"I won't have you miserable or forced into a marriage." Brooke wrapped an arm around Blythe's waist. "Heath has spoken to Leventhorpe. He's sincere about his offer, and I suspect he cares for you. Leventhorpe isn't the scoundrel I'd first judged him to be." Her mouth hitched to one side. "Though he is quite the most aloof and unreadable man I've met."

"Not at all. That's a well-rehearsed protective front. Tristan is sensitive beneath his stern mask." Blythe scrunched her brow while fingering the silky turquoise tassel dangling from the curtain tie-back and observing a pair of mourning doves that had swooped onto an elder's branch, the lone tree in the tiny side garden. "I think he's been wounded, terribly hurt, somehow."

What had happened to create such a lasting scar and the hardened barrier he kept securely around himself?

An extended silence met her oral musing. She pried her attention away from the cuddling grayish-brown birds to find Brooke staring at her, head canted to the side and a speculative spark in her dark-lashed eyes.

"What's that look for?" After running her fingers through the silky strands one last time, Blythe dropped the tassel.

"You defended him and called him Tristan." A grin threatening, Brooke adopted a maternal mien instead. She twirled a curl near her ear. "Might I ask how long that has been going on?"

"An inadvertent slip of the tongue, I assure you. But if he's to be my husband, I suppose I'd better become accustomed to it." Unless Blythe could convince him to cry off. Not likely, any more than he'd forgo that preposterous duel. The scandal wouldn't just tarnish her. The disgrace would affect the rest of the family, too, and possibly ruin Brette and the twins' chances of a decent match.

Plain ludicrous how Society believed a marriage license and murmured vows—often insincere and broken within days of their utterance—remedied the slightest hint of ruin.

"Blythe ...?" Uncertainty colored Brooke's voice. She released a hefty breath. "Mr. Burlington ...? Deuced awkward, this," she muttered beneath her breath. "What are your feelings regarding him?"

"I plopped a Grecian urn upon his conceited head last night. What's that tell you?" Twisting her mouth into a droll semblance of a smile, Blythe patted Brooke's shoulder. "Never fear. Any iota of girlish attraction I naively harbored for him vanished the instant he suggested I become his mistress."

Brooke's mouth hung slack. "He didn't."

Blythe raised a brow. "He did. After politely explaining why he couldn't marry a poor commoner."

Brooke cradled her stomach. "Oh, I'm quite furious, and that cannot be good for the babe. I hope you cracked his skull, the devious churl."

"I'm sure he's sporting a nasty, well-deserved headache." Blythe gathered a frilly pillow from the floor, and after tossing it onto the bed piled with several others, she rubbed an eyebrow. "And his heiress is welcome to him, although I feel sorry for the woman."

"As do I." Sighing, Brooke examined Blythe's gash. "How's your head today? Doctor Barclay said you weren't concussed, thank goodness."

"It's fine. Just a mite tender." Tristan meant to see this farce through, did he? A tiny part of her—truth to tell, a huge, soft, womanly chunk deep inside—thrilled that he'd defended her honor and risked censure by fabricating their betrothal. Still, he mustn't risk his life in an affair of honor.

Besides, not for an instant did she believe Phillips would fight fairly. If something happened to Tristan, she'd never be able to forgive herself. Surely gentlemen had a proviso for calling a duel off?

"How badly did I wound *him*?" Speaking Phillips's name was akin to gobbling fresh cow dung. She pressed two fingers to her temple where her head ached worse than she'd let on. The small cut, barely an inch long, was centered upon the walnut-sized, purplish lump near her temple.

"I'm not sure. Last night I didn't think his injury serious, though I may have misjudged." Straightening the pillows upon Blythe's four-poster bed, Brooke frowned then lifted a shoulder. "Lieutenant Drake paid him a call this morning to inquire who Mr. Phillips had named as his second. The Lieutenant met the physician leaving, and he claimed Mr. Phillips's wound was quite severe, that damage had been done internally. The gash has become putrid, and he battles a fever."

"I don't suppose the poker was altogether clean." God forgive her for the satisfaction that brought her.

"God willing, he'll die and the world will be spared his odious presence. And Lord Leventhorpe will be released from the duel." Brooke punched a lace-edged satin pillow. In anger or to fluff it? "I know that's horrid of me, but at this moment, I don't have a charitable thought in me."

"I might be responsible for his death then. I didn't intend to stab him." Blythe shuddered and tucked her chin to her chest. "But he deserved it, and yet I feel guilty. All I could think of was protecting myself. He meant to ravish me."

Brooke arranged the last pillow atop the cheerful green and turquoise counterpane before flying to embrace Blythe. "Stuff and nonsense. He is an evil man. Heath has told me of his reputation and that he's suspected of killing a ... a woman of ill-repute."

"My God. He is vile." Blythe may have done London and women a service if Phillips expired.

Tears glistened in Brooke's eyes, and she took Blythe's face between both hands. "You did what you had to. He isn't worthy of your sympathy. He meant to force you, and during a ball, at that. On your birthday. The man's daft as a Bedlam patient if he truly believed he'd succeed without severe consequences."

"Do you think he coerced Miss Sanford?" The iota of pity Blythe mustered was for gouty Lord Bexley. He'd seemed pleasant enough on the one occasion she'd met him, reeking of food and another other odd, medicinal odor.

"Perhaps, but she jumped at the opportunity to compromise you. A decent woman, frightened or not, would have promptly reported Phillips's suggestion. Remember, young women of quality are constantly chaperoned. Therefore, the likelihood of him carrying out his threat was minimal, as she knew that full well. I'm convinced that's why she helped him get you alone. I'd not waste your compassion on her."

"Miss Sanford spent a great deal of time with him unchaperoned. Perhaps her mother hoped to snare Phillips if Tristan avoided Miss Sanford's tentacles." Blythe pressed two fingers to her forehead. "Likely her mother's where she learned her despicable behavior."

A gentle rap upon the door preceded Brette's entrance.

"Yes, dearest?" Brooke clasped Blythe's hand.

"I've been sent to fetch you. The men grow restless. They're driving me near to shrieking with their pacing and babbling about the need for a special license in between making rather vile suggestions regarding Mr. Phillips. Each of which I agree with wholeheartedly." She raised her pert nose skyward. "I may have made a few fairly creative notions myself, one of which entailed him galloping Rotten Row atop a nail-laden saddle. Without pantaloons."

Blythe offered a wobbly smile and squared her shoulders. "Let's be about it then. From one blaze into another."

A few short minutes later, *too short*, she stood outside the study door. "Am I to speak with Lord Leventhorpe alone?"

Brooke grasped the handle. "I think that best, don't you?"

"Yes. This conversation will be awkward enough without an audience." She preceded Brooke into the comfortable study decorated in beige and sage green. Unlike the Wimpleton's darkly paneled room, Heath preferred an airier atmosphere. Yesterday, she'd trimmed the ladder ferns in their wicker stand placed before the simple linen window panels.

Freddy and the men rose at their entrance, and Heath indicated a striped armchair in verdant shades adjacent to Tristan's.

Blythe met Tristan's unreadable gaze for a fleeting moment as she made her way to the armchair, and her stomach flopped.

The planes of his face taut, he resumed his seat. Not precisely an exuberant groom.

"Do either of you require anything?" Brooke turned from the door, Heath at her side. She patted her hip. "Freddy. Come."

The corgi dutifully waddled to her, his tongue lolling and stubby tail wagging.

Given the empty brandy glass near Tristan, and the haggard lines bracketing his mouth and pleating the corners of his eyes, he could use a strong cup of coffee.

"I would dearly love a cup of my herbal tea. You know the mixture I use for soothing headaches? Would you mind terribly brewing a pot for me? The herbs are in a marked tin in the larder." Blythe managed a smile for Tristan. "Would you like coffee? We have a lovely Turkish blend."

"Yes. That would be most welcome." His reply wasn't exactly terse, yet neither was it warm. Grayish-purple half-moon shadows ringing his eyes attested to a sleep-deprived night.

"I shall give you fifteen minutes alone before I have the tea and coffee brought in." After giving Blythe an encouraging smile that didn't diminish the apprehension shining in Brooke's eyes, she swept from the room.

"I'll return within a half hour to discuss the settlement terms with you both." Heath delivered a genuinely warm smile. "I confess to being delighted that you are to marry, though, I would have bet high odds against anything of the sort when you first met."

He closed the door softly behind him, and for several interminable moments, the room remained silent.

What was Tristan thinking? Did he regret his impulsive gesture?

"You are well, Blythe?" The gentleness of his inquiry propelled her gaze to his. Compassion and something more intense emanated from his beautiful eyes.

"Yes. Other than a slight headache, I haven't suffered ill effects." Except a restless night and a reputation tainted beyond redemption. A room full of the *ton's* denizens had seen her partially clothed. It mattered not that Phillips hadn't been successful in despoiling her.

Tristan folded his hands in his lap then promptly unclasped them and laid his palms upon his black clad thighs. "You recall what happened, then?"

"If that's your way of asking if I remember agreeing that we are to be married, yes. I remember." Dragging in a great breath, Blythe jumped to her feet. She clasped her hands before her. "I feel I must tell you that I won't hold you to your offer. I know you said it to protect me in a perfectly ghastly situation."

Tristan stood as well, forcing her to crane her neck to meet his eyes. "Why were you in the library alone with him?"

"I ..." She spun away, not wanting to think about what had happened, how close she'd come to being ravished. Her knees grew shaky and her chest tightened with remembered fear as a shiver wracked her. She rubbed the raised flesh along her bare arms. "I was trying to find you."

"In the library? Why would you think to search for me there and not the ballroom or card room?"

The sunny rays filtering through the window enticed her, and she sought their tepid warmth. "I overheard Miss Sanford and her mother scheming last night and wanted to warn you of their intent to entrap you. When I entered the library, Phillips restrained me while Miss Sanford locked the door."

A robin swooped to the ground below the elder, and after giving her an inquisitive look, took to searching for insects.

"You meant to protect me? What did they plot?"

She nodded, shortly. "That you'd be found in a compromising situation with Miss Sanford at the ball and thus be forced to marry her."

He laughed, a warm, soothing rumble, filling the room and surprising her with his genuine amusement.

"You aren't angry?" She frowned, canting her head. "I should think you'd be furious."

With measured steps, he approached her, a mysterious bend to his mouth.

She dropped her gaze to the floor, afraid he'd see her love for him shining in her eyes.

"Ah, Fate had another plan, and Miss Sanford's duplicitous actions compelled me to claim you as mine." He cupped her shoulders, his large hands heavy, yet comforting. "Something I've yearned to do for weeks, though I doubted I would ever have the right."

Blythe jerked her head up and squinted. Had she mistaken his meaning? "What exactly are you saying?"

"I'm saying that I want to marry you and no other." Tristan drew her, unresisting, into his embrace. He chuckled again as she gaped, unblinking, at him. He ran his thumb along her lower lip and slanted his head at the window. "You had better close your mouth before yonder bird thinks to perch upon its lusciousness."

Her focus slid to his lips, and she pursed hers. Did she do that intentionally, to torment him?

"You've not given any indication you considered me anything other than a casual friend." Leaning into his arms, Blythe searched his face, emotions dancing across hers. "At one time, you couldn't abide me."

He firmed his embrace, edging closer until his thighs brushed her skirt, and he could feel her trembling legs. Resting his cheek against her unmarred temple, he whispered into the sweet fragrance of her hair, "You vexed the hellfire out of me, causing more intense feelings than I'd ever had for a woman. I didn't understand them for what they were."

Her expression softened, drawing him into the depths of her sapphire eyes, trapping him in their guileless, mysterious spheres. "You are the most complex man. After you kissed me, I believed you'd decided you weren't romantically inclined toward me."

"Utter gibberish." He kissed her hairline before feathering kisses down her cheek and the length of her jaw, lingering at the provocative corner of her mouth. "I never had to battle attraction so hard in my life."

Her sooty-tipped lashes fluttered closed, and she breathed out a sigh.

Needing no further invitation, he claimed her mouth, urging her lips apart with the tip of his tongue, delving into the sweetness of her mouth.

Blythe stood on her toes and entwined her arms about his neck.

Catching onto the art of kissing with alacrity, she mimicked his actions. Their tongues jousted in a timeless melody of passion, until his groin swelled uncomfortably, and they both panted for breath.

Tristan drew away first.

Tupping his closest friend's ward in the study wasn't done. Well, not before exchanging vows, in any event. Afterward ... He eyed the armchair, and an unexpected, most unwelcome flash of discomfort assailed him. Did he tell Blythe of his childhood humiliation?

No. Not now.

After they consummated their marriage, and he'd introduced her to the blissful aspects of physical joining, he might be ready to share the tale with her.

Or perhaps he never would.

That ugliness was in the past. She was his future.

Tucking her to him, he murmured into her hair. "I suppose I ought to go down upon a knee and propose formally, only I'm reluctant to release you."

Blythe chuckled against his chest, her slender arms encircling his waist. "I rather think a proposal while being held in your arms is much more satisfying and romantic."

"Blythe Culpepper, will you honor me by consenting to become my wife?" He kissed her ear, and she giggled.

"What?" She nudged his ribs. "No dramatic protestations of undying love or how I've made you the happiest man on earth?"

He drew away a fraction, drinking in her flushed features. "If that makes you happy and is what you want, I shall be delighted to do both."

"Oh. Pooh. I don't need pretty speeches. A man's actions show his affection and character much more clearly than mere words, and last night you risked everything to protect me." The look she gave him sent his pulse sprinting, and his manhood gave an eager twitch.

Whoa, boy. Patience.

"Am I to assume your answer is yes?" Tristan framed her jaw with his forefinger and thumb, caressing the silky flesh of her jaw. "I am ecstatic."

"Yes. I'll marry you." She shook her head, the silvery curls glinting halo-like in the sunlight. "I certainly never dreamed I'd be eagerly anticipating wedding the stern, rigid man I met at Esherton Green."

"Eagerly?" He waggled his eyebrows wickedly.

She gave him a coy wink. "Indeed. Most eagerly."

"Excellent. I've already purchased the special license. The ceremony will need to take place tomorrow. I know that's rushing things a jot—"

Her fair brows furrowed, and she stepped from his embrace, giving him a tight, closed-lipped smile. "I'd hoped for more time. I realize the scandal of last night prohibits a lengthy betrothal, but a week or two to prepare for a wedding—"

"I'm afraid that's impossible." He rubbed his nape. Blast, he hadn't wanted to discuss the duel on the fringes of what *was* possibly the happiest moment of his life. "The duel takes place the day after tomorrow, and we must wed first, because if I'm injured or killed—"

Blythe gasped, and balled her fists. "You mean to go through with the challenge? The day after we wed?"

He hadn't expected Blythe to be thrilled about the notion. Given the furious glint in her eye, she wouldn't concede easily. In fact, he hadn't intended to tell her about the duel until after the deed was done. That had seemed bloody brilliant when he'd first contemplated it. If Phillips bested him, she'd be married and widowed in under twenty-four hours, and she needed to know that Tristan had legally provided for her.

"You cannot meet that swine." Her chest rose and fell rapidly with her agitation. "He's a cur and a cheat. He'll not fight nobly, and you must know that to be true."

"It's a matter of my honor, Blythe." Mere moments ago, happiness and something akin to adoration had shone in her eyes. Betrayal shadowed her exquisite features now. He touched her arm. "A man is nothing if he does not keep his word. My honor is paramount to me."

Pursing her pretty mouth, she brushed a curl from her forehead. "According to Brooke, Phillips is gravely ill from the wound I inflicted. He won't be able to meet you. I'm surprised you didn't know that."

He did, yet didn't believe a word. Phillips was a bloody coward and would use any excuse to waylay the inevitable confrontation. In fact, at Tristan's behest, Drake and Whitehouse watched Phillips's residence, lest he try to sneak away. Again.

"I shall wait until he is recovered then. However, meet him I shall." Phillips couldn't be permitted to live and despoil more innocents. And if Miss Sanford had the right of it, he might be guilty of more appalling crimes. "He's escaped justice far too many times. He must be held accountable."

She closed her eyes, her lips trembling. Her lashes slowly lifted, and his heart turned to stone at the resignation and defeat in her eyes. "Then

I regret, my lord, that I must decline your offer of marriage. I'll not be married and widowed within a day's time."

"Be sensible. Your reputation is in tatters. I offer you my name and security." He reached for her, and she fled behind the desk.

Shrugging, she placed the porcelain inkwell upon its matching tray. "I hadn't intended to marry well. I'll retire to the country."

"Blythe ..."

Three sharp raps echoed outside the door before it swung open. Lady Ravensdale, Raven, and a footman bearing a laden tray stood there smiling expectantly.

The moment they cleared the entrance, Blythe bolted for the exit.

"Blythe, wait, please." Tristan's long strides ate the distance across the leaf-patterned Axminster carpet.

Lady Ravensdale swung her confused gaze between them. "Is something amiss?"

Blythe reached her, and neck bent, shook her head. "No. I simply have no desire to be widowed the day after I marry. So, I've refused Lord Leventhorpe's offer of marriage."

"You have? Truly?" Ravensdale's confounded expression would have earned a chuckle and likely a taunt or two had the circumstances been different.

"Oh, Blythe." Lady Ravensdale crestfallen countenance revealed her devastation.

Without marriage, Blythe was utterly ruined.

"I'm sorry. Please forgive me. I know what this means." She offered a tremulous smile. "I shall pack at once.

Folly whispers marriage is a scheme for contentment,
but in truth, marriage is strenuous work.
~Dignity and Decorum—The Genteel Lady's Guide to Practical Living

13

"There, that's the last of them. I feel quite wicked owning this much clothing." Early the next morning, Blythe placed the last of her unmentionables in her trunk.

Brooke promised to send the chest along later. For the journey home, Blythe would make do with a valise. Wisdom decreed she take a satchel in the event of unforeseen circumstances, although the trip to Culpepper Park could be achieved in a day.

The new house was habitable according to Brooke, though not fit for entertaining. That suited Blythe perfectly. Months might pass before she'd be in the mood for company.

Meg, Blythe's abigail since arriving in London, agreed to journey with her, though Meg had no desire to remain in the countryside and would promptly return to London. No matter. Blythe had seen to her toilette for years. She didn't require a maid.

"Are you positive you won't reconsider?" Blaike sniffled into her handkerchief.

This separation would be the first for the sisters.

Blaire tortured her square scrap of cloth, twisting and tormenting its damp length repeatedly. "This whole affair is wretchedly unjust. I don't believe I care for London after all. Such supercilious people. Why, you are the victim. How dare they judge you?"

"You should at least stay at Heath's estate. There's no staff or furnishings at Culpepper Park." Brette passed Blythe a pair of slippers. "I'll allow, I'm quite miffed that you are to go alone."

Stay in a mausoleum of a manor—Heath's unflattering description—and with strangers for staff? Dreadful, by any measure. Returning to the dairy's familiar security and comfort held far more appeal.

"I understand, Brette, but we've discussed this already." A dozen times or more. "It's what I want, and besides, our old furniture was moved to the new house." Considerable effort went into her forced, cheerful smile. "I shall be fine."

"Hmph." A vulgar noise escaped Brette.

Blythe carefully tucked the embroidered slippers underneath a gown. She'd likely never wear either at Culpepper Park. The trunk overflowed with beautiful clothing and fallals, most unsuitable for a country gentlewoman. Heath insisted she take her new wardrobe, however.

"Why shouldn't everyone leave then?" Legs dangling over her chair's arm, Blaike gesticulated into the air.

"I'm the one unacceptable to Society. If I leave immediately, we hope to lessen the shadow cast over the rest of you. If everyone departs hastily, that implies you are guilty as well, and you are not. I won't have you disparaged on my account. For respectability's sake, I shall retain one or two servants from the village, so put that fear aside."

"I thought, perhaps, you weren't averse to Lord Leventhorpe. You'd spent a considerable amount of time in his company these past weeks, and that day at Gunter's, he looked like a man besotted." Blaike sent Blaire a silent message and threw her kerchief atop the night table.

Ah, the twins had noticed the tense exchange between Blythe and Tristan that day.

"He did indeed." Scarcely pausing, Blaike launched another protest. "Won't you reconsider? Heath says his lordship is a dab hand at pistols. You should trust him."

Trust Heath or Tristan?

She did trust them both. Phillips, however, garnered the same confidence as Lucifer.

"Girls, I'm to depart within the hour. What's done is done. I've refused Lord Leventhorpe, and that is the end of it. He was most gallant to claim a false betrothal and offer to wed me to preserve my status. I do harbor a fanciful hope that since I cried off, he won't feel the need to follow through with that ridiculous duel." After all, he couldn't claim her as his affianced, and consequently the reason for his challenge no longer existed. Then again, men were so blasted difficult and prideful, he might pursue the idiocy.

Blythe had seen one way to offer Tristan a reprieve from the duel and save face as well as preserve his honor. If only he would put aside his confounded stubbornness and seize the opportunity.

God, please, let him.

If he didn't, she would pray Phillips wouldn't recover, and what manner of foulness did that make her? Wishing for a man's death?

A pout upon her lips, Brette wandered to the window. Parting the lace, she eyed the sky. "The weather has taken a sour turn. Perchance you should delay your departure. Those clouds look as ugly as the ones that brought that fierce storm the day Heath arrived at Esherton Green."

"Looking like a bedraggled puppy." Blaire grinned for the first time today.

Blaike snickered. "A cross mutt too."

"He could have caught a nasty chill." Glancing behind her, Brette frowned, her worried gaze shifting from the full trunk to Blythe. "I wish you'd wait until this bluster passes. It makes me uneasy to have you traveling in foul weather."

"In England, a cloudy sky is hardly unusual, and neither are summer rains. The road is quite passable, even after a good shower. I'm not concerned." Bless Brette's heart, she simply sought a means to persuade Blythe to stay.

For the girls' sake, she couldn't. The sooner she put distance between herself and them, the better. *Le beau monde* considered her soiled goods, and much like a spoiled piece of fruit spread rot to others nearby, her presence tainted the rest of her family. Besides, she possessed no desire to endure the speculation regarding her pathetically short-lived betrothal.

Oddly, Burlington's treachery bothered her little. She was more peeved at herself for being a ninny and judging a man by his outward appearance. It chaffed to admit she'd been shallow as a puddle.

After she'd agreed to wed Tristan, crying off pierced like a double-edged blade—deep, and lethal. Her heart had nearly fragmented when she'd told Tristan she wouldn't marry him. But if it meant his life might be spared ... She shrugged mentally and offered a conciliatory smile to the distraught girls. "Sometimes we must make sacrifices so those we love won't suffer."

"Hmph." Flopping against her chair and kicking her feet in the air, Blaike shook her head. "And sometimes, those who love you don't give a cow's stinky behind what others think."

"I must go." London held no appeal for Blythe any longer, and the sooner she departed, the sooner she could nurse her mangled heart.

Six hours later, swathed in her sensible wool traveling cloak, Blythe warmed her gloved hands before a sooty stone fireplace in The Coach and Arms common room. Damp to her marrow, she flexed her jaw to still her chattering teeth. God's bones, she was half frozen. The sputtering fire valiantly sent a plume of orange sparks skyward, failing to thaw her stiff fingers and toes.

With its bare-beamed ceiling and darkish interior, the modest inn smelled of stale ale and fresh bread. More importantly, it provided a haven from the unremitting torrents.

London's earlier blanket of pewter clouds had transformed into a churning, black tempest complete with lashing rain, bursts of lightning, and deafening thunder. They'd barely traveled ten torturous miles the last three hours; the roads had become impossibly mucky and impassable. The tenacious driver and team had pressed onward as far as they could. With the wrathful charcoal sky showing no signs of easing its tantrum, and dusk flirting across the horizon, Blythe bid him stop at the next lodgings.

Since leaving London's outskirts, Meg had sighed and complained incessantly, and by the time the carriage squished and slid to a halt in the inn's muddy courtyard, Blythe couldn't wait to send the pampered maid to the kitchen to make tea and inquire about a hot meal.

Evidently, the weather had caught several other travelers unawares as well. Besides Blythe, a young couple, who appeared to be newlywed, a kind-faced cleric, a trio of motley soldiers, and a couple of burly, tartan-clad Scots occupied the humble taproom. A formidable matron attired in crackling black bombazine, and who loudly ordered her mousy companion about, had also been present when Blythe arrived.

Every chamber was taken, excluding a miniscule, fireplace-less attic room, more closet than bedchamber, with scarcely enough space for a narrow cot, an uneven nightstand, and rickety chair.

From the dust-covered cobwebs gracing two corners, spiders had been the lone inhabitants for a long while. Grateful for a bed, Blythe didn't quibble at the exorbitant price the flustered innkeeper demanded. She hadn't slept last night, and today, the pounding winds hammering the carriage, as well as Meg's grumbling mile after miserable mile, had prevented any rest in the carriage.

What else was Blythe to do?

Sleep near the hearth or in a corner of the common room as the soldiers and Scots intended, or curl onto the carriage seat as her driver had volunteered to do?

Her head, bum, and back ached, and tears threatened constantly. Better the inadequate cupboard where she could cry in privacy then a public room where her virtue might be jeopardized.

Turning her profile to the soldiers' intent scrutiny, Blythe prayed her chamber boasted a sturdy lock or a strong bolt. Propping the chair beneath the handle might provide added protection. She bent her lips a fraction. Knitting needles were stronger than the chair's spindly legs.

Meg had fussed about having to sleep upon a pallet in the kitchen. Blythe ignored her carping and pointedly didn't invite the servant to share her tiny room. After an eternity in the carriage with the peckish servant, Blythe's head ached nearly as fiercely as her heart, and she needed the quiet and solitude the chamber promised. Accustomed as she was to years of hardship and want, the humble room reminded her of her bedchamber at Esherton Green. Besides, a pallet for the maid wouldn't fit in the chamber.

The innkeeper's red-faced wife, carrying a tray laden with heavenly smelling soup, bread, and cheese, bustled past.

"Miss, ifn' ye mean to sup, ye'll have to eat in here. The private rooms be taken, and two hirelin's, blast their lazy, ungrateful hides, didn't come to work. I can't be waitin' on ye upstairs. Yer maid will have to see to yer needs." She jerked her chins in the kitchen's direction, sending her crepey neck jostling. "Pompous chit, that one."

"In here is perfectly fine." Eyeing the occupied tables, Blythe leisurely removed her gloves. Three had chairs available, or she could take a seat upon the wooden bench below the filmy window, which rattled in protest every now and then from a gust of contentious wind.

Holding hands and murmuring softly, the couple sank onto the bench, their heads close together.

Blythe wouldn't—couldn't bear to—perch on the end of their bench and listen to their enamored chatter. To save Tristan's life, she'd relinquished her opportunity for love, but that didn't mean she couldn't yearn for the intimacy the couple shared.

Which table would it be then?

The cantankerous elderly dame? The scruffy soldiers? The fuddled Scots, already gulping their third pint since arriving? Or the pleasant-faced Man of God?

With a friendly nod, he waved her to his corner table, set slightly apart from the rest in a partial nook beside the fireplace. “Please, lass. I’d be pleased to have your company.”

Giving him a grateful smile, she untied her bonnet as she sank onto a well-worn chair. “Thank you, Reverend ...?”

“Reverend Heaven.” He chuckled softly, a merry twinkle in his warm gaze.

Disbelief must have shown in her eyes.

As if praying, he pressed his hands together. “Honestly. The name’s of Welsh origins.”

Returning his easy smile, Blythe laid her gloves and rain-splattered bonnet atop the gouged and dented tabletop. “I imagine, given your profession, it’s been the subject of many conversations.”

“Indeed. Mrs. Heaven’s first name causes a bigger stir.” He leaned forward and winked. “It’s Angel. Not Angela or Angelina. Just Angel. We named our sons Gabriel and Michael.”

Blythe chuckled. “Brilliant. You’ve no daughter?”

“Alas, no.” He pulled his earlobe while casually scrutinizing the other occupants. “But we considered Mary or Martha.”

Meg tromped into the taproom, her mouth bent into a belligerent scowl. She crossly plopped Blythe’s and Reverend Heaven’s food atop the table, sloshing stew over the bowls’ edges in her frustration. “I’m being made to help in the kitchen.”

Blythe checked her sharp retort. “It’s kind of you to lend a hand. They are short staffed, and the inn is full.”

“I care not. I am not a scullery wench. I didn’t agree to this.” She flipped a hand scornfully at their food. “First thing in the morning, I’m returning to London. You cannot stop me.”

Meg lifted her nose as haughtily as an Almack’s patroness and stamped past the soldiers.

How did she propose to do that? By post chase? Without funds?

Blythe would pay for her return to the city, but Meg would have to seek other employment. A servant with airs proved intolerable, and Brooke would be advised of Meg’s unacceptable attitude.

One scarlet-clad chap tilted his chair onto two legs and grasped Meg's arm in passing. "Interested in some company, sweetheart?"

"No, you foul oaf." Meg pushed him over then, amidst the hoots and guffaws of his compatriots, stormed into the kitchen, declaring, "I'm never leaving London again."

"That one's carrying a cartload of bitterness." Reverend Heaven buttered a piece of bread.

"She's unaccustomed to discomfort." Lifting her spoon, Blythe sniffed the stew appreciatively. "Had I known, I wouldn't have asked her to accompany me."

He tilted his head, his keen gaze assessing and nodded sagely. "You, I would venture, are familiar with hardship. I see pain and suffering in your eyes, but you haven't become bitter."

Yet.

She didn't want to become a lonely, cynical harpy.

Battling the harsh sting of tears behind her eyelids, Blythe lowered her gaze and took a bite of the savory stew rather than answer.

"I've been told I'm a good listener, Miss ...?"

Startled, she blinked away her tears, her watery gaze springing to his.

Compassion emanated from his kindly face. "And I'm sworn to confidence."

"Forgive me. I'm Blythe Culpepper, and I'm returning to my family home near Cheshire after an ... unpleasant sojourn in London."

The outer door flung open, and a gust of frigid, wet air billowed in. Blythe shivered, still not warmed. She'd likely sleep in her clothes and cloak given she'd only seen one quilt atop the thin mattress in her teeny closet of a room.

At first light, she'd be on her way. Now that home loomed near, eagerness overtook her. She'd sorely missed the country. If she had her way, she'd never venture to Town again.

"That fellow arrived upon a huge horse, just now. No luggage either." Reverend Heaven chewed his bread thoughtfully, his elbow resting atop the table. "Must be in a great hurry, or he was caught unawares. I don't envy him. He's soaked through. Must be utterly miserable. Do you mind if he joins us as well? Looks like he could use something hot in his belly and our table is nearest the fireplace."

Casting a disinterested glance over her shoulder, Blythe faltered, and her breath refused to leave her lungs.

A man, an immense man, stamped his booted feet and shook off his sodden greatcoat. Water sprayed in all directions and puddled at his feet. He pulled his hat from his head, revealing dark auburn hair.

Tristan.

A tiny gasp escaped her, and she dropped her spoon. It bounced off the table and onto the floor, clanging loudly each time the metal careened off a surface.

"Do take care, miss." The irritable ebony swathed tabby narrowed her eyes and clasped her chest above her ample bosom. "You startled me so, I may swoon. My heart is not strong. Miss Timmons, my vinaigrette at once."

Miss Timmons cast a pained glance ceilingward before dutifully rummaging in a traveling case and momentarily procuring an engraved silver vial.

"Please forgive my clumsiness." What was Tristan doing here? Blythe determinedly forced down the swell of anticipation seeing him caused.

There might've been a number of reasons he'd stopped at this inn. He didn't live far from Esherton Green. Mayhap there'd been an urgent need for him to return to his estate, and the vile weather had forced him to stop here as it had her.

Or perhaps Phillips had died—her heart pitched, bum over head—and Tristan decided to quit London rather than face the *ton* as a jilted man. She'd discerned quite some time ago that he endured assemblies and routes. He didn't enjoy them.

"Do you know him?" Reverend Heaven's question caught her off guard.

How should she answer? Yes. She knew him, and leave it at that? Yes. We were betrothed for two wonderful minutes? Yes, he was a pompous, aggravating boor, and she adored him with her entire being, enough to save his life by refusing to wed him?

Intent upon retrieving her spoon and regaining her composure before answering, Blythe bent and had clasped the handle. A pair of muddy boots appeared beside the table.

Bother and blast. And ... and damnation!

Her scrutiny slowly traveled from his mud-caked toes, past his muscled calves tucked into the dirt-pelted Hessians, skimmed his narrow waist, and followed his torso's vee to his wide, russet-covered shoulders. His size never failed to impress her.

Or others.

Every person stared their way, and Miss Timmons's mouth hung slack in awe.

I know the feeling, dear.

He'd removed his greatcoat and must have deposited the garment and his hat and gloves with the innkeeper.

She almost smiled.

Likely he didn't recognize the preferential treatment he received. He took it for granted, as did most gentry and peers.

It didn't take a scholar to recognize a nobleman flush in the pockets. No doubt the fawning hostler offered Tristan a room too, at the expense of another unfortunate guest who would have to find other accommodations or sleep before the cinder-covered hearth.

"Miss Culpepper." Tristan inclined his head the merest bit before his attention swerved to Reverend Heaven, now standing. "Tristan, the Marquis of Leventhorpe, sir. Thank you for entertaining my betrothed until I could join her."

"Betrothed, you say?" The Reverend's brows vaulted to the top of his forehead as he shook Tristan's extended hand. "I'm Reverend Heaven, my lord."

Tristan's expression didn't alter a jot at the cleric's unusual name.

"Formerly betrothed." Blythe leveled Tristan with what she hoped was an impassive stare. "What are you doing here?"

After the men took their seats, Tristan gestured for the innkeeper then summoned a crooked smile. "I called at Ravensdale's and was told you'd left for Esherton. I followed."

"You followed." She snapped her fingers. "Just like that? Had you no care for the dismal weather or your health?"

"Just like that." He grinned mischievously. "I did think to borrow Raven's greatcoat."

Reverend Heaven chuckled, his keen gaze sparking with interest.

"Reverend, I might have need of your services." Tristan patted his pocket and winked. "I have a special license. I've rather muddled things, and I hope to put that to rights."

Impossible.

Blythe kicked him beneath the table. "We've had this discussion."

Wedding him meant he would face Phillips. She could never live with herself if Tristan lost his life defending her. Far better to be alone and desolate, and know he lived, than alone and desolate if he died. Yet, refusing the thing she most wanted took her absolute resolve.

The innkeeper hurried to their table, bearing a frothy tankard. He placed the mug before Tristan and foam trailed down the pewter side. "My lord?"

"Miss Culpepper dropped her spoon. Please bring another when you serve my meal. Have you a private dining room available?"

Tristan passed the man a coin, earning a gap-toothed grin that rapidly transformed into a fretful frown. "No private dinin' room, Sir. I might be able to arrange for ye to use a chamber for a short spell. This weather has us overflowin'. I'll need a few minutes to work somethin' out."

"If we could have use of a chamber, for half an hour even, I would certainly show my appreciation." Another coin changed hands.

Blythe leaned back in her chair. "Do you do that often? Bribe your way to achieve what you want?"

"I prefer to call it compensation for extra effort. He's overworked, and from the looks of this place, he could use the coin." Tristan combed the room from end to end and gave a half jerk of his head "He'll not receive a groat more than he's earned from them, despite the hardship having this many patrons at once has caused."

"I believe you require privacy." Reverend Heaven stood. "I shall be warming myself before the fire if you should need me. Please excuse me, Miss Culpepper, my lord."

He took his chair with him, preventing anyone else from sitting at their table. Clever man. In a moment, he sat before the now roaring fire, legs extended, hands crossed atop his rounded abdomen, and eyes shut. Resting or praying?

"I have a chamber. We can talk there with the door ajar. I'll allow you ten minutes." Blythe gathered her belongings. Despite his nonchalance, blue tinged Tristan's lips, and he'd shuddered more than once. Probably soaked to the skin, and without a warm bed to sleep in, he might catch lung fever.

"That's all the time I require." Tristan nodded and stood. "Let me tell the hostler to hold my meal."

A few minutes later, and slightly out of breath from climbing three flights, she entered her miniscule chamber and immediately set about lighting the candle atop the nightstand.

Tristan leaned against the doorjamb, his arms crossed, grinning like a baboon. "I've seen carriages and biscuit tins with bigger interiors."

"You jest, but I either accepted this room or slept below." Surprised by the room's pleasant temperature, she released her cloak's frogs, before shrugging its weight from her shoulders.

Tristan moved to assist her.

He hung the cloak over a wooden peg beside the rock chimney then tentatively skimmed the gray stones nested together. Leaning against their heat, he smiled in satisfaction. "This is why this chamber is warm." He patted the rocks behind him. "The heat from the fire below radiates off them."

"That's all well and good, and I'm grateful I won't freeze in my sleep." Casting a wary glance at the open door, Blythe sat upon the mattress, its meager depth harder than frozen ground. Wiggling her bum, she attempted to find a comfortable position. A night sleeping upon this mattress and she'd ache from toe to nose. "Why did you follow me? I gave you my answer yesterday."

"You did, and at first I had determined to accept your rejection, and allow you to disappear from my life. Though, I must tell you, I've experienced gut punches that hurt less." He crossed his ankles, closed his eyes, and pressed into the rocks. "This is rather splendid. I can finally feel my fingers again."

"Tristan. Will you please make your point?" Exhausted, she had no more reserves, and the tears she'd held at bay for the past twenty-four hours stung her eyes again. "You've used five of your minutes blathering about nonsensical rubbish."

He opened his gorgeous, black-lashed eyes, his gaze slicing straight to her soul.

"I love you."

A sob escaped her, and she pressed her fist to her mouth, struggling for control.

In an instant, he was beside her then pulling her into his strong embrace. He smelled of horse and rain and sandalwood, and she'd never inhaled anything sweeter.

"I know why you refused me." He kissed the top of her head while running his huge hands over her back and shoulders.

"You do?" The great slab of his chest muscle muffled her words. "Of course you do. I told you. It's because you insist upon dueling Phillips."

"Liar." He squeezed her ribs.

Prepared to give him a set down, she stiffened her spine. "I am not—

”

Tristan settled his strong mouth atop hers, his hot, voracious kiss stifling her protest and launching it to the Earth’s remotest corner. “You will let me speak my piece, or I shall silence you with a kiss each time you open your delicious mouth.” He dropped another breath-hitching kiss on her lips. “Understand?”

She nodded, a half-smile bending her lips. “I rather like your kisses—”

In a flash, she lay upon her back, his mouth and tongue searing her senses. The cot shuddered, groaning and squeaking, underneath his substantial weight. She wound her arms around his back. Hardly the actions of a woman refusing a suitor.

But he loved her.

“I suspected the real reason behind your rejection. When I spoke with Miss Brette today, she confirmed it.” Using his forefinger, he traced her jaw, sending spirals of sensation skittering everywhere. “If we didn’t marry, I wasn’t honor bound to see the challenge through.”

“Wait until I see her—”

By the time he finished kissing her again, Blythe seriously considered closing the door, stripping him naked, and having her way with him. Where had he learned to kiss like that? To render her incapable of coherent thought as tantalizing currents sluiced through her? Punishment via kisses that turned her bones to jelly wasn’t disagreeable at all.

“Is it true? Is that why you won’t marry me, Blythe? Did you recant your acceptance in order to nullify my reason for challenging Phillips?” The anguish in his azure gaze lacerated her resolve.

“Yes.” A tear leaked from her eye, and then another. She cupped his stubbly jaw. “I love you. I’d die if you were injured or killed meeting Phillips. I know men, especially peers, have a code you live by, and I know how important your honor is to you. I’d rather live in disgrace for the remainder of my days then risk harm coming to you.”

“If you are willing to forego respectability, and face rejection, gossip, and scandal to spare me, then I am willing to live with the dishonor of repudiating my challenge.” He kissed her nose. “I don’t know whether Phillips will survive his festered wound, but if he does, I won’t face him on the field of honor.”

"Truly, Tristan?" She searched his eyes for a sign of regret and found none. "Some might call you a coward or ridicule you."

He elevated a brow. "I find honor without a cause is worthless. You are my cause. Naught else matters."

Some men might be given to flowery and romantic speeches. The sincerity of Tristan's simple heartfelt words surpassed them all.

Pressing a tender kiss against her lips, he whispered, "Will you marry me? Here? Tonight?"

Tristan waited, his breath suspended and constricting his lungs, for Blythe's answer.

Each mile he'd ridden, rain dripping into his collar and wind blasting his face with ice-cold pellets, he'd kept one goal at the forefront of his mind: to convince her that the greatest honor he would ever know would be to make her his marchioness and begin his life anew with her.

The wonder of her had crept into the recesses, the very core, of his being, and entrenched her spirit into his innermost places. Nothing that had ever come before, nothing he would face in the future, compared to the need to make her his life's partner.

He'd finally healed of his past humiliation, and though he'd never deem large gatherings his favorite pastime, the fear haunting him for almost two decades had vanished. She'd vanquished it.

Love had healed and restored him, a man filled with self-loathing.

Lips parted, plump and reddened from his kisses, Blythe peered into his soul. "I shall gladly marry you, but you need to know something about me, Tristan."

He propped his head upon his hand as he caressed the creamy column of her throat. Her breasts' perky tips taunted him below the bodice of her simple poplin traveling gown.

"And what is that?" He brushed her hair from her forehead, enjoying the excuse to touch her.

"I'm an ordinary woman of simple origins. Yes, I've endured poverty. I've also been blessed with a loving, supportive family." She entwined her fingers with his. "I haven't been scarred by tragedy, nor are there dark secrets in my past which torment or cause me angst. Perhaps couples who overcome great odds and conflict are grateful when they finally admit their love as we have, but, honestly I cannot regret the peaceful, quiet, normal life I've lived."

"Ahem. Perhaps we should commence with a ceremony?"

Tristan whipped his attention to the gaping doorway framing Reverend Heaven then chuckled as he levered off the bed. "Yes, Reverend. We'll meet you below in five minutes."

"Miss Culpepper? You are in agreement?" Reverend Heaven scratched his left eyebrow. "Are you of age?"

"I am, to both." She scooted to a sitting position. "I celebrated my first and twentieth birthday two days ago."

Reverend Heaven rubbed his hands together. "Well then, I'd say the Almighty has been working overtime arranging this storm. By-the-by, I insist you take my chamber, and I shall occupy this one." His wink wasn't the least chaste or holy. "Mine has a bigger bed."

An hour later, after having been congratulated soundly by the hostler, his wife, and the inn's occupants, who'd assembled to witness the simple ceremony, and after finally eating, Tristan guided Blythe into the reverend's former chamber.

The bed was indeed bigger. By a good six inches.

"Are you nervous?" Normally a female family member explained what a bride could expect on her wedding night. "Do you have questions about tonight?"

Blythe's smile wasn't that of a timid virgin as she stood before a cracked oval mirror and unpinned her hair. "I was raised on a farm, Tristan. I know the ways of males and females."

"Yes, well, there are differences." He swept his hand down his front. "No fur or feathers."

"Or tail." Looking pointedly at his coat, she laughed, the deep, musical chuckle that he adored. "I believe we need to be naked to do the job properly."

"Have I married a vixen?" He made short work of divesting his clothing until only his pantaloons remained. She might have been familiar with farm animal anatomy, but the engorged penis of a highly aroused man might be a mite much. Particularly a man of his stature and build.

She stepped from her dress, a bold goddess, and draped the garment over the chamber's single chair. Her stays and stockings followed, and in a few tantalizing moments, she untied one shoulder ribbon of her chemise. No false blushes or pretense of demureness.

That was his Blythe.

"Let me." He brushed her hand away while kissing her collarbone.

She shuddered and sagged against him, her breath coming in short pants. "I've wondered what it would be like to have you possess me."

The fabric slipped to her waist as he cupped her breasts from behind and continued to nibble the sensitive flesh of her nape and neck. "You've imagined bedding me?"

"Uh hum. But I believed you loathed me." Her head fell forward, and she clasped his forearms as he slowly explored her abdomen. Then lower.

A sound, half-gasp, half-moan, escaped her open mouth, as she pressed her plump buttocks against his rigid length, demanding to be freed of its constraint.

He nipped her shoulder and gave her a little shove. "Lie down."

She complied, scampering underneath the coarse sheets, her curious gaze riveted to the bulge at his groin.

He unbuttoned the falls and tugged his pantaloons off.

She chuckled throatily when his member sprang free. "I'm quite looking forward to experiencing that."

He pounced upon her. "What, no maidenly shyness?"

"None whatsoever." She lifted her arms in invitation, a saucy smile teasing one corner of her mouth. "Now, husband, why don't you introduce me to passion?"

"With pleasure, my love."

Her eyes grew sultry. "Oh, I don't doubt it will be immensely pleasurable."

And it was. Both times.

Schemes and goals motivated by love and honor are the most noble of all.
~Dignity and Decorum—The Genteel Lady's Guide to Practical Living

Epilogue

Bristledale Court, Late August, 1822

"Look, darling." Sitting at a tea table centered upon the veranda, Blythe pointed to a pair of fawns. They followed their mottled mother from the woods bordering Bristledale Court's expansive greens where Blaire and Blaike strolled, arm in arm, beneath matching white lace parasols.

The day, vibrant with sunshine and a cloudless cerulean sky, promised a sweltering afternoon.

"This year, the mallow deer herd is greater than usual." Tristan folded his news sheet, and after setting it aside, extended his hand. "Walk with me, please. I have something I'd like to discuss with you."

Blythe patted her mouth with her serviette before taking his hand and collecting her parasol. "Of course."

"You are enjoying your sisters' visit?" Tristan led her off the covered promenade and into an elaborate parterre featuring topiaries, hedges, and a circular koi pond teeming with silvery and orange koi as well as pink water lilies.

"Very much. I essentially grew up with four sisters. I miss them, and I never thought to admit it, but I miss the chaos too." A subtle fragrance perfumed the air, and Blythe bent to sniff the heather-toned lavender. Nearly time to harvest it for linen sachets.

He nodded, a contemplative expression creasing his handsome face. "I know we decided against me applying for guardianship of the twins, since Ravensdale is wholly honorable and will do what is best for them. This past fortnight, having had an opportunity to become acquainted with Blaire and Blaike, I've come to a conclusion."

Blythe sloped her parasol against the sun. "A good one, I hope."

He chucked her chin. "Never fear. I quite like your sisters. And that's why I think they need an education beyond the schooling you've told me about."

Blythe stopped short. "Are you serious? Gentlewomen don't attend higher education."

"Blythe, they are quite brilliant, and they've a hunger for knowledge I'm loath to leave unsated. I don't think I've ever encountered two keener female minds."

"Well, I don't know whether to be miffed or pleased. Are you implying I'm a dimwit?"

"Nothing of the sort. You simply aren't leaving my side. Ever."

Blythe followed the twins' progress as they occasionally pointed to a bird or plant. "They are unique, aren't they?"

"They are. Do you think they'd be receptive to the notion, or would they feel like we were trying to rid ourselves of them?" He shaded his eyes from the glaring sun and stared after the oyster-and-Pomona-green clad pair. "It's an opportunity few women have. On the other hand, I fear it may set them up for disappointment later in life by giving them a taste of freedom they may not want to relinquish for marriage."

"Hmm, I suppose it might. We'll never know unless we put the suggestion to them." She tucked her hand into his elbow, deliberately pressing her breast into his arm. "Besides, sometimes relinquishing one's freedom is quite divine."

His wicked chuckle sent a jolt of desire straight to her woman's center. Tristan had introduced her to an extremely creative and most satisfying bed sport this morning, which had restricted her liberty for several delicious moments.

"Ho, Leventhorpe." Drake waved as he, Whitehouse, and Brette, accompanied by several others, including Francine and Maddox, stepped onto the veranda.

Tristan returned his greeting. "Ah, the rest of our houseguests finally stir."

"Not everyone rises with the roosters, darling." Blythe sent him a teasing smile. "I do rather prefer sunrise myself."

"I know why you favor mornings." Tristan swung her into his arms. "You like a rousing romp first thing, Lady Leventhorpe."

"Indeed, I do." She laid her head against his chest, and he rested his chin atop her head. "Did Lieutenant Drake's news of Phillips's partial recovery cause you regret or angst?"

"Not a wit. I spent far too long fretting about Society's opinion of me, and I am enjoying the liberation immensely." He kissed her crown, giving her a little squeeze. "I'm thoroughly delighted you rendered him incapable of performing as a man. Who knew an infection could cause such damage?"

"I can't bring myself to feel the slightest regret." Fingering the button of his jacket, Blythe pursed her lips. Phillips's wouldn't be ruining anymore women, though the knowledge he'd not be punished for the viler acts he was suspected of rankled. "Surely the House of Lords has the power to hold him accountable."

"Not for despoiling a willing woman, and there's no proof of aught else." He patted her shoulder, lingering to caress the sensitive spot at the juncture of her neck that turned her knees to custard. "What think you of the other news Whitehouse divulged?

"You mean Miss Sanford ... er, Lady Bexley?" In truth, the crafty jealousy she'd meant for evil had worked for good, and Blythe owed her a debt of gratitude. Not that a formal thank you would be forthcoming. "I pity her. Widowed within weeks, and banished by the heir to the dower house with a pittance of an allowance. Once her mourning period is over, she'll be prowling about for a new husband, or cats don't meow."

"That's true, although I referred to the tattle regarding Burlington."

Cocking her head, she permitted herself an impish grin. "Mrs. Hemple is to be congratulated on her good fortune for escaping the parson's mousetrap. Wise woman, having Mr. Burlington shadowed. Three indiscretions in as many weeks. Tsk, tsk. She's well rid of him."

"I quite agree. I'd like to break his perfect nose for suggesting you become his mistress." Turning them toward their waiting guests, Tristan used the opportunity to wrap his arm about her trim waist and cup her ribs. "You've filled out a bit since we married."

"Are you suggesting I'm running to fat?" Contriving a playful pout, she swatted his arm. “Fine way to speak to your wife when she’s increasing.”

“You mistake my meaning, darling.” Casting a deliberate glance at her swollen breasts, he waggled his eyebrows and bent his sculpted lips, perfect for blood-heating kisses. “I simply worried for the babe’s and your health. I’m not complaining in the least.”

“Devilish knave.” Her contented smile betrayed her joy.

“And that’s exactly why you love me.” He dropped a kiss onto her crown. “Happy, my love?”

Blythe tilted her chin, cupped his angular cheek. “Beyond my grandest schemes.”

About the Author

USA Today Bestselling, award-winning author COLLETTE CAMERON® scribbles Scottish and Regency historicals featuring dashing rogues and scoundrels and the intrepid damsels who re-form them. Blessed with an overactive and witty muse that won't stop whispering new romantic romps in her ear, she's lived in Oregon her entire life, though she dreams of living in Scotland part-time. A self-confessed Cadbury chocoholic, you'll always find a dash of inspiration and a pinch of humor in her sweet-to-spicy timeless romances®.

Explore **Collette's worlds** at

www.collettecameron.com!

Join her **VIP Reader Club** and **FREE newsletter**.

Giggles guaranteed!

FREE BOOK: Join Collette's The Regency Rose® VIP Reader Club to get updates on book releases, cover reveals, contests and giveaways she reserves exclusively for email and newsletter followers. Also, any deals, sales, or special promotions are offered to club members first. She will not share your name or email, nor will she spam you.

http://bit.ly/TheRegencyRoseGift

Manufactured by Amazon.ca
Acheson, AB

11440202R00177